WinterTown

story and art by
STEPHEN EMOND

Ⓛ Ⓑ

LITTLE, BROWN AND COMPANY
New York Boston

Little, Brown and Company

Hachette Book Group
237 Park Avenue, New York, NY 10017
Visit our website at www.lb-teens.com

Little, Brown and Company is a division of Hachette Book Group, Inc.
The Little, Brown name and logo are trademarks of Hachette Book Group, Inc.

The publisher is not responsible for websites (or their content) that are not owned by the publisher.

First Edition: December 2011

The characters and events portrayed in this book are fictitious. Any similarity to real persons, living or dead, is coincidental and not intended by the author.

Lucy's art in Chapter 3 by Elaine Hornby

Library of Congress Cataloging-in-Publication Data

Emond, Stephen.
    Winter town / by Stephen Emond.—1st ed.
        p. cm.
    Summary: Evan and Lucy, childhood best friends who grew apart after years of seeing one another only during Christmas break, begin a romance at age seventeen but his choice to mindlessly follow his father's plans for an Ivy League education rather than becoming the cartoonist he longs to be, and her more destructive choices in the wake of family problems, pull them apart.
    ISBN 978-0-316-13332-6
    [1. Self-actualization (Psychology)—Fiction. 2. Best friends—Fiction. 3. Friendship—Fiction. 4. Dating (Social customs)—Fiction. 5. Family life—Fiction. 6. Family problems—Fiction. 7. Cartoonists—Fiction.]
I. Title.
    PZ7.E69623Win 2011
    [Fic]—dc23
                        2011012966

10 9 8 7 6 5 4 3 2 1

RRD-C

Printed in the United States of America

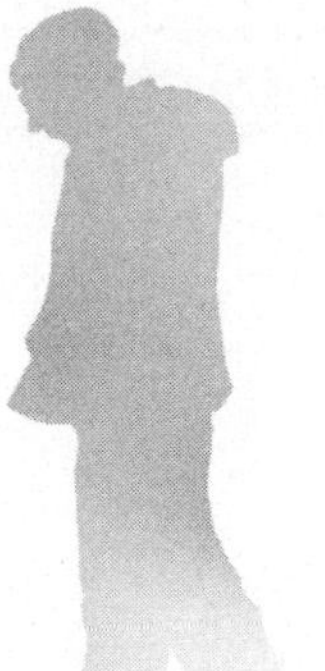

ONE YEAR AGO

"You could have at least stayed until the ball dropped," Evan said, making no effort to hide his disappointment.

They walked in the shiny street along piles of curbside snow. Lucy pulled her winter hat tight over her long, straight brown hair. Evan wished she'd wear hats more often. She looked cute in them. "It's been sixteen years, Ev. I'm tired of waiting." She cut him a quick grin.

"I *have* reached puberty, thank you," Evan said as they walked under a streetlight. The road ahead of them was wet and dark, and everything else was orange or black with touches of blue in the distance. Their voices and a droning wind were the only sounds.

"I've seen your penis, Ev," Lucy said playfully. "I'm not sure you have."

Evan's eyes widened. *She's kidding, right?* "Where's the punch line, Lucy?"

"No punch line. I saw it. It's tiny." Her eyes gleamed mischievously.

"*When* did you see it?" Evan asked, leaning over to see how serious she was.

"I remember every detail. We were six. It was summer. We were getting ready to go to the beach, and I walked into your room when you were changing, and there it was. It was just dangling there—"

"I was *six*!" Evan nearly shouted, startled by his own echo. "That doesn't even come *close* to counting! Six-year-olds have tiny penises—that's just how it is!" Evan was lanky, kind of tall, and had, as girls told him, a cute face. He rarely had to fight for his manhood.

"How do *you* know six-year-olds have tiny penises?" Lucy asked.

"I *was* one, which puts me in a position to know. I don't like this conversation."

Lucy grabbed Evan's hand, and they walked mitten-in-glove, paw-in-paw. Evan fought back a sigh. He didn't want to bring in the new year alone when his best friend was staying only blocks away. Tomorrow Lucy would be far away again. An engine sounded from down the street. Tiny white lights grew out of the horizon and crawled along the street slowly. "We're going to get soaked if we don't get off the road," Evan said, and looked for any clear spot they could move to.

Lucy stared ahead as a wash of yellow-white colored her coat and face. "Okay."

2

Evan took Lucy's arm, and they stepped cartoonishly over mounds of snow until they were a few feet off the street and shin-deep in wet-and-cold. Evan laughed. It wasn't midnight, but it was New Year's Eve and he was with Lucy, under the stars and out in the quiet, and currently looking like half a snowman. This would be their last silly night together for a while. He hated to see her go. He hated how everything had to change.

"You can probably still make it back to watch the ball," Lucy said.

"Nah, I don't know. I might try to finish my game instead." Evan was bored with it already. "I downloaded this video game. It's an old-school, side-scrolling kind of thing, and it's fun, but you have to finish it all in one sitting, and I can never do it." They crossed back into the street after the car passed. Lucy shook snow off her long denim trench coat. "There aren't really any levels. You start in this house, and you leave and go out into the woods and into this graveyard. There are bosses and stuff, but it just keeps going from one section to the next with nowhere to really save, so I'd get into the game, but then there'd be dinner or homework or a phone call or whatever. And I don't want to just leave it paused all night or anything, so I haven't finished it yet."

"God, that story sucked so hard," Lucy said, and gave Evan a soft push that caught him off guard and almost sent him back into the snow. "You just wasted my entire life."

Evan regained his balance and pulled Lucy's hat down over her eyes. "Remember when we'd have entire vacations to just play a game like that 'til it was finished?" Evan asked.

"That doesn't happen anymore." They walked quietly for a moment and leaped over another puddle—Lucy first and then Evan. She took Evan's hand again and this time gave it a squeeze.

"Well, I'll be gone now," she said, "so you'll have more time for your horrible game." This didn't cheer Evan up. "I'll be in Aelysthia. I'll be easy to find."

The name came from the street they were walking to, Alice Drive, Lucy's old home, where her dad still lived. Aelysthia was a fantasy world Evan and Lucy had made up as kids. They'd planned to write hundreds of bestselling novels that took place there. Evan's parents and Lucy's parents would meet and talk or play cards and drink, and Evan and Lucy would sit away from the adults and draw together and dream up worlds, well past their bedtime.

"So where can I find you?" Evan asked.

"Well," Lucy said. She looked forward. "You'll know where to find me because I'll be right under the vomiting sun." The vomiting sun was a staple of Aelysthia: the source of warmth, light, and a constant waterfall of vomit. The world grew sillier and more bizarre with each passing year, evolving with Lucy's and Evan's humor.

"I can't imagine a worse place for you to stay," Evan said.

"Well, maybe not *right* under it," Lucy replied.

Evan and Lucy gently swung their hands between them. They had passed the cemetery and town houses, and had turned right to walk uphill, with the lights downtown glowing behind them. Evan found he had to walk carefully on the icy sidewalk up the hill.

4

"Anyway, it's nice there. The walls of my cave are all bright from my luminous wallflowers."

"Sounds very *Avatar*," Evan said.

"No. Shut up. They stole that from me," Lucy said.

"Hey, I'll be there, too," Evan said, as if she'd neglected his existence in Aelysthia. "I'll be installing some decent lighting for you."

They reached the apex of the hill and walked toward Lucy's father's house on the left after the corner. Evan could see the ocean a few streets away, wide and dark. As they walked into Lucy's yard, she let go of Evan's hand, turned to face him, and shrugged her shoulders.

"'Til next time," she said, a silhouette now.

"Keep it real," Evan said, offering a fist bump. They shared a stilted, awkward hug, and Evan stepped back. "So this is it, then? You sure?"

Lucy touched her hair. "Yeah. I have to pack still. So."

Evan smiled at his shoes. He looked up as Lucy walked to her house, and he raised a hand in a short wave. "Happy New Year," he said, and Lucy smiled.

"You go on," she said from her front porch, lit by the porch light. "I want to watch you walk away."

Evan walked home alone.

When Evan reached his house, his driveway and the street in front of it were still full of cars. He could hear the cheer in his warm, bright house: laughter, talk, and television. He stood still for a long time, the cold stars behind him and the warm light in front of him, casting a long shadow across the street. Evan sat in a chair on the porch with his gloved hands in his coat pockets and looked up at the tiny white moon. Maybe he'd be alone for the ball drop after all.

The countdown was being shouted inside. *Four, three, two, one.*

Evan heard muffled laughter and celebration. He took a deep, long breath and exhaled slowly, and then he got up and went inside to wish everyone a happy new year.

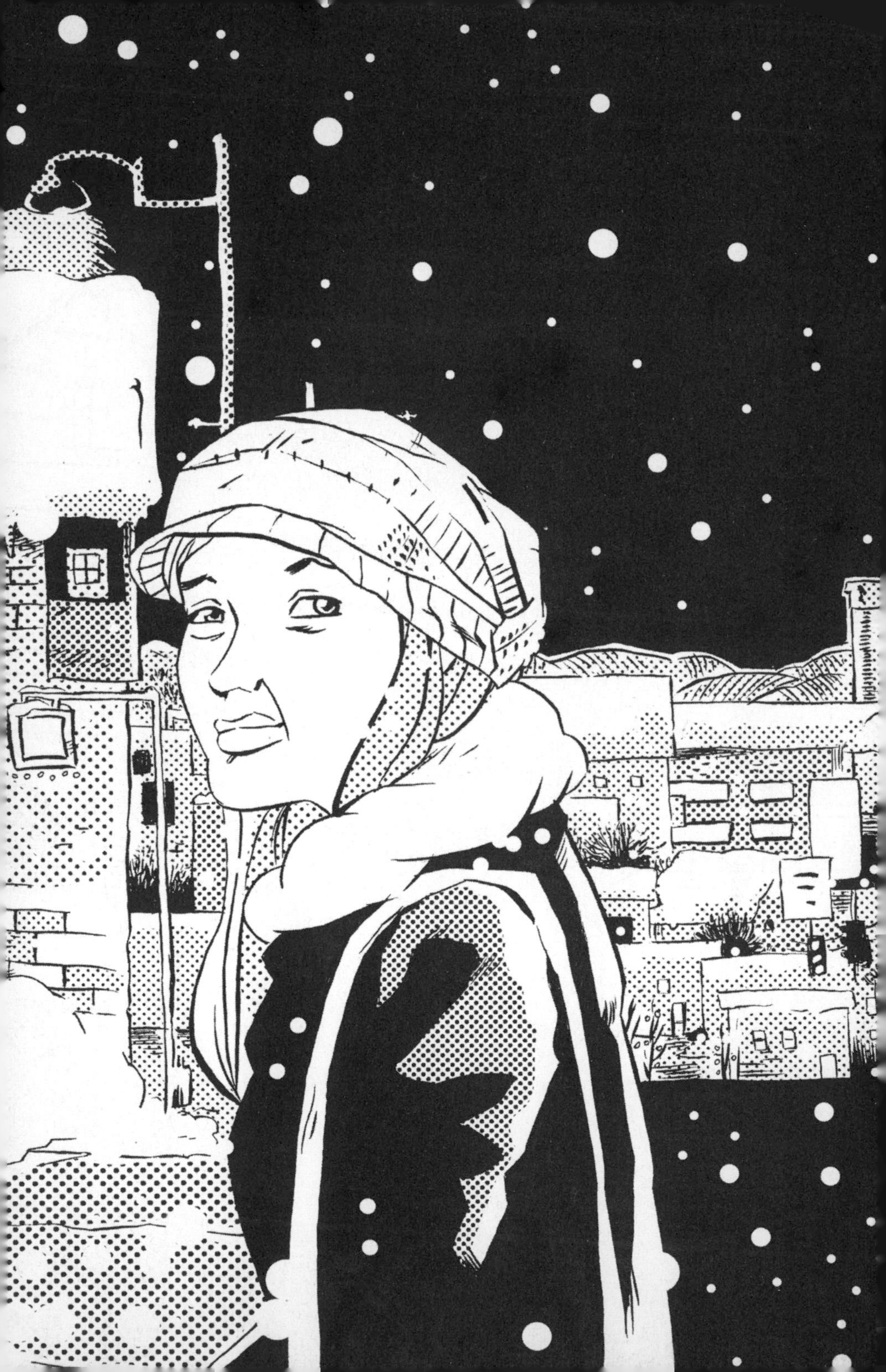

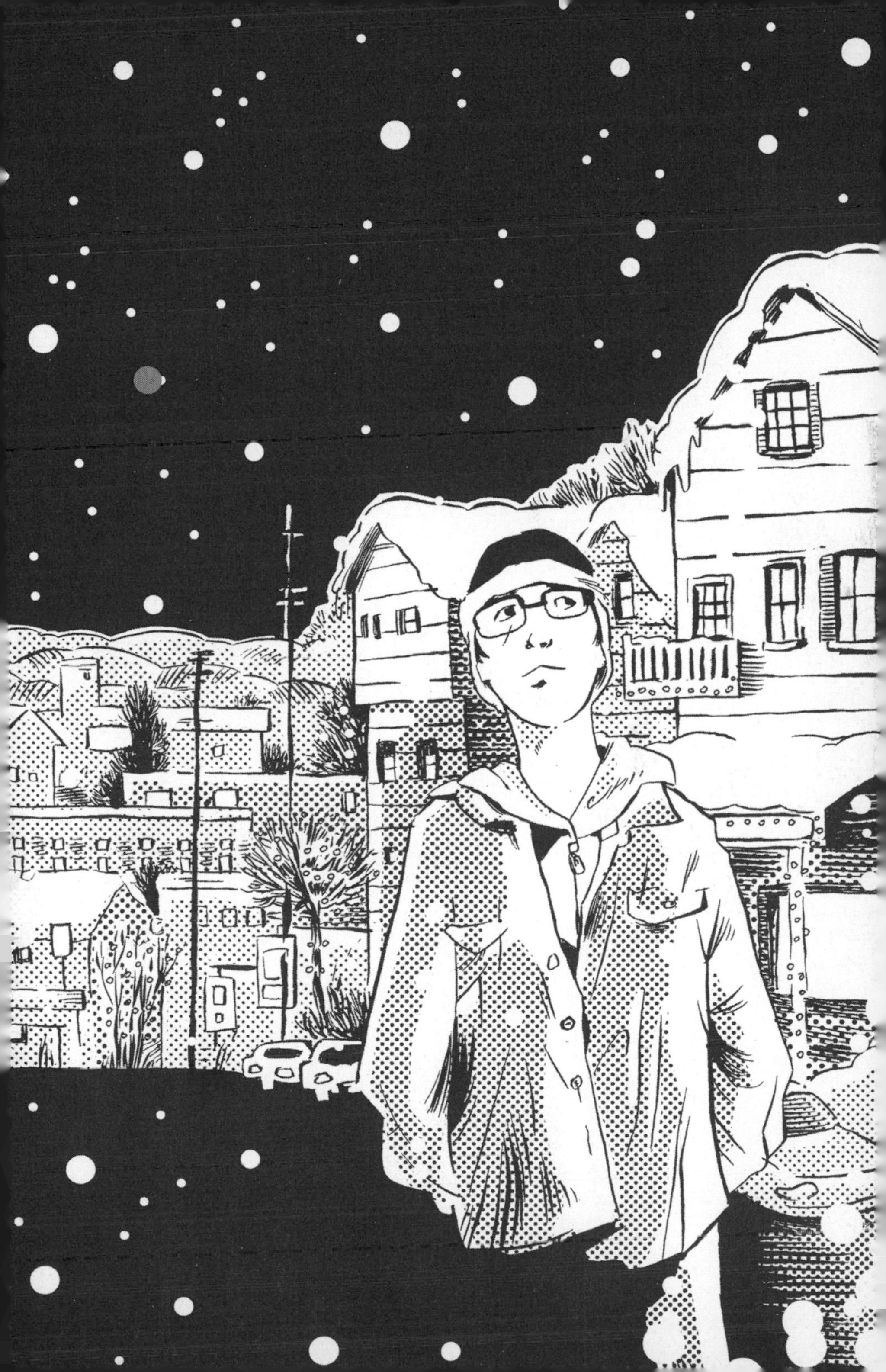

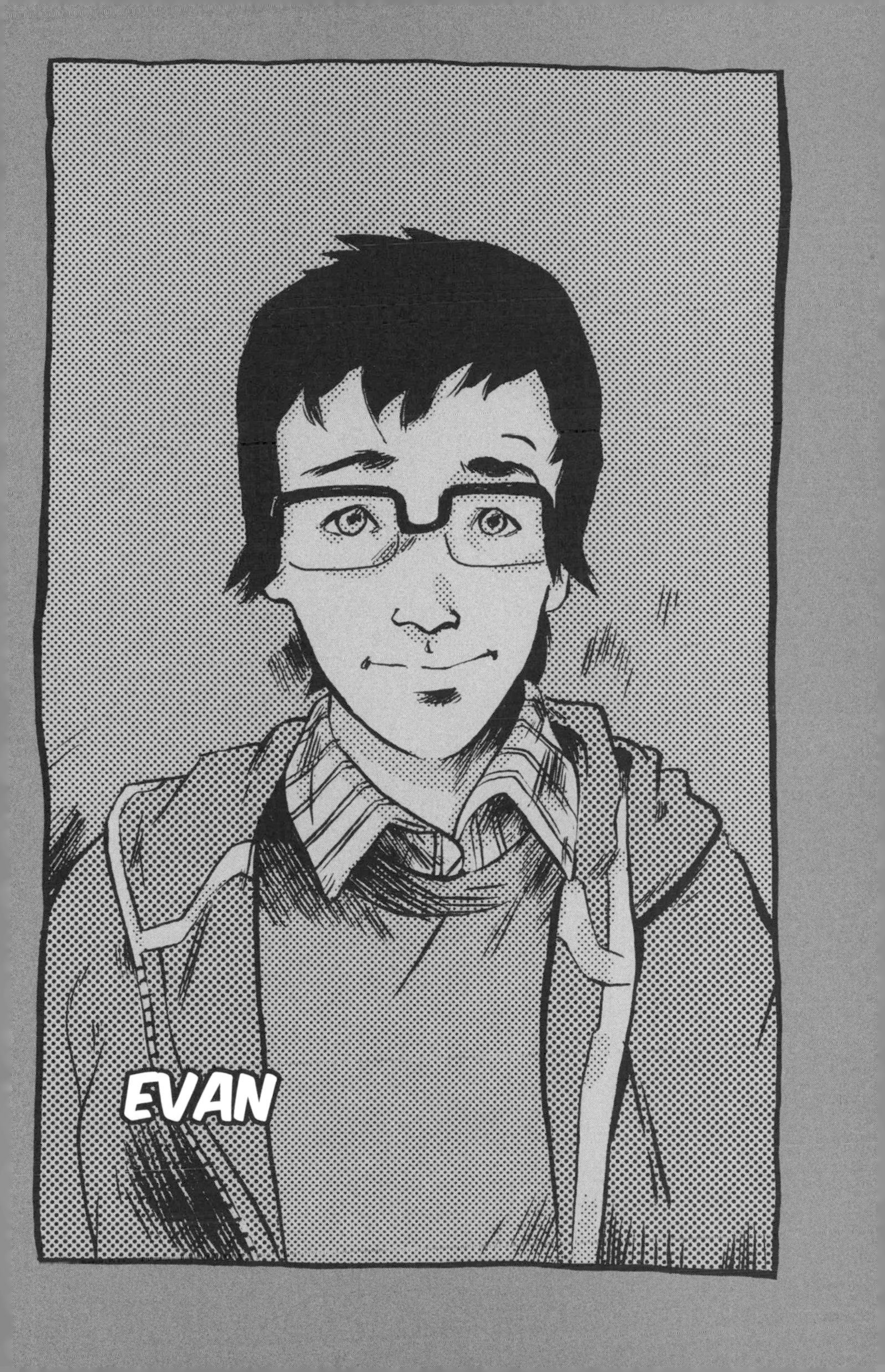
EVAN

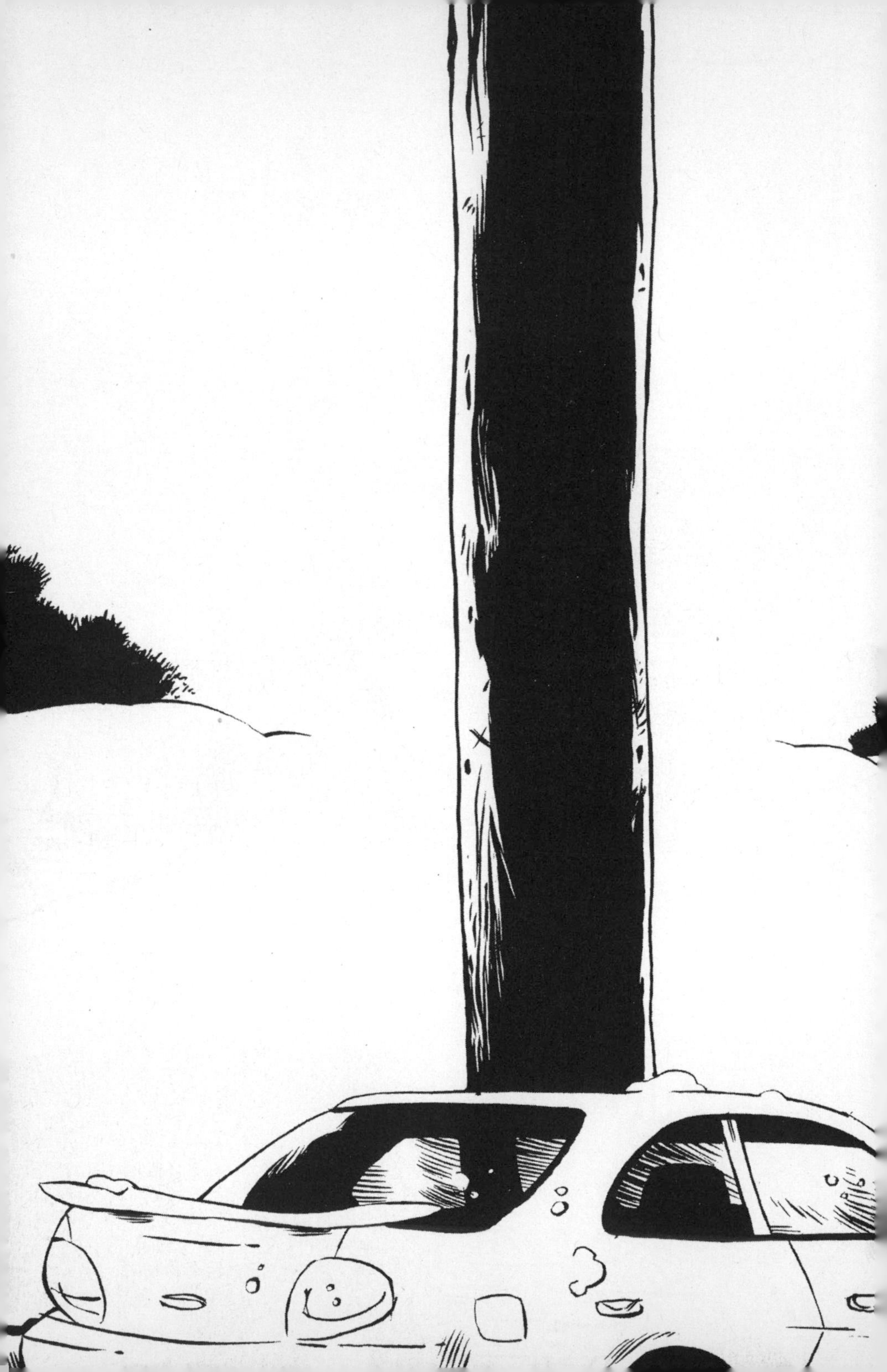

CHAPTER ONE

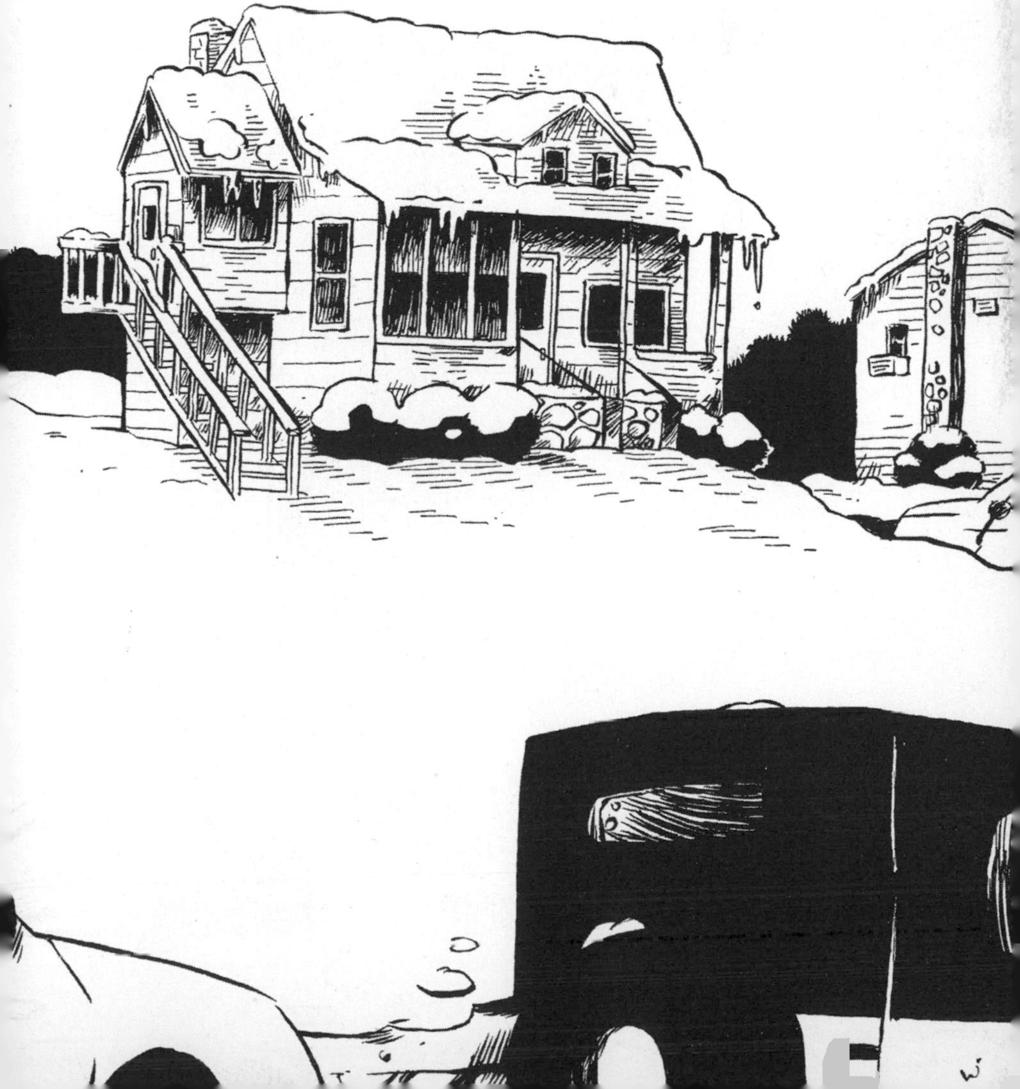

A DAY IN THE LIFE

TODAY

Back home if you're free. Evan looked at Lucy's text message as he sat in the bathroom. It was the only quiet place in the house. The last text from her had been in April, about eight months ago, and read *qwerty texting is a bitch!* Before that had been *Will be busy for the newlxt few days.* He also had a text message from his friend Marshall: *So where is this girl already?* That one was from yesterday.

"Where's the box with the wires?" Evan's dad yelled from the living room. "I need the box with the wires and lights," he repeated louder, though no one seemed to be listening. Evan's dad liked to be heard, a trait Evan had never fully picked up. Evan walked to the sink and washed his hands. Just twenty minutes ago, Evan had been enjoying himself, drawing at the kitchen table and talking with his grandmother, but those five words, *Back home if you're free*, had turned his day around. Now he felt stuck here, trapped in his own home.

The house was overrun with guests, which made it a Sunday. Family Sunday, to be exact. Meaning stay home with your family, not go out with your friend you haven't seen in twelve months. It was also mid-December, which meant his dad's winter town was being put on display. His dad was constantly fiddling with it, trying to make it just right.

"There's still a few boxes we haven't opened, hon," Evan's mom said. "It could be in one of those."

Evan stepped into the living room, where his neighbor Ben immediately began to follow him. Evan was used to being followed around the house, if not by Ben then by one of the children. Followed, talked about, or called from across the room in loud fashion. He had a close family, and that's what close families did.

There were twenty-three people in the house at the moment and one dog. The kitchen was full and the living room was full, and the couch and all the chairs were taken, with some family members watching the game, while others were talking and eating. Evan hugged the living room wall as he navigated his way toward the front of the house. The scene was especially active here as an assortment of Evan's family members were helping his dad get all the town pieces up and running in their proper places. Evan made his way into the dining room, where several unopened boxes were stacked, and he and Ben each brought one back to Evan's dad. Evan sat his box down by the large window display his dad was working on. Maybe he could get out early on good behavior.

"Thanks, son," Dad said in his baritone voice. His voice and his brow were his two most impressive features. He had the appearance of a deep-thinking philosopher. Even on *Sunday Fun-day* he wore a tie.

Conversation over the next few minutes quickly turned to Dad's topic du jour, Evan's upcoming excommunication to college. Evan was over it. He'd already spent his fall applying to ten different colleges with his dad looming over him for every minor decision. The problem was that Evan still didn't know what he wanted to do, or where he wanted to go. For all his effort and for all his good grades, Evan Owens was a man without a plan.

"What do you think about trying for an Ivy League or two?" Dad asked. "We still have a couple of weeks." He dropped and picked up a tiny Christmas tree. "You've got the grades and the extracurricular activities. If you took up a sport, you could mention it during interviews." He lined the trees up on a shelf in a perfect row around a small pond. There was a handful of boys and girls skating on the ceramic ice.

"I haven't played a sport since sixth grade, Dad. Why bother if it's not going to make the application anyway?" Evan said. The part he didn't say was that he hadn't enjoyed sports even then. Taking a baseball to the side of the head had something to do with it. Since then, he'd participated chiefly in what he called anti-sports. Invisibility was an admired trait in anti-sports. The trick was to make it look like he was having a good time, while avoiding the ball, the goal, and his teammates.

"You're in good shape," Dad said, looking Evan over as if to fact-check. "You'll pick it up fast."

Evan tried to center his eyes, which wanted so badly to roll in their sockets. His dad had to focus on *sports*, and not, say, Evan's advanced classes, homework, set-building for the theater department, tutoring, debate club, and Wednesday afternoons volunteering at SARAH, a community that helps disabled people. He had friends, he had girlfriends, he did everything right. But he didn't play sports.

"There's no time, Dad," Evan said, wondering how soon he could get to Lucy's. He stuffed his hands into his pockets and shifted his weight from one foot to the other. He hoped his father didn't realize he still had Saturdays and Mondays free.

"It'll really add another layer to your transcript." Dad stood up and scratched his head. "You've got Saturdays and Monday afternoons open still," he said, and Evan wondered if he was thinking too loudly. Would he need one of those tinfoil hats?

"Dad, you're gonna kill me." Evan plotted a quick escape to the kitchen to avoid further college talk, but his mom cut him off with a plate of cheese and crackers in hand.

"I was just looking for you," she said.

"Thanks, Mom." Evan relented and took the plate.

She gave an isn't-he-the-sweetest? smile and patted his head. Now he had to take the time to eat. Evan's mom had medium-length brown hair and red-framed glasses and what Evan would call a soccer-mom-lite look. She thought Evan was the most wonderful person to ever walk the earth and let him know it every day. With her, Evan was rocketing over the moon, and with his dad, he couldn't get off the ground. Evan imagined himself somewhere in the middle, floating along the troposphere, airplane-level. Moms coddle their children. It was nice, it was fine.

"Barb," Dad said, "what do you think about Evan taking on a sport?"

"*Dad...*" Evan groaned. "Enough with the sports."

"It's for school, Ev."

"Oh, you're going to suffocate him, Charlie. Let him go out with his friends every now and again. He hasn't met a girl in months, not since that awful Jessica," Mom lamented, exaggerating her frown. If Evan's dad was predictable in his speeches on education, then his mother brought up his social life like it was a soap opera. Not that it was salacious or even interesting; she just had a need to get her daily fix of it. Jessica was Evan's late-spring girlfriend. It had been, in all fairness, a disaster. She was the pretty, redheaded version of the baseball that had hit him on the side of the head. That was spring, though. Two seasons had passed entirely. He was over it.

Evan fidgeted some more. This talk, too, had run its course, and being the center of attention wasn't going to help Evan get out of the house.

"She could have been a lot more tactful in breaking up with you. She didn't realize how lucky she was to have you in the first place." Mom adjusted Evan's collar and brushed his sweater, as if the act of talking about relationships would lead to a date for him in the next four minutes.

"That's not *that* important right now anyway," Dad said with his hands raised. He'd heard enough of this gang-up on his son, or at least enough without his participation. "You can go out and have fun when the opportunity arises, but—"

"What does that mean?" Mom asked in sort of an accusing whine.

"Well." Dad collected his thoughts and firmed his stance. "It means he should *date*. He's a normal teenage boy, but maybe don't go falling in love, necessarily."

College and girls. At least Dad was about to pull some of the heat off him now. Evan wondered if he needed to be present for this conversation at all and decided he did not. There were two crackers left on his plate.

"And why shouldn't he *fall in love*?" Mom asked, drawing the interest of others nearby. Evan's family made a habit of talking about him as if he weren't there. "What if he meets the right girl?"

"He's not going to meet the right girl; he's *seventeen*," Dad said, giving *seventeen* all the appeal of a cockroach.

"Oh, that's silly," Evan's mom replied.

"*We* met in college," Dad said, and now he and Mom had themselves an audience in the living room. He picked a string of Christmas lights out of a box and began to unknot it. Dad spoke deliberately, like a professor, in a manner that made you want to take notes. "We were both on our feet. Confident in who we were. We were adults and capable of making rational adult decisions. What I'm saying is that it's just a better time to look at a relationship, when you can clearly and objectively evaluate what it is that you want to find in someone."

"Mr. Romantic," Mom said, fanning herself and getting laughs from the women.

"*I* think he needs to sow his oats," Evan's grandmother added, turning around in her chair across the room. "Seventeen's a little old to be a virgin."

"Aww, *Gram*...!" Evan said, and swung his head down in defeat. Ben burst out in laughter and hid his face with a couch pillow. Some conversations have a built-in stopping point, and this was one.

"Well, *these days*, I mean."

"That's absolutely not true!" Mom objected.

"You take it too far, Mom," Dad said to Gram. "This is a serious discussion."

"Who's not serious? If I'm okay with it, you should be, coming from *your* generation. And *his* generation," Gram said. She got out of her chair and walked to Evan and rubbed his shoulders. "Even if he was gay, I'd be okay with that."

College, love life, sexuality questioning. Check. Evan should be able to get out soon. "Are you guys even aware that I have to remind everyone I'm not gay every few weeks?" Evan asked. "Who started this, anyway?"

"Oh, Evan, no one's judging," Gram said. "Be young! That's all I'm saying. You should be proud you have a family so open and who cares about you. *You could date a man who's a different color and turn your willy into a hoo-hoo for all I care. I'll love you just the same!*" Evan imagined that last part, though it didn't sound out of place.

"He's not gay, Mom. He just doesn't play sports," Dad said, and put his hand on Evan's other shoulder. "And he can be young after college."

This was met with family *boo*s. Evan was on daytime talk TV. Bizarre speculations were flinging into each ear as if no one thought he was listening. Evan surveyed the other family members, his eyes pleading for help. Nothing. He'd ceased to exist in a conversation he was the centerpiece of.

"Well, I agree that it would be okay if he *was*," Mom added, "but he's too *girl-crazed*."

The living room was in stitches. Evan thought of the Woody Allen short film *Oedipus Wrecks*, in which the main character's mother disappears during a magic show and re-appears as a giant face floating in the sky. She talks all day to strangers about the main character's most embarrassing life moments. Sundays for Evan often felt a lot like *Oedipus Wrecks*.

"*Well*," Gram continued, in a manner that proved she'd given this some thought, "he's an artist, he's single, he's polite, which are all *wonderful things*, and his friends—"

"Gram." Evan cut her off. "I have close friends who happen to be gay, but that has nothing to do with me." Evan had made the mistake of inviting Tim and Marshall over to work on a project, and his grandma had spent the entire afternoon like an elderly Encyclopedia Brown, sniffing for clues and starting anything-but-subtle discussions on the attractiveness of Robert Redford.

"Well, you *do* spend a lot of time with them, and I read about something called *latent* homosexuality," said Gram. Everyone laughed again.

"So you're implying that I'm not only *gay*, but the gay third wheel to my friends?" Evan asked, afraid of the answer.

"I'm not implying anything, Evan!" she said, taking her hand off his shoulder. Evan smiled to let her know he wasn't upset. He'd always had a very close bond with his grandmother, which only strengthened when she moved in after his grandfather died.

Before the conversation continued, Dad leaned into the shelf, and a ceramic storefront building fell to the ground and broke with a tinkle.

"Oh, you see —" Dad started, and then was on the ground picking up pieces.

The room was silent for a long second before everyone huddled around to clean up the mess. They all knew how he hated to lose a piece of the town.

"I'm sorry, Charlie," Gram said. "I didn't mean to distract you."

"It's all right, Mom," Dad said, putting on a strained smile. "This just gives me an excuse to go buy a new one."

The relatives relaxed and went back to their non-Evan-centered activities.

Evan's pocket vibrated, and he took out his phone. A text read, *You home?* The text glowed like a beacon to a ship lost at sea. *It's safe here*, it said. *Come to land.* It was going to be hours before all of the Owenses' company had left, and Evan could no longer wait for hours. It was possible he could even sneak back in before they'd left. He never knew with Lucy, though. Hours could pass by completely unnoticed. This was going to be his chance. With his family members crowded around the porcelain mess or back in front of the TV, Evan grabbed his hat and coat and slipped out the door with as little noise as he could make.

The door clicked quietly shut. The sky was a pale blue as the winter sun was already starting to lower, and there were three inches of snow on the ground, from the second snow-storm of the season. Evan squinted until his eyes adjusted to all the white, reflecting the sun like a lumpy mirror covering the earth. The trees were like intricate glass sculptures, shin-ing in the sunlight, dripping water to the ground. Evan took a deep breath of sharp, cold air, which considerably cooled down his overheated body. He felt calmer almost immedi-ately. He took his iPod out of his coat pocket and put in his earbuds. He pulled his knit hat down over his messy hair and started walking.

The driveway was full of cars half-covered in snow or littered with the leaky remains from a quick dust-off. Evan waved to Mr. Jacobsen, who was almost through shoveling next door. He looked down the street and observed what was left of a man-versus-nature war—trails of snow blasted out of driveways and onto the road. A car at the end of the road was stuck, trying its best to drive over the stuff.

The walk to Lucy's house took about fifteen minutes, or four and a half songs shuffled through his iPod. A greatest-hits of Evan's Nerd Rock, as Lucy called it, played. Weezer,

Ben Folds, They Might Be Giants, Jonathan Coulton. Evan enjoyed what was left of the afternoon sun and the open air. He liked being the only one out walking. He walked fast down the long roads, in big, wide steps, burning off his nervous energy, watching the tops of trees.

Evan walked up the front steps of Lucy's dad's house and knocked. A balding Englishman in a loose robe opened the door. He looked surprised, but pleased. "Evan, how are you?"

"I'm good, Mr. Brown. Is Lucy around?"

"Evan." Doug frowned. "Call me Doug." He turned around and called, "*Lucy?* It's still Lucy, right?" He bantered with Evan, asking how his parents were doing. Then the hurricane blew by.

"Jesus, Dad, embarrass me, why don't you?" Lucy said as she grabbed her coat and walked outside.

"You want a hat?"

"No, bye, back later," Lucy said, and Evan was caught in the draft, following her out of the yard and up the street.

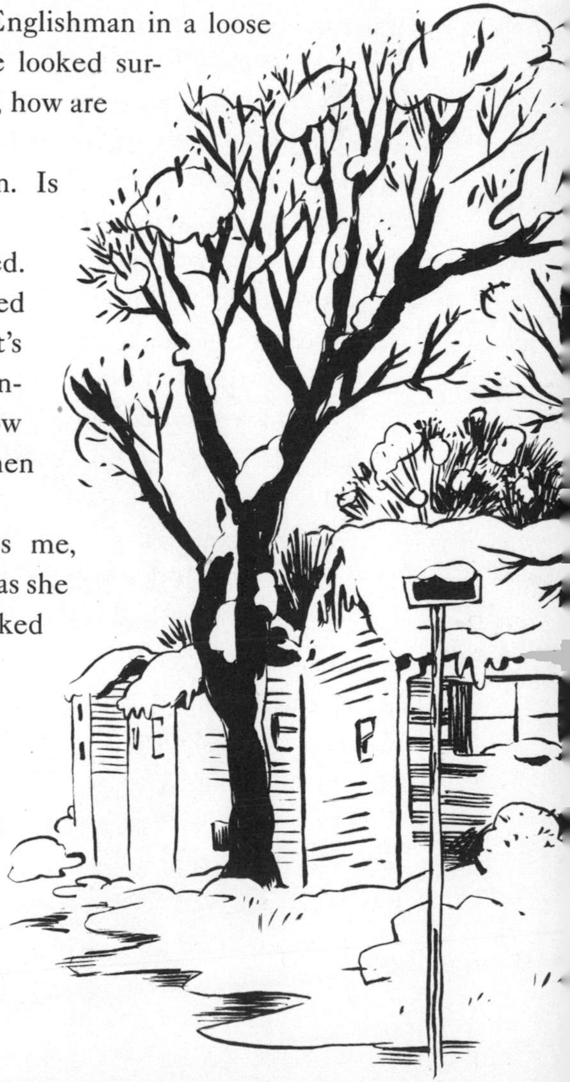

Evan said nothing as he looked Lucy over — studied her, even, like some odd artifact. She was different. Really different. Her hair was cut short — not cut but chopped off, making a statement as much as hair makes statements. Dyed black. Her eyes were covered in makeup, and her nose was pierced. The leather jacket was new, too, but otherwise it was Lucy, all right. Evan's eyebrows climbed a quarter inch. *Is it dress-up day?* Evan thought, amused. *Dress-down day?*

"Hi," she said, almost hesitantly, almost angrily, as they slowed down and walked along the dirt-and-ice-covered road.

"Hi," Evan said, his smile barely covering his surprise.

"So..." — Lucy's eyes rolled around — "you wanna go for a walk?"

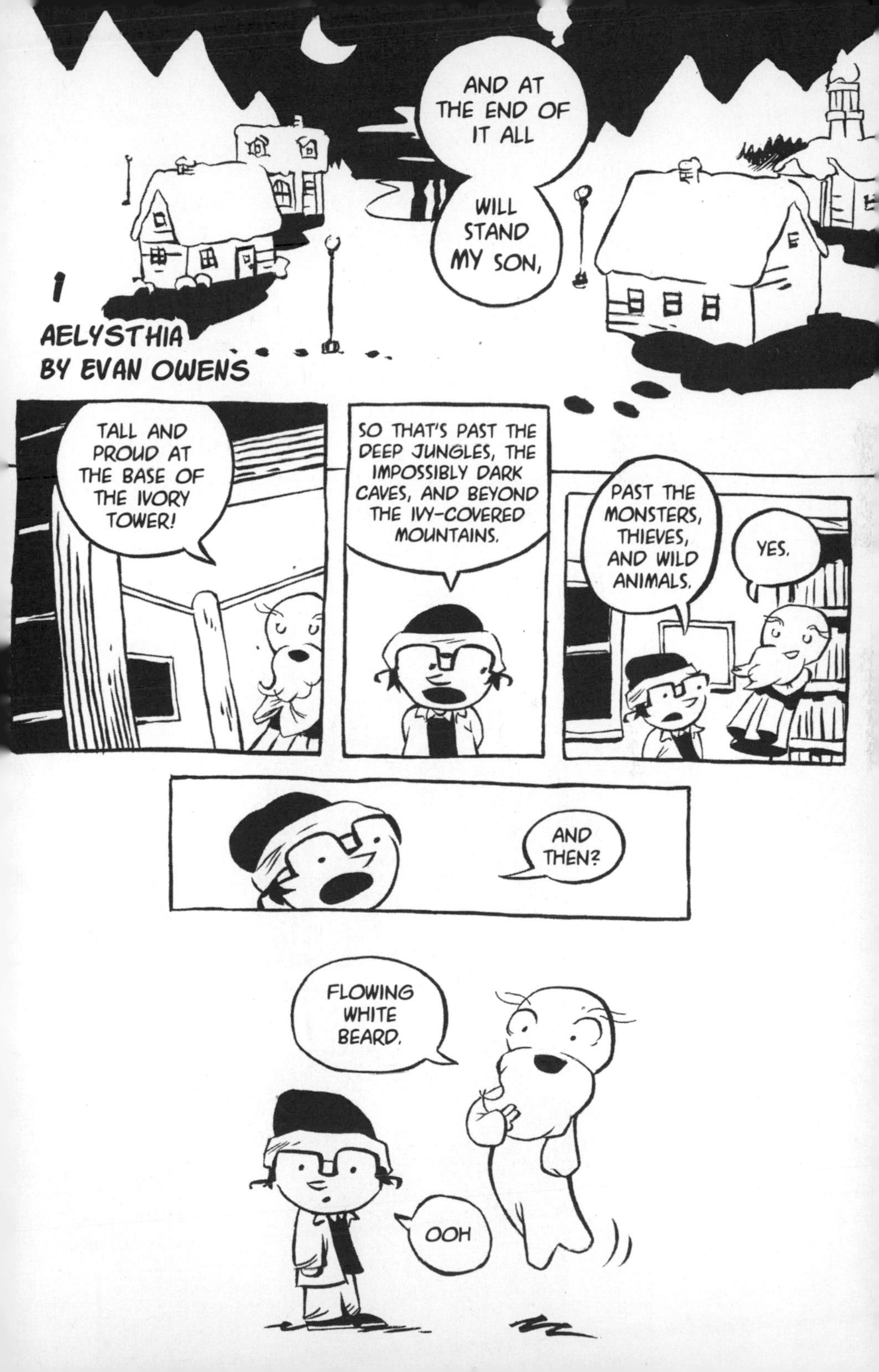
1
AELYSTHIA
BY EVAN OWENS
AND AT THE END OF IT ALL
WILL STAND MY SON,
TALL AND PROUD AT THE BASE OF THE IVORY TOWER!
SO THAT'S PAST THE DEEP JUNGLES, THE IMPOSSIBLY DARK CAVES, AND BEYOND THE IVY-COVERED MOUNTAINS.
PAST THE MONSTERS, THIEVES, AND WILD ANIMALS.
YES.
AND THEN?
FLOWING WHITE BEARD.
OOH

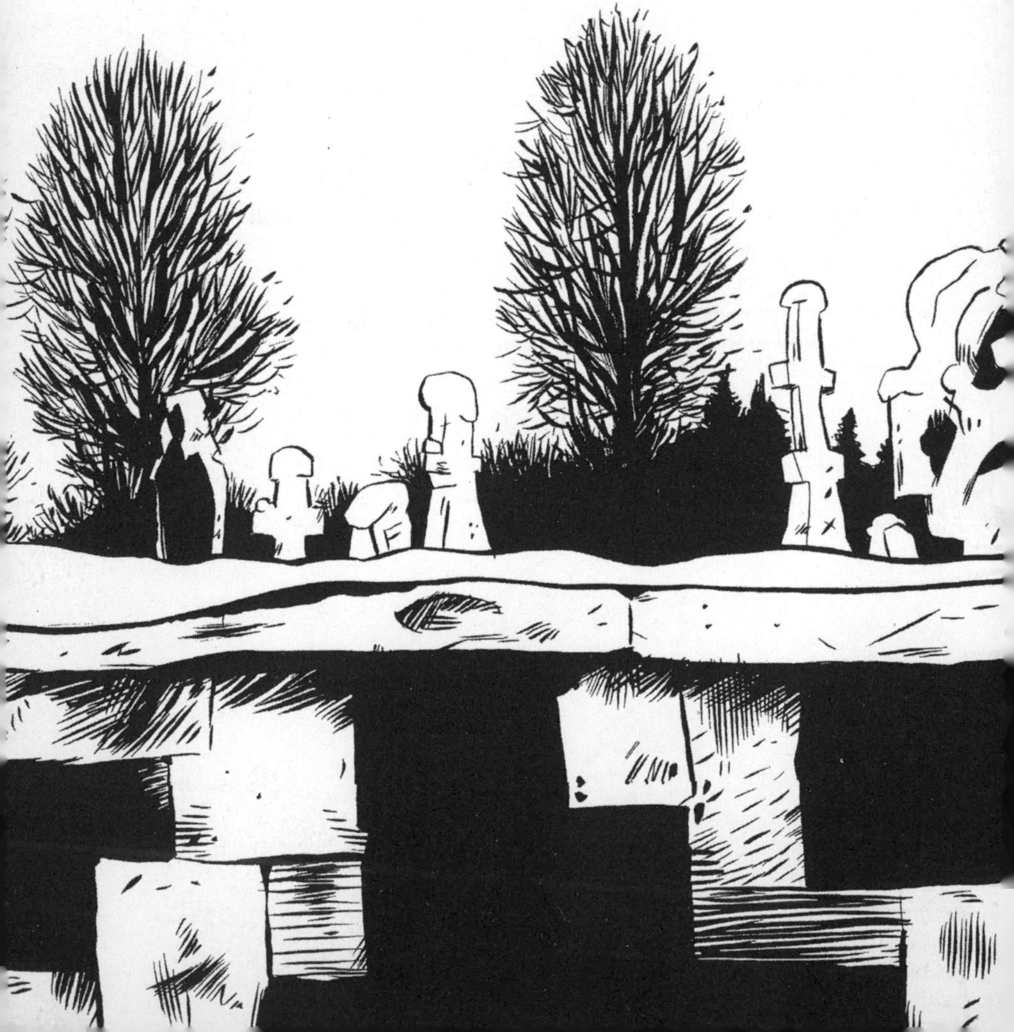

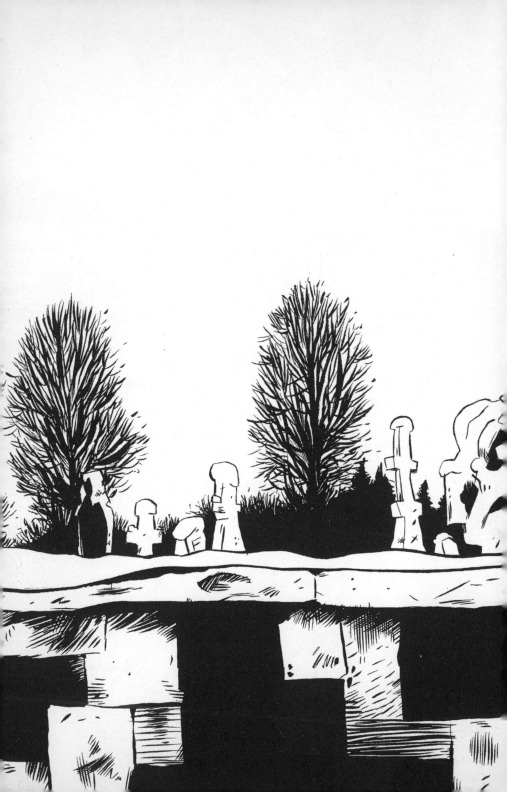

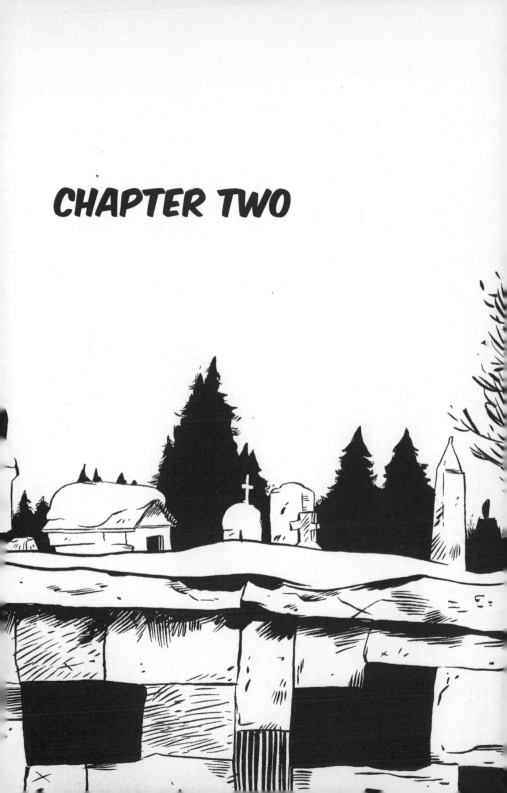

CHAPTER TWO

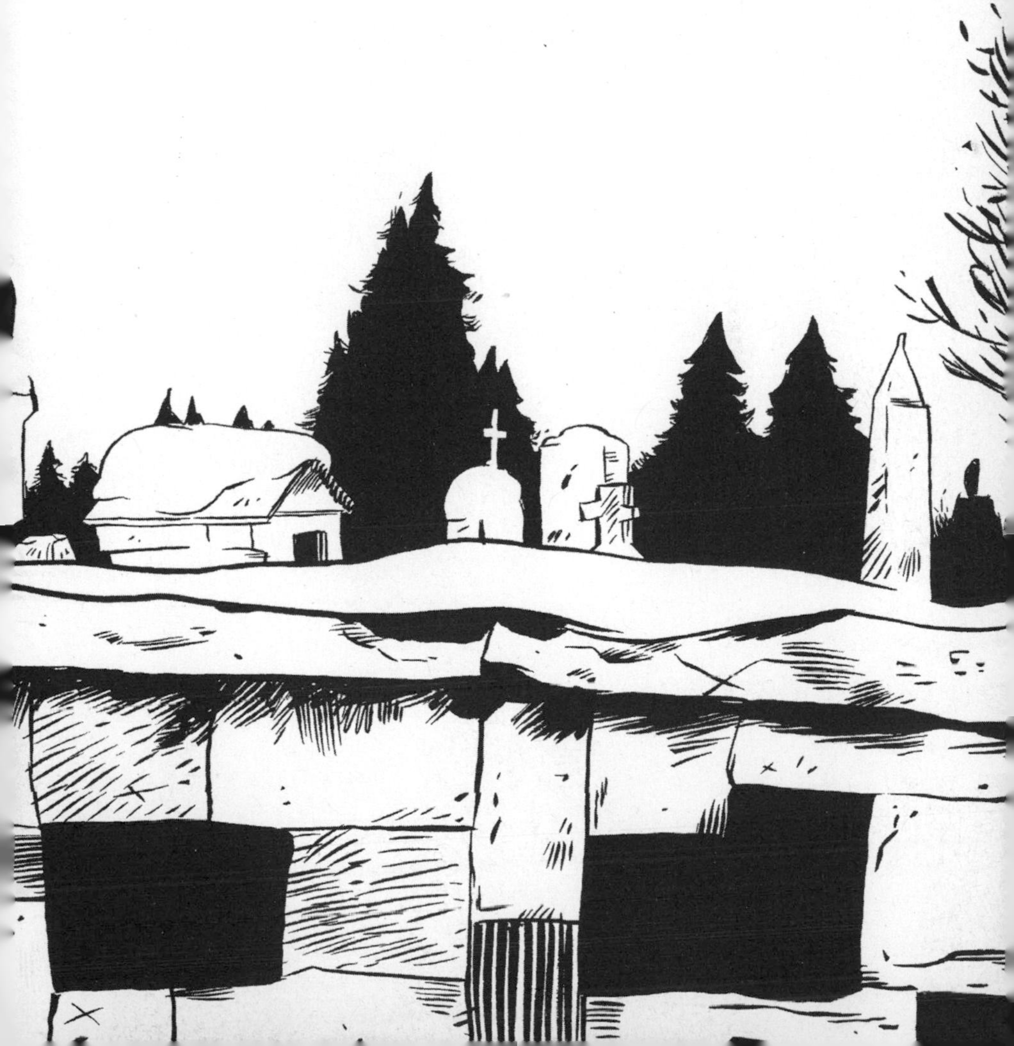

ACROSS THE UNIVERSE

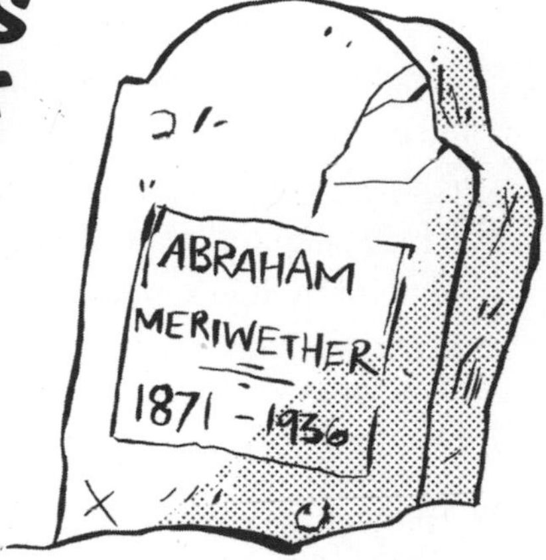
ABRAHAM
MERIWETHER
1871 - 1936

"The happy wanderers," an elderly neighbor had called Evan and Lucy when Lucy still lived there. The two would walk up and down the street and around the block for hours after school, until it got dark. They'd walk and talk about Evan-couldn't-remember-what, as if there were that many things to talk about.

The routine should have been easy enough to pick up when she visited, but for Evan, it always felt a little awkward. Conversation was always stifled at first, and this year was no different.

They walked quietly down the hill. Evan looked around at the homes spaced unevenly off the street. He always thought the houses in this area looked like they could have each come from a different part of the country. Likewise for the streets, he thought, as they walked through a "New England" intersection that looked more like a flattened X than a cross.

"This is good," Evan said. "I needed to get out of there."

"Oh, family Sunday," Lucy said, shaking her head. "Sorry, I forgot. You would think I'd remember Brady Bunch Sundays."

"No, it's fine, trust me, please," he said with increasing exaggeration. "The Brady Bunch can discuss me more openly if I'm not there anyway."

Lucy smiled.

"Can I ask?" Evan went ahead and asked. "What's with the—" Evan made a hand-waving gesture over his face and body, unable to find the words he was looking for.

"You like?" Lucy tilted her head as if she were being photographed.

"It's—it's different. I'm just used—you're just normally, I don't know what. Less…"

"You don't like. Pout."

"I didn't say that," Evan said promptly. The thought bubble floating over his head was filled with images of dragon tattoos, Hot Topic, and *Johnny the Homicidal Maniac.*

"I just thought I'd try something different."

"Well, mission accomplished, then. Congratulations." Evan held out his arms. *Voilà.*

They walked in silence for a bit. Evan kept glancing over at her. *Where'd you come from?* Her look wasn't helping them ease into normalcy. It wasn't out of the ordinary for Lucy to change her appearance (preppy Lucy, chic Lucy), and Evan did know her to develop new interests every few months (dessert baking, marathon biking). It just felt drastic. In fact, it was the complete silence, the indifference to the subject, that really fueled his curiosity. Normally Lucy couldn't stop talking about her latest obsessions. This one was a mystery. Evan knew that if he kept bringing it up, he wouldn't get any answers. But what else could he talk about? It was the Goth elephant in the room.

They turned left at the intersection and walked past the apartments and town houses, heading toward Evan's.

"I think I might be valedictorian for my class," Evan said, not bragging, but just looking for something to say.

"That's awesome. Congratulations," Lucy said with disconnect. Evan thought she was making an effort to sound happy. "I'm proud of you."

He hadn't really felt like talking about himself anyway, after the lengthy examination at his house. He was more interested in Lucy now. "You look like someone," Evan said. "I'm not sure who. Like maybe a punked-out Miley Cyrus or something." Lucy was just going to have to forgive him; she must have known this was coming.

"Yeah, right. Like if she ate a thousand pies a day for the rest of her life."

"Please," Evan said, and laughed at the image. "So your stylist, does she do any of the stars or anything...?"

Lucy punched his arm hard enough for him to feel it

through layers of sweater and coat. Evan wondered for the first time if this transformation was deeper than the clothes and makeup.

"I'm sorry," Evan said. "I'm just curious, that's all. I mean it's different. Should we be having some kind of discussion? What's the protocol?"

Lucy smiled and rolled her eyes. "You're like the guy who takes you to prom but has to ask if he can kiss you at the end of the night."

"So we *should* be discussing this."

"No. There's nothing to discuss. It would be an empty discussion. We'd be saying nothing at all."

Past the apartments was the long straight road with the cemetery on both sides. It was large and sprawling, and fences lined the entire length of it. The sky and the snow were almost the same shade of light purple-blue at this time in the afternoon. Evan and Lucy opened the cold gate and entered the cemetery without acknowledging a set course at any point, because this was just part of the walk, as it always had been. A few cars slowly passed by, their tires making a crunchy noise over the messy roads. Evan took a sharp, cold breath and sighed, and watched his icy sigh drift away.

Welcome to the Evan Owens Show. *Our guest tonight is Lucy Brown, longtime show visitor. Haven't seen you in twelve months, so tell us, Lucy, what's going on in your world? Nothing? Well, the look is something, am I right, folks? What inspired this getup? No? All right, I'm on my own tonight. Surely there's something going on you'd like to discuss. School? Family? Boys?*

Now there was something that could explain the silence —

she had met some new boy, he was on her mind, and she felt weird talking about it because when had they ever talked about relationships, especially about her and relationships? As far as Evan knew, she'd never been in one. *Of course she's shy.*

"Are you dating anyone?" Evan asked.

Lucy looked like she'd been woken up from a nap with a splash of cold water. "Why would you ask that?"

Evan was surprised. So she *was* seeing someone — he'd nailed it. If she wasn't, she'd have said no or laughed the idea off. To ask Evan why he would ask that was pretty much admitting the whole thing.

"No, are you kidding me? Boys are gross," she followed up. *Was it a cover-up?*

"You're dating someone," Evan said, a teasing tone in his voice, like a playground bully. "Who is he? What's going on? Is he tall, dark, and handsome? Is he, like, some Goth kid or something? That's it, isn't it?"

"I told you. Boys are gross. Come on, when do I date anyone?"

"So, what? Is it a crush or something?"

"Ev, God. No, there's no one. There's nothing."

The puzzle pieces really fit together, but she wasn't budging on this. Evan was still curious, though. "Why not?" he asked. "You should. Date someone, I mean. I'm sure guys ask you out. You're not unattractive or anything."

"Gee, thanks," Lucy said, clearly weirded out. Wide-eyed and with restless arms, she looked as if she were covered with spiders. "Boys are gross, end of story. Sorry to disappoint."

Lucy Brown, ladies and gentlemen, not promoting anything

today. Still single, fellas. We'll be right back! They walked slowly by rows of varied tombstones, tall and sturdy, low and crooked, some barely more than rocks. Evan didn't want to walk another five minutes not saying anything and had just opened his mouth, unsure what was going to come out, when Lucy spoke.

"Have you been drawing anything?" she asked. The first thing she always did when she visited in the winter was pore over Evan's sketchbooks and art pads.

"I guess. Just stuff." Evan had been blocked creatively lately. He added art to the pile of college and sports as touchy subjects. "I tried writing. Just this idea I had, a comic-strip kinda thing, but it didn't go so well. Turned me into a frustrated, self-loathing artiste."

"Well, the brain's a dark place to visit," Lucy said nonchalantly.

Evan rolled through his mental Rolodex, but the cards were blank. He decided on trivial conversation. "You into any cool stuff lately?"

"I don't know," Lucy said, as if Evan had asked her for the square root of pi.

Evan wondered since when had talking to Lucy been so difficult. He'd logged hundreds of hours looping these streets with Lucy and could count the number of stifled conversations they had had on one hand.

"Sorry," Lucy offered. "I just can't—brain. Coffee. What about you?" She shrugged.

"Yeah, sure, a lot of stuff. I've gotten really into Harmony Korine. He wrote the movie *Kids* for Larry Clark to direct, but the stuff he writes and directs himself is way cooler."

"Oh, okay."

"Like, the first one I saw was this movie *Julien Donkey-Boy*." Evan was animated now, his hands waving, his face coming to life. "It's about this kid who has undiagnosed schizophrenia, and it's just like nothing I've ever seen. It's not even a movie so much as a collection of scenes. It's *tonal*. There's this creepiness to it, and you keep cringing as he's playing with these little kids, and just hoping he doesn't do anything messed up, which he doesn't, but you just never know. And Werner Herzog plays his dad, and you just have to see it. He keeps asking the kid to put on his dead wife's dress." Evan was rambling, but by now he was fine with it. He'd talk until she joined him, if that's what it was going to take.

"Jesus," Lucy said, still not looking up.

"And he started this other movie that he didn't finish, with David Blaine—"

"The magician guy?" Lucy was letting him go on with this.

"Yeah, but forget about that—so he does this movie, and the whole concept is he's going to go around starting fights with random people, and he won't stop fighting without a threat of death. So he gets into six of these fights before he ends up in the hospital and calls it off. But still. He's nuts. But, like, awesome nuts."

If conversation were volleyball and Evan were volleying, then right now the sun was in his eyes and the ball had disappeared completely. Lucy was barely paying attention. He wanted her to take his hand. It felt empty. He had been so sure the works of Harmony Korine would get a conversation going.

"That's really cool." She looked lost in thought, but she wasn't sharing any of those thoughts with Art-House Evan, who was bombing, and before he could shake Lucy and demand that she *say anything, anything at all!!!* —

"Look who it is," Lucy coolly stated, raising her chin toward her and Evan's right.

They had come upon a tombstone belonging to one Abraham Meriwether, 1871–1936. Evan had never been so happy to see a dead guy.

"Abe," Evan said with a telling amount of relief and a quick glance at Lucy. "Still here."

They stopped, and Evan dusted some snow off the tombstone. "You know, I looked up his Wikipedia page," Evan said, picking up their old tradition. Even New Lucy™ couldn't resist the History of Abraham Meriwether game.

"Really? Abe has a Wikipedia?" Lucy played along. She looked briefly at Evan for the first time since they'd left her father's house. Her cheeks were flushed, and her lips were pale. They stood out from the wildly cut black hair that seemed chiseled from the sides of her face.

"Oh yeah," Evan said, pulling for a last-quarter comeback from Old Lucy. "Turns out he's a pretty famous guy. For instance, did you know he invented a prototype of the DVD-R?"

"Really?" Lucy asked, the designated skeptic. "Way back in the eighteen hundreds?"

"It was made out of stone."

"Oh, well, that makes sense, then," Lucy said, part of a comedy duo now, playing to the world's most captive audience. "I'd heard he took part in some unsavory honey-based exploits in Hong Kong. He spent the latter years of his life harassed by angry bees."

"This is true. It was the cause of his death, in fact." Evan was relishing the familiarity of the conversation. They'd been discussing Mr. Meriwether for years, his story always changing. He'd been a real-life Sherlock Holmes, a blind championship fighter, and part red fox. At times the entire cemetery had been a ruse to cover up Abraham's underground headquarters.

"Anything else on his Wikipedia?" Lucy asked, and flashes of previous years passed in front of Evan: when they were thirteen and first found Abe; when they were inventing stories for everyone buried there. But Abe was special. *Abraham Meriwether*, come on. "Sure, yeah, of course," Evan said, trying to think up something witty. "Let's see. Abe was very well-known for his activity in the *Julien Donkey-Boy* fandom." Lucy and Evan both laughed at this. "He beat Steve Wiebe's high score in *Donkey Kong*," he added.

"See, again, that seems unlikely," Lucy said with a smile. It was a slight smile, but it was genuine, and Evan knew it from the way her eyes squinted. Lucy fake-smiled often, but Evan knew the real smile was in her eyes.

"Stone tablet *Donkey Kong*," Evan said, looking away from Lucy before she noticed his glances. "That's why the council wouldn't accept his high score."

"Sad." Lucy shook her head.

"A broken heart and hundreds of bee stings, they all led him right here," Evan said. Lucy's smile was forced now. The game was over. The moment had come and gone like a passing breeze.

Lucy let out a sigh as they walked, once again in silence, aside from the crunching of leaves and branches under the snow. Evan noticed the sigh and couldn't help but think that for someone who had texted him earlier, Lucy did not seem all that interested in actually being there. He'd tried to keep her talking, but now he was thinking he should have stayed home. *Maybe she's just in a mood right now. Maybe meeting up later would have been better. Or earlier. Or any other time than right now.* They continued trudging through snow that spilled onto the path leading uphill. At the top of the hill, they turned to follow a line of trees. The icy branches crossed above them like a spiderweb against the sky.

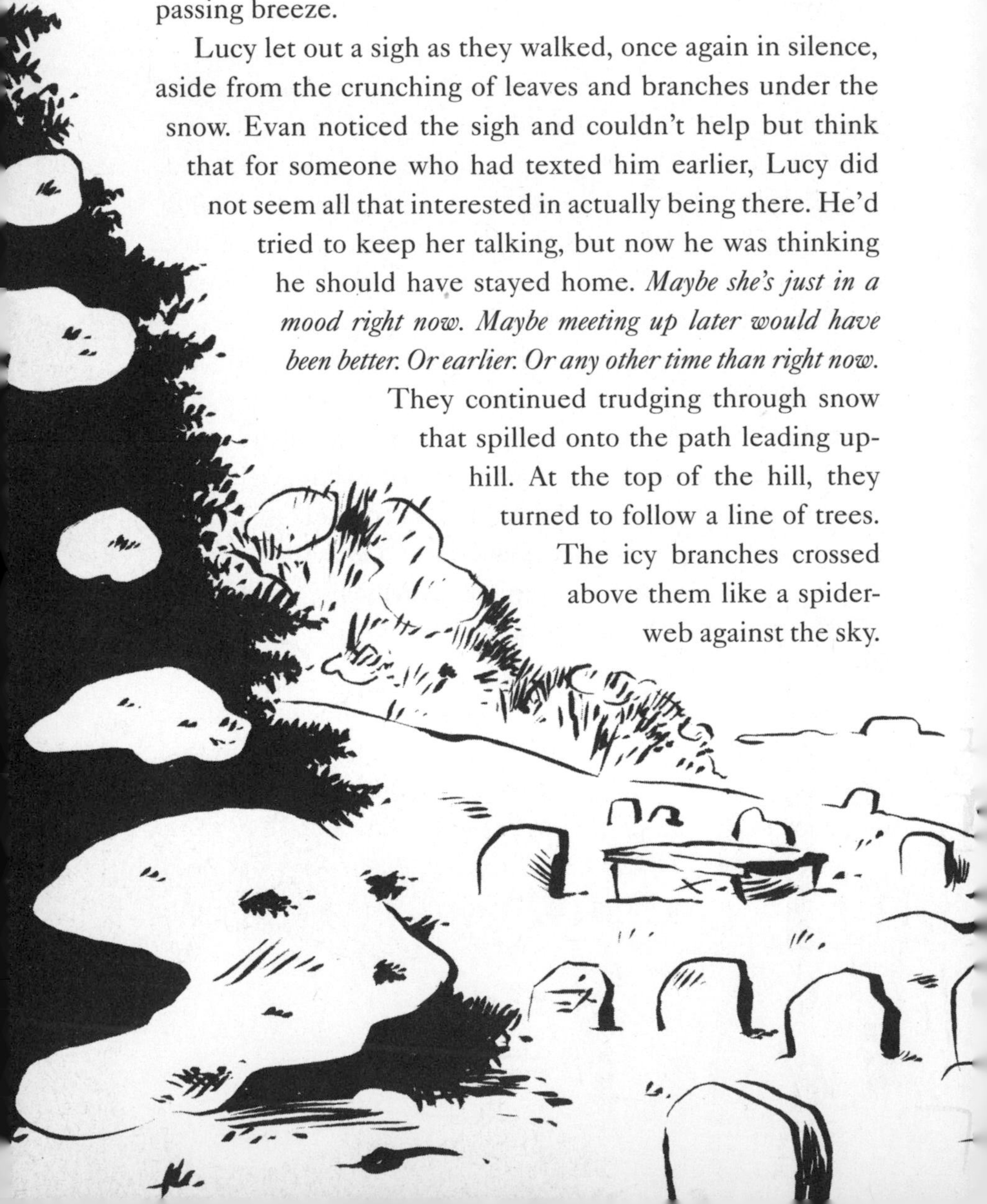

"How long have you been in town, anyway? Did you just get here?" Evan didn't want to seem pushy, but Lucy usually called him or texted the second she landed.

"Huh?" Lucy asked, like she'd just woken up from a nap.

"Well, it's Sunday now. Usually you get here on a Friday or a Saturday, right?"

"Oh. Yeah, no, I got here yesterday. My dad just wanted to spend a little time with me."

"Oh, okay." Evan saw her as infrequently as Doug did. Sometimes he felt guilty spending as much time with Lucy as he did when she was in town, but he figured it was ultimately her choice. "How is he?"

"Fine. You know. For Doug."

"Cool." As another bout of silence came on, Evan's mind started to wander to other things he could or should be doing. Like shoveling the driveway, which he didn't get to finish in the morning. Or helping more with Dad's village. He was starting to feel especially cold, too, and breathed into his gloves and placed his hands

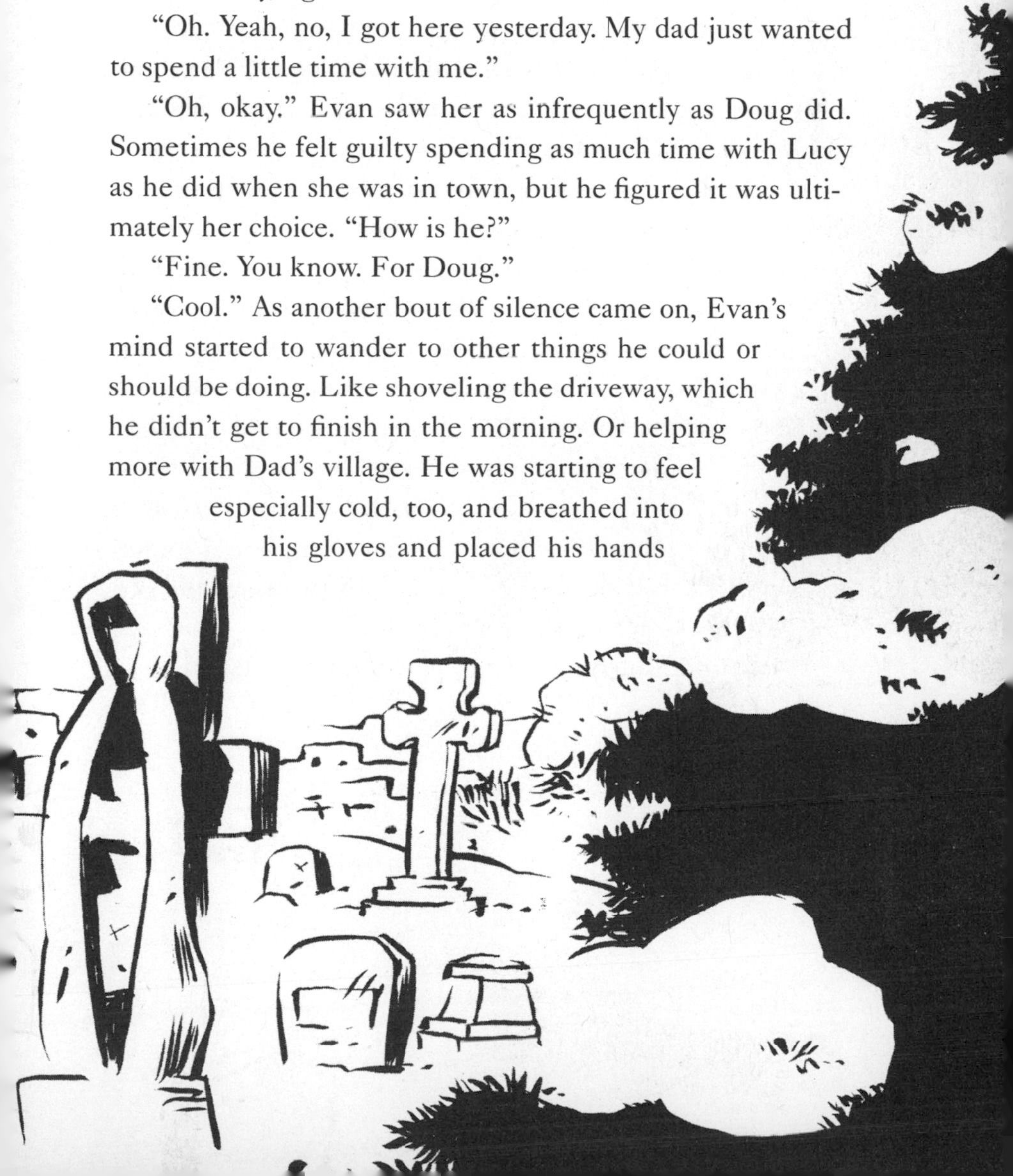

on his cheeks. "It didn't feel this cold when we started walking. You'd think the walk would have actually warmed us up a bit."

"Meteorologist Evan," Lucy quipped.

He was getting tired of making all the effort here and of getting shot down by two-word sentences. Evan thought of volleyball again—Lucy was spiking his every serve. "That would be *biologist*," Evan said, ready to match Lucy's ennui. "You aren't cold? Must not be used to the South yet. Eventually, though. You'll come back here to visit one day and you'll whine about the snow and the cold, all used to your warm temperatures, and your Georgia peaches. Probably won't want to come back here at all."

Lucy took off her gloves and fumbled through her pockets and pulled out a pack of cigarettes. "Sorry, I just really need one," Lucy said as she lit her cigarette. She seemed relieved to do it.

"What? You smoke now, too?" Evan asked.

Lucy blew her smoke out. "It's not, like, always or anything. It's just sometimes."

"Ugh," Evan said. He was already growing weary of New Lucy™. "It's such an unattractive habit."

"Who am I attracting?" Lucy asked, eyes widened, with a hint of contempt.

"Okay, forget that. What about your lungs?"

"Jesus, all right, already," Lucy said. "It's just one cigarette. I told you."

Evan glanced at her from the side of his eye. It was like

they were fighting now. *Why are we fighting?* he wondered. "It's fine. Really."

Evan looked down at his feet, buried in the snow. The bottom fifth of his jeans was soaked. *Dry jeans would feel really good*, he thought. But as long as they were out here and he was striking out, he might as well keep swinging.

"When did you start?" he asked.

Lucy let out a long exhale and closed her eyes. She took another drag and then tossed the cigarette.

"It presented itself as an option," she said, looking away from Evan. "I weighed the pros and cons and made my choice."

"Sensible," Evan said. Everything felt pointless. Lucy wasn't talking and Evan was growing tired of all the mystery, so he suggested they turn back and call it a day. It was a simple suggestion, but one that had never come up on any of their walks. Lucy looked disappointed, and Evan couldn't understand it. He hadn't made the slightest connection with her all afternoon. "I'm just cold," Evan said apologetically, and looked away from her. "And we have all that company still."

"'Kay," Lucy said, almost inaudibly. Her arms dropped to her sides like dead weight.

If he could even catch her attention for a moment, it'd be something. Lucy showed up decked out in leather and looking like Edward Scissorhands, and commanded all this attention she didn't actually want. Evan considered meeting her tomorrow with a mullet and torn jeans and an ill-fitting tank top, with uneven chin stubble and a black eye, and a hickey on his neck, with one green shoe and one red one, and a severed hand. *Some options presented themselves*, he'd say. *I made my decisions.*

Lucy kicked a rock. She was acting like a child who'd been scolded. "Seriously?" she asked. "I haven't seen you in a year, and that's it? You see your family every week."

"Well, then say something, Lucy. What the hell?" Evan had had enough. "You asked me to come out, *you*, and frankly I'm really busy right now. This is not a good time for me. I have a lot on my plate. This year has been rough. And you don't say a word, you shoot down everything I have to say, so what do you want?" Evan felt good letting off a little steam, good enough that he cut himself off there before he said anything he'd regret.

"Fine, you're right. I'm sorry." Lucy didn't return his energy. She was as quiet and aloof as she'd been yet. That made Evan angrier. He had some stranger standing beside him, practically taunting him. He hated it. He wanted her to open up. He didn't care why or how or about what at this point.

"You look ridiculous, by the way," Evan said, feeling bad immediately after he'd said it but pushing ahead anyway. "I really can't imagine what convinced you to do that to yourself."

Evan was sure she'd yell and boil over now, if she didn't punch him, but she stewed for a moment and then told him, "No, you really can't."

"Lucy, what's—" Evan started.

"I was looking forward to seeing you. Sorry I couldn't slip into a comfortable level of banter for you in twenty minutes." Lucy glared at him. "Enjoy your vacation, and have fun with your homework!" Lucy gave Evan a shove and stomped through the snow and leaves. A wind blew, pulling the light snow off the ground and into the air. She left the cemetery and headed back home. Evan watched her walk away. He didn't know what else to do.

"Lucy!" he called out when it was certainly too late.

"And where have you been, mister?" Evan's mom asked him as he walked inside, around five thirty in the evening. It was already long dark by then. A few aunts and uncles were in the living room, everyone picking at food still. They ate early at Sunday dinners so everyone had time to get home and enjoy the rest of the evening. Mom was loading the dishwasher in the kitchen. Dad's town was up and sprawling, the buildings were lit, and all the boxes were put away.

"You know…" Evan said, rolling his eyes. He walked toward the stairs, hoping for an easy exit.

"We're gonna need more details than that," Dad said from the dining room table. Evan's cousins were ready for some kind of dirt.

"I am without details," Evan said, raising his arms as if he could be physically searched for details. "I went over to Lucy's. I always hang out with Lucy when she's home. You know that."

"Bring her over sometime, Evan," Gram said from the couch by the TV. Evan didn't know how to respond. He had felt embarrassed the whole walk home. He had yelled at Lucy for dressing differently and not having anything to say because he was stressed about college choices and history reports and the Christmas town and having to sneak out of the house because of a dinner his family had every single week. He knew he hadn't been fair.

"How is she?" Dad asked. "And how's the homework paper going?" This is what Dad really wanted to ask. Anything else was just a dance to get there.

"She's fine. You know. It's always a little weird at first." He wasn't sure if he'd see her again to prove that right or wrong. "I haven't started the paper yet. Sorry."

"Say good-bye to your aunt and uncle," Mom said, standing in the kitchen doorway. "They're loading up the kids in the car. Are you gonna watch a movie with us after dinner?"

"Or you could get a head start on your paper," Dad said, and glanced at his watch. "It'll be early still."

Evan looked at his mom and then at his dad. He felt angry still. Too angry to work on a paper. Maybe he could get lost in the movie. Maybe that would help.

"Watch a movie with us," Mom said. "You've got all vacation for homework, right, honey?" She looked at Evan's dad, who shook his head and took his plate to the dishwasher. Then she turned back to Evan.

"Sure, sure." Evan relented and gave his mom a peck on the cheek. He had a hard time saying no to his mom anyway. She seemed so excited. After their company left, they ate some cookies she'd baked earlier and watched *It's a Wonderful Life*. The perfect image of a loving family during the holidays. Evan couldn't pay attention to the movie, though. He was still on edge. He felt rotten over Lucy, and he was annoyed with his dad, and his to-do list was looking less and less like a list and more like a big mountain of dirt he had to dig through. By nine, Evan's blinks were lasting a full second each. His dad had been asleep in his chair for the past half hour, his snore as loud as the TV.

When Evan got to his room, he clicked on his drawing-table clamp light. The table was tilted slightly and held a few loose sheets of paper. Along the sides it shelved water-colors, brushes, pencils, pens, and ink. Evan fell into his chair, stared at a blank sheet of paper, picked up a pen, and tapped it against the table. His notebook and history book sat waiting for him on the right. He was so tired. To his left was a half-finished watercolor depiction of Aelysthia with odd-looking creatures at war with one another. Evan brushed his finger over the painting. He liked the texture of watercolor paper. He reached over to his bookcase, where on top of his hardcover Harry Potter collection sat his college applications pile. Evan placed the unruly stack of papers and pamphlets on the table and let his head fall on top of them.

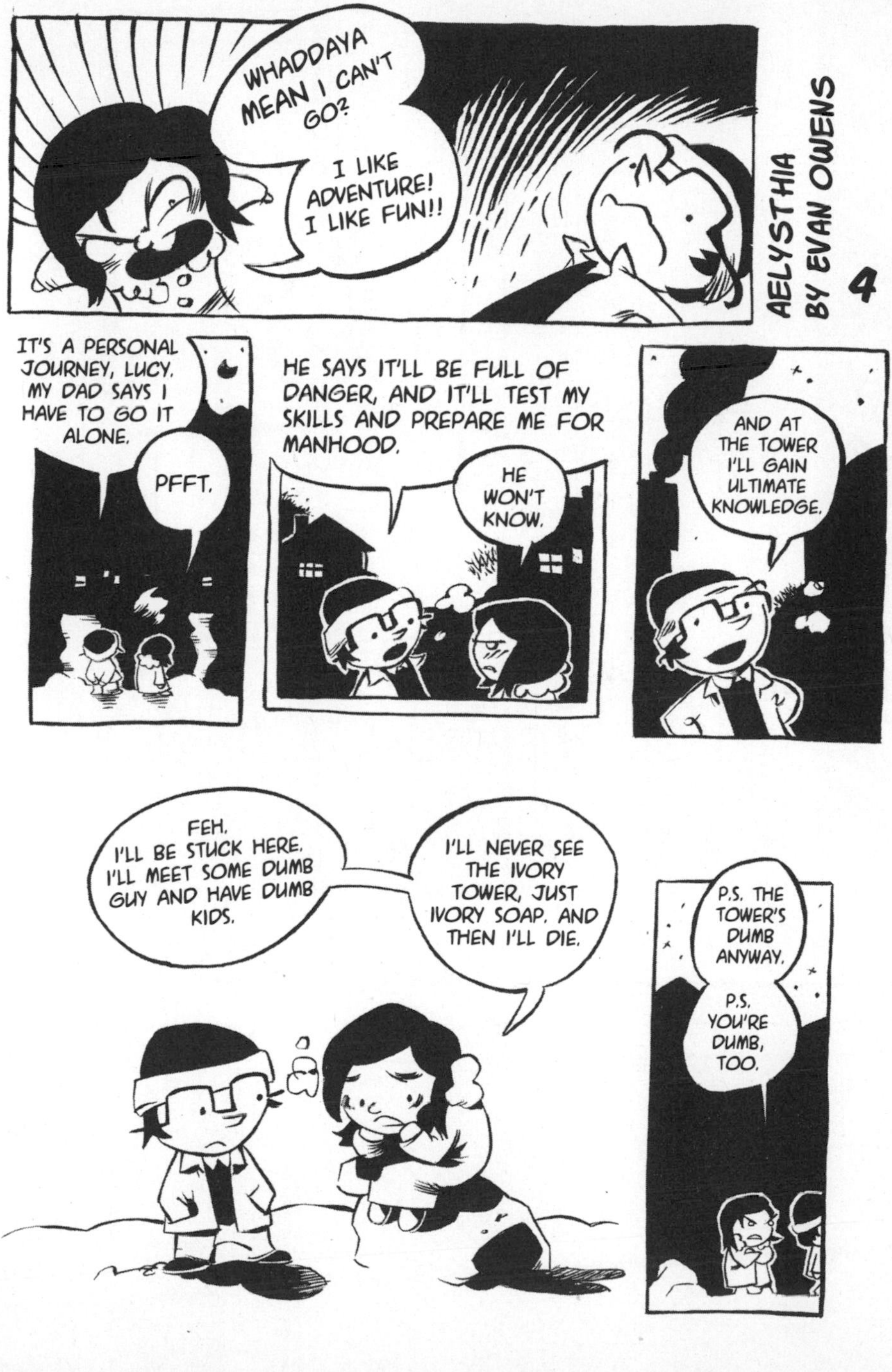
AELYSTHIA
BY EVAN OWENS
4
WHADDAYA MEAN I CAN'T GO?
I LIKE ADVENTURE! I LIKE FUN!!
IT'S A PERSONAL JOURNEY, LUCY. MY DAD SAYS I HAVE TO GO IT ALONE.
PFFT.
HE SAYS IT'LL BE FULL OF DANGER, AND IT'LL TEST MY SKILLS AND PREPARE ME FOR MANHOOD.
HE WON'T KNOW.
AND AT THE TOWER I'LL GAIN ULTIMATE KNOWLEDGE.
FEH. I'LL BE STUCK HERE. I'LL MEET SOME DUMB GUY AND HAVE DUMB KIDS.
I'LL NEVER SEE THE IVORY TOWER, JUST IVORY SOAP. AND THEN I'LL DIE.
P.S. THE TOWER'S DUMB ANYWAY.
P.S. YOU'RE DUMB, TOO.

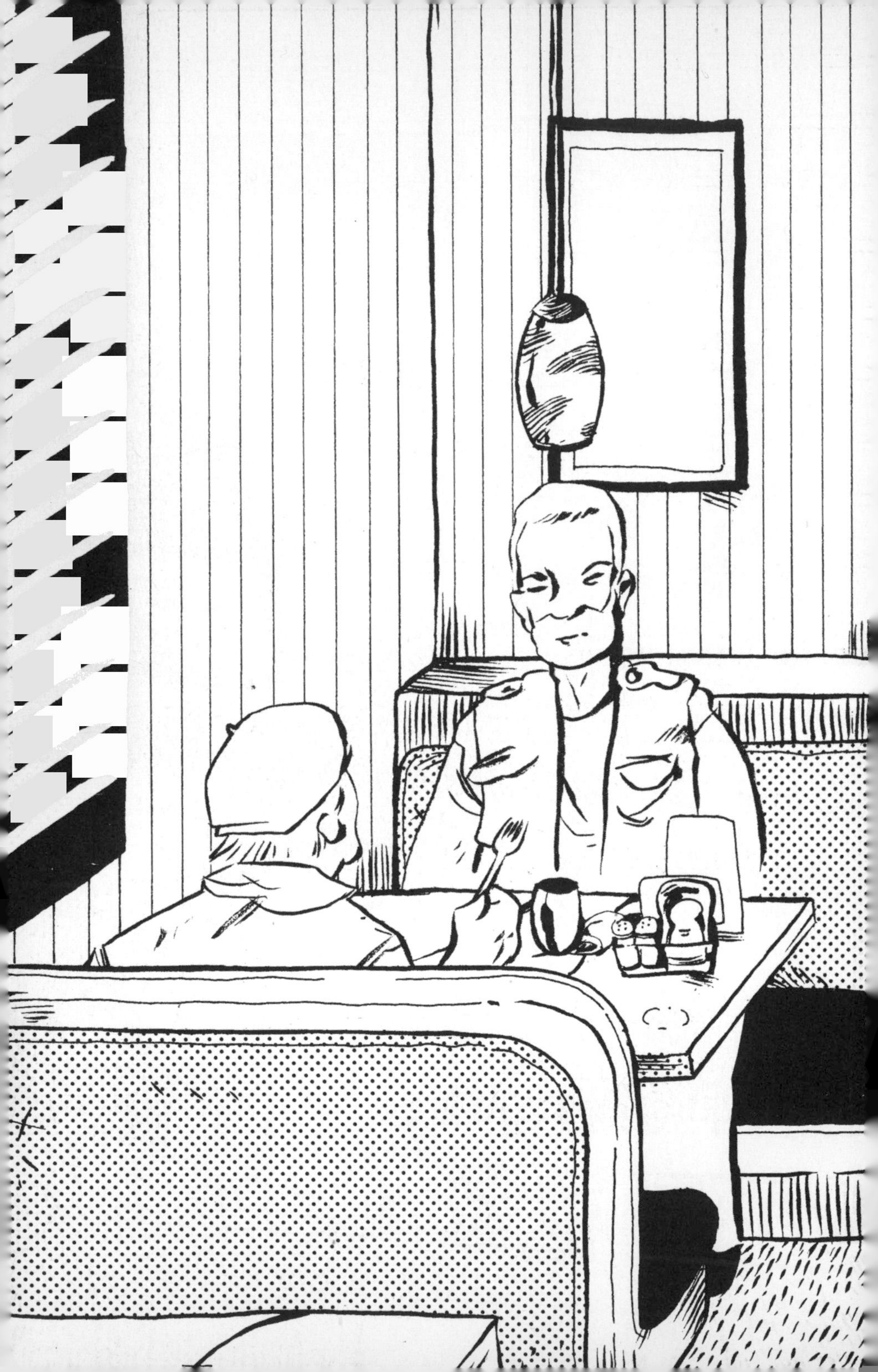

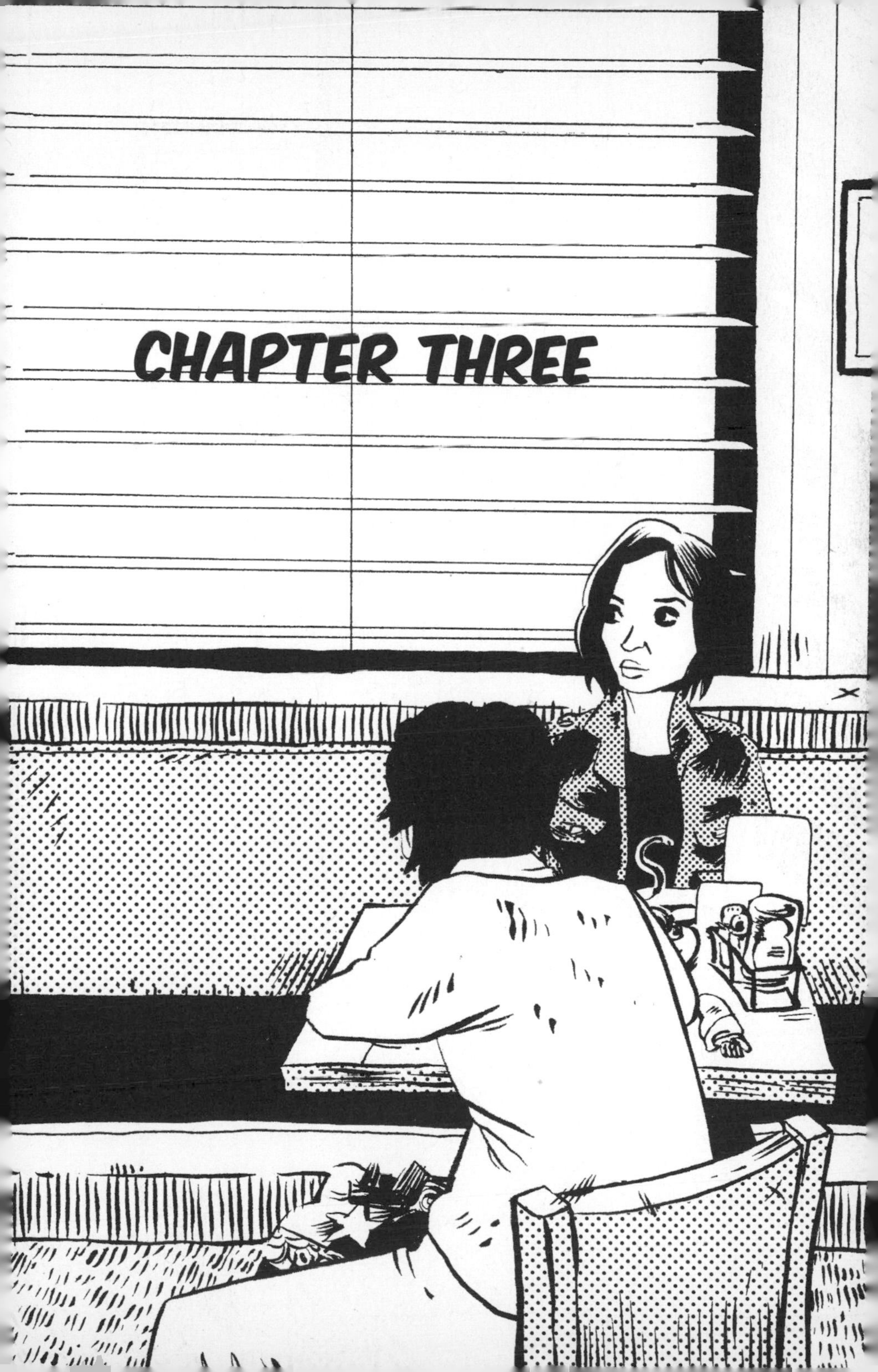
CHAPTER THREE

I'M LOOKING THROUGH YOU

"Hi, Evan, I'll be right with you," the waitress at the small diner Evan liked to frequent said. She gave an extra mumbled hello to Lucy, who sat quietly across from Evan like a ghost. A moment later, she flew past them again. "Sorry I'm taking so long. One minute!"

"It's all right, Tracy. Take your time," Evan said, and Lucy gave him a cold stare. This was the third time the waitress had said *One minute*. Dishes were clanking in the kitchen, and assorted smells wafted by. The coffee and bacon smelled good. The eggs not so much. "She's nice," Evan said, as if that were reason enough to let her take her time.

How did we end up here? Evan thought. So far, breakfast with Lucy was much more subdued than their walk had been. Lucy had shown up on Evan's doorstep in the morning, where she'd sent Evan a text message in lieu of, say, calling or knocking on the door. Evan hadn't brought up Lucy's Goth getup yet, or the fact that the last time they had talked she had shoved him away and ditched him in a cemetery. Their conversation was the better for it. Evan knew a cry for help when he saw one, though, and wasn't ready to let Lucy's odd behavior go completely just yet. He could subtly nag her into submission, for instance. He decided to test it lightly at first and stared at Lucy for a couple of seconds. He was only thinking *Holy hell, what's all that on your face?* but said nothing.

"*What?*" Lucy barked.

Evan snickered to himself and decided he'd back off.

Lucy sighed a gust of air that reached across the table. Her old brown hair would have reacted to the sigh, but her sculpted black hair sat lifeless. She took her phone out of her purse and looked at it for a minute before shutting it off and putting it back in her purse. Evan checked his own phone for messages, but he had only another text from Marshall: *She's obv back, seeing as you've fallen off the face of the earth. Response, plz. M.* Evan put his phone away.

"Marshall's dying to meet you. You really don't remember him at all? Sullen, Gothy, looked kinda like you do now?"

A quick eye movement told Evan to shut up. "If I did know him, it was pre–middle school," Lucy said. "And I've completely blocked out those years by now. Sorry."

Two men were having a loud conversation on Apple and Microsoft and laptop technologies. The rest of the diner was maybe a third populated, so Evan wondered why the hostess had seated him and Lucy right next to these guys.

Evan pushed away his napkin roll of a fork and a knife, and laid out a grid of boxes on a blank page of his sketchbook. The paper stuck to the table, which was still damp from a wiping. He laid out twelve panels, three across and four up and down. Evan and Lucy often spent time waiting for food or for a movie to start doing these jam strips, one-page collaborative comics. Evan would choose a topic and draw the first panel, Lucy would take the second panel and continue the story, Evan would draw the third, and so on. With an even number of panels, one gets to start the comic, and the other gets to finish it.

The morning sun was seeping in through the half-shut blinds of the diner window. There was a row of neighboring stores across the parking lot that were partially obscured by giant hills of plowed snow. The sun was bleaching them pure white. Evan drew the square panels fast and loose, as was his style. He used a pocket brush pen, which gave the appearance you'd get by using a brush dipped in ink.

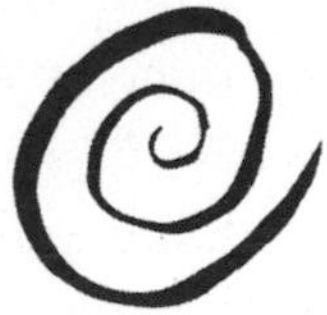

Evan started the first panel while Lucy observed the busy diner. She looked down at her fingers, which were twirling the paper place mat in large circles.

"We're supposed to get a snowstorm today," Evan said, passing the sketchbook to Lucy to continue.

"It's New England—what else is new?" Lucy said in a flat tone, looking at Evan's panel.

"It's just odd because it's sunny," Evan said. *Not this again.* He looked out the window at the stores across from the diner. It looked cold, and it was, but otherwise it seemed pleasant.

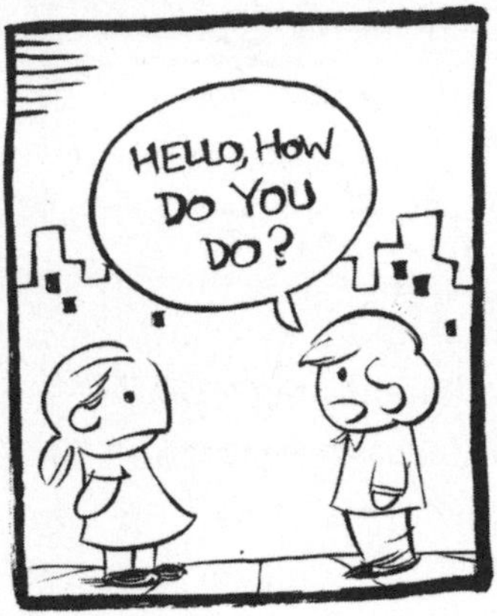
HELLO, HOW DO YOU DO?

"Better go buy five shovels and a fifty-pound bag of salt," Lucy deadpanned. "We'll stock the pantry—might be trapped for the winter."

Evan found himself placing any observation of Lucy into one of two categories: Old Lucy and New Lucy™. Sarcasm was borderline, but he'd give it to Old Lucy. New Lucy™ was moodier and quiet, and, dare he say, *emo*. It amused Evan to know how much she'd hate it if she knew he was thinking this. She'd probably give him a bruise somewhere. *That's so Old Lucy.*

"I'm just being a bitch," Lucy said.

"'S all right. I miss your bitching." It was definitely better than the long stretches of silence.

"It'll get old. Trust me."

Evan watched Lucy draw. She took a lot of time and care to try to match Evan's style. She stuck out her tongue while she was focused, an old habit Evan had noticed years ago. Evan wondered if it helped in some way, if she was aware of it, if he did anything similar when he was drawing. Because when he was focused, he was gone. He could be thumping his leg and sitting in his underwear for all he knew.

Lucy passed the comic back to Evan.

Evan held the pocket brush pen to his chin while he thought of the next panel. The sun moved behind clouds.

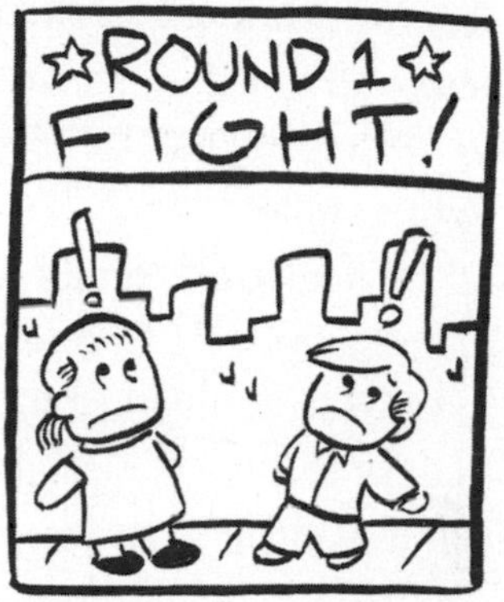
☆ROUND 1☆
FIGHT!

The waitress approached Evan and Lucy. "Hi, sorry for the wait. Can I get you guys something to drink?" she asked with a large grin. Evan ordered an orange juice, and Lucy asked for a coffee.

"Sure, I'll bring those right out," she said, and gave Evan a wink. He figured she must have thought he was on a date.

"Tracy, this is Lucy," Evan said, and Lucy waved. Tracy smiled and said they'd met last year.

"Did you?" said Evan. "Yeah, I guess you would have. Lucy's my best friend since childhood. She's in town for vacation."

"That's so awesome. Well, be sure to enjoy it," said Tracy. Before turning around, she noticed the sketchbook. "Evan, I didn't know you could draw. Are you both artists? May I?" Evan passed her the sketchbook, which she thumbed through. It was mostly jam strips, dating back a few years, with a few random drawings Evan had done on his own interspersed. Evan remembered that some of the jam strips were pretty dirty. He hoped Tracy wasn't looking too carefully.

"*He*'s the artist," Lucy said, pointing to Evan. "I just pretend."

"We *both* are," Evan said, embarrassed. "She's the modest one, and I'm the braggart."

"It's really good, very impressive. *Both* of you," Tracy said with a smile.

"Thank you, thank you," Evan said, playing rock star. Lucy sat quietly. She vacantly looked over the menu.

"Are you guys ready to order, or do you want me to get your drinks first?"

"I'm all set," Evan said. "Lucy?"

"Yeah, you go first," she said, still mulling over her choices. *Not big on small talk*, Evan thought. He looked up at Tracy and ordered a sizable selection of pancakes, sausage, hash browns, and eggs (sunny-side up). Lucy opted for the more economic side of toast. *Plain, please.*

The waitress left, and Evan started drawing. "Not hungry?" he asked.

"Not really," Lucy said. "What about you? Did you just cross a desert or something?"

"I'm a growing boy," Evan said with a wink. He passed the sketchbook back to Lucy.

Lucy, a lefty, started drawing, twisting her arm around the page, turning the sketchbook sideways, her head cocked at a forty-five-degree angle. "You'd think I lack thumbs, looking at my art. I draw like those dogs that paint with brushes attached to their paws."

Evan laughed. "What? What are you talking about? What dogs are these?" He leaned forward, resting his chin on his hand, ready for an explanation.

Lucy relented and laughed herself. "I don't know. Forget that. I was going for something."

"You missed it by a mile."

"Screw you."

Lucy handed him the sketchbook.

"You know you deflect, like, every possible compliment?" Evan said, resuming his drawing. "You used to be so *confident*. What happened to that Lucy?"

"Do I get an example?" she asked, leaning her head on her fist, looking tired.

"Well, I don't have any off the top of my head," Evan said, retreating. He couldn't think of one. He was sure she was confident, at least she was in his mind. Maybe that was just some ancient remnant from eight-year-old Lucy he was holding on to. Shooting her water gun in her mom's face, climbing that tall tree in her yard. Maybe she hadn't earned the confidence moniker in a while. Evan put down the pen and passed the sketchbook back to Lucy. "In general. No, all right, I'll think of something, give me a second." Evan leaned back in his chair, looking down at the table in front of him.

The waitress came back with the orange juice and coffee. Lucy grabbed the coffee, closed her eyes, and took a sip. "Mmmmm."

"How about that talent show?" Evan asked. "How old were you then? You got up onstage and sang in front of our entire class. That was ballsy. That was so Lucy!"

"That was really embarrassing, and it was, like, the worst moment of my life, ever. My parents *made* me do it. You suck. That was an awful example."

"All right, well..." Evan fumbled for words and clung to the next idea that popped into his head. "Your parents. What about when your parents divorced? You were so strong about it. I would have cried like a baby."

"Jesus, Evan. It's like you're trying to be offensive."

"No, I wasn't —" Evan laughed nervously, and then apologized for it quickly when he saw the expression on Lucy's face.

Lucy put the pen down. "Yeah, I didn't cry, but your family isn't fucked up like mine." One of the Apple and Microsoft guys looked over. "It sucked, but I knew it was better that way, too. If your mom and dad divorced, it'd be like going from the perfect parents to some crappy divorced-kid life, but I had the crappy divorced-kid life all along."

"Perfect parents aren't all they're cracked up to be, if that's what my parents are." Evan wondered how many children of "perfect parents" crashed and ended up as meth addicts or convenience store robbers. "Look. You're right. I'm wrong. I have learned my lesson, and I retract all previous statements. Like, ever." Evan knew this wasn't the right time to back down, though. She was finally talking. About real stuff. *Maybe she'll open up about this lifestyle makeover*, he thought. "I shouldn't assume anything. It's just—We just never really talked about any of that."

"Well, I was twelve," Lucy said, shifting her eyes. "I didn't want to talk."

"Sure," Evan said, taking baby steps and happy with the progress. "That's completely acceptable. I've made things awkward here. This is a lame breakfast now, isn't it?" Evan waved his napkin in front of him. "See this? This is my white flag. I'm waving it."

Lucy broke into a smile. "It's fine. You're just a big dork. I'm used to it."

Evan was content with that answer. *Big dork* was a strong compliment in their world. "If you ever do want to talk, you know, about anything—"

"It's like this," Lucy said. "If my nose wasn't pierced and my hair wasn't dyed, we wouldn't even be having this conversation." Lucy started drawing again. "You're just used to the long brown hair and the preppy clothes. This is more who I am. This is who I've always been."

Lucy finished her panel in silence while they waited for the food to arrive. Maybe she was right. Maybe it was just the clothes and the makeup. They felt extreme and sudden. They did leave an impression.

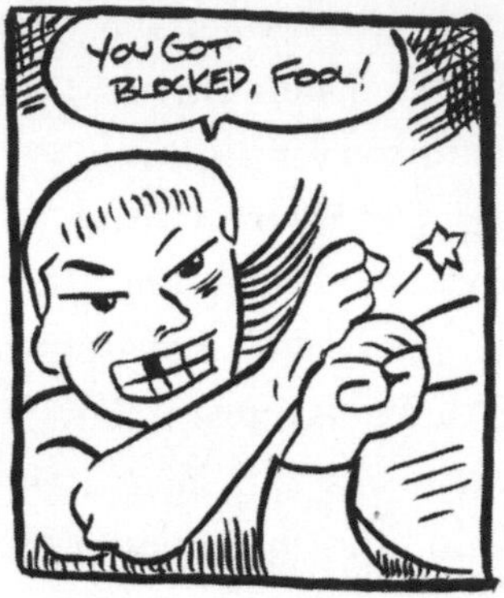
YOU GOT BLOCKED, FOOL!

The waitress brought out the food and set it on the table. Lucy's toast, and Evan's feast. "Here you are. Careful, plates are hot. Can I get you anything else?" she said, standing up straight and smiling.

"No, I think we're good," Evan said, distracted by the thought that maybe Old Lucy had been New Lucy™ all along. He pushed the sketchbook across the table.

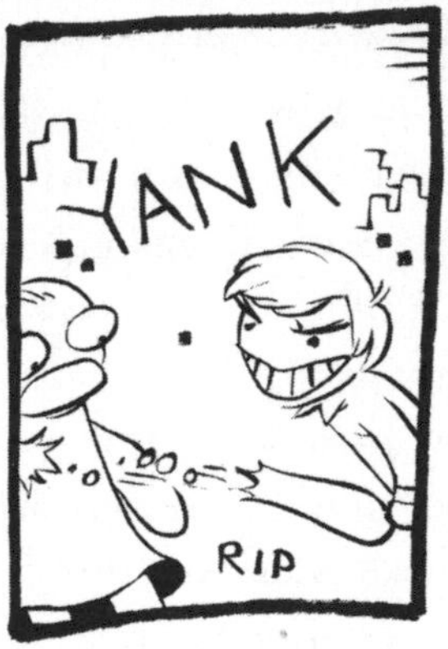
YANK
RIP

"Thanks," Lucy said, and picked at her toast, looking at the jam strip. She picked up the pen and started to draw.

Evan surveyed his multiple plates of food, comparing them with Lucy's heated bread. "I feel like a fat ass now."

"Don't, it's cool. I'm just not hungry."

"Old Lucy used to *eat*," Evan said, gulping the orange juice and hoping she hadn't caught the term *Old Lucy*.

"Okay, can we stop that now? I feel like you're picking on me again today."

"Picking on you?" Evan asked, looking at Lucy's last panel and chuckling. "I complimented you."

"You're right. I'm just crazy." Lucy shook her head and

looked groggy. She nibbled on her toast, holding it with both hands. Her face dropped to a pout. Then, suddenly and with direct eye contact: "Look, I'm sorry about the cigarette thing

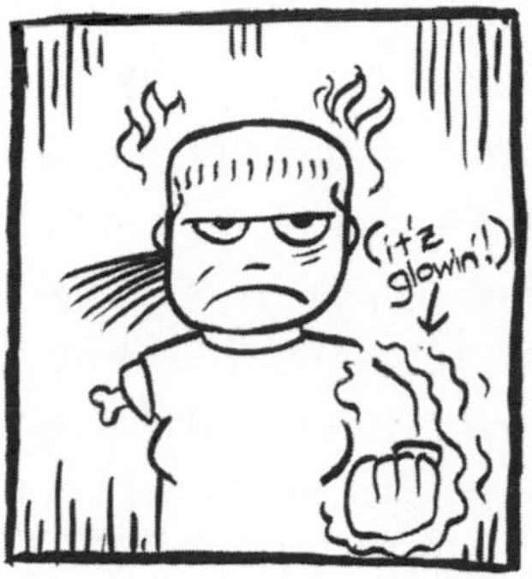
(it'z glowin'!)

yesterday. If it freaked you out or whatever."

"No. It didn't," Evan said, alarmed at the concern. He was glad she wasn't still mad at him for blowing up. Before she'd said that, he'd forgotten about the cigarette ordeal completely. "It's fine. Really. Serious this time."

"Okay. I thought maybe that was why you were mad at me," Lucy said. She ran her finger around the edge of her plate, which still held a piece and a half of toast. "I had been thinking on the plane ride here about the time you stole your dad's car to come get me. It was still on my mind while we were walking. Do you remember that?"

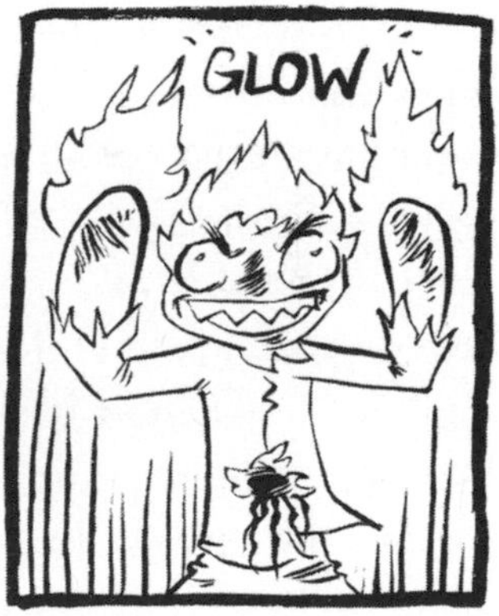
GLOW

The memory flashed in front of Evan like a bad dream. "God, don't remind me. That was terrible."

"Come on, you didn't even get caught," Lucy said.

"I was scared to death. Are you kidding me? We were *fifteen*. Not only did I barely know how to drive, but I was also scared for weeks that my dad was going to find out and run me over to teach me a lesson. Not to mention it was illegal. Can you imagine if it had been printed in the police blotter?"

"I guess." Lucy seemed to dismiss his rant. "It's still one of my favorite memories."

"Seriously?" Evan asked, surprised. "If I recall this correctly, you got into some huge fight with your grandparents, and you were hitchhiking out of town when you called me. How could that be a favorite memory? I was furious with you."

"But you came out and saved me," Lucy said quietly, looking up.

"Well, yeah," Evan said, his eyes shifting down. "I wasn't going to let you get killed or anything."

"You stole your dad's car and you drove out to get me. It was so sweet. You wouldn't talk the whole way back because you were afraid you'd crash into a telephone pole or something. You were all frozen and nervous and shaky.

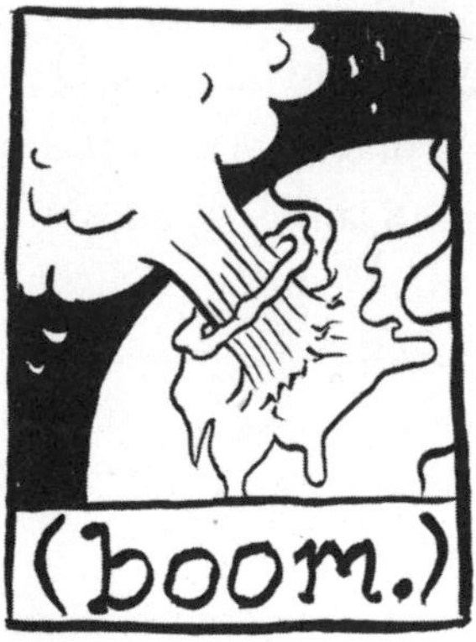
(boom.)

"It was pretty amazing. It's not easy to pull you out of that comfort zone." Lucy started wrapping up the comic. She went at it like the ending was already written in her mind, written several panels ago, when she saw where the comic was headed.

"What?" Evan asked. "That's not true. I like doing new things."

"Pfft," Lucy said. "You don't know you well enough to

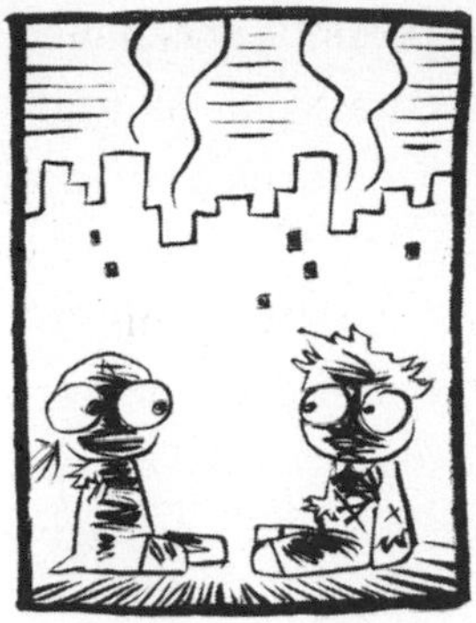

make those kinds of claims. You want a cigarette?" she asked, pulling the pack out of her pocket.

"Get rid of those things." Evan waved her off. "That's not change. That's suicide." He quickly completed his panel.

Lucy helped herself to some of Evan's hash browns. "What's this now?" Evan asked.

"We're gonna be here all day waiting for you to finish that!"

"I'm gonna starve!"

"Waahmbulance," she mocked, sipping from his orange juice. "Wanna brave the crowds and hit the mall?" Lucy asked, her eyes squinting a little.

"Yeah, definitely," Evan said, taking his wallet out of his pocket. Lucy slid the finished jam strip back to Evan.

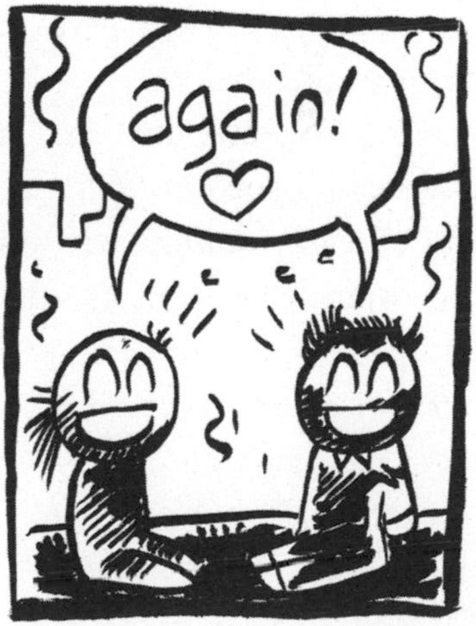
again!

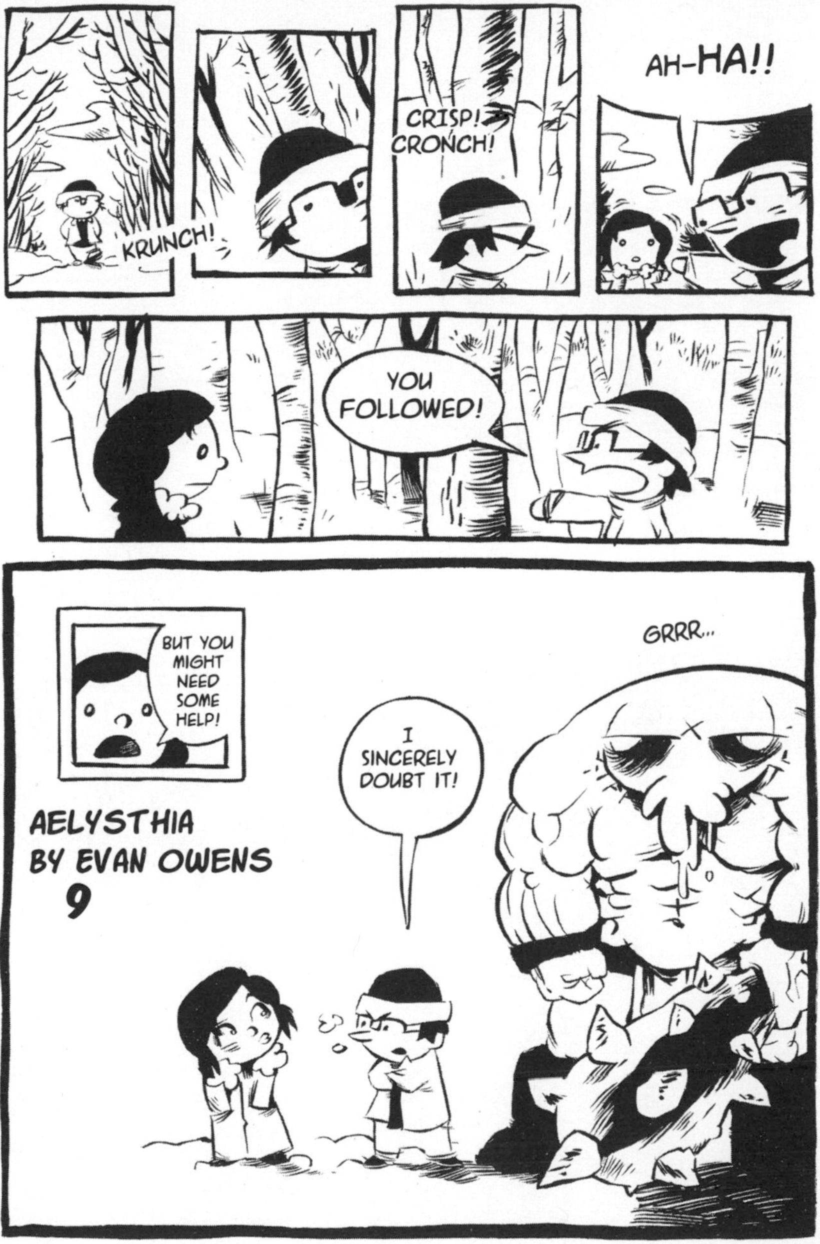
KRUNCH!
CRISP! CRONCH!
AH-HA!!
YOU FOLLOWED!
BUT YOU MIGHT NEED SOME HELP!
GRRR...
I SINCERELY DOUBT IT!
AELYSTHIA
BY EVAN OWENS
9

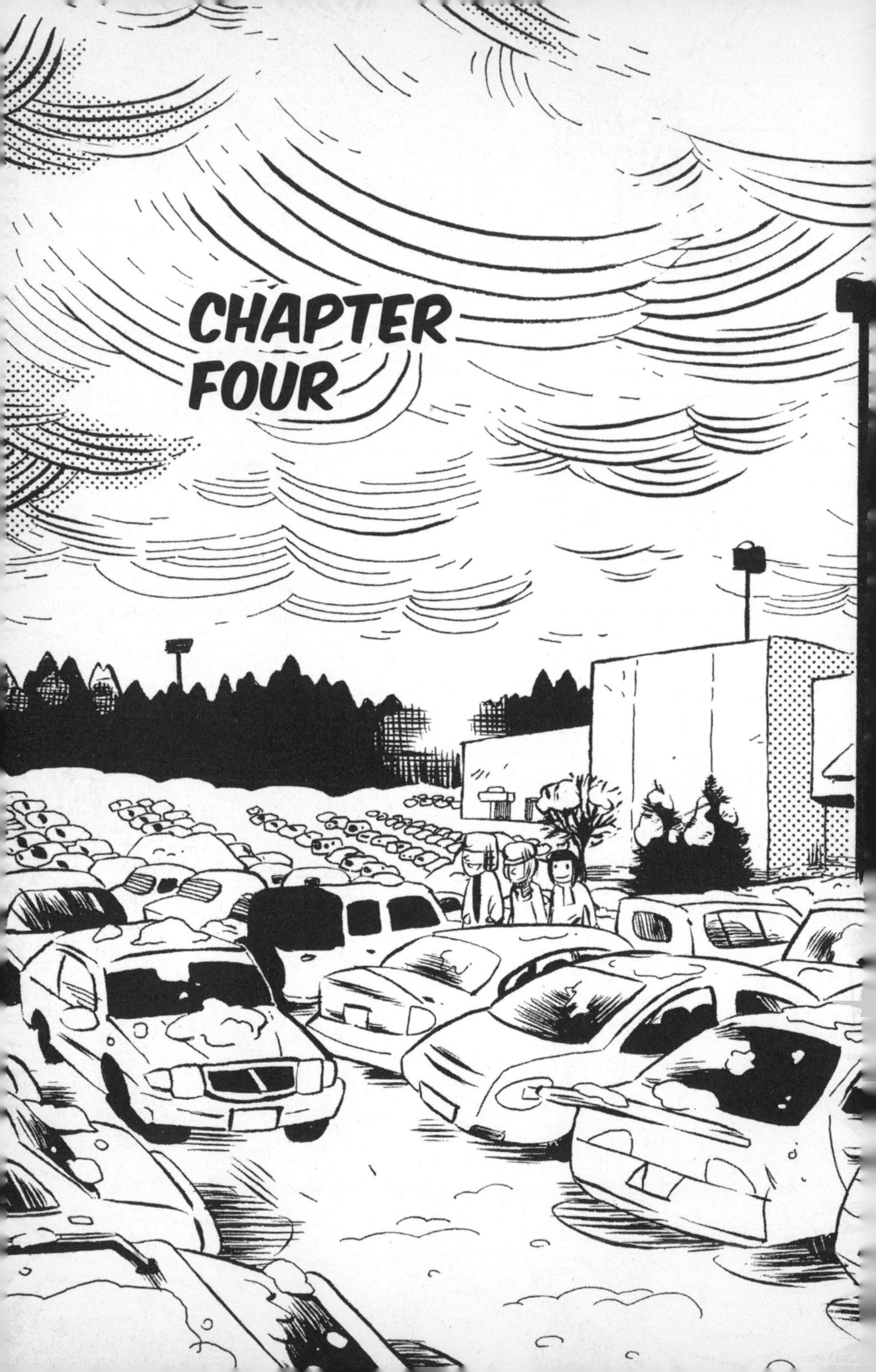
CHAPTER
FOUR

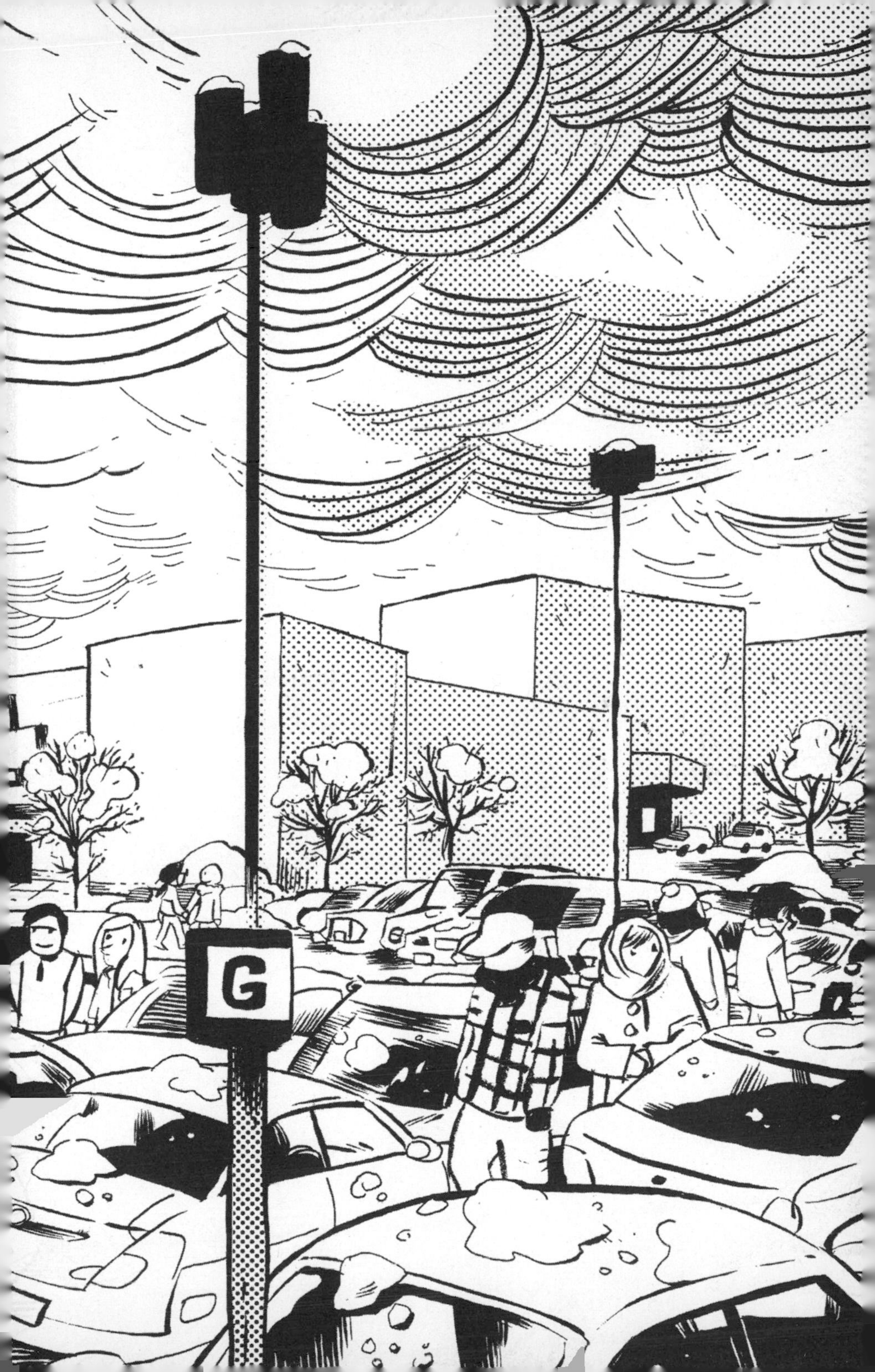
G

CARRY THAT WEIGHT

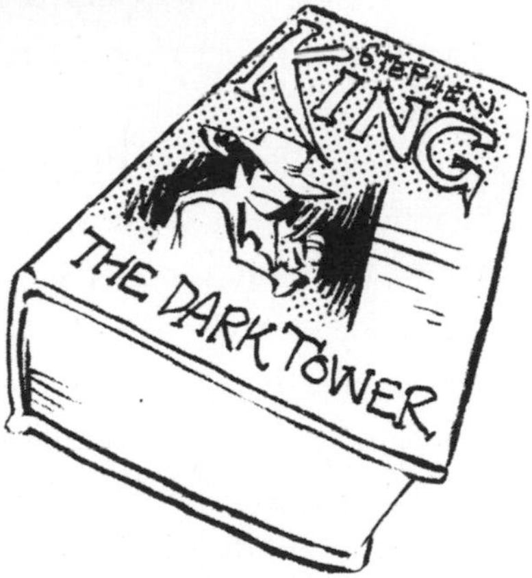
STEPHEN
KING
THE DARK TOWER

The mall parking lot seemed at capacity. Evan had to park as far away from the mall as possible. Even the pressing air of storm all around couldn't keep the crowds away. He found it hard to imagine there was anyone in town who wasn't there.

Evan stepped out of the car and looked up at the clouds billowing—dark and light and swirling together. The wind was strong, and it was just starting to snow. Evan felt like he was caught in a perpetual slap, his cheeks stinging. He felt woken up. School and research papers and graduation slipped away. He looked at Lucy, who lowered her head and sped up her pace. Evan caught up. They started the trek through the sea of parked cars, heading toward the mall, that tiny box off in the distance.

"*Gawd*," Lucy said.

"This is good," Evan said in his outdoor voice. "You can walk off that piece of toast."

"So how many Dark Tower volumes are you going to get?" Lucy yelled over the loud whooshes of air. "I suggest getting at least the first three. You'll finish them all before you come back here."

Lucy buried her hands deep in her jacket pockets and leaned against Evan as they walked. Evan knew he'd have to read those damn thousand-page tomes eventually. He and Lucy had always delved into fantasy epics together. It was like they shared a dozen hidden universes and it was imperative they both spoke the same languages. Even a book like *The Hobbit*, though, which is far less dense than *The Lord of the Rings*, had a certain heft to it. These things didn't come short.

"I don't have the *time*," Evan whined. "That's seven large books!"

"Tell you what, read the first four, and I'll just explain what happens after that."

"All right, what can I get you to read, then? If I'm going to give up the rest of my year chasing the Tower, you've got to read something, too."

"I'm listenin'."

"Okay, this is pressure now. This has to be good." Evan winced at a rush of cold wind against his face. "I want to say

Gunnerkrigg Court, but that's a Web comic and you can read it in, like, a day. Same goes for *Achewood*."

"All right, keep thinking. And I already read *Achewood*."

"It's so good."

"I know! You could do an *Achewood*, too, though."

Lucy could sound like a broken record sometimes. It wasn't that Evan didn't like drawing or didn't feel he had some talent at it. There were other issues. Like time. Or energy, or commitment, or having anything to say. Evan always thought of drawing as more of a hobby.

"It's just not my thing," Evan said, exasperated.

"Again with this!" Lucy said, giving Evan a push. He strayed a few feet with the momentum before curving back to Lucy. "What are you going to do with that talent? It's senior year. I know you have some kind of plan in mind. You can't make art because you're going to be a big-shot lawyer and collect Christmas toys and marry someone just like your mom?"

"I make art." Evan felt attacked. Evan didn't want to be like his dad. He didn't think so, at least. "Where'd that come from?"

"Come on. It's so obvious you want to be like your dad. It's fine, I just want to hear you say it."

"I'm just…" He wasn't sure what he wanted to be.

"Mm-hm," Lucy said quietly.

And he wasn't sure what Lucy wanted to hear. "I guess I could be an artist."

"You should be. And you can have legions of little teenybopper fans groveling at your feet and tearing your clothes everywhere you go," Lucy said. "I'll be the first one. I'll tear the sleeve right off your arm."

"Here's the thing, though," Evan said, trying to ground this pep talk in some level of reality. "It's a hobby. No one makes any money doing comics. It's like being a poet or a mime or something. It's cool and all, but you can't really make a living off it. You can't raise a family from it."

"Evan, do you want to be a mime?" Lucy asked, concerned eyes effectively cutting the tension that was building. Evan laughed. "I looked into it, yes."

"And who cares about money? Where's the compulsion to create and showcase and put it out there?" Evan and Lucy crossed the street to the mall sidewalk. Evan left a dollar with the Salvation Army Santa. "You should see some of the people in Georgia," Lucy said. Evan let her continue. She didn't often talk about Georgia. "I know some friends of friends who go to SCAD, the Savannah College of Art and Design. Like this one guy Matt makes these xeroxed-and-stapled comics, and every year he goes to the MoCCA festival in New York and sells them. He doesn't live off it—I can't imagine he even recoups the cost of getting a table there. But he meets all these other artists and trades comics with them, and he's part of this whole community. It's not their primary source of income, but it's a big part of their lives and it makes them happy. And this other kid there does this Web comic about computers and stuff, and I know that's not your thing, but he has all these people who visit his site and communicate with him, like he has his own fan

74

club. One of my friends is in a sketch-comedy group. I don't know that anyone sees their stuff, but they have a lot of fun with it."

It really didn't sound bad. It just sounded like a TV show where all the characters have great apartments and nice clothes and attractive friends but never work. "Are you in this sketch-comedy thing?" Evan asked.

"Eff no," Lucy quickly said. "I'd melt the camera film."

"They probably do it digitally," Evan said, aware of how quickly Lucy dismissed any focus on herself. For someone who just spent a few minutes dishing out a pile of analysis, she sure didn't like to take any.

"Then I'd melt the"—Lucy gave it a quick thought—"computer chip."

"Come on. You're the big dream chaser. You'd be good. I can see it." Evan pictured Lucy in various wigs and mustaches, talking about crunchy frogs and cheese shops. The more he thought about it, the more he realized she should be on TV. She was watchable, unpredictable, sharp, and certainly theatrical. Give her a stage and she'd command attention. Lucy was a star in waiting.

They entered the mall, where a vent blasted hot air from the ceiling. They stood under it and thawed.

"I need to warm up," Lucy said, out of breath and red-faced. A crowd of people came in from the parking lot and trafficked past them into the mall.

"You never told me about any of these people," Evan said, curious about Lucy's suddenly blossomed social life. He really didn't know much about it, but then again, she didn't know much about his, either. She hadn't met most of his current friends. Their time together always went quickly, and the rest of the year Lucy was the off-line type. Evan usually heard from her only a handful of times.

"I'm a girl of mystery, Evan Owens. I don't tell you everything."

"I guess not," Evan said. He raised an eyebrow. "You ever *date* any of these guys?"

"Maybe," Lucy said, letting the intrigue linger a moment. "No. I did tear this one guy's shirtsleeve off, though."

"Yeah, I'm not sure what to make of that," Evan said.

Surrounded by shiny reds, greens, silvers, and golds, Christmas trees, large candy-cane sculptures, and signs that shouted *SALE! SALE! SALE!* Evan took in the Christmas spirit. There were signs on every window, and Evan knew that eventually the walls would be bare and the crowds would be gone and there wouldn't be all the excitement. January was always a depressing month. Evan was glad to be doing something familiar with Lucy and glad that she had suggested it. It meant to Evan that things were getting back to normal. This was something they did every year, although Evan was pretty sure he wasn't going to get a picture of Lucy on Santa's lap like they'd done their freshman year of high school.

It was hard to get anywhere in the mall or in any of the stores. People of every age were walking the same subleisurely pace. Evan huffed and reached his head around, looking for any clear path to walk comfortably. He felt a hand grab his and pull. Lucy, being smaller and used to having

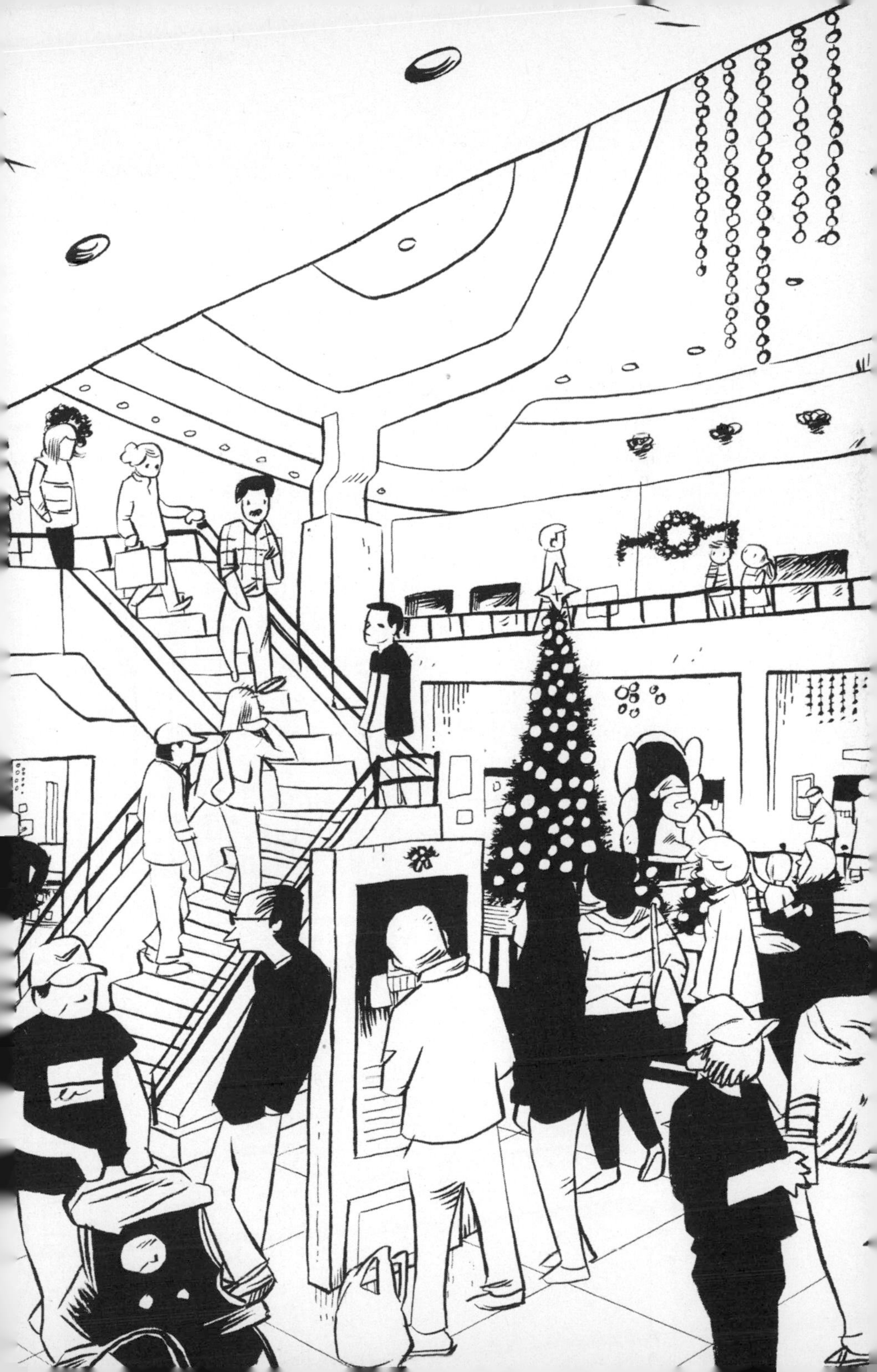

easier access in situations like this, pulled him through the crowds. *Sorry. Pardon. 'Scuse me.* It was the only way they were able to move.

They ran from store to store like they did when they were children. Or like they would have, if Evan's parents hadn't been with them. Unsupervised kids. Evan felt an urge to be bad. They dashed into Best Buy, and he loaded Lucy's arms with things she wasn't buying.

"Beats by Dr. Dre, you *need* these," Evan said, placing a box of the expensive headphones on her already-growing pile of things she'd have to put back.

"I don't even have an iPod! Do these plug into a record player?"

"Why don't you have an iPod?" Evan asked, picking up a tricked-out wireless mouse. Lucy needed this. "Let's go find you an iPod!"

Evan and Lucy were making their way through a

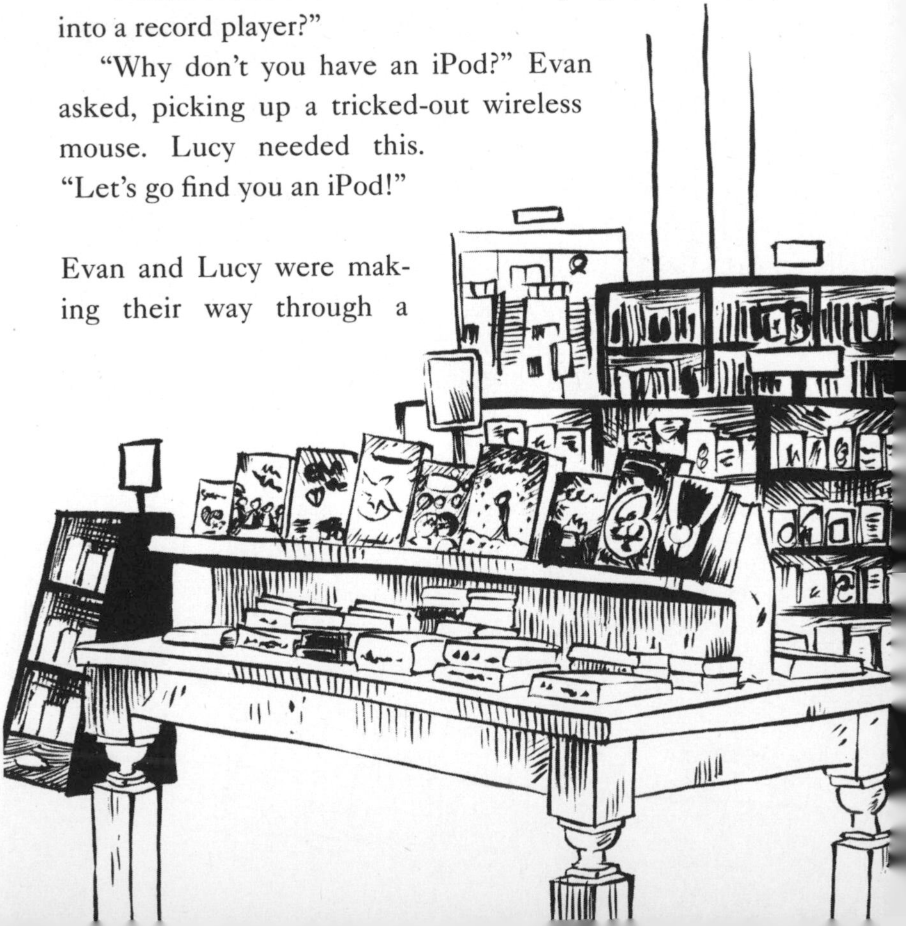

Barnes & Noble when Evan spotted someone with brown hair and blue-framed glasses duck down by the magazine shelf. He knew those glasses. Suspicious, Evan surveyed the area quickly and saw a familiar old-style hat with earflaps poking out above a low shelf. They were being followed.

"Are you guys stalking me?" Evan asked, approaching Marshall by the magazines. He was surprised, but excited to introduce them to Lucy.

"Evan!" Marshall said. "And you must be Lucy!"

"You're stalking me!" Evan repeated, and Tim came over.

"Oh, hey!" Tim said, and then shook Lucy's hand. "Hi, I'm Tim. Do you like Duran Duran?"

"Um, not really? Sorry?" Lucy said, confused. Tim looked disappointed.

"How could we be stalking you?" Marshall said. "Last I got was a text from you saying you were at breakfast, with *no* mention of the mall, even though you know we love the mall. In fact, you might be stalking us."

"It's not like we just showed up at the diner to surprise you guys, and you were just leaving so we tailed you to the mall or anything," Tim said. "We do have lives, you know."

"I want to know everything about Lucy," Marshall said. "Evan says you're more badass than Wonder Woman."

"I wouldn't say that," Lucy said. "But I do have an invisible aircraft that's kinda like hers."

"I'm so jealous!" Marshall said. "I want to see it!"

"Well, you can't, because, you know, it's invisible."

Evan was glad to see Lucy warm up to Tim and Marshall in record time. He had known they'd hit it off, but watching them talk and laugh, Evan felt like she'd always been a part of the gang. Evan almost felt like a third wheel.

"Hey, I have a question, if you guys will humor me," Lucy asked as they walked aimlessly through the store. "Actually two questions. One, why Duran Duran? And two, since I never get to see Evan's friends, what's he like? Like when you guys hang out, is he all *Waaah, I have too much homework to do!* Because this guy is way too into his schoolwork."

"Yes! That's definitely Evan," Marshall said.

"Aww," Tim said. "He can't help it. He's in all the advanced classes."

"I knew it! You're a buzz-kill!" Lucy said, and gave Evan a poke in the ribs.

"Evan's a lot of fun as long as you can plan it out. He's a man with a plan," Marshall said. "He's going to help us film a horror movie. So, what's cooler than that, right?"

"I'm starring in it," Evan said, beaming a little, showing off for Lucy. "I'm going to be pantsless."

"I am so impressed with you right now," Lucy said. "I'm looking at you a little differently. Pantsless movie star Evan Owens."

"*Ow!*" Tim said, celebrating Evan's newfound awesomeness. "Oh, and I just thought if you liked Duran Duran, then we could bond over it or something."

"We'll find something. What about Tears for Fears?"

"I'm onboard," Tim said. "We're, like, best friends now. We're bonded by eighties music. It's like superglue."

"We'll leave you two kids alone, but first…" Marshall

turned to Lucy. "We're having a Christmas Eve party, and I do hope you plan to attend."

Lucy looked at Evan, caught up in the whirlwind of fun that was Tim and Marshall. "I guess? Sure!"

"Of course she'll be there," Evan said. "Unless you guys have graduated from stalking to flat-out kidnapping by then."

Evan sat in the food court a half hour later, holding a table while Lucy got mall sushi. Lucy had been full of energy since meeting Tim and Marshall, who had that effect on people. Things were going really well now. He was glad she had come over that morning. All the stress he'd felt was falling away. Evan supposed that was Lucy's effect.

"Is anyone...?" a tall Asian man asked Evan, pointing to the empty chair reserved for Lucy.

"Someone's sitting here," Evan told the man, the fourth person to ask in as many minutes. Evan looked around at the volume of people. Large families spreading over generations sat together, eating and laughing. Children ran around restlessly, ready to go back into the stores. Evan liked this time of year. It may have been artificial or designed by companies, but it gave everyone an excuse to be happy and to go out and enjoy one another's company. Evan began to eat his slice of pizza when Lucy arrived.

"Oh my God, the freaking lines," she said, placing her food on the table. "Goddamn lady had to pay for sushi with a check. Who uses checks?"

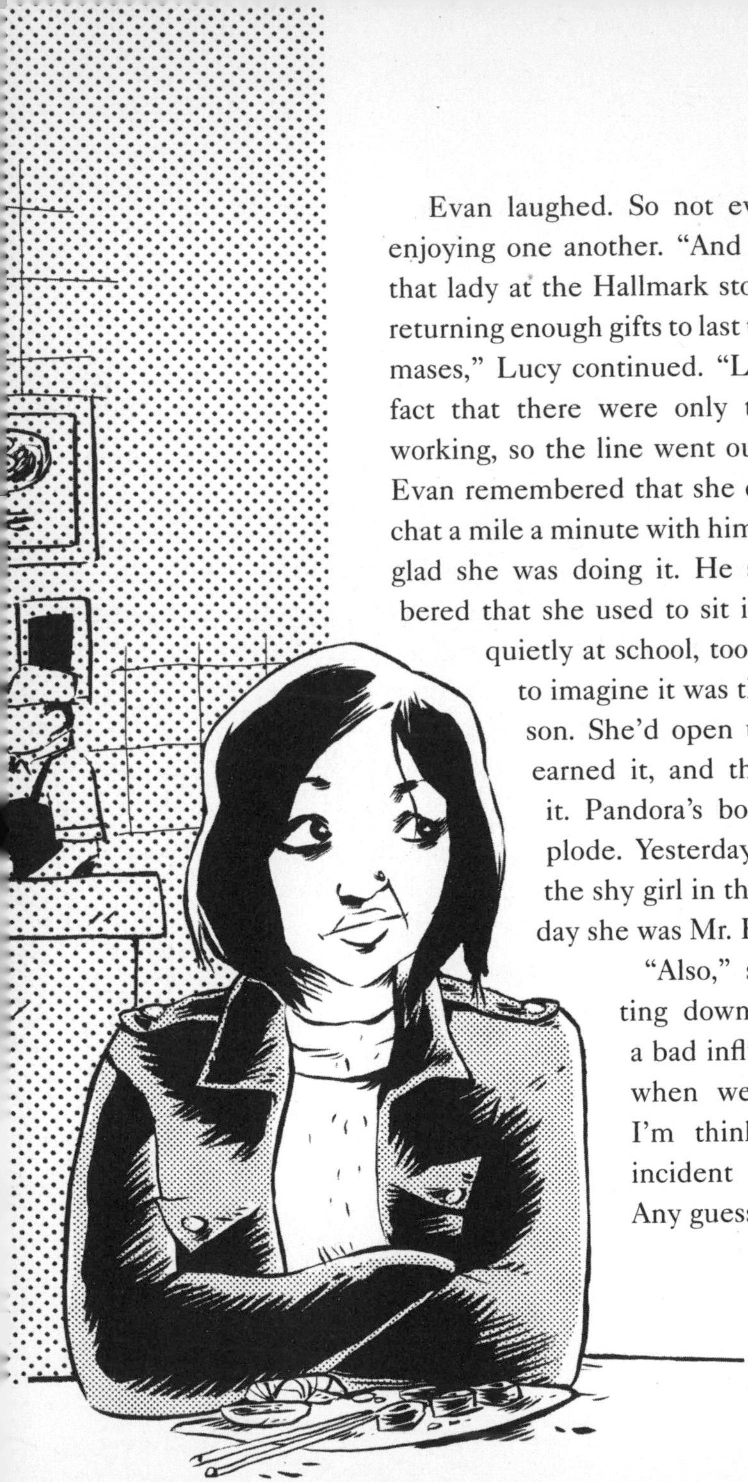

Evan laughed. So not everyone was enjoying one another. “And did you see that lady at the Hallmark store? She was returning enough gifts to last three Christmases,” Lucy continued. “Let alone the fact that there were only two cashiers working, so the line went out the door.” Evan remembered that she could always chat a mile a minute with him, and he was glad she was doing it. He also remembered that she used to sit in the corner quietly at school, too. It was hard to imagine it was the same person. She’d open up once you earned it, and then that was it. Pandora’s box would explode. Yesterday she’d been the shy girl in the corner. Today she was Mr. Hyde.

“Also,” she said, sitting down, “you were a bad influence on me when we were kids. I’m thinking of one incident in particular. Any guesses?”

"That doesn't seem probable," Evan said, diving comfortably into her non sequitur. He gave it a quick thought but came up blank. "No guesses."

"The rock in the street?" Lucy raised her eyebrows. "You made me roll a giant rock into the middle of the street at night. We could have seriously messed up someone's car, or worse!"

"Come on. You know it was cool." Evan turned a little red. Lucy went from shy girl to chatty, but Evan went from placing giant rocks in the road to being on-target for class valedictorian.

"Not cool, Ev. And Mr. Genovese? Threatening to tell our parents?"

"That's right. 'What's the matter with you, Lucy? You know better than that!' Oh, he was pissed." Evan looked at nothing in particular, with the ghost of a smile still on his face as he pictured the scene. Evan had been the more aggressive of the two when they were kids. He was a little hyper, and spontaneous. He

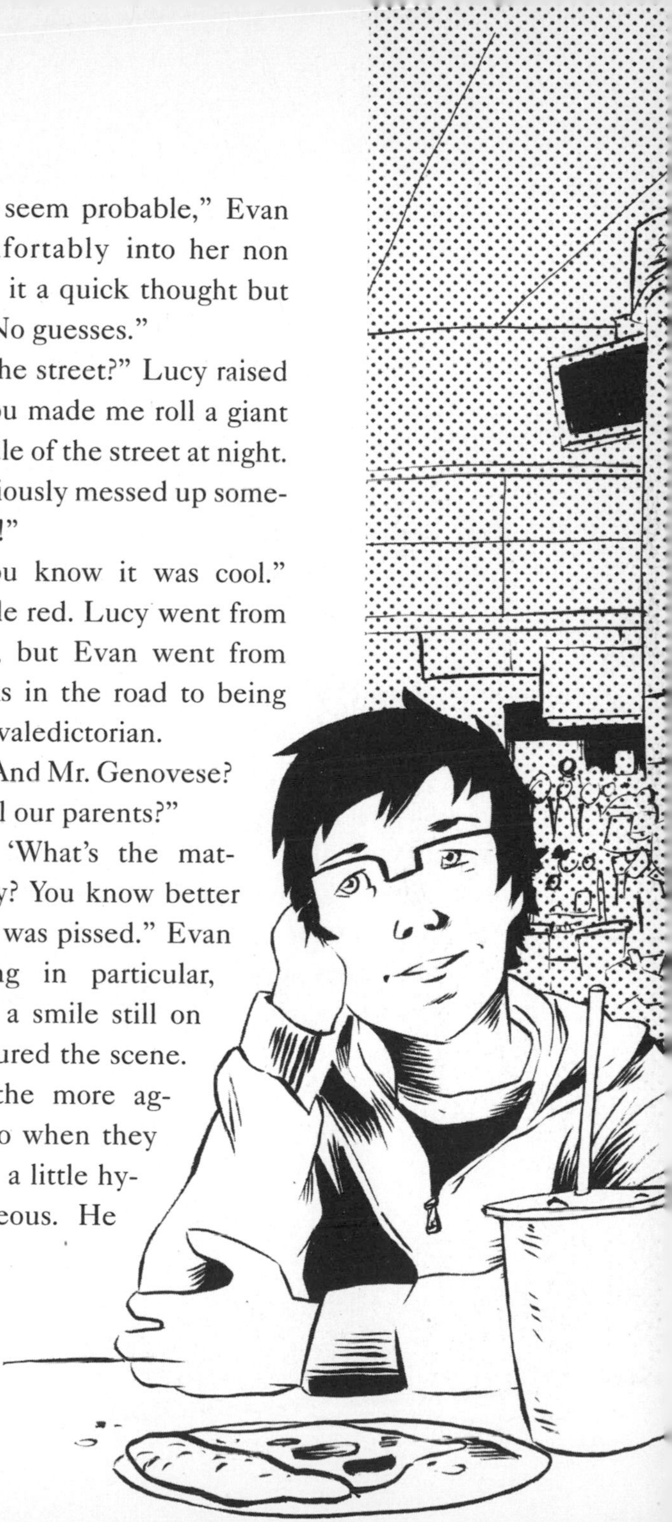

always wanted to be outdoors and exploring, or spying on people. Lucy was the quiet one, and it always took some egging on to get her to act. Evan looked at her disheveled appearance and thought of his straight-A persona and wondered if they were slowly changing places.

"What were you thinking?" Lucy asked as she drank her Sprite.

"That's a really good question," he said. "Another is this: Why would you agree to that? Clearly ten-year-old Evan's attempt at impressing you succeeded."

"Oh, yes," Lucy said, lifting a piece of sushi. "To this day, I'm searching for the man who's gonna roll a large rock out into the road for me."

"That's really crazy. God, what else did we do?"

"Laser tag," Lucy offered.

"Oh, that's *right*!" Evan said. It was hard for Evan to imagine current-day Nega-Lucy drumming up enthusiasm for laser tag. "Remember that kid? I was supposed to be the traitor on our team, and that kid got so pissed off at me when I shot him. He said he was going to kick my ass."

"He wasn't going to do *anything*," Lucy said. "I would have beaten him up before he got the chance."

"Remember, he was following us around all night and you kept saying I should just fight him and get it over with, but I didn't want to, because I was a chicken. *But.* Then I did go look for him because I knew you'd never let me live it down if I didn't."

"That's right...."

"And then we found him, and he was eating ice cream with his mom and dad and sister."

"It's hard to be tough when you're ten," Lucy said.

"I should have clobbered him with a chair in front of his whole family," Evan said coldly.

Lucy snorted with laughter.

"I'm serious," Evan said with a smile. "Now I'm angry again. I want to find that kid."

"*See*, you're a bad influence still. Total hard-ass."

Evan wondered why he hadn't brought any of this up yesterday. They had years between them. How could they have nothing to talk about? It was fun. It felt good. It was easy to pretend that they were kids still and that nothing had changed. This was nice.

"Remember the caves?" Evan asked. "We'd have to walk through half of our neighbors' yards to get to them, behind that big hill. And we thought it was like in *The Hobbit*, and if we went far enough into the caves we'd find some giant dragon. Sleeping on a bunch of treasure. I'll bet if we went there now, we couldn't even fit in the caves. We should really go there, just for the hell of it."

"We're seventeen," Lucy said, about half done with her lunch. "I don't know if we can get away with tramping through everyone's property anymore."

"We could make a comic of just this, of our old stories and stupid stuff we did as kids." Evan felt inspired suddenly. This was easy, telling old stories, and they were practically a comic strip already, with their long walks and ruminations and witty banter. The only question was which one was Calvin and which one was Hobbes. And with Lucy involved—

"Oh, that would be *awesome*!" Lucy said, her eyes widening.

"We could do a series about the laser tag, and you and I would be the main characters. And the caves. That'd be cool, right?"

"Anything you draw is cool. And I get to be part of it! Ooh, I want to be a character!"

"Well, yeah, you're half the story." Evan took the last bite of his pizza. The cemetery walk was feeling more and more like a fluke. She'd been gone for a year, really, so it only made sense that it would take a day or two to adjust. Lucy was Lucy still. Case closed.

"I think it's more interesting if we make the dragon actually there. All my memories of the caves involve a dragon. This is good! This can be, like, a whole thing. We can make a comic of Aelysthia!"

"Oh, no, not Aelysthia. What is this turning into?" Evan laughed. The days of Aelysthia being bold and colorful enough to inspire volumes of books were long gone. Half of the material had been thought up when they were children, and half of it grew out of sarcasm and boredom. Some of it could land them in a mental asylum for having thought it up. Evan had to think they could do better.

"Yeah, yeah, but we take all that stuff, and we mix it up with our own childhood, we make us the protagonists, we write out a whole story for it, you draw it, and we put it online!" Lucy bounced in her chair. She was getting increasingly excited over the idea, and her excitement was contagious. Her involvement made it easier for Evan to sign on.

"Okay. I like it," Evan said. "Because I suck at stories."

"That's the easy part. We'll do it together, it'll be fun. Promise. I want to be an ass-kicker. My character is brutal."

"That sounds right," Evan said, and slapped the table. "I'm in!"

Evan and Lucy walked back to the car. The snow had gotten heavy. Already, the parking lot was in need of a plow and the cars were covered in thick snow.

"So what does my character do?" Evan asked, holding his hand over his head to protect it from the wind. "Maybe he's, like, an artisan or something."

"That's perfect! Like, you can draw stuff and it comes to life." They reached Evan's car, which was sleeping under a white blanket of snow.

"Or I can build stuff out of snow. Like *weapons*," Evan said, thrusting a pile of the snow off the hood of his car and onto Lucy.

"Let me help you clean off your car," Lucy said. She pulled in a lump of snow and heaved it Evan's way. "I'm the *ass-kicker*, remember?"

The snow hit Evan, who ducked behind the car. He laughed and leaned over the hood, knocking more snow her way.

Soon the car was clear of snow and ready to be driven, and Evan and Lucy were cold and wet and tired.

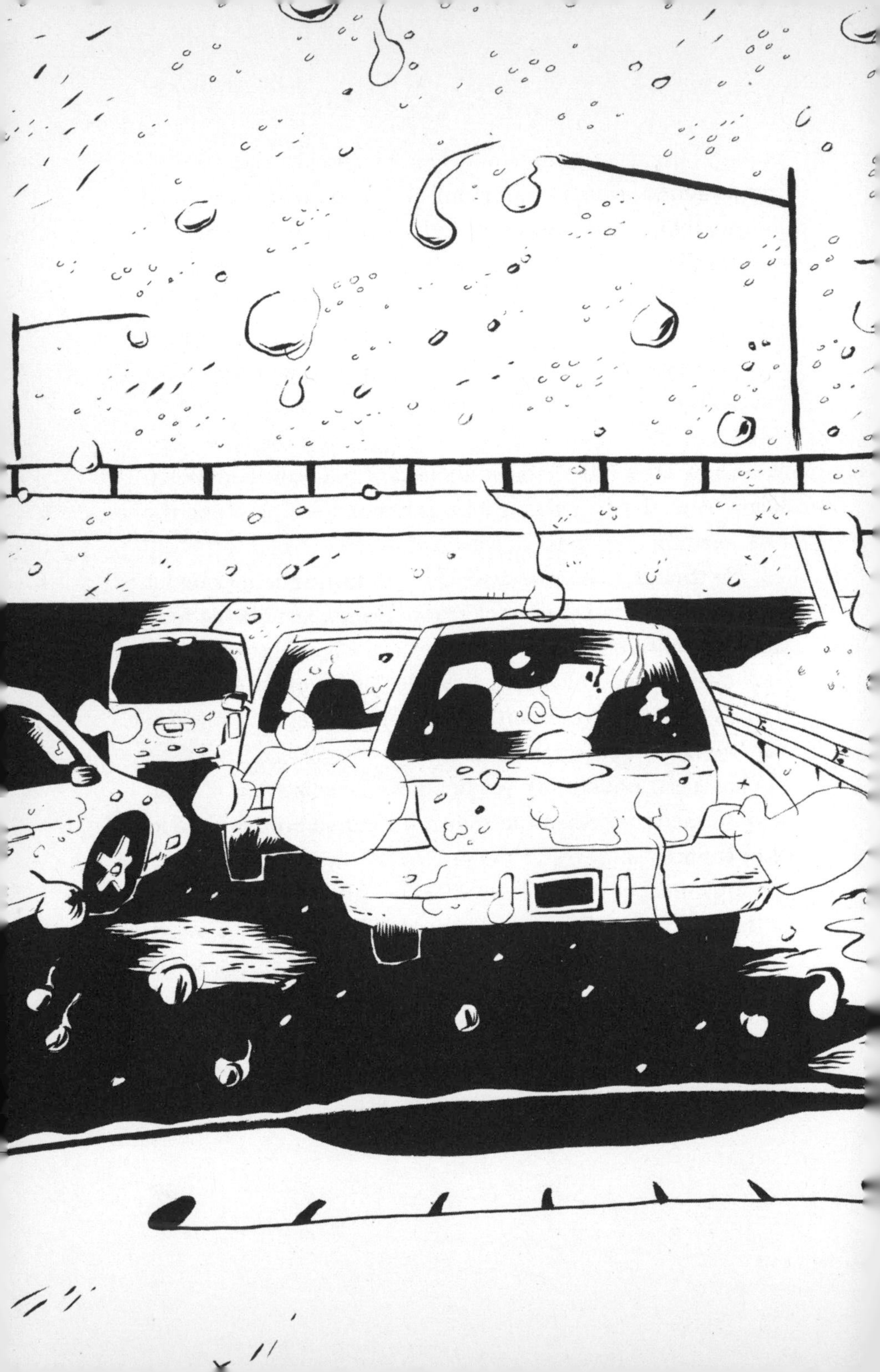

*   *   *

It doesn't take much more than a flurry to cause traffic, and this was an official snowstorm. The highway was backed up for miles as Evan and Lucy sat in Evan's mom's Honda. They'd just passed a particularly troublesome highway entrance and were now heading toward a bridge. The afternoon had a blue quality, blue, white, gray, and wet, with flashes of red taillights all around. The inside of the car was toasty as Evan had the heater running on high. They edged farther along, one wheel rotation at a time, and Evan wondered how much faster they'd get home by walking.

Evan tapped the gas and brake pedals alternately, slowly and rhythmically. He was patiently following the chain of cars ahead, leaving plenty of space. Hands at ten and two. He was comfortable, and the quiet was nice. He and Lucy were talked out at this point, but it felt okay to be quiet now. It had stopped being an uncomfortable silence. There didn't need to be talk for talk's sake. Instead, he reflected on the day and took a sip from the peppermint mocha he'd gotten to go. Evan tapped his fingers against the steering wheel to "Let It Snow" playing on the radio. Lucy leaned against the window.

The jolly DJ said to expect several more feet of snow in the next twenty-four hours and to keep off the road if at all possible. Too late for that.

"I have to do this paper thing for school still anyway," Evan told Lucy. "I should probably take tomorrow to work on it."

"Okay," Lucy said, her head tilted away, eyes fixed on the railing on her side of the road.

Evan looked at Lucy and wondered briefly what she was thinking, and if she was all right with taking a day off, and if she felt as comfortable as he did in the car at that instant. He wondered if she was having fun. He thought, for a moment, to ask her how she was feeling, but then thought better of it. Then he thought about what he was thinking about and felt less content.

Evan got home after Dad. This meant he would run into him, which would mean some kind of lecture, likely on the history paper he still hadn't started. Dad's primary form of communication was the Lecture. Evan knew that it was just his way of looking out for him, that it was Dad's way of expressing concern, but a lecture is a lecture. They're seldom enjoyable.

Evan came in through the back door into the kitchen, took off his wet, dirty shoes, and got a glass of milk.

"Is that you?" Mom called from the living room.

"It's...it's *me*," Evan called back. "If by *you*, you meant *me*, then yes." Evan drank from his glass and wiped his mouth. He started looking in the cupboards.

"Dinner's going to be soon, so don't eat anything," Mom called.

"Hey, champ," Dad said, walking into the kitchen and dropping his briefcase on the table. He also went for a glass of milk. "Coming down hard out there," he said, looking out the window. He loosened his tie as if it were choking him. "Maybe I'll work from home tomorrow."

"The firm won't miss you?" Mom asked, entering the kitchen, and she and Evan shared a knowing look, certain he'd be going into the office, snow or not.

"We'll see," Dad said, and took a drink from his glass. He turned to Evan. "How's your paper coming along?"

"Good," Evan said. He leaned back against the counter. Evan didn't understand the need to check in daily. It implied some kind of mistrust, or that he was expected to fail at this task. Evan was top of his class. He could write this paper in his sleep, and he had a whole two weeks to do it. And Dad knew this, too. Evan wondered how much of this was about the paper and how much was about Lucy. "I'm still researching. You know, figuring it out."

Dad nodded. "I want to take a look when you're done."

"Yeah, sure, Dad," Evan said.

Dad ruffled his hair. "I'm gonna keep bothering you on this 'til you finish, just so you know. Could be a long vacation."

"Dad, I'm working on it," Evan said with a laugh. "Promise."

The sun had set, dinner was eaten, and upstairs under the light of his desk lamp, Evan watched his history book sit like a brick. It wasn't that he hated homework or was bored by history, or even that he was stuck on ideas for his paper. The problem was that his head was racing with ideas and images for his comic with Lucy. It was like there was a need to purge them from his brain immediately before they dulled or disappeared. If he could just get the images out of his head and onto paper, then he could focus on the history report and make headway there.

Evan pushed the history brick to the side, pulled his sketchbook over, and started sketching. He drew quick ovals and rectangles over stick figures, looking for shapes, appealing sizes. He filled out the stick figures and connected the shapes, making realistic faces and cartoony ones, elongated bodies and short, squat Calvin-and-Hobbes-style characters. He took out his brush pen and added details — clothes, facial expressions, hair, Lucy's nose ring, Lucy with her cropped black hair, Lucy with long brown hair, Evan himself with all sorts of hats. He drew a tiny Evan carrying a large rock,

with Lucy trailing behind. He liked this cartoon—he liked the characters small and round, ageless, like a comic strip you'd see in the paper. Once he had the style figured out, he wanted to make it better, draw it bigger and with detail. This was ready for the expensive paper.

Mom knocked on Evan's open door. "Yeah, Mom."

"Hi, hon, whatcha working on?" Mom said songfully. She stepped inside and looked around the room as if it were a spaceship. Mom peered over Evan's shoulder as he closed his sketchbook. He didn't want to explain that he was working on a comic strip or why he was drawing pictures of Lucy. It would lead to art-gushing and romance-gushing and a myriad of awkward looks, and, really, it would just be embarrassing.

"Just doodling before I work on the paper," Evan said.

"Oh, good. Your dad would be a lot more comfortable if you just got something down on paper, I think, even if it's not finished or good. He just wants to see that you're working on it."

"Yeah, no, I'm working on it. I'll write something tonight. I'm gonna start now."

Mom wasn't exactly the best motivator; where Dad was adamant about work and structure and success, Mom was keen on seeing Evan enjoy himself. She sounded guilty asking about the paper, and Evan was sure his dad was waiting on a full report from her. He considered tossing the whole thing and playing his video game, but, alas, that was not the Evan Way.

"Okay, well, have a good night, sweetheart," Mom said, kissing the top of Evan's head and exiting the room.

"Good night, Mom," Evan said. He leaned back for a second, exhaling audibly. He opened a drawer in his desk and pulled out a fourteen-by-seventeen pad of bristol board, a heavy, smooth, bright paper, and his good brush and ink. He opened the pad to a clean sheet of paper and drew a fast, loose, round sketch with a sharp, hard pencil, ready to make something good.

11 AELYSTHIA BY EVAN OWENS

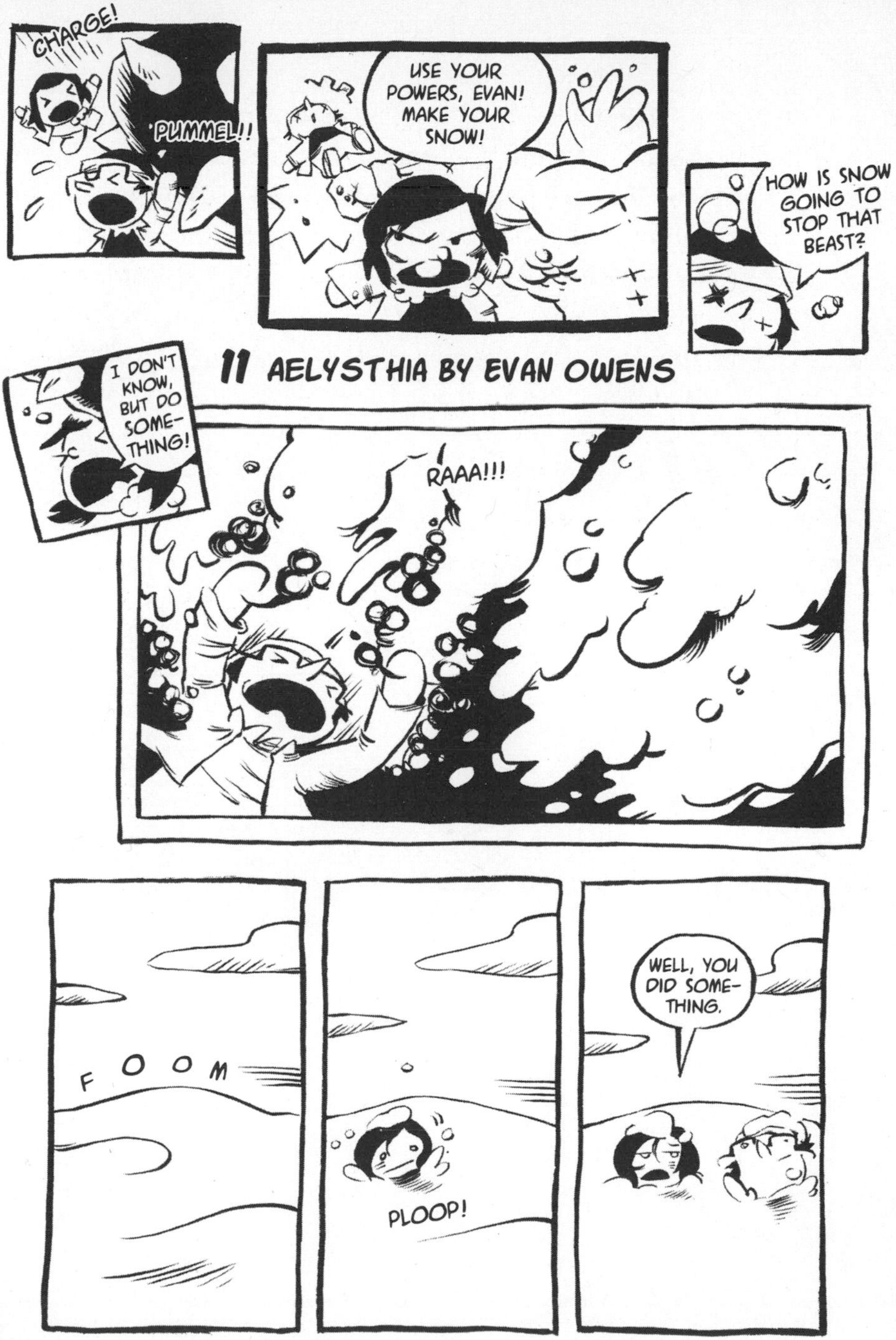
CHARGE!
PUMMEL!!
USE YOUR POWERS, EVAN! MAKE YOUR SNOW!
HOW IS SNOW GOING TO STOP THAT BEAST?
I DON'T KNOW, BUT DO SOME-THING!
RAAA!!!
F O O M
PLOOP!
WELL, YOU DID SOME-THING.

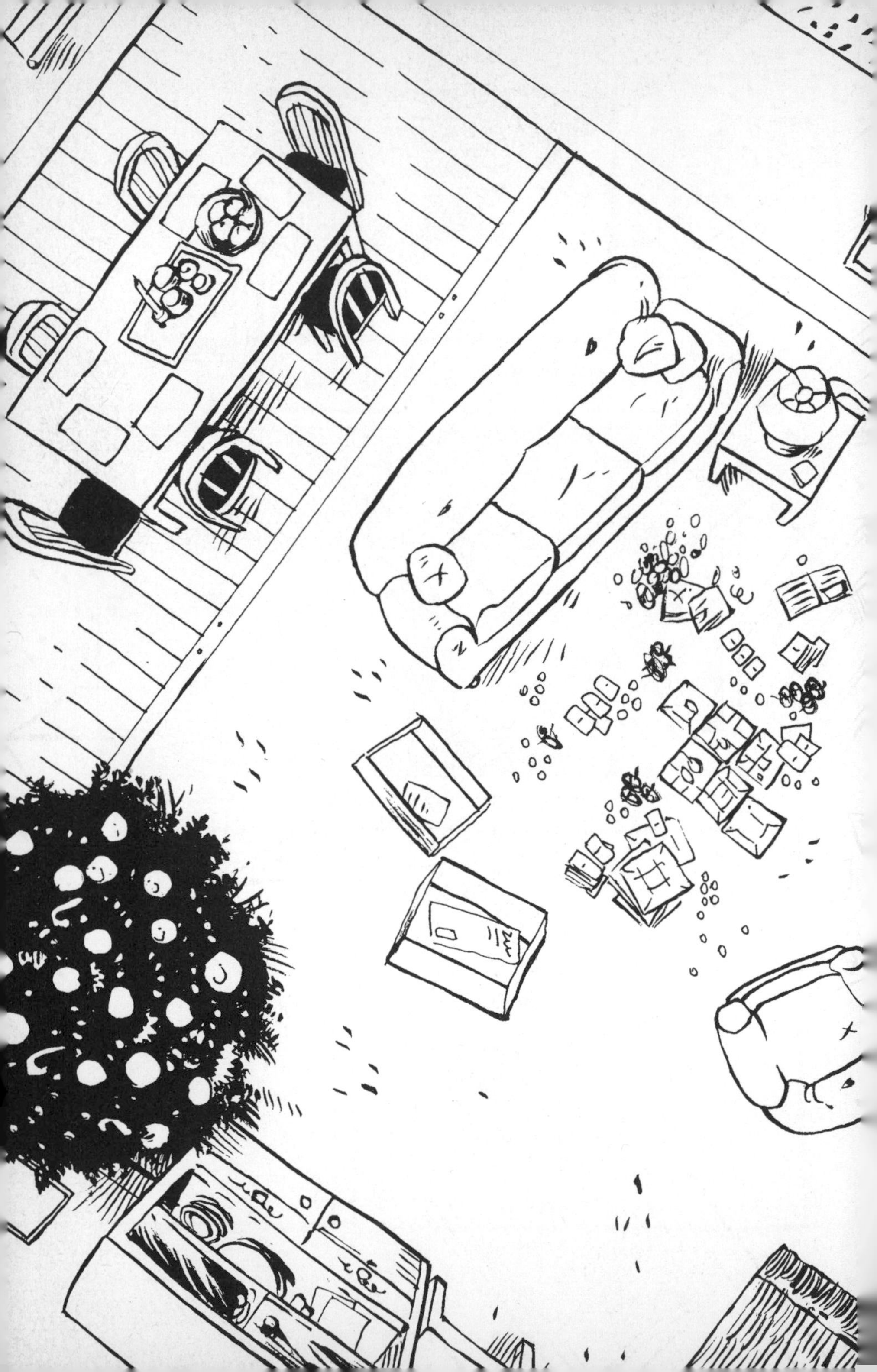

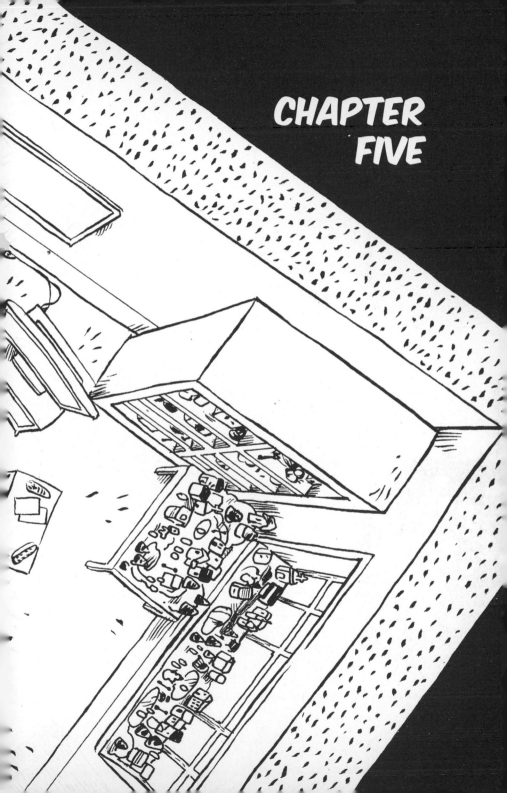

CHAPTER FIVE

SHE CAME IN THROUGH THE BATHROOM WINDOW

It was eight o'clock when Evan woke up. His bedroom window was a quarter covered with snow, and daylight just barely made it through. Evan rolled out of bed and stumbled down the stairs.

Mom had already put the coffee on. She stood by the counter in her bathrobe, looking out the window at nothing in particular. Gram was up, too, reading the paper at the kitchen table. Evan said his good-mornings.

"Dad left already?" Evan asked his mom as he entered the kitchen in his pajamas.

"*Already?* He'd been waiting to leave for an hour before the plow went by."

"So why *doesn't* he just work from home?" Evan asked.

"Because he's your father."

Evan knew that Dad came from the school of thought

that said work and home were never the same thing. A man goes out to work and comes back home, simple as that. Mom worked, too, as a nurse. She'd take off a day or two a year when the weather was this bad, since all the other nurses lived near the hospital in the city.

Evan savored the smell of the coffee, something he had always enjoyed, even before he learned to like the taste. He'd found coffee bitter at first, but an especially gruesome finals week in junior year had made him a coffee pro.

"How's Lucy doing?" Mom asked, pouring coffee for herself and for Evan. "When is she going to come over and say hello?"

"Uh, I don't know," Evan said. "Soon?" He wondered if it was even a good idea. He'd adjusted to Lucy 2.0, but now his mom would have to: *Bye-bye, sweet Lucy.* Only his grandmother, despite being several generations removed, was likely to accept her. Evan was still having trouble explaining to her that a straight male can be friends with a gay one, though. And of course there was Dad. The uncertainty of his reaction was a sign of just how negatively he'd view her.

The phone rang, and Mom handed Evan his cup and picked up the phone. "Oh, okay, glad to hear it. Love you, too," she said, and turned to Evan. "Your father's at work. He made it in okay. I didn't want to say anything, but I was really worried. Look at it out there."

The road was already covered in a layer of white snow again, and activity outside was nonexistent.

"Well, I'm going to try to finish that report," Evan said,

sliding back his chair. "I don't know why I've been dragging my feet on it."

"Oh, go play. It's vacation," Gram said. "What are they giving you homework over the holidays for, anyway?"

"I guess to keep us sharp," Evan said.

"Any sharper, Evan, and you'll cut yourself," Gram said. Evan thought that if he were younger, he'd go out and do something dumb, like place a giant rock in the middle of the road, but he was determined to finish his paper. "God bless you, but I don't know where you got those studious genes from. Not your grandmother, I'll tell you that much. I get tired just watching you sometimes."

"Oh, that's Charlie, one hundred percent," Mom said.

"I suppose it is," Gram said. She watched Evan for a few seconds. "This is the same boy who used to run away in stores and hide in coatracks and climb on restaurant tables."

"Sounds like I needed medication," Evan said.

"You were mischievous but always good-hearted. You were a fun boy." Gram placed her hand on Evan's.

Upstairs, Evan spun around slowly in his chair. His bookshelf passed through his line of vision, and then his table, and then the door. The window floated by, and there was his bed, and two more windows. Then his dresser and the TV and the computer, and, hello, there's the bookshelf again. And there was the table, holding his history book.

Evan clicked his mouse and turned on the monitor and speakers and played "Move," the first track off Miles Davis's

Birth of the Cool. No lyrics, no visuals, no distractions. The idea was to cancel out the thoughts and the noise and to focus. He had a playlist of jazz albums and movie scores that he had conditioned himself to associate with homework.

Evan kicked off the wall, rolled in his chair to the window, and looked outside. The snow was coming down fast, wet, and thick, and it was sticking to the ground and piling up quickly. The plow had pushed the early snow off the road and onto cars parked along the curb, making the street and hill look like a luge track.

Back to the desk. He put his book square in the middle of the desk, opened it up, and began to read. The first paragraph went slowly, but by the second, he was gaining focus. Evan pulled the highlighter out of his pen holder and started highlighting useful phrases. A page went by, and then another. When he was not highlighting, he was holding the end of his marker to his chin, and he knew his concentration was where it needed to be. Twenty minutes slid by as paragraphs and chapters were compressed into ideas and facts, and a paper began to form in his head.

"Evan! Lucy is here!" Mom called, and the locomotive in Evan's head hit the brakes, raising a deafening rusty squeal as the train derailed and cartwheeled down a hill, flattening a storefront and emptying a dozen citizens into the street, running and screaming. It would take hours for the dust to clear.

"Evan!" Mom called again.

Evan put down his marker and looked at his highlighted and marked-up page. He took a deep breath and pushed away the book.

*   *   *

"Honey, you *walked* here?" Evan heard his mother asking
Lucy as he got to the stairs, still in his pajamas. Lucy was
standing inside the door, wet and cold and pale, her makeup
a mess and her hair flat along her face. She looked like a
helpless dog that had come in off the street. Or like a child
in grown-up clothes.

"We're having a blizzard out there, Lucy. Look at you!"
Mom said, taking Lucy's leather jacket off her. All her motherly instincts must have been on red-flag status.

"Hey, Lucy," Evan said, trying to conceal his surprise at
seeing her there. "Everything all right?"

"Yeah, I was just, you know, bored," Lucy said with
a dead stare and a shrug of the shoulders. "Am I bothering you?"

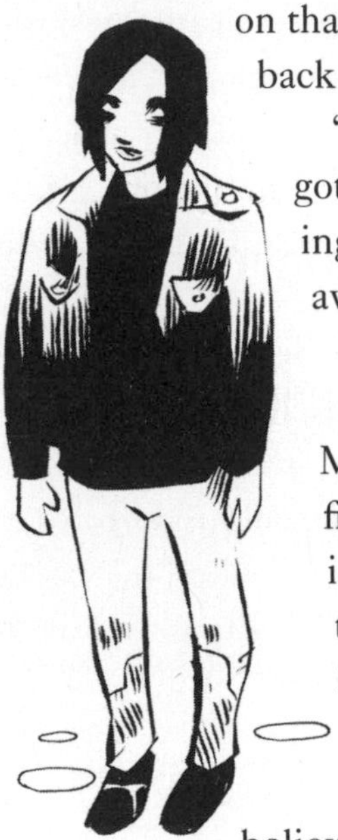

"No. No, of course not. I was just working on that paper," Evan said, pointing his thumb back to his room.

"Oh, God, you're right. I'm sorry, I forgot about that. I'll leave," Lucy said, starting toward Mom, who'd taken her coat away.

"No, don't go," Evan said.

"You're not going anywhere, missy," Mom said. "Evan has the whole break to finish his paper. First thing you're doing is taking a hot bath, and I'm gonna take those clothes and dry them. Come over here." Lucy looked at Evan with semi-wide eyes as she sluggishly did as she was told. Evan stifled a chuckle. "I can't believe your father let you come out in this weather."

"He doesn't really care what I do," Lucy said.

"I don't know about that," Mom said. "But you're here now. Let's get you dry and warm, at least, and I'm going to call your father and make sure he knows you got here okay. Did you eat yet?"

"I'm not hungry—" Lucy started before Mom took over.

"You wash up and I'll fix you breakfast. Will you eat pancakes?"

"I'll have some pancakes, Mom," Evan said from the bottom of the staircase.

"Hush, you. Lucy?"

"Sure," Lucy said with a blush.

"Leave your clothes at the door, honey, and I'll put them in the dryer for you, okay?"

"Okay. Thanks, Mrs. Owens."

"Don't you worry about it, sweetie. I'm a nurse and a mom. This is what I do."

The smell of food filled the kitchen. Not just pancakes, but bacon and eggs, too. Evan sat at the table and poured himself a glass of orange juice.

"I'm going to ask you a personal question now," Mom said. "Is she all right, really? I'm worried. Just tell me not to worry and I'll stop, but I have to ask."

"Who, Lucy?" Evan asked.

"No, Oprah Winfrey. *Yes*, Lucy!"

"Yeah, she's fine," Evan said, before taking a big gulp of his orange juice. He had figured this conversation would happen at some point. "I mean, I think so. You don't?"

"I don't know," Mom said, moving pans and adjusting the stove heat. "She looks different, and I don't like her walking out here in a snowstorm. I need to call Doug. We haven't had him over in a while anyway."

"It's just the hair and makeup." Evan shrugged. "It threw me off at first, too. It's not that long of a walk anyway. I'd have probably walked it if I hadn't been planning on writing today."

"Well, never mind that," Mom said, scrambling the eggs around in the pan. "You can work on it later. You want any chocolate milk?"

"No, Mom, thanks," Evan said, smiling. He hadn't had chocolate milk in years.

"She could have waited, or I could have picked her up," Mom said, and turned toward Evan. "I should let her know that — maybe she didn't feel comfortable asking me. It's just so strange, walking out in the snow."

A simple concern about Lucy's well-being could escalate into a full-fledged investigation of his entire history with her. Which, of course, would be a waste of Mom's time. It was best to play it simple.

"I've compelled young ladies to do worse, Mom."

"Listen to you, mister. You're dreaming." Mom took the pans off the heat and got plates out of the cabinet. "So you think she's okay, and I should stop worrying, then?"

"She didn't tell me anything. I asked her when I saw the new look."

"Were you tactful?"

"Tact—? Yeah, I was tactful." Evan noticed her twist her face into a semiaccusation. "What?"

"Oh, brother," Mom said, pouring the scrambled eggs out of the pan and onto the plates. The thought passed through Evan's mind that maybe Mom actually could find out what was going on with Lucy. Maybe it was girl problems, something Lucy couldn't talk about with him. Maybe she really needed a mother figure to talk to. Lucy's mom wasn't exactly June Cleaver, after all. The thought passed. He'd rather involve his parents as little as possible.

"Want me to ask again?"

"You'd really better not, dear. No offense to you."

"None taken," Evan said, finishing his OJ and pouring another glass.

"If there's anything to tell, Evan, I'm sure you'll be first in line to hear it when she's good and ready," Mom said. *I would be, right?* he wondered. "Will you watch the pancakes? I think her clothes should be dry."

"Yeah, sure, Mom." Evan stood up and walked to the stove. He looked down at the bubbling white batter on the griddle and realized he had no idea how to tell when pancakes were ready.

Evan watched Lucy survey his book collection. Her finger ran along the spine of each book. Lucy examined his room each year as if she'd never seen it before. He did add to his myriad collections frequently and changed his furniture around every year or two.

"*The Stand*, but not the Dark Tower books? Are you serious?" Lucy said, lifting the heavy hardcover.

"I'll read them, already! Promise!"

Lucy gasped. "Gaiman! I remember when you were obsessed with *American Gods* and it was, like, all you'd talk about for a month." Evan filed her immediate involvement with his bookshelf under "Old Lucy." The only change was that she now looked like a character out of Gaiman's Sandman series.

"So what would I like?" Lucy asked, looking back at the shelf.

"Hmmm," Evan said. He spun his chair to face the bookshelf. His eyes scanned the titles, looking for fantasy, edgy, cool, layered, quirky. "There are a few graphic novels you might like. I'd recommend *Dead@17* or *Swallow Me Whole*."

Lucy picked up *Dead@17*, impressed with the girl holding a large ax on the cover.

"*What Is the What* was good. . . . I can't think of any fantasy to recommend."

"That's not *all* I read," Lucy said. "I'm not some stuck-in-la-la-land-pathetic-faerie-princess-wannabe dork or anything. I can appreciate a book without goblins. I just think they make books *better*, is all."

Lucy continued to poke around the bookshelf, pulling books out, opening them, closing them, and putting them back. Evan wondered what she expected to find beyond blocks of text and illustrations. The majority of them were graphic novels, fantasy books, and sci-fi. She knew that. Maybe she was looking for signs of evolution. Maybe she had noticed his copy of *Thus Spake Zarathustra* and thought he was turning some new existentialist leaf. He looked down at the history book he had been perusing earlier, still open on his desk.

"Oh, your paper," she said, and touched her lower lip. "Do you want to keep working on it? I can be quiet."

"No, I'll just do it tonight," Evan said. "You're here, so we might as well hang out."

"I can read," Lucy offered, seemingly eager to please. Evan wondered again why she had come over. He was glad to have the company but wasn't sure what to do with her. Lucy seemed content, but almost guilty. Had she really forgotten about the paper? "I'll just read one of your suggestions, and you work on your paper—then we both win. Everyone wins. Yay, winning." Lucy raised her hands shoulder-level in the world's tiniest celebration.

"Yeah?" Evan looked at the history brick again. "I mean, only if you really want to."

"It'll be more fun than sitting at home," Lucy said, one eyebrow raised.

"If you're sure. It'd be good to get this out of the way," Evan said nonchalantly. If he looked too excited to work on a history paper, Lucy might take offense.

"Then it's decided. You go work, and I will reaaaaaad..." Lucy ran a finger along her choices and raised *Dead@17*. "The Adventures of Ax Girl! Starring me."

Evan laughed. "Fair enough. Enjoy. I'll expect a full report."

"And I'll expect a full *history* report, from you. Cleverness." Lucy dropped to Evan's bed with a bounce and turned on the reading lamp. She looked cute with her hair all wet and none of the eye shadow blocking her eyes. He didn't understand why she needed it. It had everyone wondering if she was okay, and clearly she was fine.

Evan shook his head and spun his chair back to face the desk. *Where were we?* The train was back on track, and the cargo was being loaded. Time to start it up again. Evan reread his highlighted passages, leaning over the book, ready to devour it. The train, follow the tracks. History-town, here we come, all aboard.

Evan read through the chapters he needed to read, highlighting and making notes. He started to jot down the broad strokes on what he wanted to say in his notebook. Time passed and Lucy was quiet, just breathing, softly at first, and then deeper, and steady, in and out, full deep breaths through her nose. The sound of someone really comfortable…the sound of someone fast asleep. Jealousy set in. It just sounded *good*. To close your eyes, and breathe in, breathe out, and slip away…

Evan dropped his book on the hardwood floor. The deep rhythmic breathing stopped.

"*Why?*" Lucy grumbled.

"I'm sorry, did I wake you?" Evan leaned over and picked up the book.

"You know damn well what you did, meanie." Lucy rolled onto her side and let an arm drop off the bed.

"You were snoring, it was distracting. It was like a buzz saw going over a pile of bricks."

"I was *not*!" Lucy said. She took a small pillow off the bed and threw it at Evan. He deflected the pillow and laughed.

"It's all right. It's a cute snore. You're safe. You're not gonna scare off any prospective mating partners or anything."

"You're walking, like, twelve thin lines right now," Lucy said with her eyes closed and her head on a pillow. Evan grinned and turned once again to face his book. He'd made a little progress, but there was a long way to go. "What's Zombies?" Lucy asked.

Evan turned to see her looking up at a box on top of his bookshelf. "See, now you've done it. Now I can't work,"

Evan said, thinking she was probably bored anyway. Thinking he was definitely bored.

"No, I'm sorry, I didn't say anything," Lucy pleaded. "I don't care about Zombies, whatever it is. Actually, I'm deadly curious, but no, you have to work."

"I can't believe we haven't played Zombies. This is inexcusable," Evan said.

"No, go back to your project. I'm going to feel guilty now."

But Evan was already up and reaching for the game. This was perfect—another great classic Evan-and-Lucy event. "Nope, we're playin' Zombies, my friend."

Evan sat in the living room with Lucy, his mom, and his grandmother. The couches were pushed apart, and all the game parts were sprawled across the floor. There were a few stacks of cards, a pile of square tiles, red and blue dice, army figures, and one hundred little plastic zombies. Mom and Gram took the couch, Evan had a chair, and Lucy insisted on sitting on the carpeted floor.

"This is my first time playing without Marshall and Tim," Evan said, straightening everything up and placing one of the square tiles in the middle of the table. "Hopefully I don't mess this up."

Evan explained the rules. You roll the dice and move your army guy, then roll again to move the zombies. When you land on a zombie, you need to kill it and put it in your bin. The goal is to kill twenty-five zombies or reach the

helipad to es-
cape. If you get
killed, you go
back to the start
and lose half of
your zombies.
Evan's longest
game with Tim
and Marshall went
four and a half hours.

"I want to play as a zombie," Lucy
said.

"Not an option," Evan replied.

"I'd let you be a zombie, Lucy,"
Gram said.

"Thank you," Lucy said with
her best manners. "I motion to re-
move Evan from the game."

"I'm the only one who knows
how to play!" Evan complained, and
Lucy waved the instructions at him.
Duh! Evan went first.

"This game is kind of morbid,"
Mom said. She was looking at one of
her event cards, which read, THE KEYS
ARE STILL IN IT — MOVE UP TO TEN SPACES
INSTEAD OF MOVEMENT ROLL. The picture on
the card showed a zombie's severed hand
holding the keys in the ignition of a jeep.

"You and Charlie used to love your *Night of the Living Zombies*," Gram said.

"*Night of the Living Dead*," Mom corrected.

"This is nothing. You don't want to know the kinds of games they make these days," Gram said.

"Really? And how do *you* know?" Mom asked. Lucy and Evan glanced at each other and giggled.

"I'm on the Internet. I stay informed. They let old people on the Internet, you know."

Lucy rolled the dice and moved her army man. Evan thought back to Sunday nights when he and Lucy were still kids. Every Sunday, Evan's extended family came over, his aunts and uncles, his cousins. One of Evan's cousins (the unfortunately nicknamed Chumbawumba) and Lucy would team up and chase him around the house. After dinner everyone would play a board game or a card game. It was always festive and cheerful, and Lucy was like a part of the family. Evan had grown out of game nights, which happened rarely now, but with Lucy there, he felt like they were nine years old. He moved to sit on the floor by Lucy.

After a few rounds, the masses of zombies were building. It wasn't so hard to take down a zombie or two, but if you found yourself in a herd, the game got pretty difficult. Gram found herself in such a pickle. She used her last bullet and her last heart.

"I don't need this kind of stress at my age," Gram teased.

"Wait, where did that come from? Are you cheating?" Evan asked, pointing at a heart Gram pulled from under the tile nearest her.

"I certainly did not cheat!" Gram said. "It's not cheating unless I steal it. Hiding it is my own business," she said matter-of-factly.

"Evan and his dad are both sticklers for rules," Mom said, moving her army man around the board.

"Oh, don't I know it," Gram agreed.

"Dad used to play games with us, so Lucy knows about his rules," Evan said. Lucy gave a weak smile. "He used to keep the rules right by him, ready to contest anyone. He must have them all memorized by now." Evan noticed Lucy withdrawing from the conversation and did his best to keep her included. "Lucy's up," Evan said, handing her the dice. "She's gonna take down her twenty-five zombies right here — you watch."

At this point, the game was beginning to take over the floor around them. It was a warm scene — family, games, Christmas in the air. His best friend. Of course she'd want to come over — what was she going to do at home? Now she had people and comfort and zombies. This was like old times.

Lucy looked pale but threw the dice. Was she feeling okay? Or was he just used to the makeup? Evan wondered. She found herself in a swarm of zombies. She survived the first two but was on her last leg after the third.

"This is painful," Evan said, taking on the role of announcer. He looked at Lucy, whose total concentration was seemingly on the game. "Not looking good, folks. *Not looking good.*"

"Come on," Lucy said, rolling again. Lucy moved out of the zombie pile and into a clearing.

"Yes! She lives!" Evan clapped his hands and gave her a celebratory nudge. Lucy offered no reaction, looking blankly at the game board. It couldn't be because of Zombies. Zombies was rad. "Remember when we used to make our own board games?" Evan asked Lucy.

"I remember," Mom said. "I used to take you both down to the craft store so you could buy those giant boards and paints, and God knows what else you found in that store."

"They were terrible," Evan said, laughing. "What games did we make? I'm trying to remember."

"Life Sucks, parenthesis, and Then You Die, parenthesis, trademark," Lucy mumbled. Evan was spending the holidays with twins, an old friend and her dark sister. New Lucy™ made Evan anxious because she was distant. Evan couldn't relate; he couldn't read her. He didn't know her, and that worried him.

"That's not real, is it? I remember the Batman game we did," Evan said, focusing on the positive.

"Attempted Suicide, Home Version," Lucy said, in her own world. "Roll three sixes and win."

"Oh, Lucy," Mom said in a sour tone. "That's not funny." Evan had almost forgotten Mom and Gram were sitting there. They'd been officially introduced to New Lucy™.

"I'm sorry," Lucy muttered, and stood up. "Excuse me."

She walked briskly to the bathroom. There was a moment of silence, and Evan struggled to lower his eyebrows. "She has a dark sense of humor," Evan offered. It was all he could think of. What do you say when your best friend breaks down in front of your mom and grandmother? He sulked against the couch and sighed.

"Oh, I hope she's all right," Gram said, rolling the dice and taking her turn. "I've always liked her."

During the next fifteen minutes, they shared small talk and waited for Lucy to get back. No one inquired aloud what she was up to, but Evan feared they were all wondering. He officially broke up Zombies, as it had clearly been replaced by the return of the game Is Lucy Okay?

"Maybe we should make some lunch," he said. No sense in sitting there dwelling. At least in the kitchen they would be busy and could maybe focus on something else. "Counting the most zombies bagged, Mom, I think you won."

"If you're ever in a crisis of the undead, you call me," Mom said with a wink.

Evan was sitting at his desk, lost in his paper, when Lucy appeared in the doorway and knocked on the wall. Evan glanced at the clock on his computer. Another thirty minutes had passed since the game had ended. He was surprised he'd been able to pick up on his report so easily. But with Lucy in his sight, history floated away.

Lucy sat back down on the bed. "Your family thinks I'm crazy."

"Nah." Evan lifted his head, shrugging her comment off with a wave of his hand. "It'd take a lot worse than that."

"Probably. Sorry." Lucy looked at the rug by the bed. "Anyway, I apologized to your mom and Gram."

"You didn't have to. It *was* kind of funny," Evan said, turning his head back to his book. "Want a sandwich? I brought one up. I didn't think you'd swing by the kitchen." Evan held up a small plate with a tuna-fish sandwich on it.

"I ate with your mom and grandma downstairs," Lucy said softly.

"Oh." Evan took a bite of the sandwich. That explained the missing thirty minutes. "My mom thinks you're, like, upset or depressed or something."

"Oh. Yeah, well. Who isn't?" Craftily dodging any discussion again. "Do you need to work? I can read some more."

"Eventually. Hey, check this out." Evan opened his art drawer and pulled out his sketchbook with the quick drawings he had done of himself and Lucy the night before. This would cheer her up. Lucy walked over and touched the paper, running her finger along it. There was cartoon Evan, his round face in a battle roar, his stubby cartoon arms in the air, a sword made of snow in his hand. Cartoon Lucy was also combat-ready, poised for action.

Lucy's eyes gleamed, her mouth hung open in overly dramatic awe.

"So we're really gonna?" she asked.

"Well, yeah, if you still want to."

"Dude. Yes. Can we start, like, now?" Those eye crinkles, and the way her cheeks suddenly pronounced themselves—her smile was contagious. Evan would draw right through vacation if it kept her smiling.

"Yeah, I guess. I mean, what better time, right?"

"Yes!" Lucy exclaimed. She sat down on Evan's bed pretzel-style, and Evan rolled his chair over and clapped his hands. This was a good reason to share his art. If everyone in the world reacted like Lucy, he'd have a great career going. Lucy and Evan sat, neither sure how to progress. Outside Evan's window was nothing but white, with a slightly brighter white torrent of close-by snow visible.

"All right! So. How do we start?" Evan asked.

"Let me think," Lucy said. She looked like a caricature of *The Thinker*, her brow quizzical, her fist holding her chin.

"We have characters," Evan said. "Me and you. We have a genre. That's fantasy. Right?" Evan put his feet on the bed. With his pen, he tapped the sketchbook he held in his lap.

"A quest," she said. "We need an angle, a hook. What's the main thrust?"

"I have no idea," Evan said. Evan looked up, like he expected a thought bubble to float above his head with the answers inside. The invisible thought bubble burst. This was how creative writing always went for him. He had thought maybe having Lucy to bounce ideas off of would help, but it hadn't. He was a failure. "I told you I suck at this."

"We're, like, ten seconds in. Be patient," Lucy said. She suggested they think up a theme, then a motif, before settling on anything at all. Anything that could be classified as an idea was good. She looked out the window. "Snow." She looked back at Evan. "I think of winter when I'm here. I think of snow when I think of you. So we should make it a winter story. And I like your idea of the snow-weapons thing."

Evan looked at Lucy, nodded, and then wrote *Winter Story* and underlined it. Now there was progress. Snow. Why couldn't he have thought of that?

"In a snowy land," Lucy continued, "everything is white and clean and untouched. And your character's, like, the snow master anyway. So maybe he gets his power from the land."

"But it's an epic," Evan reminded Lucy. "There's going to be lots of travel, so he'll be leaving home, right? So what does he do when he leaves? His power would be useless." He was still punctuating his points with his pen. He was contributing now, but ruining the story, too. This was frustrating.

"Well." Lucy thought about it. She smiled. "That's what my character is for."

"Maybe Evan's family sends him on a quest. And along the way he meets Lucy."

"No," Lucy said flatly. "Evan and Lucy have always been friends. Lucy just decides to go along with him."

"Okay," Evan said. It was only fair that she'd decide the role of her own character.

"I'm the best friend. And I sneak away and follow you. You go off on a quest to find a dragon, and I follow you and we find the dragon, but he's friendly and the dragon needs our help in defeating this colony of bad dragons, so it's, like, good dragon versus bad dragons, and we're in the middle of it, or maybe I join the bad dragons and we have to fight in the skies." Lucy looked at his sketchbook. "Are you writing this down?"

"Yeah, that's basically what I was thinking anyway," Evan said, and started scribbling notes. He decided if he wasn't fit to be a writer, he could always be a court stenographer.

At five thirty, Evan, Lucy, Mom, and Gram watched the news in the living room. The room was warm and cozy from the fire Evan and his mom had started. The snow had just begun to let up after accumulating ten inches. The door opened, letting in a chill, and Dad stepped in. His hat was dusted with snow from the short walk from his car. He took off his coat and hat, surveying the living room scene.

"No dinner?" he said.

"Oh, honey, I didn't know when you were going to get home with all the snow out there," Mom said, getting up to welcome him. "I tried calling your cell, but you didn't answer."

"I was in traffic, trying not to drive off the road." He threw his keys onto the hutch. "I'm not going to talk on the phone while police are everywhere out there." Dad realized everyone was looking at him, uncomfortable. "Hi, Lucy, how are you?" he said. "Didn't realize we had company."

"Hi, Mr. Owens," Lucy mumbled.

Dad and Mom walked to the dining room area, closer to the kitchen. Evan glanced at Lucy, with her wide-eyed child-in-trouble look. He shrugged his shoulders as an apology.

"Barb? How's she going to get home?" Dad asked quietly, but not quietly enough that everyone in the living room couldn't hear. "I imagine I'll be going back out? I already put the car in the garage."

"You cook, I'll drive. I can do it."

Dad walked into the bathroom and shut the door. This was about as bad a reaction as Evan had feared. The entire situation was not the optimal New Lucy™ Meet-and-Greet. Evan thought of sneaking Lucy out and driving her himself, but that would just get everyone more upset.

"I'm sorry," Lucy said to Mom from across the living room.

Mom put on her best smile. "No, don't worry, sweetie. Let me take you home. Just put on your boots before Mister Cranky-Pants comes back out. He's always like this right after work."

"Okay." Lucy grabbed her coat and sat back down with her boots in hand.

"I'll be back in a bit, hon," Mom said to Evan, who was still on the couch, leaning on the armrest and feeling embarrassed. This was like the end of a preschool playdate.

"Drive safe, Barb," Gram said, and patted Evan's knee. They shared an understanding look.

A few minutes later, Dad walked back into the living room.

He eyed Evan silently for a moment. Evan knew this look. He hadn't done anything wrong, though. His dad had been at work; he didn't know a thing that had happened that day. Evan felt the target on his forehead. Dad was going Terminator on him. *Suspect: Evan Owens. Seventeen. Neglecting studies to invite troubled girl over. Punish at all costs.*

"Again?" Dad said. "I thought you were going to do your paper today." He walked back into the kitchen and started slamming cabinets, looking for something to cook. "Did you finish?"

"No, not yet," Evan said, looking away from the kitchen. He wished he could be done with that paper. He should just lie about it. No. He wished he'd kept working instead of bringing out that board game. It *was* his fault.

Dad walked to the kitchen door.

"Huh?"

"Not yet, Dad. Sorry."

Dad gave Evan a disappointed look and walked back into the kitchen, making noise. Gram pulled herself off the couch. "I'll go help with dinner," Gram said.

"I'll do it," Evan said. He called out toward the kitchen. "You want some help, Dad?" It was an effort toward peace.

Dad shut each of the cabinets he'd opened and turned on the stove. "Yeah, all right, get in here."

Evan turned off the TV and went into the kitchen. Dad patted his back, and Evan helped him fix dinner.

Dad had calmed down a little as he and Evan made dinner, but he was still hunched over and surly as he sat at the table with Gram and Evan only an hour later. When Mom returned, tensions flared again.

"So is there anything we should be concerned about?" Dad said. He took a bite of his steak. "Regarding Lucy?"

Evan wondered why he'd bring that up now while there was a tableful of people. Because there was a tableful of people, obviously. "No, of course not. Why?" Evan asked, jabbing his fork into several green beans.

"I'm only asking that you leave some time for school-work, Evan. You can't keep to evenings? Or maybe just the phone for a day? You should be done with your homework by now. And what's going on with the nose piercing and the hair? Seriously?"

"People get piercings," Evan said quietly.

"Well, you aren't kids anymore, Ev. You can choose your friends."

"She *is* my friend," Evan said, jabbing his fork again and hitting the plate.

"All I know is she starts coming over and you stop doing your work. We're talking your senior year here, and you want to get into an Ivy League school."

Evan looked down at his plate. "It's just a nose ring. Besides, she's only here until New Year's. Just like every year."

"Is she having some kind of rebellious phase?" Dad said. Evan felt like his answers were being studied and didn't want to reply at all. Dad had trouble seeing things in any way other than his own. He'd nudge and nudge until Evan came around and saw things his way, too.

"She is a little troubled, Evan," Mom said.

"Let's not gang up on the boy," Gram said, placing her fork down.

"You know as well as anyone she has family issues," Mom said to Gram. "She can be a handful."

"She was raised in a less-than-stable environment," Dad agreed, and filled his and Mom's wineglasses. "And then she ended up with her mother, of all people."

"I think Doug settled too easily with that one," Mom said.

"If it hadn't been Dawn, it would just have been some other version of Dawn," Dad said. "It always was."

"I really don't need to hear this," Evan said. It was as if his parents and Lucy's parents were all still in middle school.

"Lucy was always running away," Dad continued. "And then she'd turn up here. I'm sure she broke into our house once."

"Dad, let it go," Evan said. They had been twelve then, and yet it still came up from time to time.

"I think she's cute," Gram said to Evan, and then turned to his parents. "They're young, and they're figuring themselves out. Let them be kids."

"That's the problem, Mom," Evan's dad said. "They aren't kids. I'm not sure you can trust kids to be kids anymore."

"This isn't worth discussing," Evan said, pushing his half-finished plate away. "Besides, I'm seventeen. I think I can choose who I'm friends with, and when I do my homework and where I'll go to college."

"Were they supervised today?" Dad asked, and Evan felt invisible again.

"We're not making out or anything."

"Oh, Evan. You must notice the way she looks at you," Mom said. "She's definitely sweet on you, honey."

"All right, I'm done." Evan stood up and headed to his room. His parents had abandoned Lucy and her whole family when her parents split up. When was the last time they'd spoken to her dad? How would they even know what she was going through? Evan had a history with Lucy; they shared a childhood. No one ever seemed to get that. Evan and Lucy held hands, they gave knowing looks and had random bursts of giggles, and they spoke their own language, but they had always done those things. This wasn't the first time someone had mistaken their closeness for something more, and Evan knew it wouldn't be the last.

"Oh, Evan, don't do that," Mom called after him. "Come back and finish your supper, we're just talking. No harm, no foul."

"Charlie?" Evan heard Gram say as he walked through the living room.

"Yeah, Ma."

"They *are* still kids."

Evan was on the phone with Lucy as he got ready for bed. He grabbed his sketchbook, climbed into bed, and doodled as they talked.

"Oh my God, they did not," Lucy said, a tiny voice on

the other end of the phone line. Evan imagined the shocked and horrified expression on her face.

"I know, can you believe it? Evan and Lucy, Owens house gossip item," Evan said.

"Well, that settles it. I'm never coming over again."

"Stop."

"No, you don't understand. I can't ever look at your mom again, and your dad already hates me."

"Does not."

"Send me a text when your entire family's dead, and then we can be friends again."

"That's morbid."

"Everyone dies, Evan. We'll still have a few good years."

Ten minutes passed, and Evan's page filled up with sketches. His feet were on the windowsill, buried in thick, poufy slippers. The window was open a crack, and he could feel a chill. His nightstand light dimly colored the earthy greens of his room. His history book lay on his desk, ignored.

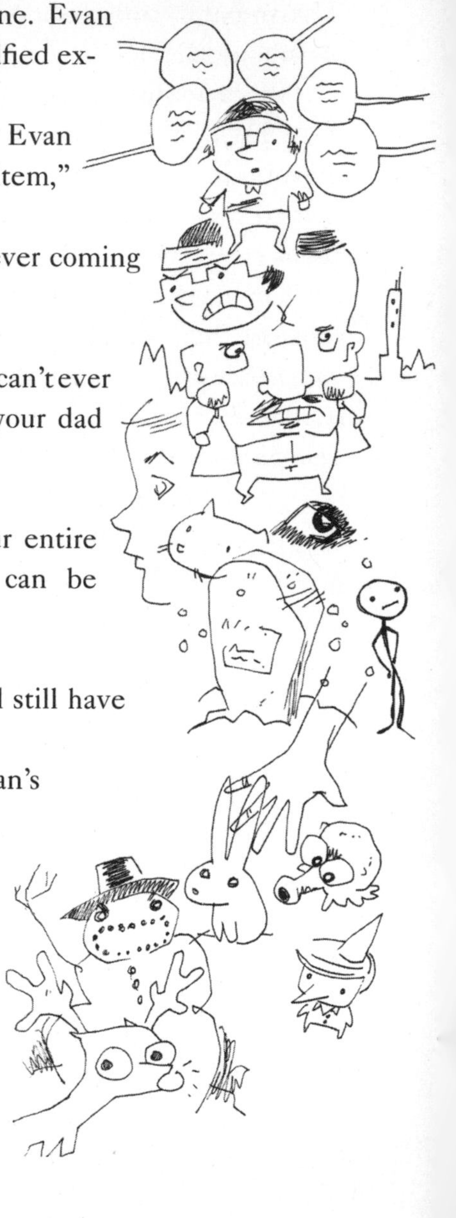

The sound of dishes clanking wafted upstairs and through the open bedroom door.

"What about tomorrow?" Evan asked. "It's Wednesday. I have SARAH in the afternoon. Like, not the person but the organization. Basically we hang out with some handicapped people. Ben will be there. They're all great, really. You'll like them."

"Oh, wow," Lucy said. "That's kind of awesome. All right, but you come over here for breakfast, then."

"*It's a date*," Evan said, and shut his eyes tight, for a moment pulled back to the conversation over dinner. *Hopefully Dad didn't hear*. Evan laughed.

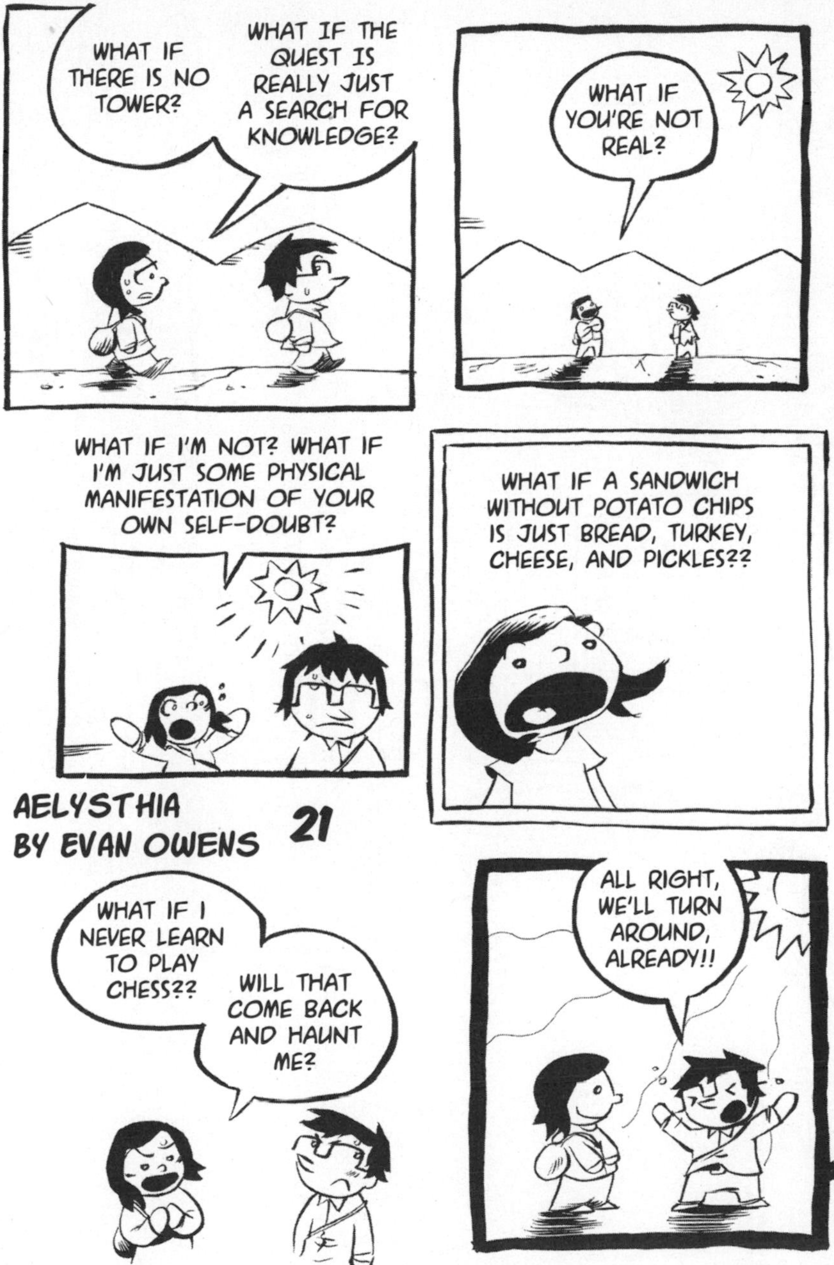
WHAT IF THERE IS NO TOWER?
WHAT IF THE QUEST IS REALLY JUST A SEARCH FOR KNOWLEDGE?
WHAT IF YOU'RE NOT REAL?
WHAT IF I'M NOT? WHAT IF I'M JUST SOME PHYSICAL MANIFESTATION OF YOUR OWN SELF-DOUBT?
WHAT IF A SANDWICH WITHOUT POTATO CHIPS IS JUST BREAD, TURKEY, CHEESE, AND PICKLES??
AELYSTHIA
BY EVAN OWENS
21
WHAT IF I NEVER LEARN TO PLAY CHESS??
WILL THAT COME BACK AND HAUNT ME?
ALL RIGHT, WE'LL TURN AROUND, ALREADY!!

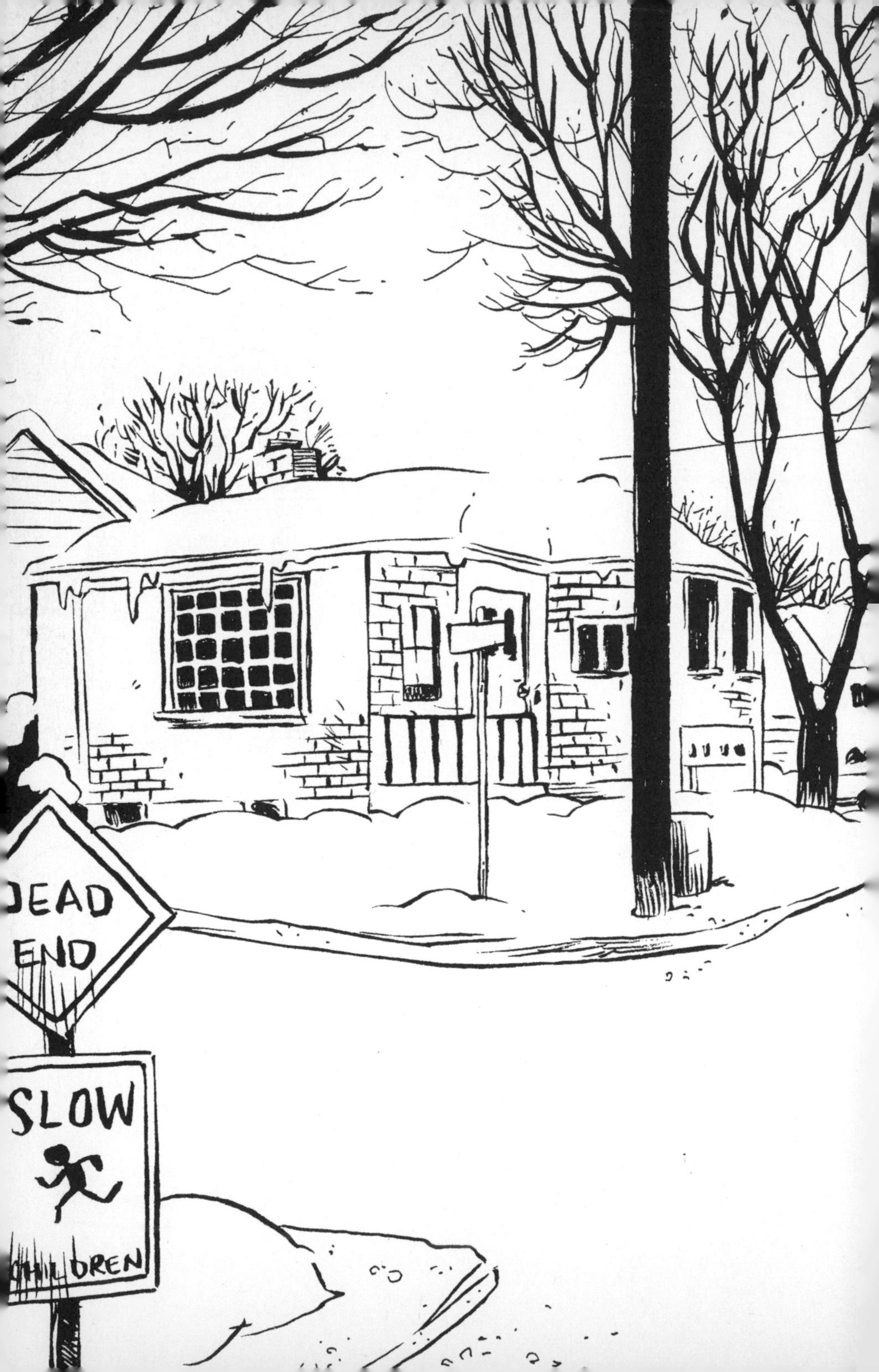

DEAD END
SLOW
CHILDREN

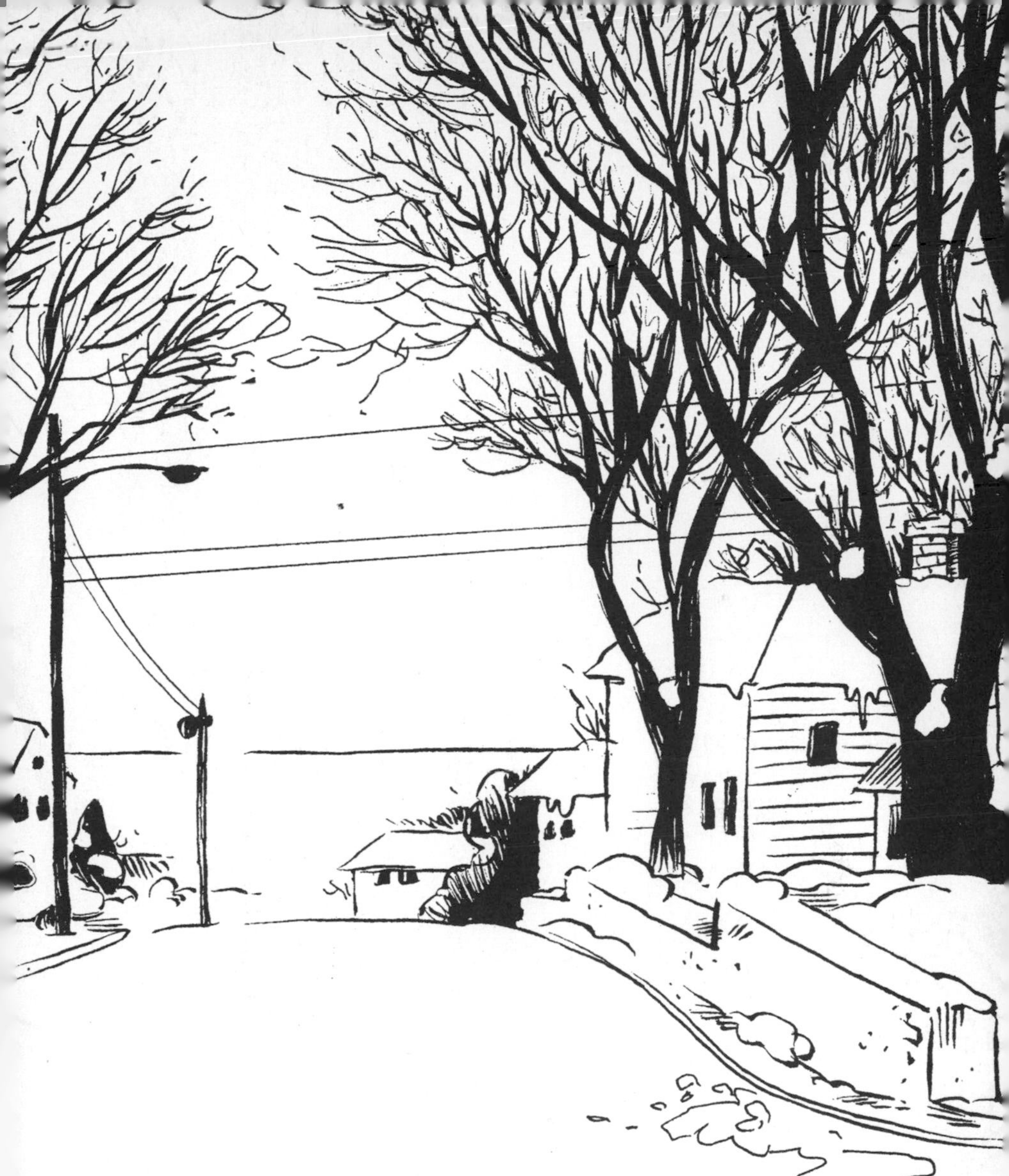

CHAPTER SIX

FIXING A HOLE

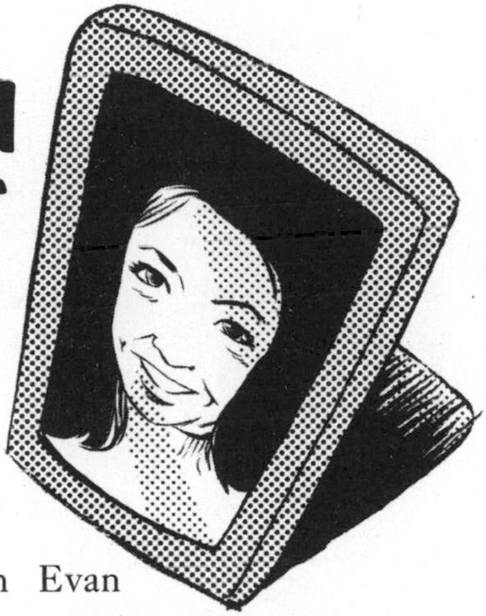

It was still cold when Evan stepped outside the next morning but considerably warmer than it had been the past few days. He slipped out quietly before breakfast so he wouldn't have to listen to any more Lucy dissertations over family meals. As Evan pulled out of the driveway and into the road, the car half drove and half slid over what amounted to flurries layered on salt layered on dirt layered on ice covering more dirt on snow over street.

Lucy's father's house, or Lucy's old house, was a few turns away. The beach down the street from the hill was painfully white, and Evan almost had to close his eyes. He pulled into the driveway and walked a shoveled path that cut through the knee-deep snow. He knocked on the door, and Lucy's father answered, wearing a loose robe and looking not at all as if he were expecting company. His face was stubbly, and his head was on its way to bald, as it had been for as long as Evan had known him. The look of not expecting quickly melted into not surprised.

"Evan, come on in," Doug said, shaking Evan's hand and patting him on the back. He mumbled in the heavy British accent he still had after decades living in America. "Place is a bit of a mess, sorry."

Evan stepped inside the house. The air was thick and stale with cigarette smoke. Magazines and newspapers piled up on any flat surface that would hold them. It felt like an old house. It felt a little bit older each year he visited.

"Lucy!" Doug called, and then said to Evan, "Let me go get changed. Help yourself to some breakfast. Nothing fancy, but we have a few boxes of cereal."

Lucy came out, and Evan and Lucy sat down and had a bowl of cereal each. Happy-O's. Doug came back out and joined them at the table.

"How's school?" Doug asked Evan.

"It's good," he said.

"Still doing the activities? Yearbook, chess . . ."

Evan wondered if this was how people viewed him. *The activities kid.* "Never did chess. Skipped yearbook this time. I've been working on sets for the school play this year."

"Oh, yeah? What show are they doing?" Doug asked.

"*Rumors,*" Evan said, sure Doug would not be attending opening night.

"*Rumors*," Doug repeated, and nodded. "How are your parents?"

"Same old, I guess."

"Same old," Doug said. "That'd be Charlie and Barbara all right."

Evan wasn't sure how to take that, so he nodded and continued to eat.

"How's your mom?" Doug asked Lucy, leaning forward over his large bowl. Evan had noticed the picture of Lucy's mom on the hutch when he came in. It was the one object in the house not taken over by clutter. The photo was professionally taken. Dawn looked much younger in it than he remembered her, but just as tanned, with the same dark brown hair. Evan hadn't seen her in years.

"Dad, seriously?" Lucy asked, looking away. Evan thought maybe he should have prolonged the school-play talk.

"Well, we've hardly gotten to sit down and talk, Lucy. I'd just like to know how the mother of my kid is. She dating anyone?" Doug asked, as if it were a casual question and not at all loaded with history and implications. Or, you know, kind of creepy.

"Dad…" Lucy said, rolling her eyes.

Evan ate quietly.

"It's all right," Doug said, letting it go. "I wish her well, you know that."

Everyone sat in silence for a moment, Lucy leaning on her hand and swirling her spoon around her bowl.

"You can tell me, if she is," Doug said. He faced Evan. "I really did love her. I wish things had worked out different, but..."

Evan tried to eat a little faster.

"If it's meant to be, right?" Doug said, and offered a hopeless smile.

He was likable enough, but just so *sad*. It was hard to even feel empathy for him, looking around the house. It was as if Doug and the house were stuck in some perpetual limbo, as if he and Dawn had split up only weeks ago. It had been years, though, and Evan wondered if the house had been cleaned at all in that time. Or if anything had been moved. He wondered how much of Dawn's stuff was just lying around like she still lived there.

Evan looked at Lucy, who was still playing with her spoon and bowl as if they were a Nintendo game, and wondered why she wanted him here for this. It wasn't a planned breakfast. Maybe she thought her dad would be a little more dadlike with company. Maybe she felt the house just needed some more people in it. Or maybe she felt Evan would understand her a little better.

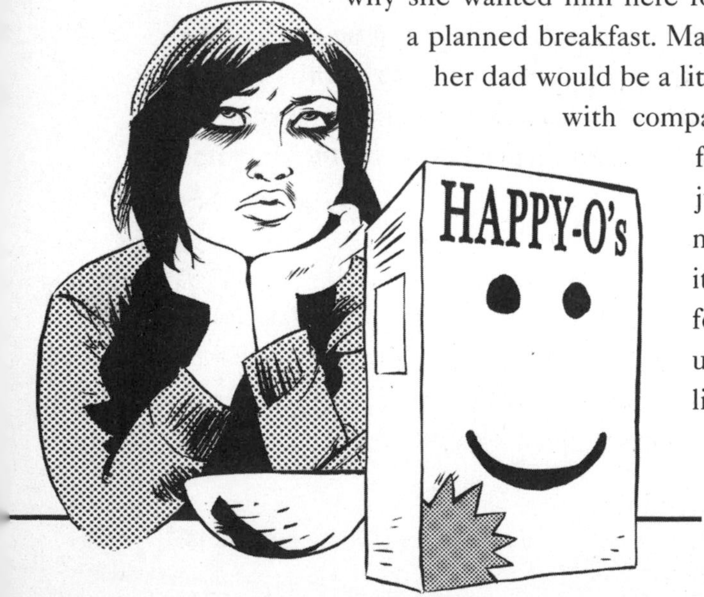
HAPPY-O's

Lucy sat, her

leg bobbing up and down, her hair a mess, her dad a mess, her house a mess. Evan thought of Lucy as this unbearably bright spot in this broken, dark place, like a full moon lighting up a dark night sky. She had so much beauty and smarts and potential and wit. She was better than this place. Evan wondered if she knew that. He wanted to take Lucy away, and bring her home and give her all the love and support and all the opportunity he'd had. He wanted to be her knight in shining armor.

Things had been anything but clear with Lucy so far, but one notion, one idea, started to shine to Evan like a beacon. He knew that he wanted to save her.

Evan and Lucy were back at the mall, this time with Ben and his friend Katie, both from the SARAH group, in tow. The mission: to find Ben some CDs to listen to. Ben was already happy and hyperactive, oblivious to the crowds of people, tugging on Evan's shirt until Evan pushed him off, and then bothering Katie. Evan hadn't mentioned this to Lucy—that nothing gave Ben so much joy as pissing people off.

"Look over there," Ben said to Katie, pointing to the right with his arm in front of her face. Ben had very short blond hair and large front teeth, and while Evan wore a heavy coat, hat, and hood, Ben wore a T-shirt and thin jacket. Katie had a short bobbed haircut and thick-framed rectangular glasses.

"Look at *what*? There isn't anything there!" Katie yelled, fed up already. Fed up was almost a personality trait for Katie.

"Aren't they kind of like us?" Evan asked Lucy, trailing

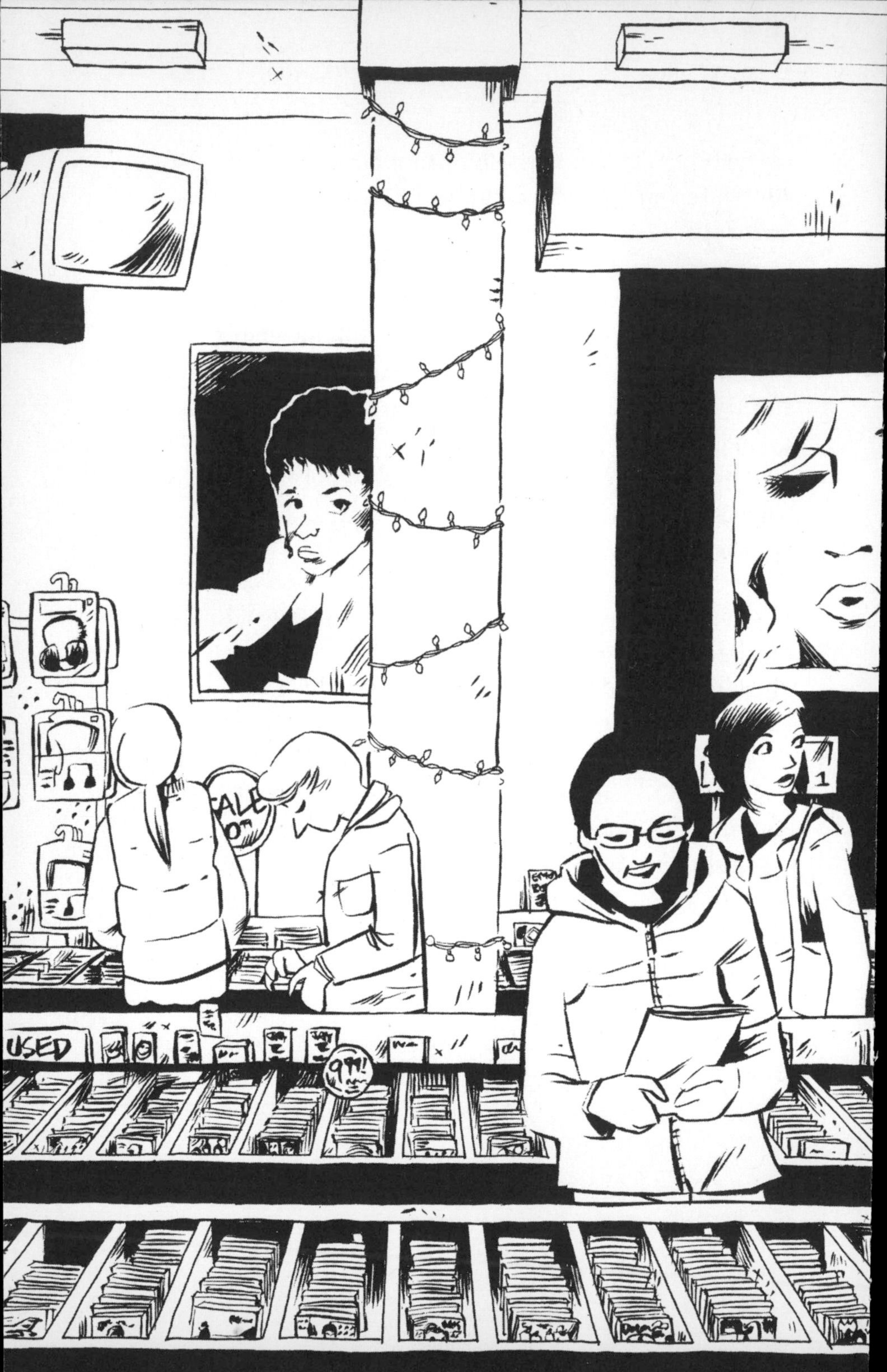
USED

a few steps behind them. Lucy said Evan would have more bruises if he were any more like Ben, who was staring at Katie now.

"You can tell him to knock it off, Katie," Lucy said.

"*Miss* Katie," the now–Miss Katie told her in a scolding voice. Evan mentioned, belatedly, that Katie liked to be called that, especially at first.

"Miss Katie, you can tell him to knock it off."

"*Knock it off, Benjamin!*" Katie yelled at a still-too-close Ben, who did not seem to notice or care. "He won't listen!" Katie complained to Lucy.

"Maybe they are kinda like us," Lucy said, amused.

They went into the f.y.e. store to browse for music. Even when she was cranky, Katie loved the mall and loved watching all the people. She smiled for the first time all afternoon when they walked into the crowded store, which was playing some upbeat, current-day Christmas music.

"She's adorable," Lucy said.

"I really like doing this," Evan said. "Of all the things I have to do after school all week, it's the most fun for me personally. It's almost like my little 'take that' at my dad. He was doing some legal work for SARAH and put this whole thing together as something to put on my résumé and college applications. And it was something for me to do at the end of the summer. To get out of the house and all. I can't imagine the thought that I'd actually like it ever crossed his mind."

"Does Lady Gags do comedy?" Miss Katie asked, looking at a CD.

"That's Lady Gaga," Evan corrected.

"Just kidding," Miss Katie said quietly, and pushed Ben a comfortable distance away from her. Lucy fawned over Miss Katie.

"There's a handful of other guys at SARAH I guess you won't get to meet," Evan said to Lucy. "But they're all really sweet, and they're genuinely excited when I come over. There's a sense of fun with them that I really don't feel anywhere else."

Evan started to comb through the CDs himself now, looking for something for Ben. Ben told him to look for something classic, so Evan knew just where to start. "What do you like, Ben? Kanye West?"

"*Evan!*" Ben said as if he were being teased.

"No Kanye. You're missing out, though. Who do you like? Celine Dion?" Ben rejected this idea, too. "All right, Ben, I gotcha. You're a classics kinda guy. The Beatles."

"*Evan!*" Ben said again.

"Hang on, I'm not playing. I don't play when it comes to the Beatles. You'll learn this about me. Let's find a good one," Evan said, shuffling around before pulling out *Rubber Soul*. "Here we go. This was my first Beatles album. You're gonna love it."

Evan scanned the disc in the sample area, and Ben put the large headphones on, then stood blankly while the album gave him a preview in ten-second installments.

"So that's your big eff-you to your dad—to enjoy doing what he tells you to do?" Lucy asked Evan.

"I guess it's not much of an eff-you when you put it that way," Evan said.

"There's this guy Ian I know in Atlanta who would throw these crazy parties and empty out his parents' liquor cabinet and basically trash the place whenever they went away. Now *that* was an eff-you."

"Did you attend these parties?" Evan asked, intrigued. "Who's Ian?" Lucy took a second too long to answer, like she was trying to come up with something.

"Oh, he's just some guy in Atlanta," she almost mumbled. She didn't even have a good answer.

Evan looked at her quizzically. Why was Atlanta always such a big secret? She'd never mentioned an Ian before. Ben took off his headphones, so Evan scanned in the White Album; Ben put the headphones back on. "Ben, listen to this, let me know if you like it." And then back to Lucy: "You mentioned that. But who is he? Is this a boyfriend?"

"Look at you, Owens!" Lucy said. "You're so jealous!"

"I'm not jealous," Evan said, giving her his full attention. "I'm just curious about what you're up to, that's all."

"Nothing." Lucy shrugged. "Ian is no one, and you're a jealous boy. This is very interesting."

Ben took off his headphones. "Evan likes Lucy!" he said, and laughed.

"Ben, listen to music!" Evan took another CD out; he didn't want to go far. He chose Boston, scanned the CD, and put the headphones back on for Ben. Maybe Evan was jealous. Or just curious. Where was the line between them?

Semantics and games. It felt like Lucy was playing a game with him he did not enjoy.

"Are you guys boyfriend and girlfriend?" Miss Katie asked. She'd been standing there so quietly that Evan had almost forgotten she was there.

"No, Evan's very sweet, but we're not dating," Lucy said. "Right, Evan?"

"Nope," Evan said. This conversation was going about as well as Ben's music selection was going.

"Good," Katie replied.

Lucy feigned shock. "She doesn't like me! I'm heartbroken!"

Ben took off the headphones and shook his head. Evan was glad. The CD shopping experience was quickly getting awkward. Evan put back the Boston CD. "So in recap," Evan said to everyone, "Ian is no one. I'm not jealous. Lucy and I are just friends. Lady Gags does not exist but would be awesome if she did. And, worst of all, Ben does not like the Beatles. Now that is upsetting."

"He's a Stones fan, definitely," Lucy said.

Ben walked to Evan's side and tapped his shoulder. "Can we go?" he mumbled, looking down at his feet. "The guys from my bus stop are here," he said, barely audible.

Evan raised an eyebrow and looked away for a moment. "Really?" he said. Evan used to walk with Ben to the bus stop every morning until this year, when Evan was able to drive and had a parking spot at the school. Since then, Ben had told him a few freshmen teased him some mornings.

"What?" Lucy asked Evan. "Who are the guys from his

bus stop? What's going on?" Evan didn't want to involve Lucy, fearing she'd — "Who are the guys from the bus stop?" she asked Ben now. Ben told her the full story, in more detail than Evan had heard, actually, which was impressive. Maybe Evan hadn't pursued the conversation hard enough in the past, or maybe Lucy in her ten minutes with him had formed a stronger bond than Evan had. Or, more likely, Ben just really liked talking to girls.

"The guys" were two fourteen-year-old boys, one thick, with a faux hawk, and one skinny and tall, with a baseball cap. Per Ben's story, they gave him a hard time while he was waiting for the bus, asking dumb questions and laughing at his answers. Just a couple of punks. Evan hadn't really ever considered a time when he'd actually be confronted with them, and he was unsure what he should do. Ben had never gone to the principal about the issue, which Evan had suggested.

"I'm gonna go talk to them." Lucy had her eyes locked on the guys.

"Wait." Evan placed a hand on her arm. She turned to face him, and he took it off. "Don't get crazy. There are rules here. We're basically the face of an organization right now, don't forget. We're not supposed to get into fights in the mall. Let's just get out of here. Ben doesn't want us making a scene." Evan took a step toward the door.

"Ben, can I go say something to them?" Lucy asked him directly. Ben nodded and looked excited. "All right, you guys wait over here. I recommend sampling some Wu-Tang Clan."

Jesus, Ben, anything for a girl, Evan thought. He was nervous now, preferring to have a plan when jumping into a situation.

"Do you really think those kids should go on teasing Ben every morning?" Lucy asked Evan once they were out of earshot of Ben.

"No, of course not." Evan couldn't help feeling uncomfortable about it, though.

"They're a couple of fourteen-year-olds; you're twice the size of either of them. What's the worst thing that could happen?" They might want to fight. He could lose his volunteer work at SARAH. Dad would throw a fit.

Evan sighed. "All right, let's go."

The two boys were talking loudly to each other when Lucy approached them, Evan in tow. The store seemed crowded suddenly. Evan felt like everyone was watching them. The walk across the store took an unusual amount of time.

"Do you guys know Ben over there?" Lucy asked them casually, nodding back in his direction. Evan stood behind her, the hired help, the goon. In case things got out of line. He'd be the one to shout *Look over there!* and pull Lucy in the opposite direction.

"Oh, yeah," Faux Hawk said, leaning forward to look at Ben, who was facing away. "He takes the bus every morning."

"Do you think it's *cool* to make fun of people?" Lucy asked crossly.

"It's not cool," Evan added. No Silent Bob over here.

"We don't make fun of him. We're just messing around," Faux Hawk said.

"Yeah, chill," Baseball Cap added. "He knows."

"That's *beyond sick*," Lucy said. "You shitheads are all that's wrong with this world." Evan tried to look tough.

Faux Hawk and Baseball Cap laughed uncomfortably. "You don't even know us," Baseball Cap said.

"Sit there and laugh," Lucy said. Evan saw where this was headed and was prepared to pull Lucy away if she lost her temper and abandoned reason. "He's a *person*, he is sweet and kind, and he feels everything you or I do and then some. He's seventeen, and he's had enough shit heaped on him in his life *without* dealing with you two. And I've only known him for a day, but I can guarantee he's brought a lot more positivity into this world than either of you ever have or will."

They continued to snicker. Evan was ready to punch them himself now. "Have a nice life," she said suddenly and coldly, and she and Evan left. Evan was surprised, proud, and maybe even a little let down. He wanted those guys to run home and stay there. He was no Lucy, though. "Nice line about it's *not* cool," Lucy said to him.

Evan and Lucy reconvened with Katie and Ben, who had found himself a copy of *Exile on Main St.* Lucy wrapped her arm around Ben's as they passed the two boys on the way out. Evan was proud of her, though he wasn't sure what his dad would say, or what the rules actually were in that kind of scenario. *Aww, to hell with it*, Evan thought.

"Lucy is cool," Ben whispered to Miss Katie.

"*I know*," Miss Katie said. "She's my *best friend*, for crying out loud." Evan knew what she was feeling. He was looking at Lucy a little differently himself.

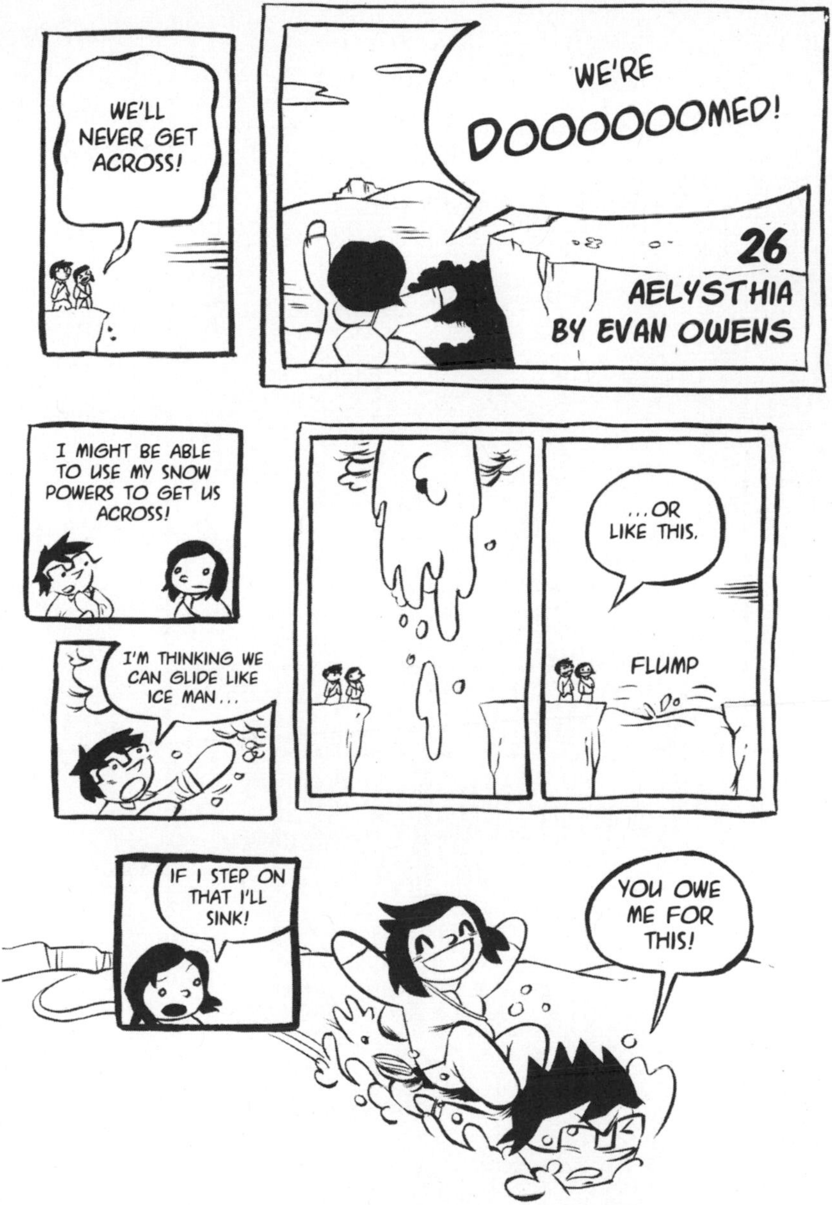

WE'LL NEVER GET ACROSS!
WE'RE DOOOOOOOMED!
26
AELYSTHIA
BY EVAN OWENS
I MIGHT BE ABLE TO USE MY SNOW POWERS TO GET US ACROSS!
I'M THINKING WE CAN GLIDE LIKE ICE MAN...
...OR LIKE THIS.
FLUMP
IF I STEP ON THAT I'LL SINK!
YOU OWE ME FOR THIS!

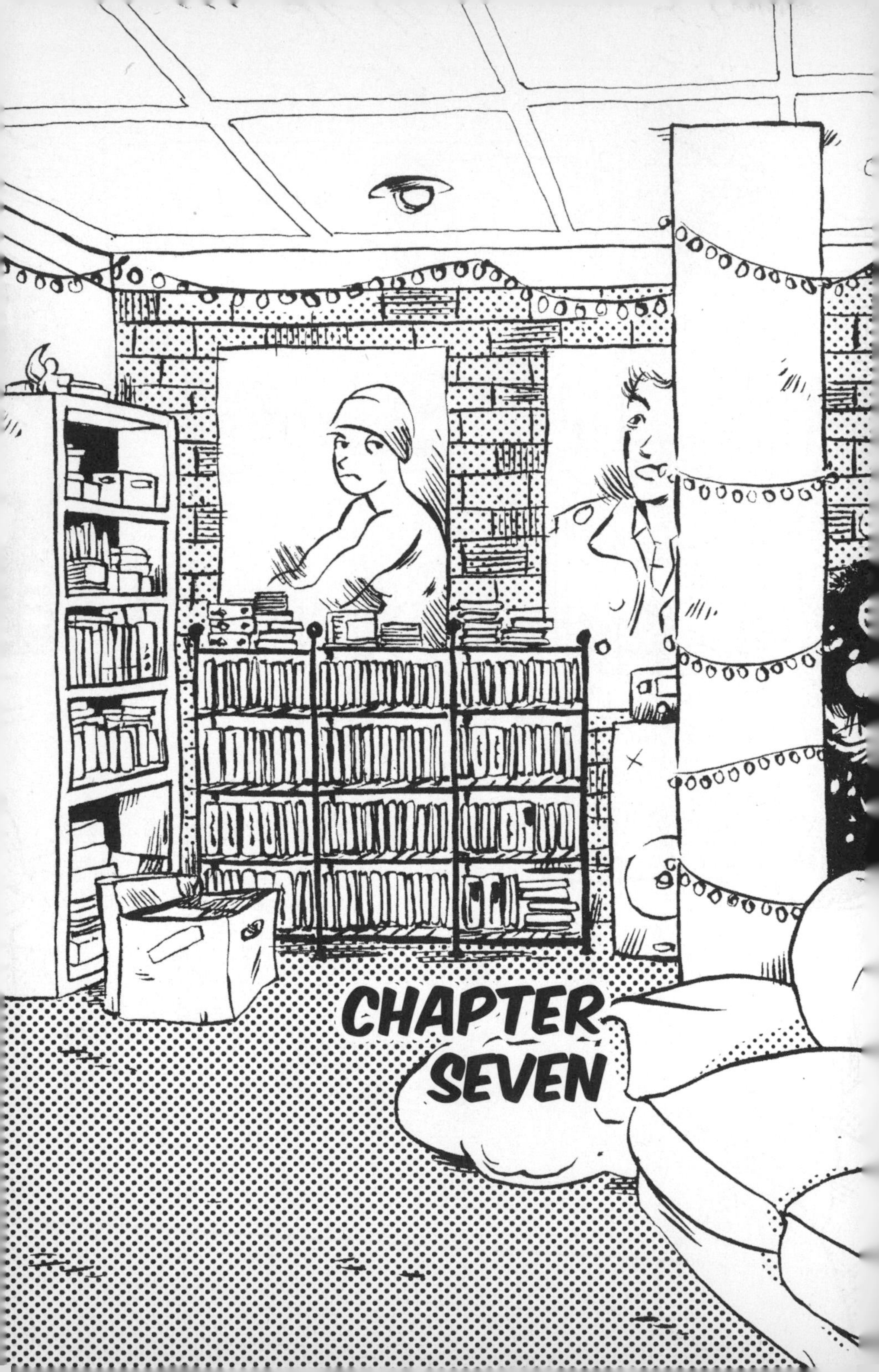
CHAPTER SEVEN

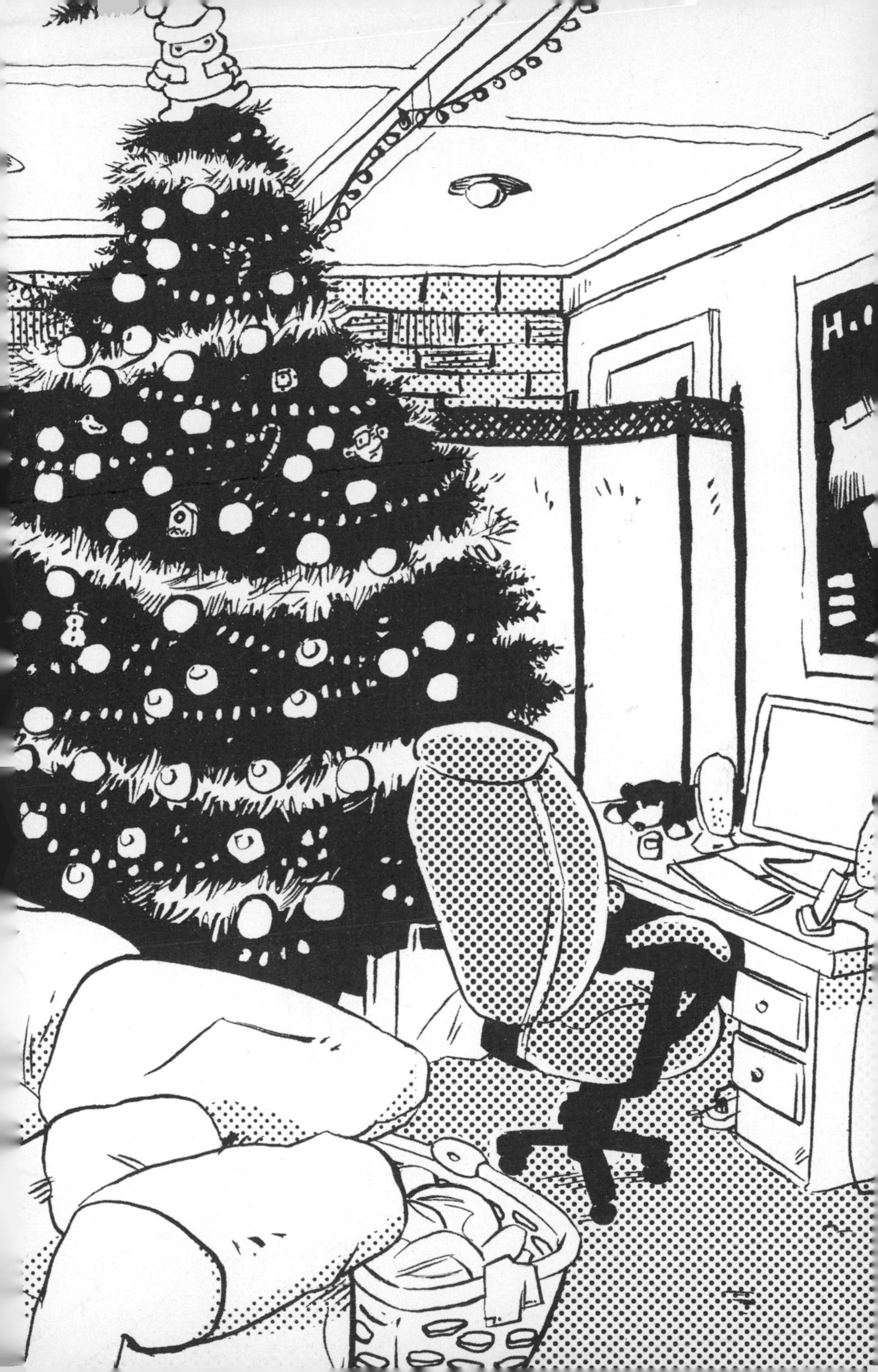

NOWHERE MAN

Lucy and Evan arrived at Marshall's basement Thursday afternoon for the first annual Christmas Eve Extravaganza, which promised vomit-inducing saccharine Christmas cheer. Standing in the basement doorway before them was Tim, his hand in a bloodied bandage, his arm stained red.

"What's wrong with your hand?" Lucy asked.

"Oh, nothing, I just thought it would be, like, a cool reintroduction for us," he said. "Do you like it? No?"

"It's pretty damn cool," Lucy agreed. "I wish I'd had warning. I'd have come in theme."

Marshall's basement was like the North Pole for homosexuals. A giant Christmas tree lounged in the corner, relaxing its limbs as far as they'd reach, spilling out on the floor. One of the walls was brick and held large Gap posters of shirtless men. Lights spread along the walls like rainbows, pink and purple and blue and red.

"We were kind of hoping you guys were Christmas carolers," Marshall said. "But, you know, you'll do."

Marshall and Tim were wearing matching snowflake sweaters. "Do you love our sweaters?" Tim asked Lucy and Evan. "They're going to double for our bad-sweater party. You guys should totally come."

"I wish I could," Lucy said, laughing. "If we could combine that with bloody appendages, it's like my dream party."

"Oh, you have to meet Fern!" Tim said. "He'll be so excited. There are never any women around here."

Fern was Marshall's guinea pig, and, sure enough, he couldn't have been more excited to see Lucy. Marshall took him out of his cage and he did backflip after backflip. "He's trying to impress you," Marshall said.

After Fern's performance, they went upstairs for the baking portion of the day. The plan was to make red-and-green cupcakes, wreath cookies, and hot chocolate to wash it all down. Evan imagined that by the end of the evening they'd be running up the walls and jabbing themselves with insulin.

Marshall gave Lucy the full story of how he had met Evan. He told her about Art Studio 3, the class they had shared. They had bonded over comic books and talked all class about Marvel superheroes. They had collaborated at the

end of junior year on a series of fine paintings of Spider-Man in the styles of artists like Lichtenstein, Monet, and Picasso.

Evan told her about the movie Tim and Marshall had been plotting for as long as Evan had known them, the movie with no script or real scenes or characters or ideas. It was just about ready to shoot, Tim told her. This much was known: It was a *horror* movie. There would be a *pantsless Santa*. Tim wanted *gore*. Marshall was more keen on *psychological* horror. Evan was playing Santa.

Lucy wanted in. "You have to do it before I leave! I want to be in this more than anything!" Lucy groveled. This was the most active Evan had seen her since she'd arrived; she was almost like an entirely new person. Or an entirely old person, as her personality now felt more like Old Lucy than he'd seen in a while. They settled on finally filming this cinematic masterpiece next week, before Lucy went back home. Talk of Lucy's leaving made Evan's stomach drop like an anchor, but he knew there was still plenty to do before then. They'd have a horror short filmed, for one thing, and then she'd always be just a DVD away.

Evan, Lucy, Tim, and Marshall munched on cookies and cupcakes in the basement as the Christmas classics marathon began.

"You're going to *love* this," Tim told Lucy, searching the

DVD rack. "It's about a little boy, and he's bald and no one likes him, but you're going to want to take him into your home." Tim continued to talk up Charlie Brown as if no one had ever heard of him, and Lucy cracked up and joined the fun.

"Is his dog boring?" she asked.

"Oh, *heavens* no," Tim said. "Charlie's dog can turn into all kinds of different characters, and he can make his doghouse fly. He's going to change your whole life." Evan and Lucy and Tim and Marshall talked and laughed all through Charlie Brown's anxiety-ridden holiday.

"Now *this* guy," Tim said, changing the DVD after Snoopy won his Best in Competition prize. "*This* guy is a bad kid and he has ADD and he's no Charlie Brown, but I think you'll love him all the same. And don't be frightened, but he's a *talking chipmunk.*"

Marshall's dad came downstairs after the cartoons had ended. He was short and portly, had curly receding hair, and wore glasses. His eyebrows curved in a way that gave his face a constant look of worry, despite his large smile. Marshall and Tim had warned Lucy he might drop in. Mel was what Marshall and Tim called a weeper, and he did not disappoint.

"Hey, guys, is it cool if I drop in or am I ruining the party?"

"Hi, Mr. Catalano," Tim said.

He raised his eyebrows and paused before saying, "Tim, you can call me Mel."

"Sorry, Mel," Tim said, blushing.

“Hi, Mel,” Evan said, standing to shake his hand. “This is Lucy.”

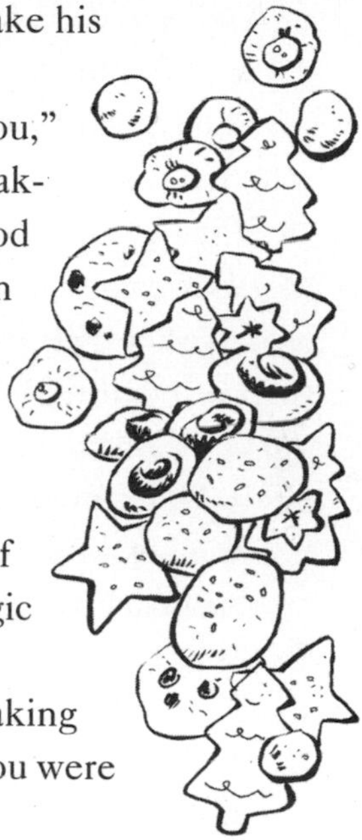

“Hi, Evan, hi, Lucy, nice to meet you,” Mel said with a big, nervous smile, shaking their hands with both of his. Mel stood up straight, holding an already half-eaten cookie. He took a big, deep breath and looked around at the Gay North Pole. He took another bite of his cookie. His cheeks were rosy and the smile never left his face. He surveyed the scene as if it were a Polaroid, already some nostalgic memory.

“Seems like just yesterday I was baking *you* cookies, Marshall,” Mel said. “And you were just a little boy.”

Tim and Marshall shared an embarrassed look. Evan enjoyed Mel, though; he thought he was a sweet guy.

“Now you’re all grown up,” Mel continued. “You’ve got your own friends, your own life, your own parties, and your own *cookies*.” Mel was laughing. “Aww, look at me, I *am* ruining your party.”

“It’s all right,” Tim said. “You’re not ruining anything.”

“No, no, you guys have your fun. Merry Christmas, Merry Christmas.”

“Love you, Dad,” Marshall said, waiting for him to go back upstairs.

Marshall exhaled after his dad took the last step up the stairs and went down the hall. It was like a tornado had run through the party, and now it was time for recovery efforts. "Sorry about that," Marshall said. "He's really sensitive."

"That's fine," Evan said. "He could have stayed and watched movies with us."

"Please, he breaks down crying watching *The Simpsons*," Marshall said. Lucy told him about her dad and his inability to move on with his life since her mom had left him. Marshall responded that he didn't know what his dad was going to do when he went off to college in the fall. He'd be living in New York, and the thought of Mel just wandering the house alone broke his heart.

"At first I was sad because my dad was, but now I'm just sad in general. I need to stop growing, like, now," Marshall said.

"Me too," Lucy said, her shoulders slumped.

"Let's just all stop growing," Tim contributed. Suddenly, Evan felt he was on the outs here. He liked growing up. He was looking forward to college and life after. He figured he'd see his parents and Gram often enough and they'd keep busy. Last Sunday had proved he didn't need to be physically present to be a part of family conversation. He leaned back into the couch and listened.

"*You've* changed the most," Marshall said to Tim. "You weren't even gay until last year."

"I know, I was so straight, right?" Tim said. "I got to have my big moment, and call all the people I hadn't talked to in forever to let them know. I told my parents, and my friends. I thought everyone was going to hate me, but apparently they all knew already. But *I* didn't even know!"

156

"They stole your moment!" Lucy said, commiserating.

"I had *no* such issues," Marshall said, crossing his legs. "I was born a gayby."

"Aww, you were a *gayby*?" Lucy gushed.

"I seriously was," Marshall said. "I was allergic to breast milk."

Everyone laughed. Evan was glad Lucy was getting along with his friends. He wished they had more time, that she could come along on their Anything-Goes Fridays or have lunch outside with them in the fall and spring. She'd fit right in.

"Still," Marshall said, uncrossing his legs and remembering he was depressed, "I'm way too mature now. Being a gay *kid* is basically being an *alone* kid, and sitting in my room, sullen and mopey and expressing it through Goth clothing and eye makeup and whatever. It was really pretty awesome. I miss it."

"Again," Evan said, looking at Marshall and Lucy, "it's like you have the same life. Lucy, are you a gay boy?"

"I think I am," Lucy said, and laughed.

Marshall sighed. "It's like I'm adapting to society, or society is adapting to me. It's so *boring*!" Marshall stuck out his tongue in distaste.

"We're *all* changing," Evan said, sinking into the couch and putting a foot up on his knee. "I have issues, too. I'm scared to death to even apply to a college because I feel like it's declaring my entire future in such a small step." Evan backtracked on the complaint. "It'll be good. It's just…it's such a *big* change for such a tiny action."

"I didn't know you were having doubts," Lucy said, looking at Evan.

"It's not like it's just me or anything," Evan said. "I wish there was more *time*. I really don't know what to do." He was surprised to hear himself say that. He'd been moving along without missing a beat. Mostly following a path, though; his mom and dad picked out most of his activities, suggested schools. All of that was like a flashlight in the dark. He could see the light where they shined it, but outside that circle was darkness, and he didn't have a damn clue what was in it.

"Okay," Marshall said, leaning forward and clasping his hands. "It's ten years from now. Where do you see yourself?"

Evan thought of the darkness outside his spotlight. "I don't know."

"*Wrong answer*, try again!"

Evan thought harder. "I guess I'd like a family," he said, and he could see his mother smiling. The light grew a little. "A house. I don't know. A kid? A dog?"

"All right," Tim said, barely accepting this, but encouraging more.

Evan thought of his dad. "I'd like to be financially secure. I'd like to be successful at something, respected in my field."

"So you want family," Marshall said matter-of-factly. "A high-paying job, respect, yada yada yada. That about it?" Marshall sounded tired just reading off the list.

"Basically," Evan said, and laughed. "That's normal, come on."

"All right, just say you'll be doing some kind of art, at least, okay?" Marshall pleaded. The flashlight jerked to the left. "I *live* to express myself. My dream in life is to do a one-man show, and I live out my entire being through monologue and song and dance and I scream and cry and by the end of the show I run into the audience and beat the hell out of every person there."

"I love you so much, Marshall," Lucy said. "You can beat the hell out of me anytime."

"Aww," Marshall said. "I love you, too. You'd totally get a pass."

"I don't have that much to express," Evan said. The flashlight was turned off. "I'm generally pretty content."

"Your demons are just hidden well," Marshall said. "We'll pull them out of you. We can do an exorcism." Tim and Marshall and Lucy all looked at Evan like he was ready to explode and take out everyone.

"Stop it," Evan said, laughing. He was pretty sure he was demonless. In this group, feeling content was a bad thing, and dysfunction was a badge of honor. Evan wouldn't want a chipper, straight Marshall, though, or a sports-playing, straight-As Tim. He wouldn't want Lucy to be any less spirited and independent. He'd even grown to appreciate her appearance. The nose ring was kinda cute. Evan wondered what they found appealing in him. Where was *his* quirky dysfunction?

"You just need to come to NYU with us," Marshall said, "and the creativity will fall right out of you and you won't be able to stop it. You'll have a diarrhea of art."

"Ew," Evan said, and frowned.

"People go to New York to find themselves," Marshall

said. "The city is full of people chasing their dreams and finding other people chasing their own dreams, and chasing them together."

"Will you guys go out with me?" Lucy asked them, starry-eyed. "You're like my perfect two gay boyfriends." Evan retracted from the conversation and wondered what dream he'd chase in New York City. It was abstract. Art, love, life, they were big shapeless ideas, and that made them scary.

They all sat on the couch together and watched *Black Christmas*, the 1977 version, and then *Bad Santa*. Evan felt scared for a while. And then he stopped thinking of colleges and cities and dark open spaces. Then he had a sugar crash and fell asleep on Marshall's couch, and woke up covered in tinsel.

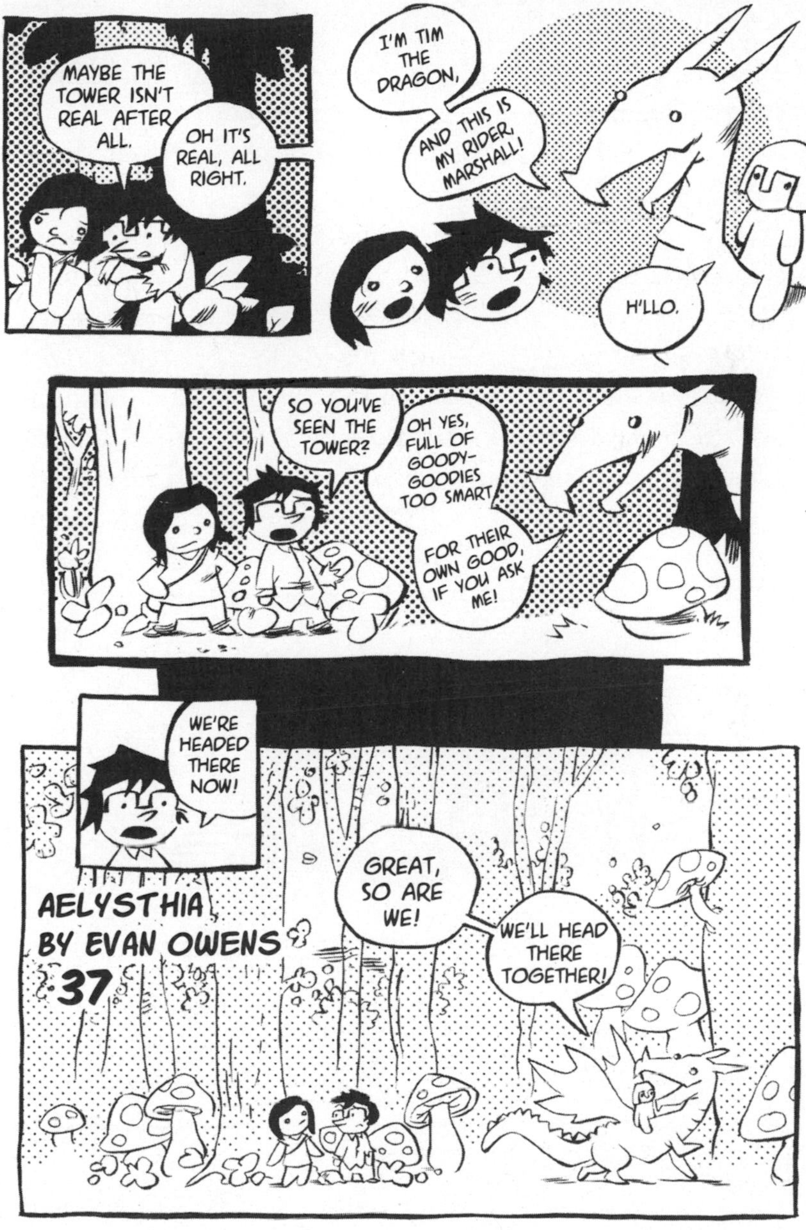
MAYBE THE TOWER ISN'T REAL AFTER ALL.
OH IT'S REAL, ALL RIGHT.
I'M TIM THE DRAGON,
AND THIS IS MY RIDER, MARSHALL!
H'LLO.
SO YOU'VE SEEN THE TOWER?
OH YES, FULL OF GOODY-GOODIES TOO SMART
FOR THEIR OWN GOOD, IF YOU ASK ME!
WE'RE HEADED THERE NOW!
GREAT, SO ARE WE!
WE'LL HEAD THERE TOGETHER!
AELYSTHIA
BY EVAN OWENS
37

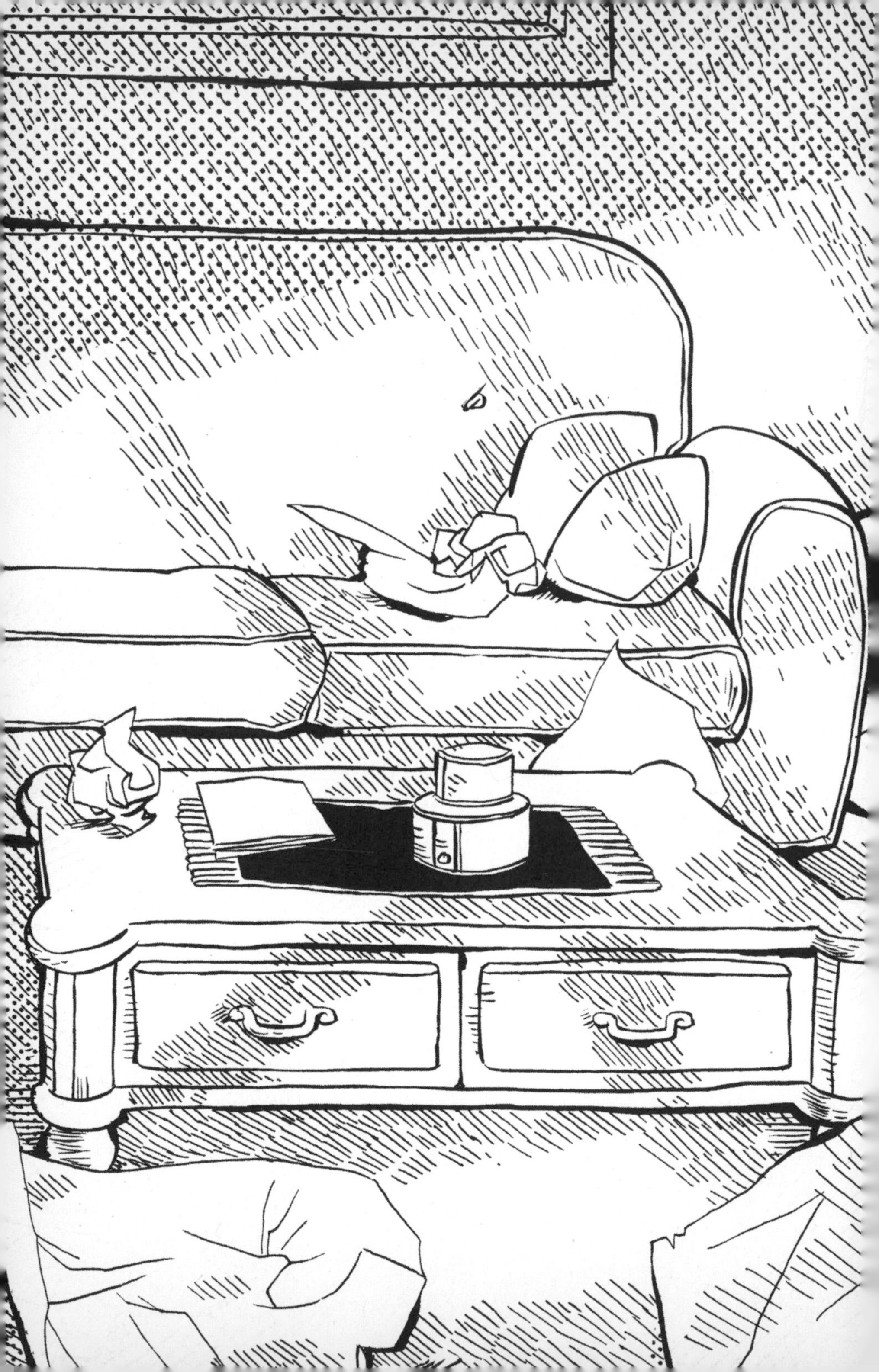

CHAPTER EIGHT

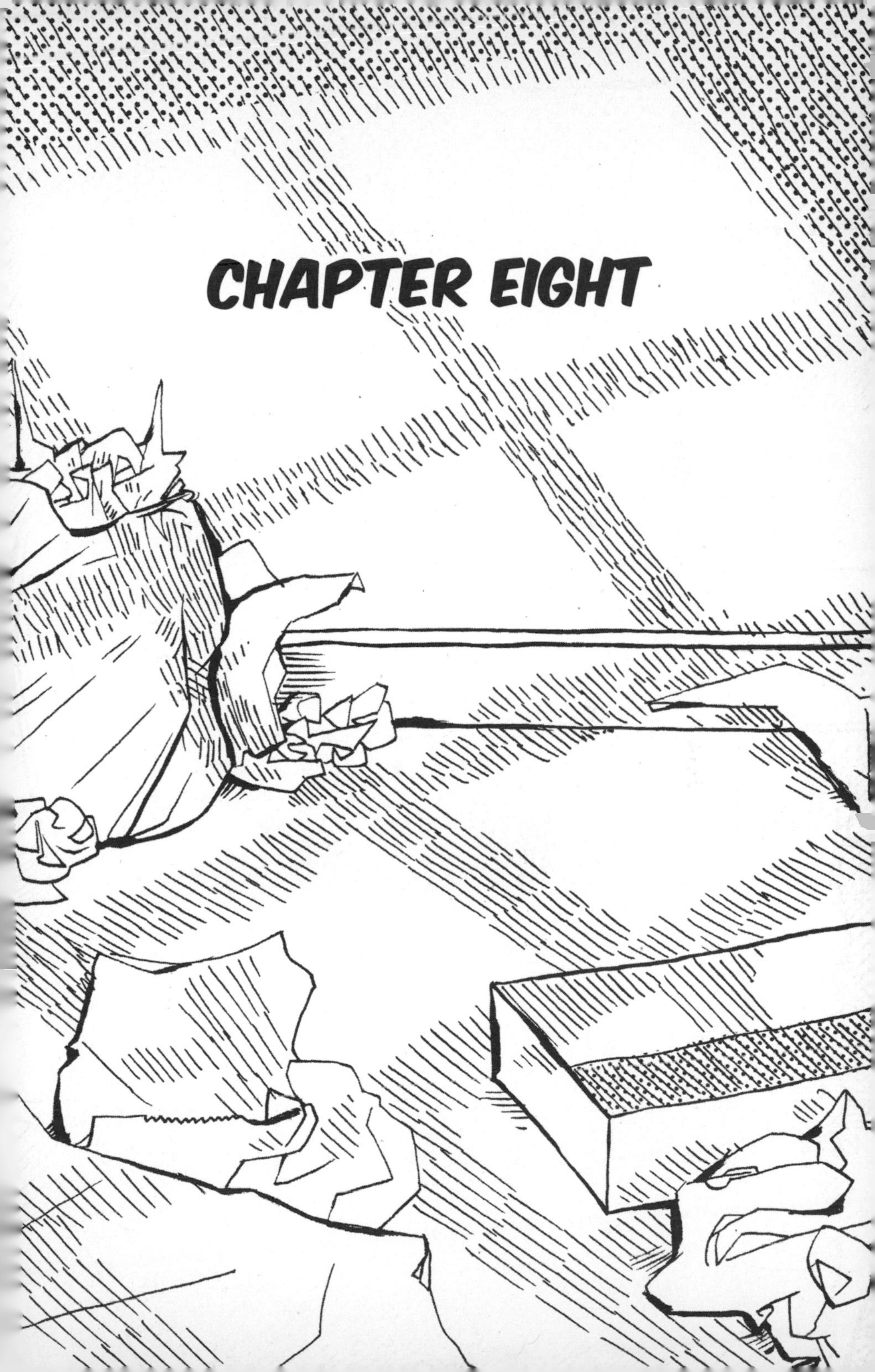

IN MY LIFE

Evan woke up around seven, as he did every Christmas morning. He walked downstairs with his hair a mess and sleep in his eyes. His parents and Gram were already awake, waiting for him in their pajamas. The living room was dark, though the blinds on the windows were open and light bounced off the snow from outside and onto the ceiling. The tree was lit in the corner of the room and hid a spread of presents, which Dad and Mom handed Evan with smiles as he sat on the floor between them. Mom held a large garbage bag to take all the wrapping paper as Evan went through his gifts.

Evan got: a netbook, for college; a microwave, for college; a thesaurus. All Dad gifts. Sweaters, pants, shirts (for college), new socks and underwear, two new hats, and a pair of gloves. Mom gifts. A couple of books, several pads of the expensive paper he liked to use, gift cards to iTunes and Amazon.com; thanks, Gram. And luggage, for coming home from college (Dad). Christmas was always big for the Owenses. Even years when money was tighter, his parents managed to go all out for Christmas. They'd say things like *For working so hard this past year* as they handed him gifts.

Evan got a cappuccino maker for his parents, which he'd been planning for months and which he also considered a gift for himself. He drew a comic strip for his grandmother, which he was sure would be framed and viewable for the next twelve months.

Everyone hugged and Evan had his hair ruffled.

By ten, visitors had begun to fill out the house. Children ran around with their 3-D video-game pets and dolls that had larger wardrobes than the kids had themselves. Evan's hair was combed nicely by then. He wore a blue sweater over a light button-down shirt. He sat on the end of the couch in the living room, reading one of the books he'd gotten, Haruki Murakami's *The Wind-Up Bird Chronicle*. The Walt Disney parade was on TV, and a teenager with piles of hair and frozen red cheeks was singing love songs to a dark gray Muppet with long blond hair.

There was food everywhere: pigs in blankets, shrimp, deviled eggs, tortillas and salsa. Evan's cousin's dog was running back and forth from the living room to the kitchen, where all the adults were, his nose raised high, waiting for the food that would inevitably fall to the floor. Evan got down on the ground and wrestled him into submission, rubbing his belly until he was in dog heaven.

Evan went into the kitchen to wash his hands. His parents and grandmother were there, as well as an aunt and uncle and a few of his cousins. His grandmother was telling them all a story from back in the summer, when she'd been out shopping with Mom and they'd come across a heavily tattooed young woman. His grandma had always been fascinated by tattoos, so she asked the woman about them, and eventually asked to see the large tattoo design that took over her back, prompting the woman, glad to be asked, to lift up the back of her shirt for Gram to see it fully. Gram was a ham at these parties. She loved her family and she loved telling stories.

"I always wanted George to get a tattoo for me and he never would," she said of Evan's late grandfather. "*For Christmas*, he'd say, every time. And every Christmas I thought, *This will be the year*, but it never was. Now I'll never get my tattoo."

This could have been a morose scene, but the family knew that Gram had long come to terms with his passing, which was peaceful and natural and all you could ask of such things, so Evan knew this was all said in good spirits.

"What I really wanted was my name tattooed on his arm—that'd really let me know how much he loved me. But oh, well."

"I'll do it, Gram," Evan said, joining in the conversation.

"Oh, Evan," she said. "I'd be absolutely touched if you did."

Evan hadn't expected that answer, and neither had anyone else, as they all laughed.

"Now you *have* to do it!" his cousin said. "Didn't think of that, did ya?"

Evan walked back into the living room to find Lucy there, standing uncomfortably by the door.

"Hey, I didn't hear you come in," Evan said. "Merry Christmas."

"You look nice," Lucy said, and touched his hair, as if to see if a gentle poke would send it right back to its usual mess. They stood for a moment, and then hugged, unsure if you were supposed to hug after spending the last few days together. Evan smelled alcohol on Lucy's breath as he got in close.

"Have you been drinking?" he asked her quietly.

"I don't know," Lucy said. "Jesus. Merry Christmas to you, too."

They sat on the couch. Evan shifted a little to face her. "Get any cool presents?" Evan asked her.

Lucy shook her head. "Santa was still asleep when I left, so if he got me anything, it's waiting on the roof with Rudolph. It's fine. What about you?"

"Not much," Evan lied. "Laptop for college, some clothes."

Gram came into the living room not long after with an

envelope for Lucy and a box in her hand. "I thought maybe your friends Timmy and Marshall might have come over. Maybe you can give them this for me, then." She handed Evan the box.

Evan was hesitant. Of course she'd mean well, but he would have to know what was in the box before he gave it to anyone. Sometimes Gram was too open-minded, and this gift could be just about anything.

Gram sensed the hesitation. "It's a couple of scarves," she said. "Not because they're gay, but because everyone should have a scarf."

Before handing Lucy her gift, Gram asked her what she thought of Evan getting her name tattooed on his arm. Lucy was all for it, and said she'd get a matching tattoo herself. Gram handed Lucy the gift to open.

"Oh," Lucy said. "I didn't buy anything for you."

"Oh, *please*," Gram said. "You're kids. Save your money for something good." Lucy opened the envelope and pulled out a Starbucks gift card. "This is so you can take some handsome young man out for coffee back home." Gram patted Lucy's leg.

"Oh my!" Lucy said with a laugh. She stood up to give Gram a hug and Evan clenched, hoping his grandmother wouldn't smell the alcohol on her breath. There was no mention of it, no awkwardness at all, and Lucy sat back down just as the front door opened and another set of Evan's aunts and uncles came in with three more children. The children ran into the house, screaming and shredding more wrapping paper. Their parents spotted the mistletoe overhead and shared a kiss and wished everyone a Merry Christmas.

Mom walked into the living room to give Lucy her gift next, which was in a perfectly cubed box. She wished Lucy a Merry Christmas and gave her a hug and a kiss and handed her the present.

"Your dad said he'd stop by today, honey," Mom said. "He didn't come with you?"

"No," Lucy said, and shrugged her shoulders. "He wasn't awake when I got up."

"Well. You stay here as long as you like. Have some food. We made too much," Mom said, looking around to get something for her.

Lucy opened her second gift of the morning. She tore the wrapping paper and opened the box to find a loosely stuffed dark brown bear, slouched over and looking up at her.

"You're never too old for a stuffed friend," Mom said.

"Thank you, that's very sweet," Lucy said, and gave Mom another hug.

Evan took the bear out of the box and walked him around on his and Lucy's legs.

"Did you know?" Lucy asked.

"No, I had no idea," Evan said. He wiggled the bear around, facing Lucy, and got a chuckle.

Evan's cousin's daughter Jana crawled onto the couch and onto Evan's lap. She had a bow in her hair, and her face and fingers were sticky. She looked at Lucy and smiled hesitantly, and Evan laughed and sat her up properly.

"What do you think, Jana?" Evan asked. "Do you like Mr. Bear?"

Jana shook her head no, and Mr. Bear mauled her with his cuddliness. *"Rawr!"* Jana laughed.

"What do you think now?" Evan asked her. "Do you like Mr. Bear now?"

Jana nodded and put all her fingers into her mouth. Her eyes moved to Lucy, and, deciding Lucy was a friend, she reached her wet, sticky fingers out slowly toward Lucy's face.

The bathroom door opened, and one of the children stepped out, surveyed the room, and made a run toward the other children.

"I'll be right back," Lucy said, dodging messy fingers and making a quick dash to the unoccupied bathroom, taking her pocketbook with her.

Evan sat on the couch, waiting for Lucy and holding his book, keeping his end of the couch warm. On the TV Santa Claus was waving to the masses as the parade ended. The doorbell rang. One of the kids ran to the door and looked through the glass window and saw a tall man standing there. He gave her a goofy smile, and she laughed and ran away. Evan answered the door.

Before Evan stood Doug Brown, a far cry from the robed, unshaven man he'd been the other day. His remaining hair was tidy, his face shaven, and he wore a nice shirt-and-pants combination. *The sly bastard*, Evan thought. *He could still pull it together!* The Browns certainly had a capacity for change.

"Hi, Doug, Merry Christmas," Evan said with a large grin, and opened the door fully. "Come in."

"Evan, Merry Christmas to you," Doug said, shaking

Evan's hand. Doug had a bag of gifts with him. "Hold on, I have something for you."

Doug found the gift with *Evan* written on it and handed it to him. "I hope you like."

"Wow, thanks," Evan said, opening the gift. It was a knit hat, something Evan collected. He did like.

Lucy came out of the bathroom, looking worse than before. Evan glanced at her, worried that a scene was inevitable at this point. Lucy held her gaze on her father, though, and Evan thought she looked like a small, sticky-fingered child looking at Santa standing before her with a sack full of presents.

"Dad?"

"Merry Christmas, sweetheart," he said.

Lucy walked slowly over and gave him a hug, her head placed against his chest.

"Kind of embarrassing," Doug whispered to her. He handed Lucy her gift. "Slept right through the alarm. There's more back home."

Lucy watched him as she unwrapped it. It was a hardcover collection of *The Divine Comedy*. "I know it used to be your favorite. The old one was looking a bit ratty."

Lucy looked up at her father, as if the idea of him all cleaned up and handing out presents was too much to process. "Thank you, Daddy," she said quietly.

"What's going on?" Evan asked Lucy, sitting down beside her on the couch a little later. She clutched one of her books tightly and shushed him. She was eavesdropping on her father's conversation with the Owenses. Evan joined her in listening. Doug sat at a table with Dad and Mom and the three of them were reminiscing about old college adventures. A glass clinked, and there was a commotion as if someone had just spilled a drink.

"Oh no," Mom said, disappointed. "Oh, I'm sorry, guys."

"Not at all," Doug said calmly, quickly standing up. "There we go."

"Always cool," Dad said.

"Oh, it's true," Mom said. "Nothing ever fazed you."

"Tut tut and all that rut," Doug said quickly. "It's the British temperament, I suppose. I had my moments, though. We both did."

"Well, you never showed us," Mom said.

A chair squeaked, and Doug sat back down. "Where were we?" he said, and for a moment they all laughed.

"Cool British temperament," Dad said.

"Oh, right," Doug said. "I suppose when Lucy was born things became a little less mellow."

They all laughed knowingly. "I think that's allowed, hon," Mom said.

"Oh, not just the birth," Doug said. "She was always a handful. I think she ran away at least once a month for a few years straight."

Evan turned to Lucy. "Maybe you should at least go in there and join the conversation," he said. Lucy waved him off.

"I remember one time," Doug said, "she ran away because she'd been punished for the *last* time she ran away.

We wouldn't let her attend some sock-hop party with her Girl Scouts and she ran off. We hadn't heard back from her for hours, we phoned the police, we went out and searched the neighborhood. I got home and there were cookies left out in the kitchen, so we knew she'd been home. She was either in the house or nearby. She finally came home an hour later, and I swear I could have just killed her. I yelled and yelled 'til I was red in the face. I just loved her so much." Doug paused for a moment. "So. Not always cool, no."

It sounded like a far cry from the family Evan had known. He looked at Lucy, who was eyeing the bathroom again, and put his hand on her purse. "Leave it," he said.

Lucy covered her mouth quickly, but her cheeks puffed out and a small amount of vomit fell onto her shirt. Startled, Evan let go of the purse, which she grabbed as she ran back to the bathroom.

When Lucy emerged five minutes later, Evan took her arm and pulled her quickly upstairs. Lucy looked angry but didn't have enough sense left in her to do or say anything about it. Instead, she pouted like a child and tripped over stairs. Evan continued to pull.

"Are you crazy?" Evan asked, shutting the door behind Lucy as she stumbled into his room. "People are going to notice! Your dad is down there."

Lucy stared at Evan, fuming, her fists closed, her upper body heaving, her mouth clenched tight. Her black eyeliner was smeared from crying, and her foundation and lipstick were a mess from wiping vomit off her mouth. She looked like she had a million things to say but couldn't remember one. So instead, she cried. She sobbed and moaned, and she shuffled her feet over to Evan and she grabbed his sweater and pulled it to her face and rubbed her blotchy makeup and tears all over it.

"Lucy," Evan said, and repeated her name several times. "Lucy…" He held her shoulders and then gave her a hug and walked her over to his bed, where he sat her down and she cried hot tears on his shoulder.

"Shh," he said, hoping nobody would hear and come check on them. He petted her hair like she was a puppy.

They reclined on the bed; Lucy lay on half of Evan, grasping at his shirt and sweater and wrinkling the sweater, pulling the breast of it into a ball. The sobs became sniffles and the sniffles became groans and the groans became heavy, labored breathing, and then she fell asleep. And then Evan fell asleep, too.

After twenty minutes and an ounce of drool had passed, Lucy rolled over onto her back, taking up what was left of the bed.

"I didn't buy anyone presents," Lucy mumbled.

"'S okay," Evan said quietly. It was late afternoon. The room was dark with shadow, and the white Christmas lights outside Evan's window had been turned on. Evan figured there was too much going on downstairs for anyone to notice they were gone. That was a lucky break.

"I'm selfish," Lucy said in a whisper. Her eyes were closed.

"You're brave, though," Evan said, looking down at the

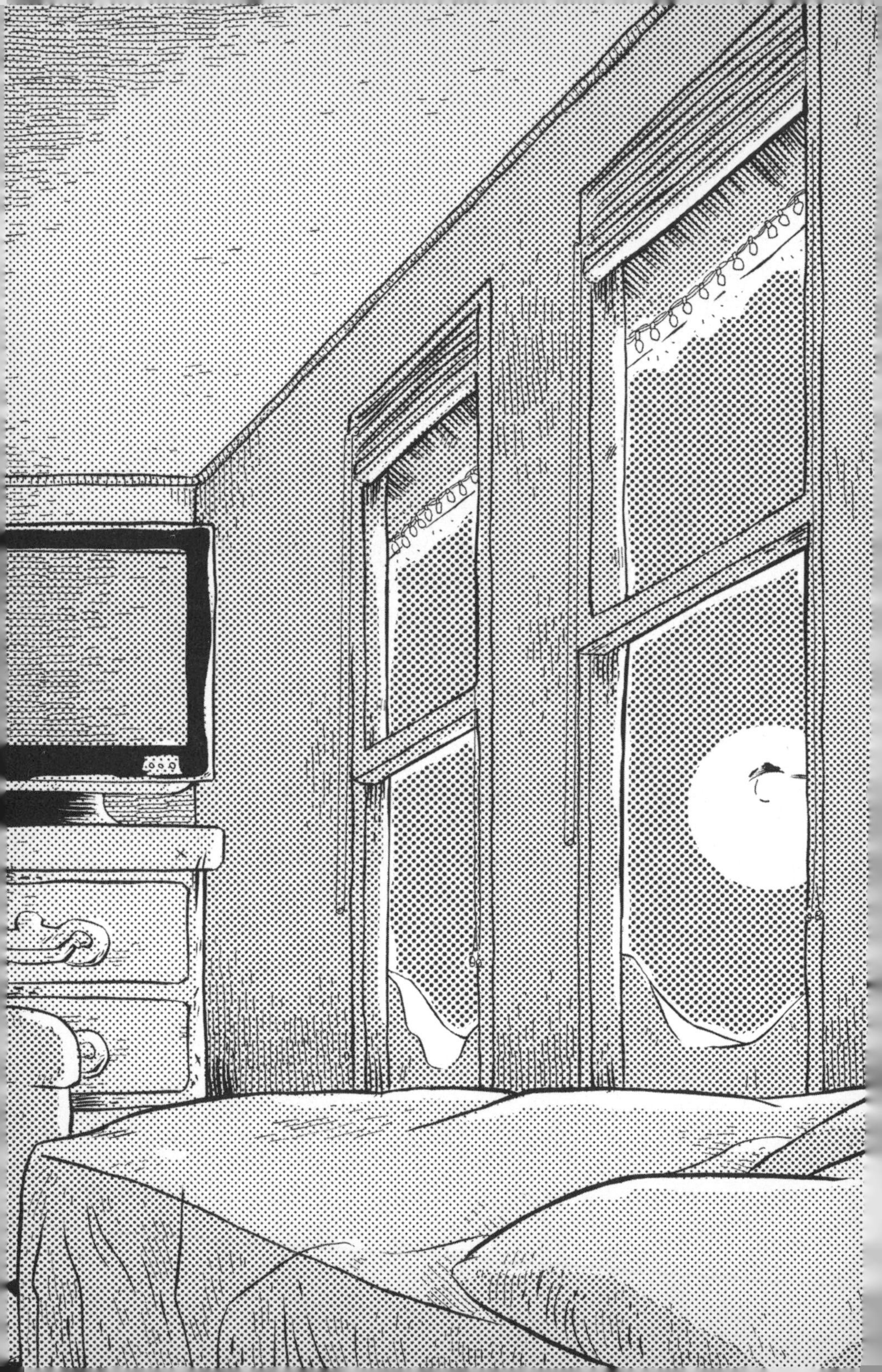

top of her head. "And confident. You know, usually."

"I'm not either of those things," Lucy said in a childlike voice. Like someone who'd just thrown a tantrum and tired herself out. "I'm a mess."

"You're pretty," Evan said, ignoring her self-deprecation. "You've always been so pretty, even with your hair all messed up. Even with all this drool."

Lucy didn't say anything to this.

"You know what's my favorite thing about you?" Evan asked her quietly. "There's no one on Earth like you. You're just a complete *individual*, and that's the biggest compliment I can think of. I can live another hundred years and I'll never meet another person like you. And that makes me feel just really special to know you, you know?"

Lucy stirred a bit at his side, pulling her head back to look up at him. "Do you know what I like about you?" she asked.

Evan smiled. "No, what?"

"That you're my home. And my rock." She put her head down against his shoulder and her hand on his arm. "And you're warm and stable and you make me feel safe. And you're so *smart*, and so talented. I mean…you don't even know how much I look up to you."

Evan turned red. He'd never heard that kind of compliment come from Lucy. About anyone, let alone himself. She seemed like a different person, but one more like herself than any of the new or old Lucys.

"I didn't give you your Christmas present. Hang on." He wasn't even sure he wanted to give it to her. He thought maybe it was lame or corny, but at the moment it felt right.

"Huh?" Lucy asked, as Evan got out of the bed and turned his desk lamp on. The movement woke Lucy up a bit, and she held her upper body up on her elbows. Evan rummaged through his art and pulled out the drawing he'd done of them as cartoon characters for their Web comic. It was painted in watercolor, and said *For Lucy, Love, Evan.* Evan took it back to the bed, where he sat down, and Lucy leaned up to look at it. Evan watched her touch the painting, nervously waiting for her reaction. She looked sad for a moment, and she looked up at Evan, and she looked sad and confused. Lucy leaned forward and kissed Evan on the lips, and Evan kissed her back, and he let go of the drawing and put his hand over hers, and she held the back of his head and they kissed each other for the first time in their lives.

"I'm sorry I threw up," Lucy said quickly and quietly between kisses. "I didn't plan on this."

Evan held his head against hers, and she pulled her head back and her sad eyes looked into his. "I always wanted to do that," she said.

And they kissed again.

AELYSTHIA BY EVAN OWENS 40

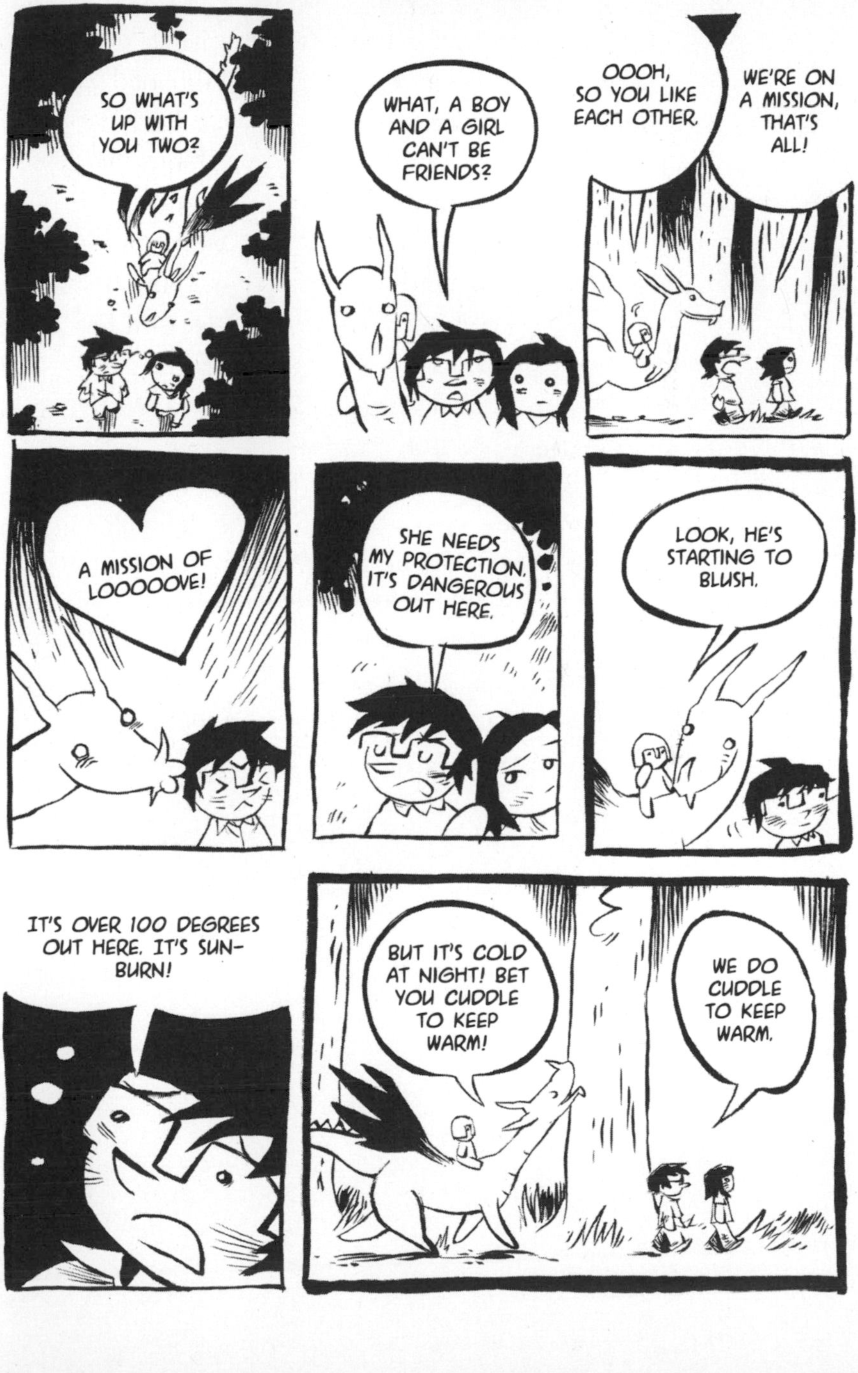

SO WHAT'S UP WITH YOU TWO?
WHAT, A BOY AND A GIRL CAN'T BE FRIENDS?
OOOH, SO YOU LIKE EACH OTHER.
WE'RE ON A MISSION, THAT'S ALL!
A MISSION OF LOOOOOVE!
SHE NEEDS MY PROTECTION. IT'S DANGEROUS OUT HERE.
LOOK, HE'S STARTING TO BLUSH.
IT'S OVER 100 DEGREES OUT HERE. IT'S SUN-BURN!
BUT IT'S COLD AT NIGHT! BET YOU CUDDLE TO KEEP WARM!
WE DO CUDDLE TO KEEP WARM.

INTERLUDE

THE LITTLE GIRL I ONCE KNEW

Shortly after Evan had walked home from Lucy's father's house one year prior, Lucy was on a plane to her home in Georgia. She arrived at the Atlanta airport on a bright Saturday morning. To her surprise, it was not just her mother who met her, but her mother and another. The "another" was Bill, Lucy's mom's new boyfriend. He had hair that was practically molded to his scalp like a sculpture, a plastic smile, a pressed shirt. He was the type of southern conservative Lucy would go miles out of her way to avoid. Lucy didn't trust a thing about him. As they drove home, her mom turned back in her seat to face Lucy, a matching plastic grin like she'd never seen before. Lucy thought she'd been abducted by pod people. She was ready for the car to hover and blast off into outer space at any given minute.

Lucy's mother wasn't motherly by any stretch of the

imagination—she was always much more of a friend than a mother. The same could be said for her dad. Lucy never had any rules; she was rarely watched or held to any standard. Her sense of humor, her spongelike ability to absorb knowledge, her ambitions in creative fields—they could all be credited to one person: Lucy.

Lucy's mother, Dawn, was simply too distracted with her own life to pay much attention to Lucy. And, at the moment, her mom's life revolved around Bill. This wasn't her first boyfriend, of course; her mom had dated many men since leaving Lucy's father five years ago. Some of them lasted awhile. David lasted one year, and he got along with Lucy. He recommended books and movies, he was an intellectual, and Lucy would have loved for her mom to settle down with him. David was weak, though, like Lucy's dad was before him, and a stronger man pulled her mom away. And that affair lasted about two weeks, much more in line with her mom's average relationship length. Which was a good thing because when her mom was dating, Lucy found it insufferable. Lucy would have to spend her time out at the library, at the park, at a diner, or at school. *Just stay out of the house for a while*, she was repeatedly told. And when she was home, she'd spend all of her time alone in her room.

Bill moved in by spring. Late winter had been a series of odd interactions and judgments passed between Bill and Lucy, comments on wardrobe, or choice of activities, the occasional backhanded compliment. Once Bill had moved in, though, he felt it was his right to dictate what Lucy did, and that did not sit well with her.

The first was mandatory church on Sundays. Lucy had no problems with Bill going to church, and she didn't even tell him that her mom had never attended a day of church in her life before him; that was their business. But now he was insisting she go because *There is a lot you can learn there*, and *A little God never did anyone no harm*. And then there were the sweet things he did for her, like picking out nice sunny little dresses and clothes a *proper lady* would wear. Her mom actually thought this was sweet. *You look like a whore* is what he said when Dawn wasn't around. No, there wasn't a sweet thing about him. He was manipulative, condescending, and controlling.

In June, Lucy met Ian.

She'd decided, with her friend Tess, to go into the city to a party half her class was attending. Not that she liked parties, or even wanted to go, but this was a good chance to show Bill who was boss. The party itself was awful. Lucy sat in silence while Tess and everyone else one-upped one another on how cool and grown-up they were because they could drink beer.

"So what's your deal? Why are you so quiet?" Ian had asked her as she sat at the bottom of the living room stairs. "I always see you around, but you never say anything." Lucy laughed because she didn't know what to say and because she was a dork and hated social situations, but she knew Ian could be a good thing, so she let him do his little sweet-talking thing. Ian and Lucy grew close very fast.

That night was the first time Bill tried to "ground" Lucy, which she laughed at, stumbling home at three in the morning. Bill grew irate and called in her mom, and she took Bill's side. *No more trips to the city* was the punishment they'd decided on.

Lucy continued to see Ian. He was large and loud and aggressive. He was a football player—not at all the type of person Lucy had pictured herself with. He was good-looking, but not great-looking. Lucy was socially nonexistent and she knew she might not be anything more than sex for Ian, but he got her out of the house. When she wasn't there, she wasn't a problem. Her mom barely noticed anyway. Bill was Dawn's family now; Lucy was just boarding.

As the relationship went on, Ian did develop feelings for Lucy, strong ones, and even if she didn't reciprocate those feelings, she at least felt somewhat safe around him. She stopped seeing people or going to the library; she dropped off the face of the earth. She came home late, preferably when her mom and Bill had gone to bed already. She was grounded a lot and ignored her punishments as frequently. And as she became ingrained with Ian's crew, she smoked and she drank. She drank a lot, actually. *Why did no one tell me there was a drink that made Bill just go away?* she thought. This was all very interesting to Lucy. She found that with just the right amount of smoke and drink, all the songs she listened to were about her. And TV actors became her friends. *Everyone* was her friend.

Lucy was out drunk with her friends when she cut and dyed her hair and pierced her nose. *Take that, Bill.* He'd told her she looked like a clown, but no punishment—he didn't say much else on the subject.

Lucy stayed with Ian for two weeks at the end of August when his parents were away on vacation, and she and Ian were drugged out of their minds for the majority of the time. When she came home from this blissful vacation, her mom informed her that she and Bill would like her to leave. "We tried, Lucy. You know we did," she'd said, standing across from the couch with Bill, who was looking smug and victorious while Lucy sat.

"Leave?" Lucy asked. "And go where?" Her dad was away for Navy business most of the year, and her grandparents were either dead or in nursing homes. For better or for worse, this was her family.

"Well, you didn't have any trouble finding a place to stay the last two weeks while I was looking all over for you." She'd said it so coldly. She wouldn't even give Lucy the courtesy of looking at her while she essentially made her homeless. And Bill was worse, standing there silently, his arms crossed. It was all his doing.

So Lucy stayed with Tess in her loud and violent home, and she stayed with Jennifer and her seven brothers and sisters, and she dated Ian, though she felt cold toward him now, and she failed classes in school. She got quiet, very quiet. She didn't know what to do with her hair. And she smoked and drank and cried and did her best to forget it all, and then it was December. And then she kissed Evan.

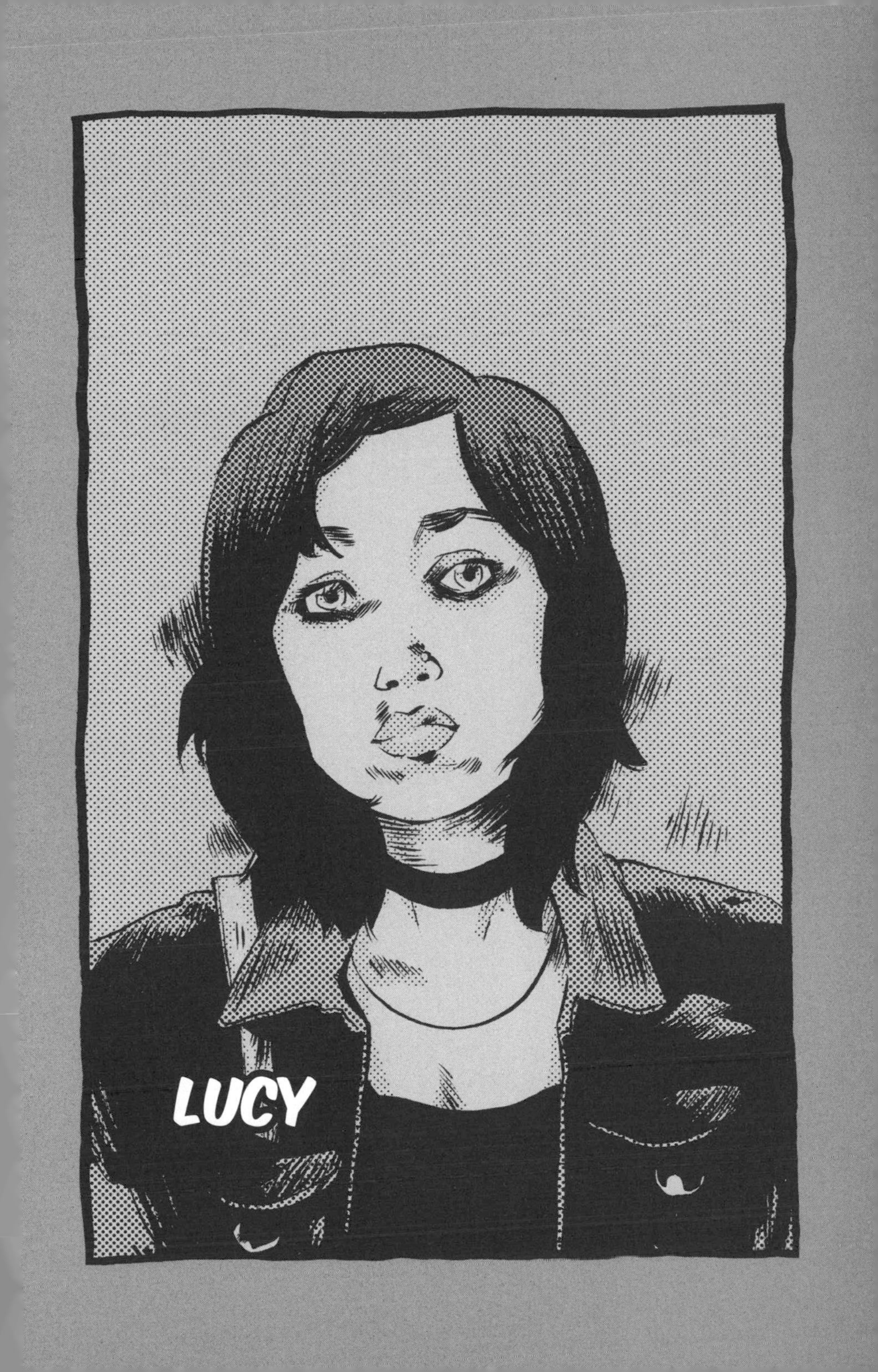
LUCY

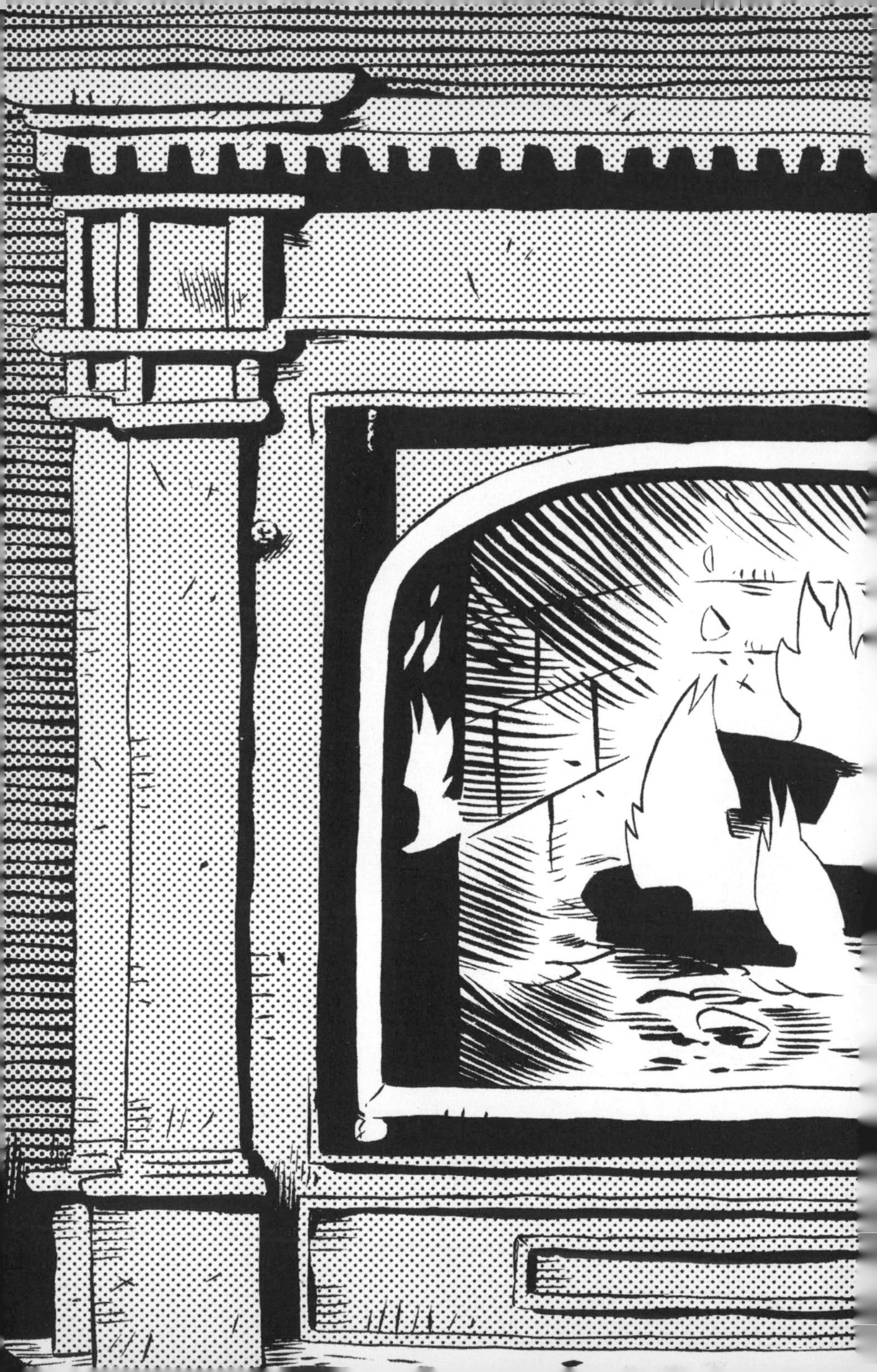

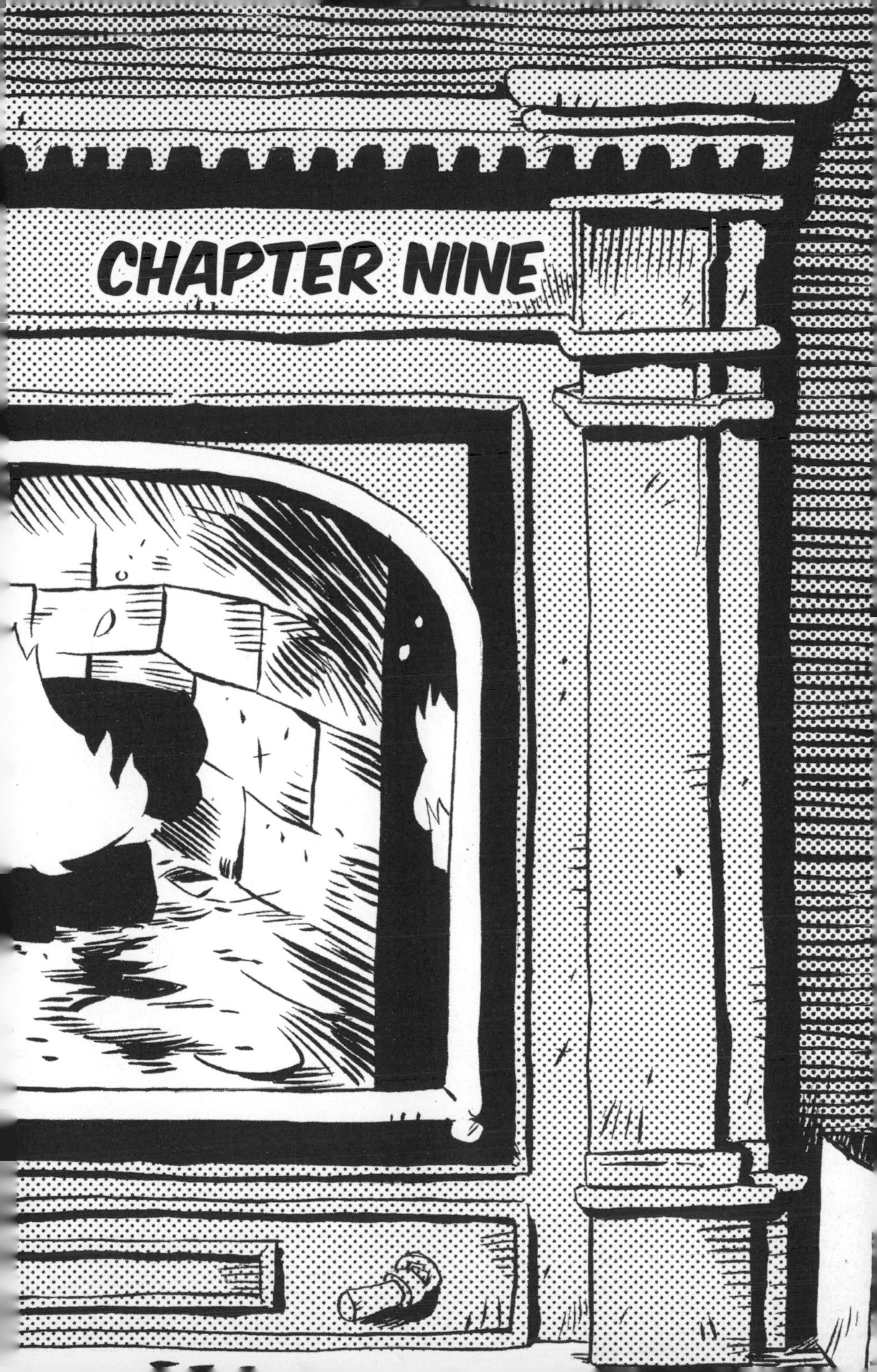
CHAPTER NINE

HEROES AND VILLAINS

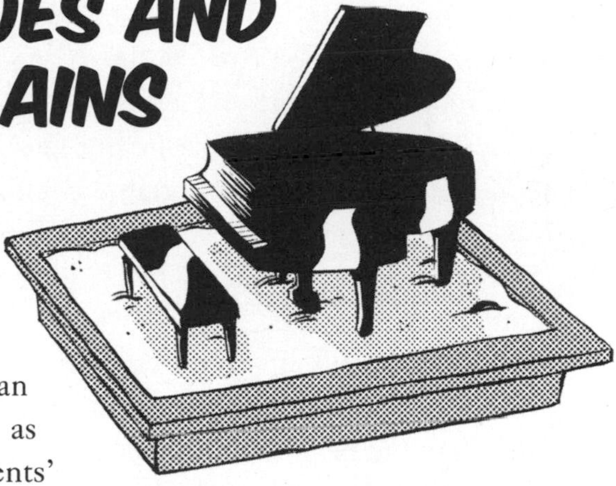

Lucy caught Evan glancing at her as she sat in his parents' living room, her legs curled under her on a comfortable, blue, cushioned chair, reading Brian Wilson's autobiography, *Wouldn't It Be Nice: My Own Story*. Evan looked back at his book (*Peepshow: The Cartoon Diary of Joe Matt*) and smiled, not a wide goofy grin but a respectable acknowledgment of the perfectness of the moment. The fire swirled in the fireplace and snow fell softly outside the window. Lucy smiled a bit herself, but barely perceptibly, just a curl around the edges of the mouth. She watched Evan. He was so cute, his hair all a mess from that hat he wore all the time, his shirt half untucked under his sweater. He was sprawled out on the couch, his feet up on the armrest.

"Come here for a second," Evan said, scrunching up on the couch. He leaned over toward Lucy's chair.

"What?"

"Nothing, just—" Evan pulled himself clumsily over the armrest and kissed Lucy on the lips—what would have been a romantic moment if Lucy hadn't pulled away.

"Let's not…" Lucy said. She put her book down on the coffee table. Lucy was comfortable coming over as long as his parents were away. She still felt like an evil succubus in the Owenses' household. "What if your mom walks in or something?"

"So?" Evan said, his face a contortion of happy and con-fused. "They'll be happy. I mean, my dad might have some-thing to say, but my mom would be through the roof about it. And if we needed a tiebreaker, Gram is *all* about you, defi-nitely."

"No, I mean, I just feel weird about it myself."

"About us?"

"No. Yeah. I don't know." The truth was, Lucy had always had a little crush on Evan, and kissing him didn't feel as strange as she'd thought it might. Even when they were both kids, Lucy had imagined they'd end up married someday. Every time she visited for Christmas she thought of it as a fun flirtation, not that anything could ever happen, but it was something she thought of often and it made her smile. And here they were, a bona fide—what? Couple?

Boyfriend and girlfriend? Friends with benefits? Or was it still just a fun flirtation?

"Well, what do *you* think?" Lucy asked Evan.

"What do—I don't know. I mean…we *did* kiss," Evan said, with *kiss* being an odd mumbling like if he said it too loud it might not have happened.

"Yeah," Lucy said with a smile.

"We'll take it slow," Evan said, and looked her right in the eyes when he said it.

Lucy smiled and nodded, and Evan touched her knee and smiled before picking his book back up and sliding into a recline on the couch.

"What are you reading?" Evan asked, still looking at his own book.

"Brian Wilson's autobiography," Lucy said, looking at hers.

"Is he in the sandbox yet?" Evan asked, referring to the infamous sandbox the former Beach Boy had built for his piano.

"Please," Lucy said, placing the book on her lap. "You've never even listened to *Pet Sounds*, so you don't get to talk about Brian Wilson."

Evan put his book down and turned around to show Lucy his puppy-dog expression. "I'm just playing. Tell me about it."

"It's actually really interesting," Lucy said, crossing her legs and getting comfortable. "The book itself is devastating and beautiful, but the kinda interesting thing is that the entire book was written under the supervision of Eugene Landy. Now this guy was a psychotherapist hired to help Brian Wilson out of this crippling depression he was in—he was on drugs and overweight and afraid of water and barely making music at this point. So you read this book, and you'd think this Eugene Landy is a saint or some kind of miracle man. He fixes Brian's life, gets him off drugs and to lose weight, and even gets him making music again. Both of the other Wilson brothers died and by all rights Brian should have, too, but he's saved by this Landy fellow. And in the book the Beach Boys come off as evil, trying to keep Brian suffering and miserable, and they just want him to write hit songs and whatever. But in reality, like I said, Eugene Landy was heavily involved in the writing of the book. He actually was in control of everything in Brian Wilson's life—he controlled his money, who he could see; Landy was living big off this one client. He was successfully sued by the other Beach Boys and lost all contact rights with Brian Wilson. So in the end you can't tell whether this guy saved or ruined Brian Wilson's life, or if it's a little of both. Brian Wilson has pretty much disowned the book entirely, which is a shame because it's absolutely heartbreaking."

Evan smiled. "So should I listen to *Pet Sounds* or read this book?"

"*Both*, duh."

There was silence for a moment before Evan said, "I still think it's funny"—he rolled over on the couch, now hanging over the armrest—"I mean you were named after a Beatles song. I'd think you'd be more into them. Forget that, even without the birth-name tie-in, how is anyone just not into the Beatles?"

"They're fine," Lucy said. "'Goo goo g'joob' and all that. 'I wanna hold your hand,' good stuff."

Evan smiled like he was thinking, *You must be a closet fan.* Lucy actually was, but she found Evan's taking offense at the situation humorous.

"They're, like, the greatest band of all time," Evan continued, as if this time he'd convince her. "Who else in history has accomplished a tenth of what they did? They rewrote music! They were everything for a full decade and barely repeated themselves the entire time. Even after breaking up, they went on to distinctively successful solo careers. Who else can claim that?"

"I suppose only they can," Lucy entertained Evan. "Eminem sells a lot of records, too. I guess I should become a fan."

"You're totally a fan," Evan said, and Lucy laughed.

"Just because my parents named me after an ode to acid," Lucy said, "doesn't mean I have to be a Beatles fanatic. Look, they're all right. I don't even dislike them. I'm a casual fan!"

"No." Evan dismissed the idea. "There's no *casual* Beatles fandom; you're either a fan or you're off the bus."

"All right, bye, then!" Lucy waved the bus good-bye.

Lucy had been shooting down Evan's Beatles obsession for quite a while — when he tried to convince her the surreal "Yellow Submarine" was like no other song in existence, or had her listen to the pretty, acoustic "Blackbird," and she listened and liked them. She liked early Beatles. She liked "In My Life" a lot, and she liked "The Fool on the Hill," which reminded her of Evan, tying the music into her life. The best music for her was always the stuff you could relate to, the stuff that spoke directly to you and twisted and knotted itself so far into your life you couldn't tell where art ended and reality began. Evan liked the Beatles so much because their music was the soundtrack to his youth; it was what was playing when she'd come over all summer and his mom would be cleaning the house, and she was sure it was what he had heard on long family road trips. It was his mom and dad's music, so it was there for all the key moments, all the defining memories. The Beatles were his mom and dad, so they were him, too.

Lucy liked the Beatles. But she *loved* the Beach Boys. That's what *she* grew up with.

Lucy picked up her book. She looked at the page but couldn't remember where she'd left off. She looked at the page before — nothing. *No, none of this page looks familiar*, she thought. She turned another page back. And another. *I didn't read any of this.* She'd been moving her eyes and a few words had been registering and the pages had been turning, but Lucy hadn't actually been reading at all. *I was in my head that entire time*, she thought. *Well, of course I was, look at what's going on. Forget the book. This is all crazy.*

She watched Evan, reading contentedly on the couch, and breathing suddenly became difficult.

No, I'm *what's crazy. Like I could sit here and read when I'm going to ruin his life. I'm* with *someone. Someone who'd beat Evan to a primordial soup if he knew we had kissed, let alone if he knew how I actually felt. I'm a crazy nobody who's dating a 'roided pothead and I'm going to mess up things with my best friend. He'll never talk to me again. If he knew half of what I've done the past year he wouldn't be talking to me now. And he's looking at me like that and touching my leg and smiling like he knows who I am, like I'm cute little Lucy and everything's worked out just right for us, fate and destiny and true love.*

Evan turned the page of his book slowly. Oblivious to everything. Lucy couldn't bear the sight of him and closed her eyes tightly.

And now I'm completely making up how he feels. I'm projecting. He's probably just playing it by ear; it just happened for him. I'm the one with the stupid fantasies. I'm the one who needs to grow up.

Lucy's eyes opened and darted back and forth across the page of her book, trying to will some kind of focus, but nothing was coming. She was too far gone.

I'm here for less than a week more. And then I'll be off again, back to the land of Bills and Ians. I won't see Evan again for another year at least, and he'll be in college then, far away from here, and what am I going to do? Evan's going to be in some Ivy League school, and I ruined my chances of going to any college with the way my grades are. I can't ask him to not go to school. And I can't go with him and drag him down and pull him away from his schoolwork. I can't and wouldn't.

I act like I'm good for Evan and like he'll be so happy with me, but I'm messing up his life. I'm lying to him. I'm lying about every little thing, and when he finds out he's going to see me for the disgusting, worthless rodent I am.

Lucy took a deep, sudden breath, like she'd been punched in the gut. Evan glanced over at her, and she pretended it was a yawn.

"Tired?" Evan said.

"No," Lucy said, trying to hide all the fear inside. She gave him a brief smile. "Just trouble focusing on this book."

"I thought you were engrossed in that thing."

"No, I am, I just...I don't know."

Hearing him speak and seeing the calmness in his eyes helped. *Just breathe*, Lucy thought. *This is going to be okay. Just enjoy this. You've earned it.*

Lucy stared at Evan vacantly for a brief moment, and just before Evan could ask if anything was wrong, she asked, "Do you want to go to a movie?"

Evan looked at her for a moment while the idea clicked into place. He picked his phone up off the coffee table to check the time. "We could."

"I think some air would wake me up."

Dear God, I hope some air wakes me up, Lucy thought.

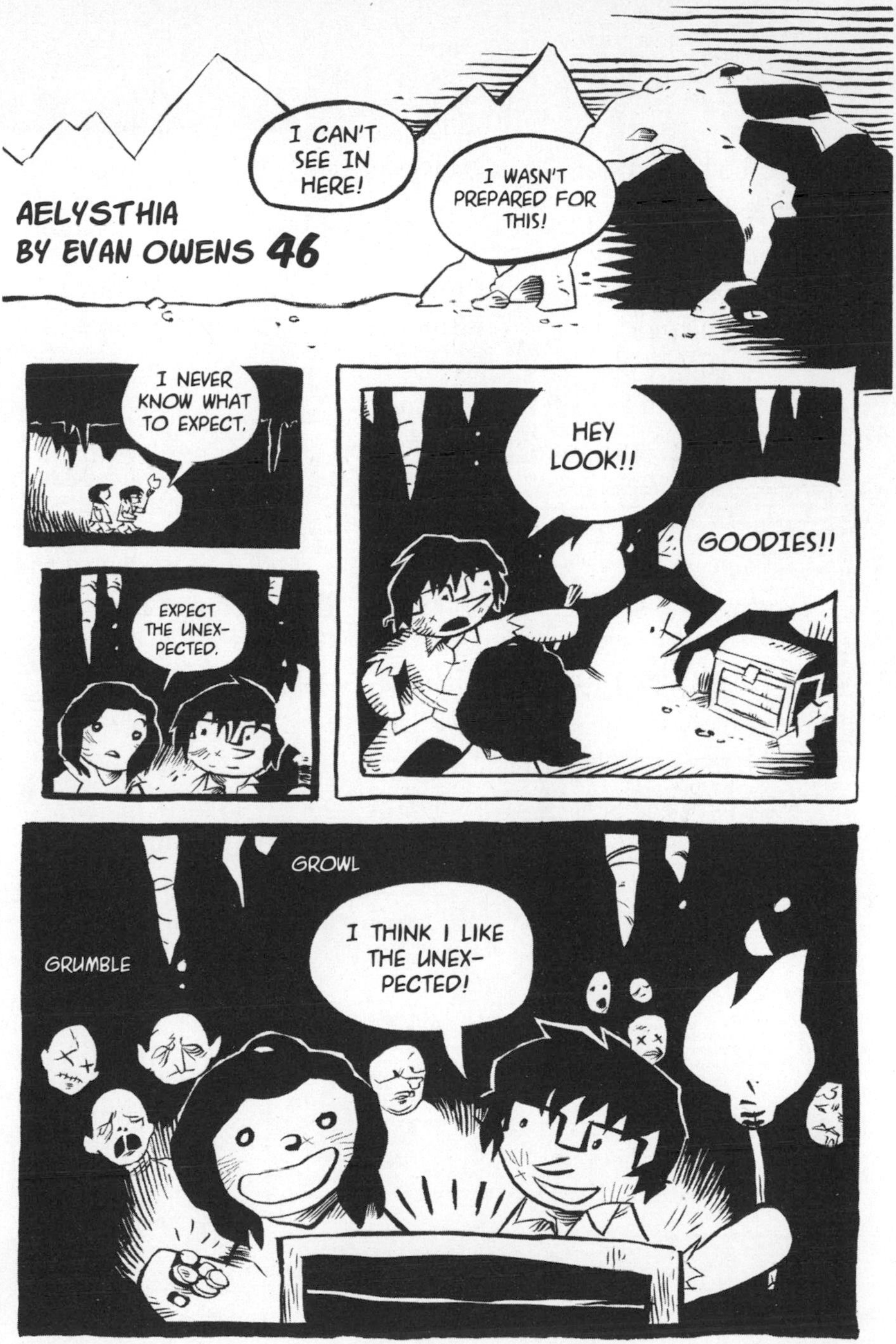
AELYSTHIA
BY EVAN OWENS 46
I CAN'T SEE IN HERE!
I WASN'T PREPARED FOR THIS!
I NEVER KNOW WHAT TO EXPECT.
EXPECT THE UNEX-PECTED.
HEY LOOK!!
GOODIES!!
GROWL
GRUMBLE
I THINK I LIKE THE UNEX-PECTED!

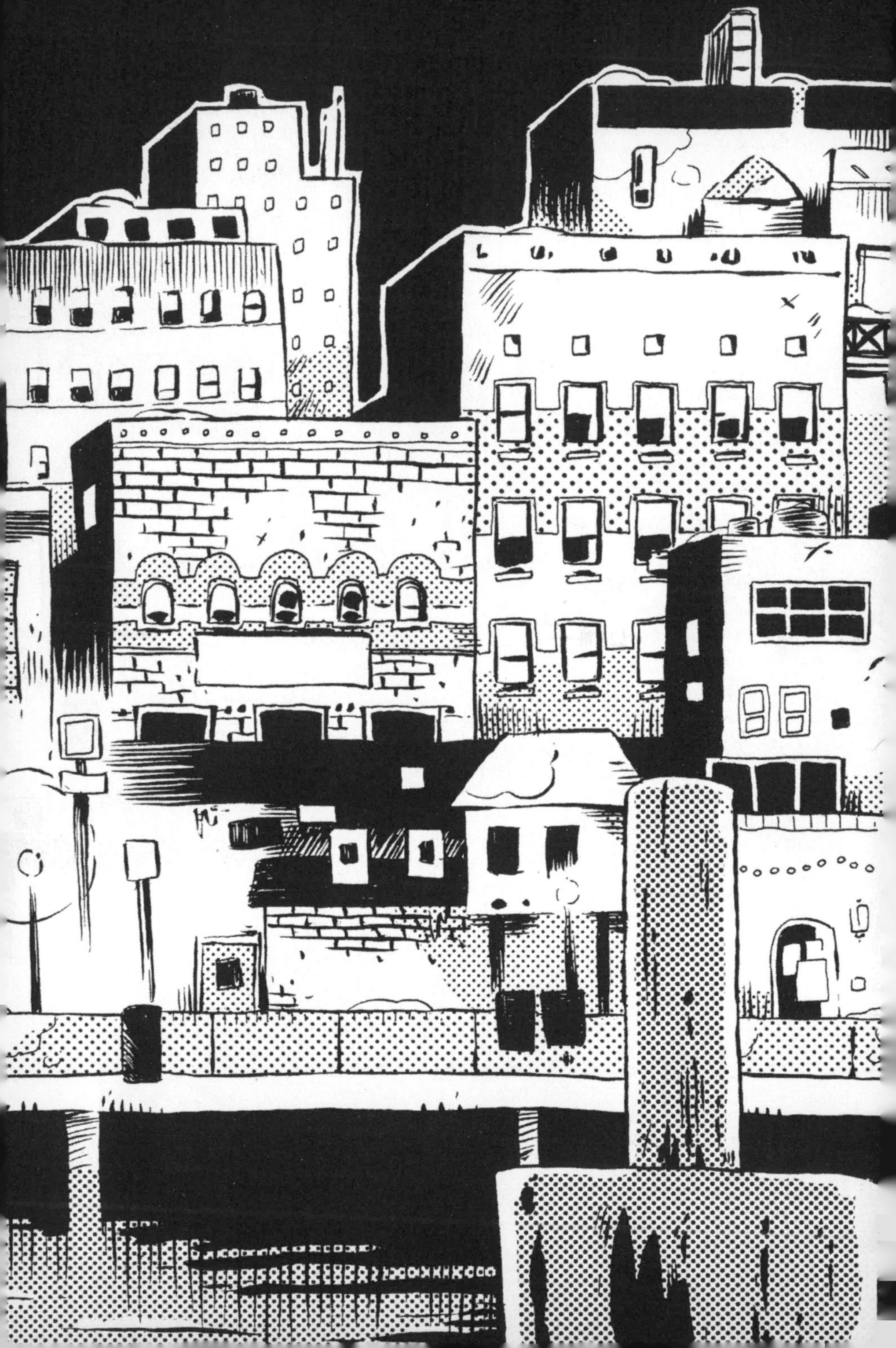

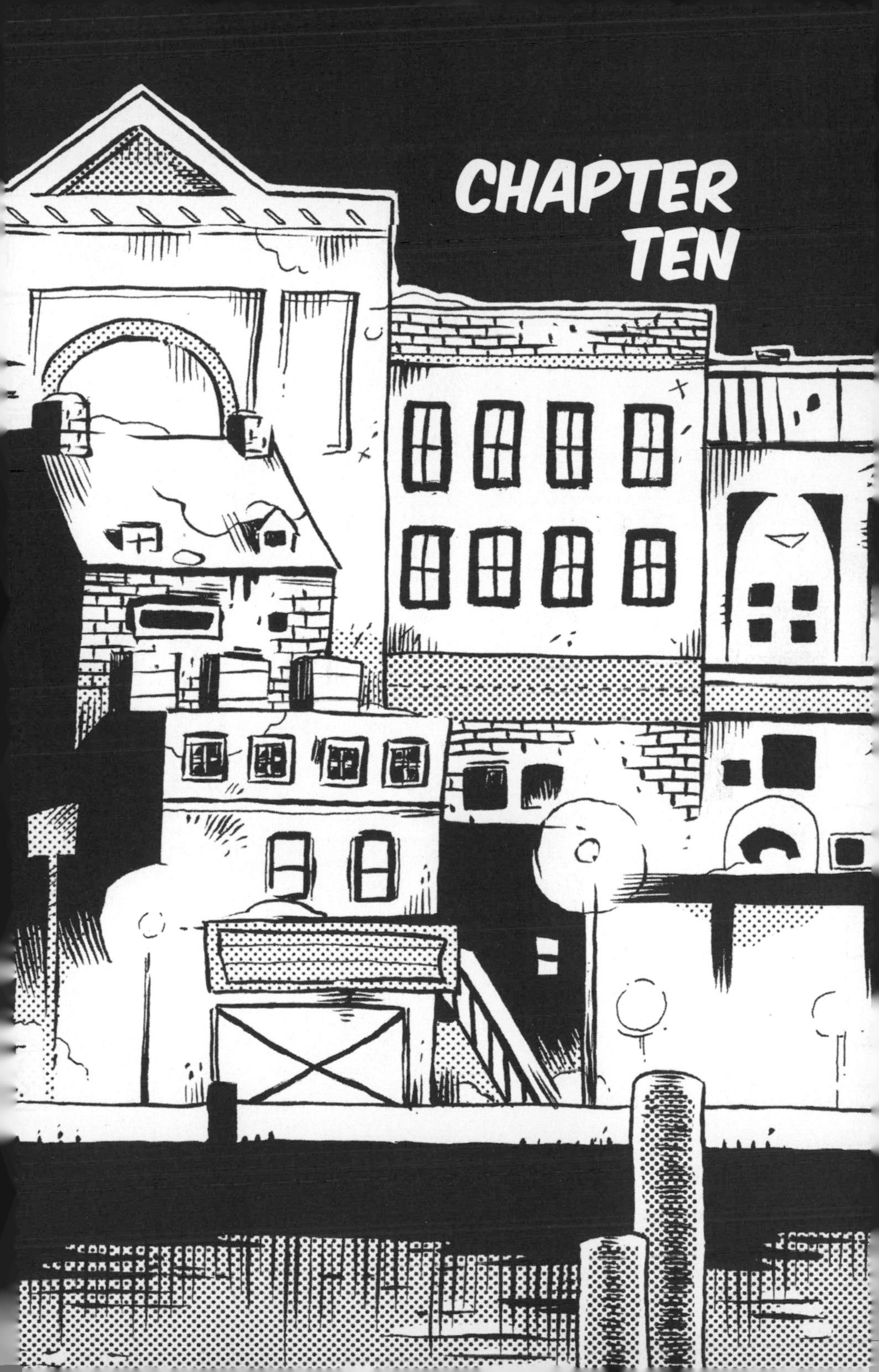
CHAPTER TEN

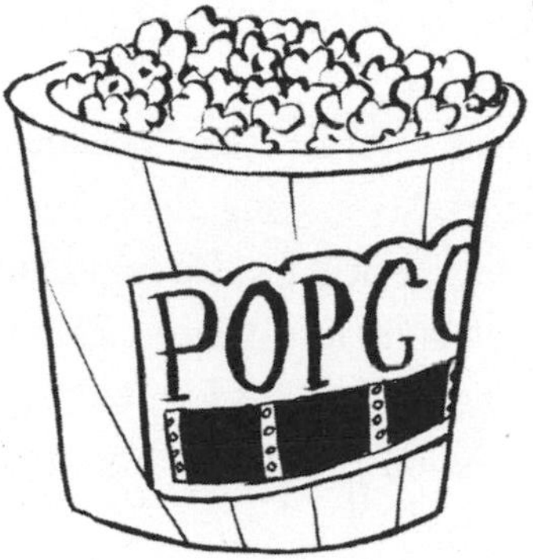
POPCO

LET'S GO AWAY FOR A WHILE

The cold outside gave Lucy a quick shiver and a burst of energy, and the angst she had felt only minutes earlier quickly shattered away. It wasn't long before the energy became a spike of mania and Lucy couldn't walk fast enough, almost prancing through the slush scattered over the street. She was anxious to get downtown.

The afternoon had turned to evening, and the sky, which had been full of dull light, monotonously matching the land, was now a dark blue. Lucy liked the contrasts against the dark sky as they reached downtown—the bright whites and yellows of the streetlights and apartment windows, the neon of the storefronts, which spilled color into the streets. White Christmas lights were still strung around store windows and sidewalk trees, and they crossed streets like a festive spider that had scurried through town. The buildings came to Evan and Lucy like old friends, and the harbor behind them reflected light in joyous squiggly lines. The activity and number of people out shopping or getting dinner or coffee increased with each street passed.

As they got farther downtown, traffic picked up, and cars stopped at each red light, headlights casting sharp shadows and brightening features. Lucy grabbed Evan's hand and he looked down at her, and it was a little different this time. Lucy closed her eyes and leaned up to give Evan a real kiss like the one they'd shared Christmas night. To her great relief, it felt wonderful.

"I hope my nose isn't runny," Evan said, touching it with his gloves and sniffling. "I can't feel it."

"It's not," Lucy said. Her breath hung brightly in the air before floating off like a ghost. She got on her tiptoes and kissed his nose. "Don't you feel *alive?*" Lucy asked Evan. She took a great big breath and smiled fully. She talked loudly over the murmurs of dialogue and the sounds of cars stopping and starting and all the running engines. "There's so much going on, so many *people!*"

"There are a lot of people," Evan said, looking around as though unsure how to contribute.

"Like, even if we don't know any of them, we don't *need* to. Just being in the same space and time with them feels less lonely, feels like we're a part of something."

"I wasn't lonely," Evan said with a sheepish smile. He pulled Lucy closer to him. "Were you lonely?"

"No, that's not what I—" Lucy felt a pinch of guilt. "You

know what I mean. Come on, I'm in a rare good mood. Let me enjoy it."

Evan hung an arm around Lucy and looked up at all the light. "Sorry. Enjoy."

"Sometimes back home—other home—sometimes I'd go into the city just to get out and feel like I'm a part of it. Sometimes I'd go alone and do my homework in Five Points or I would go with my friend Tess, and we'd go shopping or to the museum, but mostly we'd just sit and people-watch and walk around with everyone." She did miss some things from back home. She did have a few close friends, as was her way. Tess was trouble, too, probably the only person to have it worse than Lucy did, but she was as loyal as friends got. Lucy preferred to keep her northern and southern lives separate, though.

"That sounds nice," Evan said, and Lucy wasn't sure if it did sound nice to Evan or if he was just saying it to appease her. She decided he meant it.

"They were filming a movie this summer," Lucy said. "I might be in the background. I can't remember the name of it, but if you hear of a movie that's a *Breakfast Club* for today's kids, look for me."

"Am I looking for short-hair Lucy or long-hair Lucy?"

"Long hair," Lucy said. "They had to come talk to Tess and me because we kept moving with each shot to try and get in the background again, and one of the assistants said if we were going to stay and watch we had to pick one spot and stick there. But we'd been doing that for thirty minutes already by that point."

Evan laughed.

"It was fun. Something you don't see every day. But there's always something going on there that you don't see every day." Lucy nestled her head into Evan for a moment and then perked up. "I wish I could take you back with me," she said. Not that she would. She didn't want to go back herself. She would take Evan back to a more ideal Georgia—a postapocalyptic version, where they were the only two living humans left.

"I don't know. I don't have a lot of desire to migrate south," Evan said, scratching his head. He adjusted his hat. "Maybe you should come back here."

"We need someplace new," Lucy said, looking ahead at nothing in particular, and then she smiled. "I want to go to New York. We can live there with Tim and Marshall, in a rad loft apartment."

"Can we afford it?" Evan said.

"Oh yeah. Well, you're the big moneymaker. We write our comic together, and it takes off, and we print some collections, start a few new books, Hollywood comes calling, because, I mean, every comic book gets at least optioned these days, and we get a movie made, and suddenly we're in demand, but you're painting, too. You're not satisfied with our hacky stories. You find you have too much to say."

"I'm liking this," Evan said, and Lucy beamed.

"We'll have to film our own movies, 'cause Hollywood doesn't get us right, so we shoot things and Marshall is our set designer and costume guy, Tim is our director, we write and star in it, and look, I'll be honest with you, it's not a hit.

But it's a *cult* hit, because not everyone's going to get us, and that's just a sign of how awesome we are. And we write and draw and make stuff, and we live very fulfilled lives." This was the most optimism she'd felt in a while. She'd forgotten how good it could feel. She felt physically lighter.

"Is there anything else we do...?" Evan asked, and Lucy felt herself blushing.

"Evan Owens! This is certainly a new side of you."

"Hey, this is your fantasy here. I'm just trying to get a full view," Evan said.

"*Yeah* you are," Lucy countered, and smiled. "If you think you're getting any this week, keep dreaming."

"I'll take that as per-

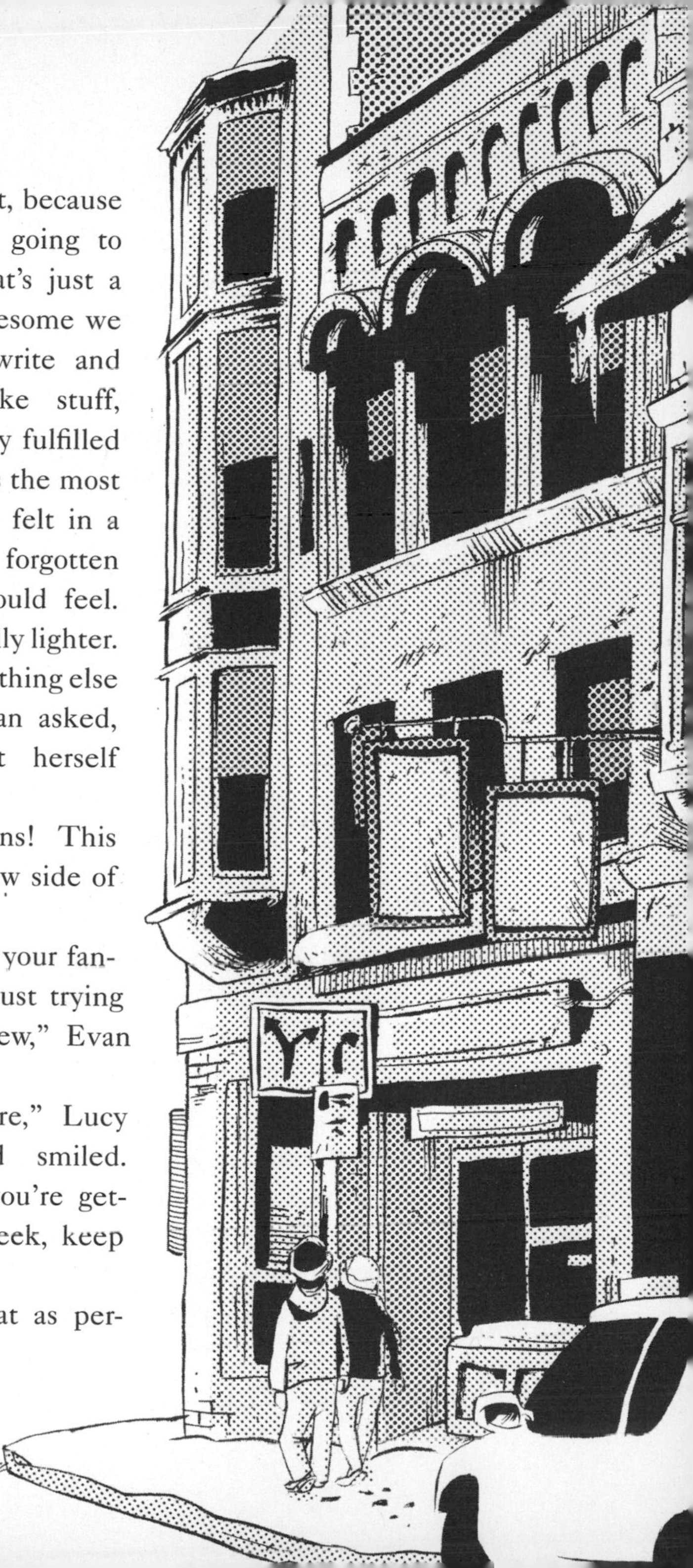

mission to do just that, then," Evan said, and Lucy was both embarrassed and impressed by his sudden bravado. "So yeah, count me in. Of course we'll have to go to school first."

Lucy knew it would come up at some point. Evan wanted to coordinate their list of schools, and his consisted of Brown and Dartmouth and places Lucy knew she no longer stood a chance of getting into. Even before Bill and the Year from Hell, Lucy's grades had slipped. She wasn't the straight-A student she used to be.

Lucy wasn't interested in talking about school, or about how close New York is to New England—*really just a train ride away*—and now her head was full of thoughts of being separated and alone again and of the doomed nature of the future. Lucy wanted to leave life up to this point behind, and run to New York or California or maybe even out of the United States, maybe go to Paris or Italy or somewhere romantic, and start fresh. Anywhere she hadn't been before.

"New England isn't the same for me as it is for you," Lucy said, afraid to make eye contact. She feared Evan wouldn't understand or that this would be a deal breaker. He was a homeboy. The type to wear some stupid New England sweatshirt with a maple leaf on it or something.

"It's beautiful here," Evan said, once again looking up at the lights and the water. It *was* beautiful, Lucy agreed silently. "I thought you were excited to come back."

"I'm always excited to come back, but mostly to see *you*." She slipped her hand into his. "My family broke up here. My thoughts of this place involve a lot of fighting and not fitting in and wanting to disappear. It's not a happy place for me."

"They're just locations, you know," Evan said. "New York and New England or Georgia or wherever, they're all just places. The fighting and not fitting in and all that, that's in your head, it's your history. It's going to be wherever you go."

He was right. She had thought coming back here would help her forget about her summer in Georgia, but it had followed her. It was only the scenery that changed. Neither place ensured any kind of happiness. She'd be miserable anywhere. Poor Evan.

They reached the theater and Lucy leaned into Evan under the marquee, which was brightly lit and rendered them silhouettes. People came out of the theater and passed them on either side, but Lucy just stood there in Evan's arms, weak and just *okay* for now.

The theater was a small downtown arts cinema. It had only two screens and usually played stuff the megaplexes didn't touch: low-budget indies, the occasional Oscar-bait drama, and sometimes—

sacre bleu!—something with subtitles. It was an old-school theater, the kind with a window kiosk for tickets and a long ramp leading in. It was quaint, and cute. Despite its anti-quated feel, lack of variety, and small size, it was always full because of its prime spot downtown, and because it showed films that moviegoers often couldn't find anywhere else.

Evan's school friends John and Mitch were working this night. John was tall and outspoken, and Mitch looked to Lucy like a young Woody Allen with the nebbish qualities to boot. Not bad. Evan told her they were both movie buffs and could get them in for free.

"Owens," John said, and he shook Evan's hand. "What are you seeing?"

"Hey, John. We're thinking of *Mickey Lee*," Evan said, re-ferring to an indie that the theater was replaying.

"It's good," Mitch said with a smile, ready to review it.

"But not great," John quickly added. "Frankly, I think he phoned in a lot of favors to get it made, because the script feels half-assed at best."

"We're playing it here after several years," Mitch added. "So someone liked it."

"I said it isn't great. But it is *good*."

Evan introduced Lucy and told Mitch and John that she used to go to school with them. No one remembered her. Lucy gave Evan points for playing it cool and not being *hands all over* with his supposed new girlfriend in front of his friends. Lucy wasn't surprised they didn't remember her, though she did have recollections of Mitch and John, who hadn't changed much. John seemed to have sported some facial hair. Truth was, Lucy wasn't ever highly visible and often went out of her way to keep it that way. She liked people, but she liked them as an observer or as an anonymous participant, she liked to watch from the outside—a wallflower. Evan was the one who would know everyone by name, learn their stories, and keep up with them over time. True fact—Lucy's Facebook friend total: 37. Evan's Facebook friend total: 574.

As Evan talked to John and Mitch, going back and forth from light conversation to quickly escalated heated debates, Lucy walked down the aisle and looked at the art on the walls. It was all done by one person, a local artist, she figured. The pieces seemed to all belong to the same series of paintings of distorted perspectives and chaotic lines. They were really eye-catching. Lucy thought downtown was quite a venue for local artists, with the theater and all the coffee shops and store windows offering a large amount of space for art displays. The comic-book store alone was a gold mine. Lucy came back to Evan, who was having a tough time with John.

"I'll get you guys in," John was saying, "but you have to come to my Hitchcock marathon."

"All right, all right," Evan said. "Just e-mail me a reminder. When is it?"

"Oh, whenever you're free," John said.

"I can clear my calendar," Mitch added. These guys weren't quite at Tim and Marshall's level of coolness, Lucy thought. But friends at the theater and free shows? *Not bad, Owens.*

Evan turned to Lucy. "You ready? The movie's going to start."

"I'm ready," Lucy said, and gave Evan a kiss on the cheek. Why not give the fellows a little show.

Mitch gave a virginal smile and John elbowed him. *Knock it off.*

Lucy's heartstrings were more than tugged as she sat in the darkened theater—they were yanked and torn. She was trying hard to hold in tears, unsure why she wanted so badly to cry in the first place. Lucy glanced over at Evan, who was watching, enthralled. Maybe it was just a really good, powerful movie.

Lucy wasn't fully paying attention anymore, though. She'd disappeared into her head. She was thinking about Evan, and how he liked these movies. But he was strictly a spectator. Evan liked art, but he couldn't write it. He was afraid to make it. He could draw these amazing things and then hide them in a box as if he were ashamed of them. Lucy thought of their talk with Tim and Marshall, and how they were so right. There's a human need to make art, and she wasn't great but she had it, and Marshall sure as hell had it, so what was wrong with Evan that he was so content and willing to just blend in? It's not that every artist has to come from a broken home, and it's not like he was perfect anyway. She loved the guy, but she could list a dozen things wrong with him. The problem was that he liked art, but he never suffered for it. He liked it, but he never *lived* it. And that's why he couldn't write it or make it. Lucy had an Evan breakthrough. She stared at him from the corner of her eye, but his eyes stayed fixed on the screen. He could watch the images on the screen and appreciate them just fine but he couldn't invest in them. He couldn't fully understand them, even if he thought he could. He didn't know pain enough to relate to it honestly. Lucy felt dirty examining him like this. She couldn't stop, though. She felt an urge she wanted badly to resist—an urge to *hurt* Evan, not just to hurt him and not in a mean-spirited way, but to hurt him so he could feel alive, so he could have a full life experience, so he could appreciate these beautiful moments, so he could understand her. So he could be full, and complete. And in a weird way it might work for them as a couple. They'd be equal then.

Somewhere in Lucy's mind a seed had been planted, to break Evan's heart. And it made her sob uncontrollably then, and loudly, and Evan held her hand tightly, looking concerned. People began to turn in their seats to look at them.

"Shh, shh, shh," Evan whispered. *"It's just a movie."*

Lucy came home to a cluttered living room that seemed to be missing a floor. You know, those things for walking on. In place of the floor were a million tiny fragments of computer guts. In the center of them was Lucy's father, with the shell of the computer opened like a book. Only the living room was lit, and sparsely. The house was barely decorated for the holidays. There was one small Christmas tree that fit on a tabletop. Lucy tiptoed through the computer parts to the couch, which she fell onto heavily, flat on her face. She moaned to herself for a moment.

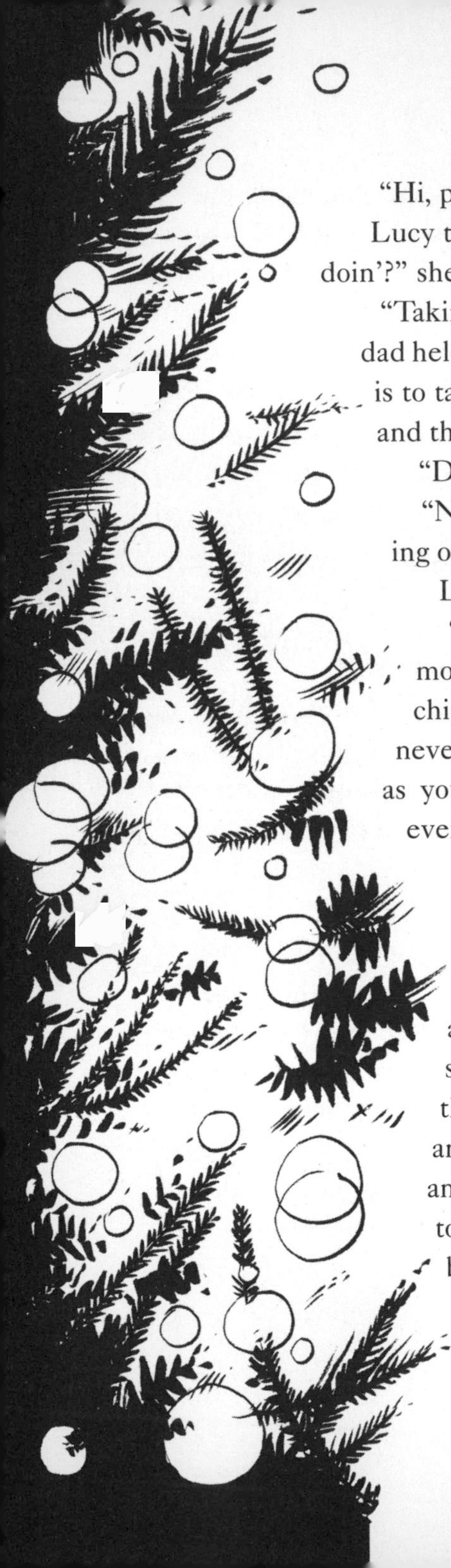

"Hi, pumpkin," her dad said.

Lucy turned her face sideways. "Whatcha doin'?" she asked.

"Taking a look at this old computer." Her dad held up a board of some sort. "The idea is to take it all apart, see how it all works, and then put it back together."

"Does that ever work?"

"Not so much, not yet, anyway. Feeling okay?"

Lucy groaned again. "Emotional."

"Enjoy it," he said, his attention mostly on a multitude of computer chips on boards in front of him. "You'll never feel quite so emotional again. Not as you get older and stop caring about everything so much."

"Is that true?" Lucy asked.

Dad was quiet for a minute, thinking about it. "Nah," he said.

"I want to get old," Lucy said, and sluggishly lifted her arm to the small Christmas tree and snapped on the lights. She looked up at the blue and orange and green and red lights, and let them fall out of focus. "I want to take computers apart and put them back together."

Lucy looked at her phone. *Life*

is so boring w/o u! Plz come save me. Luv u. She had received seven texts from Tess back home that she still had to reply to, and one from Ian that gave her shivers. The farther she was from that situation, the more she couldn't believe she'd ever gotten herself into it. When she'd lived here full time, she'd never have imagined her life where it was now. She shut her eyes tight. She was on vacation and didn't want to deal with Georgia matters. She wasn't without guilt, though. She had no shortage of that lately. She did hope Tess was okay. Lucy drooped her arm to the ground and picked up a computer part at random.

"What's this one do?" she asked.

"Honey, I really haven't the foggiest."

"You're weird, Dad."

"You wonder why I hung on to your mother. Not many women would put up with me." He gave a sad smile.

Lucy shut her eyes and rubbed her feet together, kicking off her shoes.

"Dating any boys at school?" Dad asked.

Lucy groaned.

"I only see you once a year, I have to ask. Indulge me."

"Boys are stupid," Lucy said sleepily, figuring it was a true enough answer to his question. If not factually true, it was emotionally true.

"We are, aren't we?" Her dad studied a piece of plastic before tossing it behind him, dismissing it as not useful.

"Have you heard from Mom at all this year?" Lucy asked, and opened her eyes again.

"Not so much, no. We don't really talk much, Lucy. I'd

like it if she would contact me, but I trust her with you. And you're here now after all, aren't you?" He turned his head to face Lucy and smiled, and she smiled slightly herself.

"Would you take Mom back if she asked nicely?"

He put down his toys. "Well, I don't know. It depends on whether or not I'd think she'd really changed at all, I suppose."

"Do you think someone can change? Like maybe in a year or two? Like, do you think if maybe two people aren't right for each other right *now*, maybe they could be later?" Lucy walked her fingers along the carpet.

"I don't know, pumpkin. It's a nice thought, though, isn't it? I can't figure out how a computer works. Human beings are far more complicated, I'm afraid." Dad smiled again, as if this were somehow a warm and encouraging statement. "You're really not dating anyone?"

"I told you boys are dumb."

"And...girls?" he asked, and adjusted his glasses.

"*Dad...*"

"I'm just asking, that's all." He looked with distaste at the large mess he'd made. "I think this computer is about rubbish now, don't you?"

Lucy mumbled an agreement.

"You look different this year," Dad said, not quite facing Lucy. "Do you think you've changed?"

"I don't feel very different," Lucy said. "I feel like the same old. Do you think I have?"

"Oh, I think you've changed every time I see you," he said with confidence. "It's easier when you're young, of course."

This was comforting to Lucy, and she smiled. "Did you have dinner?"

"Oh, I might step out and get something to eat in a bit."

"Dad, it's ten o'clock."

"Is it?" He seemed surprised. "Damn."

Lucy sat up. "I'll make something for us."

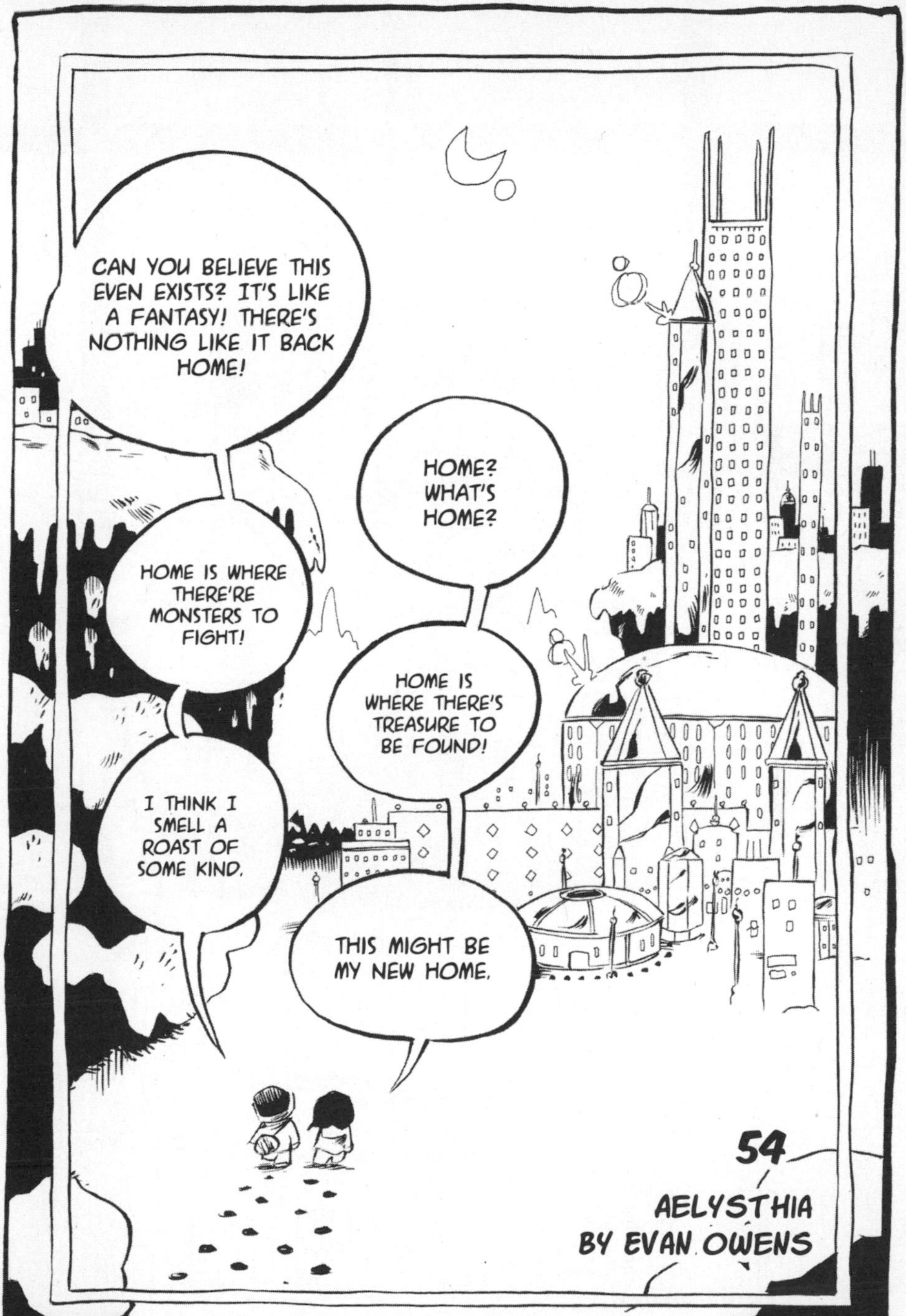
CAN YOU BELIEVE THIS EVEN EXISTS? IT'S LIKE A FANTASY! THERE'S NOTHING LIKE IT BACK HOME!
HOME? WHAT'S HOME?
HOME IS WHERE THERE'RE MONSTERS TO FIGHT!
HOME IS WHERE THERE'S TREASURE TO BE FOUND!
I THINK I SMELL A ROAST OF SOME KIND.
THIS MIGHT BE MY NEW HOME.
54
AELYSTHIA
BY EVAN OWENS

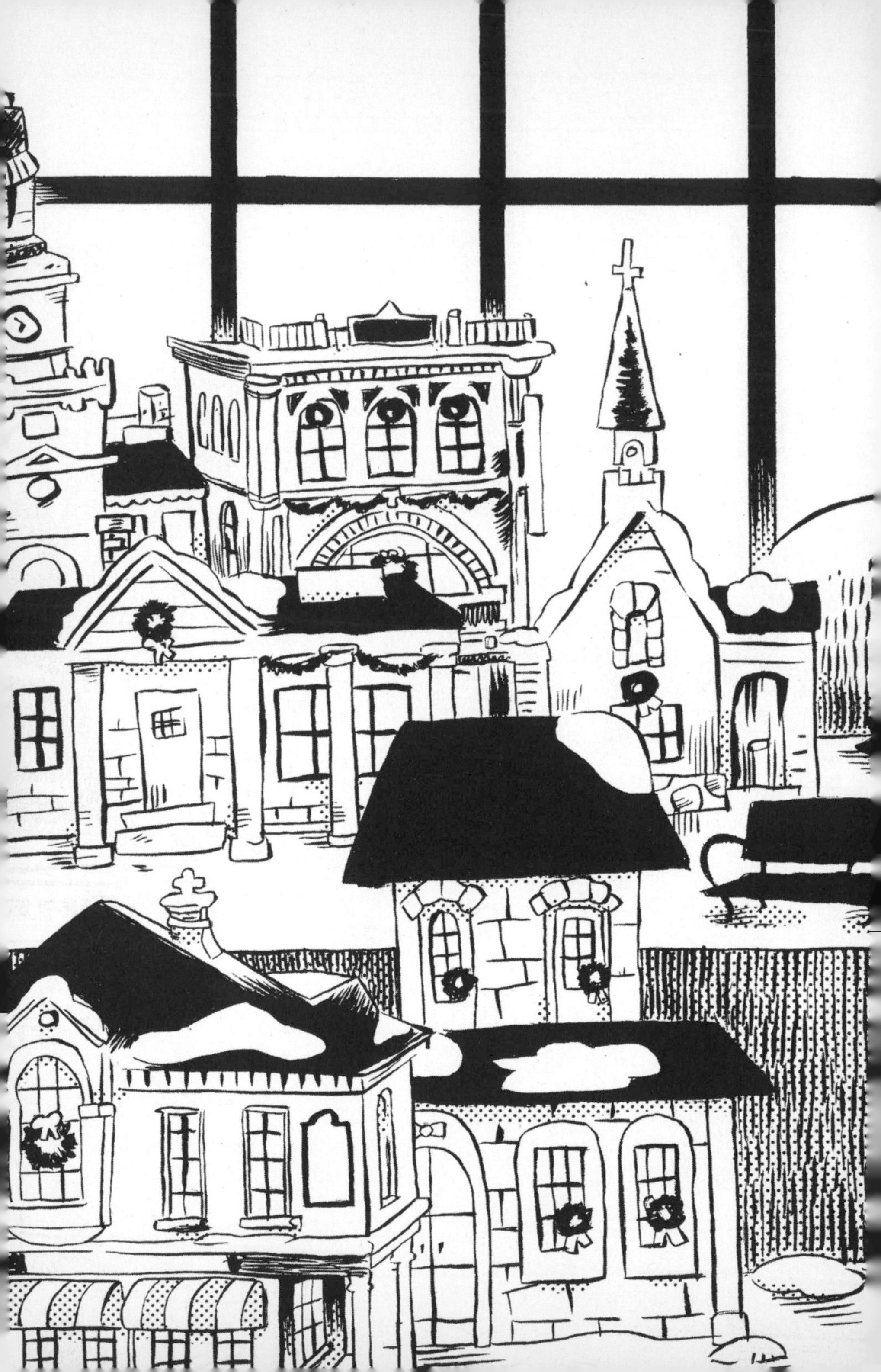

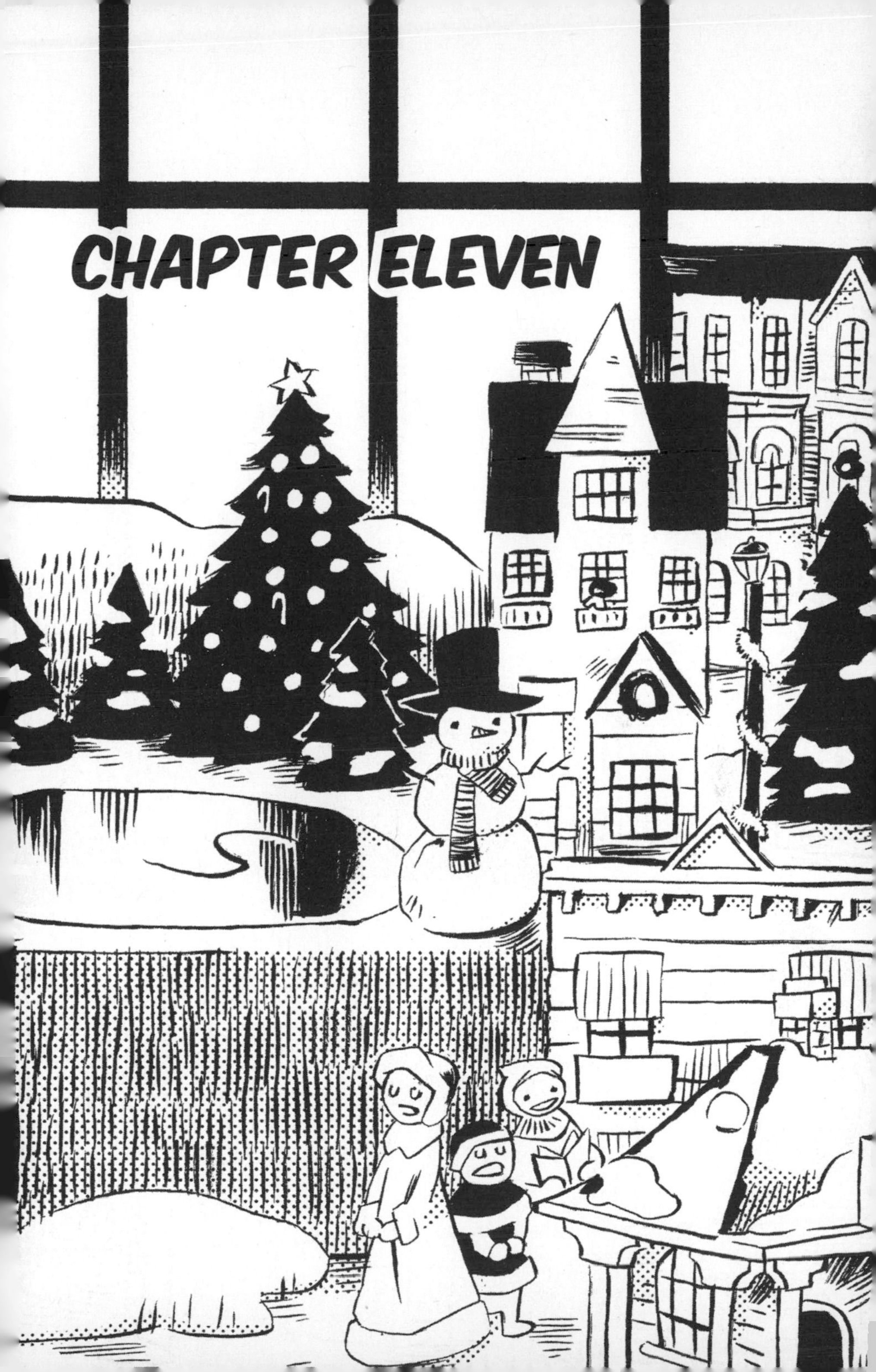
CHAPTER ELEVEN

FAIRY-TALE MUSIC

Lucy hung out with Evan as he worked on his paper the following afternoon, sitting at the dining room table under the chandelier. She tried to keep herself busy and quiet, and found it very difficult. She was looking at Charlie's village, which she'd seen a dozen times before, but she looked at it now with new eyes. She imagined herself as one of the — there must be a hundred of them — tiny people found on the circumference of the main set pieces. And as one of the tiny people, she started off skating across the lake. She walked along the pure white snow paths and under the bridge and followed the bright path lit by streetlamps; she followed them past the church and into town. Everyone was happy and singing, with their eyes shut and their homes unlocked.

The cars here never evolved past 1945, and the policeman directed traffic with delight, the families walked the streets with glee, and little Joey didn't mind shoveling the sidewalk one bit. There was a gigantic clock in the middle of town. They were all too happy for Lucy's comfort and she stuck out like a sore thumb here. She was a Grinch, and no, her heart would not grow three sizes that day. All the people set their eyes on Lucy and it made her uncomfortable, so she grew into a giant and observed the town from a distance. She tromped through town at a quicker pace now, and she noticed all the churches here, and all the hospitals. Everyone seemed to live within a short distance of a hospital. Such a need for medical care suggested a lot. There was pain here, beneath those frozen grins. Maybe the pond didn't quite hit the freezing point and bodies were drowning left and right. Maybe the outskirts in the corner of the room, where the light never fully reached, hid some secrets. Maybe there were gangs. Giant Lucy zoomed in on little Joey, holding his shovel, his face beaming—with menace?

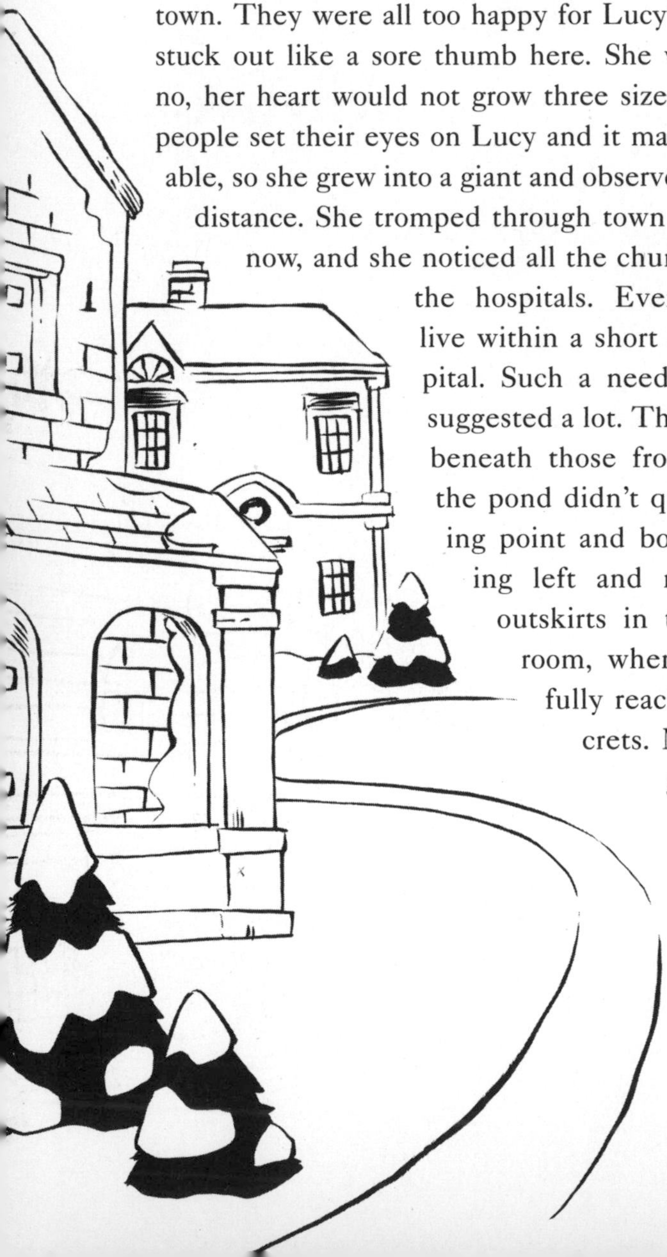

Evan turned a page of his book and coughed. *Mr. Studious. WinterHat BoringPants. Bookus Reporticus. Evan the Librarian. Shush! Silence!* Lucy looked back at little Joey. Yes, she could see only evil in him now. Lucy groaned audibly. She was bored.

"Hey, *Bookus Reporticus*," she called.

"What?" Evan asked with a smile, not looking up. "Is that me?"

"Yes. I think Joey killed the neighbor boy."

"You're getting really involved with my dad's town, aren't you?"

"Maybe."

"Well, solve the crime, Nancy Drew," Evan said, typing something into his new laptop.

Lucy began rotating all the figures in the front window display to face her. *You have done well, little Joey. You are in my good graces.* Lucy stood up, and they all stared at her in awe.

"I'm their god now," Lucy said to no one in particular.

"Do you want me to put on the TV?" Evan asked.

"Blech," Lucy said, and picked up a small figure and tossed it over her shoulder. It landed behind her and rolled across the floor. "This one doesn't accept me."

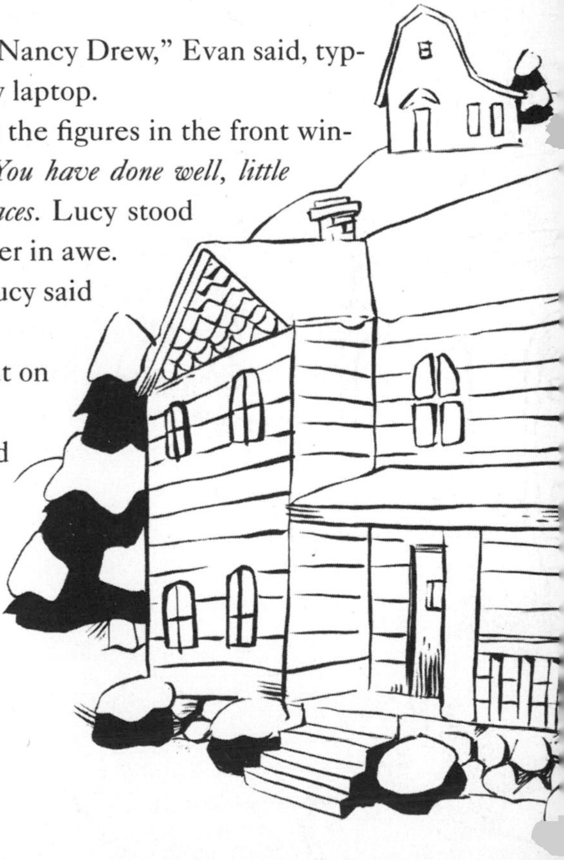

"Hey," Evan said. "Careful."

She threw another one. "It's all right. I'm just making an example for the others."

"Lucy, come on. Those are my dad's."

"You are the *angry* god. They fear you more."

Evan got up from the table, picked up the two figures, and brought them back over to the village and placed them with the others.

"You are Mothra," Lucy said, "and I'm Godzilla. We must fight."

Evan sat in the nearby recliner and Lucy smiled at him.

"Which one's Joey?" he asked, and Lucy faced Joey toward Evan. Joey grinned evilly, brandishing his shovel like a weapon. "Oh yeah, I see what you mean."

"The real tough guys are in the corner over there," Lucy said, and pointed toward the dark corner of the room.

Evan leaned forward and moved the jolly snowman over to where Joey was standing. "This is where he hid the murder weapon. It's inside Frosty." Frosty smiled innocently, his wooden arms outstretched. *I got nothin'!*

"They have no idea what's going on," Lucy said, "with their idyllic Christmas festivities day in and out. A murderer is among them, and they don't even know to look for him, let alone who he is."

"Oh, but they know," Evan said, nudging two nearby Christmas carolers forward. "Mother and sis saw the whole thing."

"*Joseph!*" Mother said, in a voice that sounded like Evan pretending to be a southern belle.

228

"Yes, Mother," Joey said, a young British lad.

"Joseph, I see you've shoveled this nice little mound of snow, but I can't figure out why, seeing as there's no driveway to keep up."

"Oh, yes, Mother." Lucy wiggled Joey back and forth as he said this. "You see, I merely intended for me and my fellow children to have a little jump in the snow, see, young fun and whatnot!"

"Well, Joseph, you and I both know you *have* no friends now, so let's not lie."

"Yes, I do hate them so. In fact I'd made this snow pile here for me to have fun in alone, and you know, *rub it in*, with all the fun I'll be having."

"I suppose that *could* be true," the mannish-sounding belle declared. "So you wouldn't object to me taking a dive into your pile, no?"

"Oh, ha, well, you wouldn't want to ruin your lovely dress, seeing as it's zero degrees outside and the snow is *sure* to be even colder."

"Nonsense, you do know I partake in the ocean plunge once every winter. I find it does the heart good. In fact I might just take this dress off right here and now if you don't mind!"

"There's a dead body in the snow, and I killed him and I'll kill you, too, you bloody old sod!" And with that, Joey slapped the lady right off the ledge and into the fiery pits of carpet below.

"You were always a shitty son!" she yelled as she met her untimely death. Evan and Lucy laughed, and Evan kissed the top of her head.

"I'm sorry, but I really do have to finish this stupid paper. I'm *so* close. *So* close."

Lucy leaned against the wall and smiled and blushed a little. Evan walked back over to the table where his books and laptop were and sat down, and watched Lucy for a moment. She picked up the fallen figure and put her back onto the ledge. She felt less bored now. That was fun. That was a nice break. Lucy felt guilty for the things she'd been thinking about Evan and wished she could take those thoughts back. Evan was who he was, and there was room for study and room for play. He could read and he could come be silly and he could kiss her on the head, and all those things could coexist just fine.

Lucy started moving the townspeople around in a tribute to the events of the afternoon. The mother lay on her back, Joey standing over her, shovel in hand. Sis watched, stunned. Joey's schoolmate lay covered in cloth snow, and Frosty lumbered behind Joey, his dark accomplice. The rest of the townsfolk closed in, curious about the goings-on, searching for the next piece of small-town gossip to dish out over Christmas dinner.

There was an hour until Evan's dad came home. She'd have to leave soon. The figures would all be back in place by tomorrow, Lucy knew. *Dad would kill me*, Evan would say. *I can't mess up his village!*

When Lucy came by the next morning, it was all back in its place.

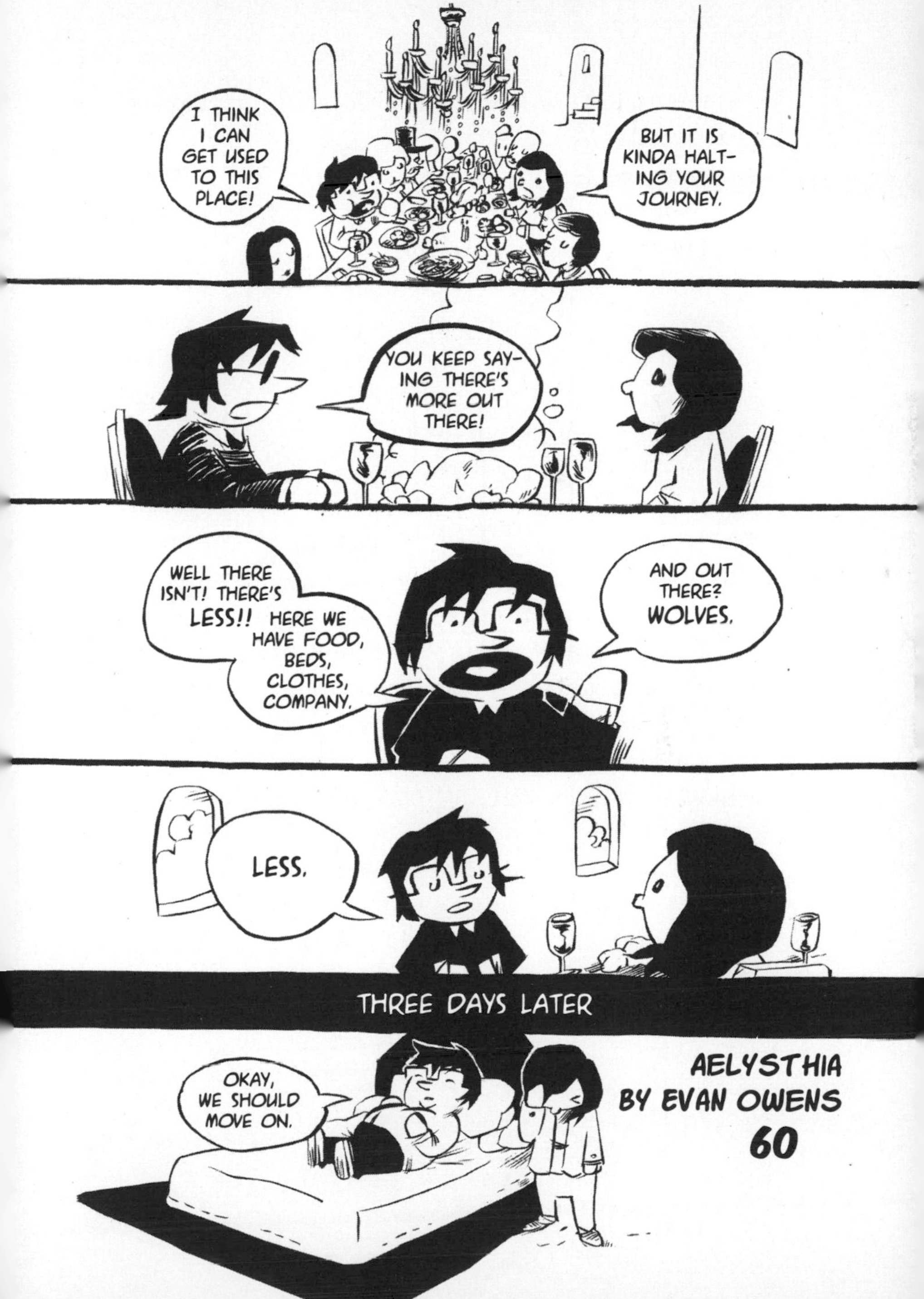

I THINK I CAN GET USED TO THIS PLACE!
BUT IT IS KINDA HALTING YOUR JOURNEY.
YOU KEEP SAYING THERE'S MORE OUT THERE!
WELL THERE ISN'T! THERE'S LESS!! HERE WE HAVE FOOD, BEDS, CLOTHES, COMPANY.
AND OUT THERE? WOLVES.
LESS.
THREE DAYS LATER
OKAY, WE SHOULD MOVE ON.
AELYSTHIA
BY EVAN OWENS
60

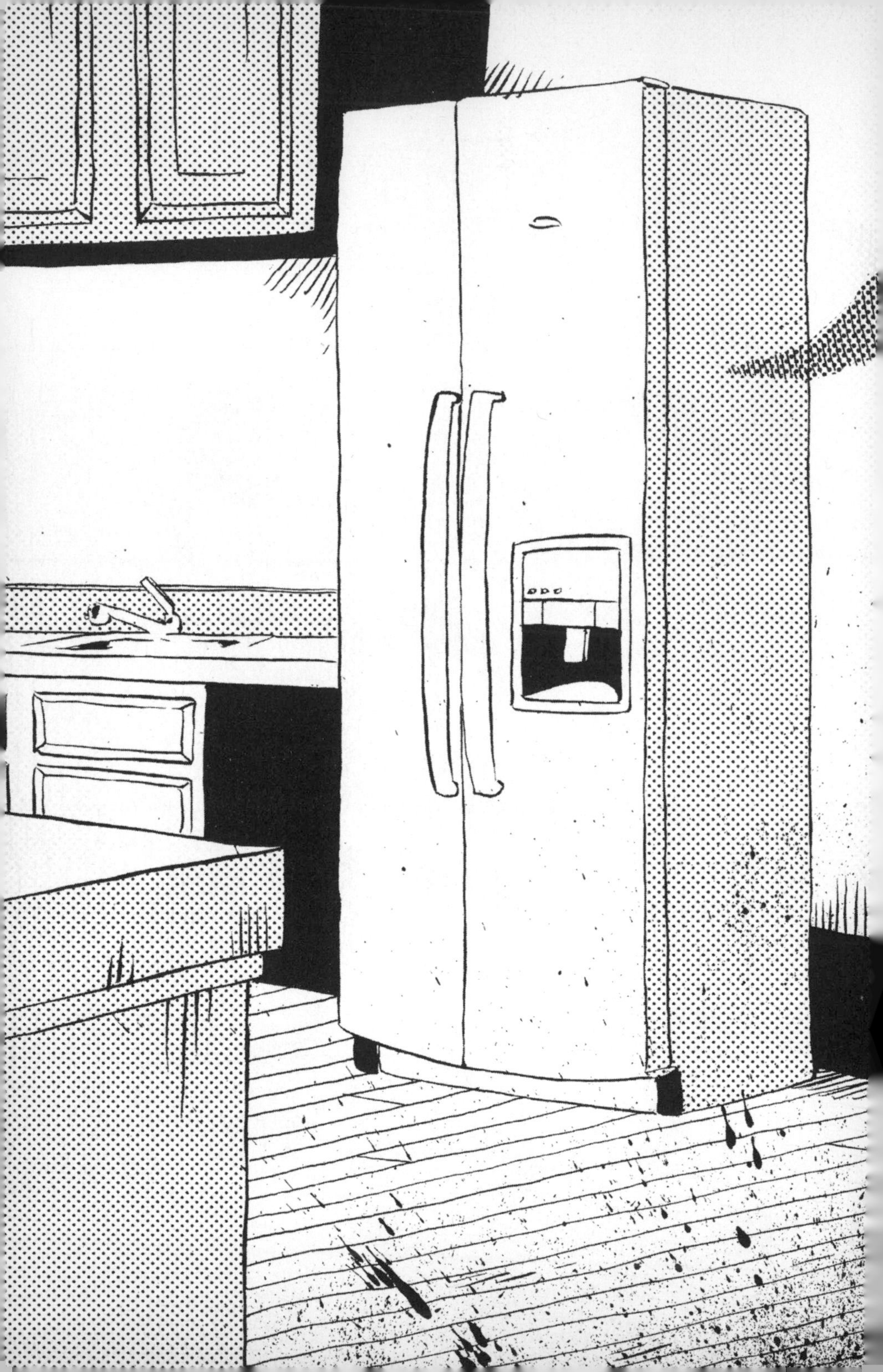

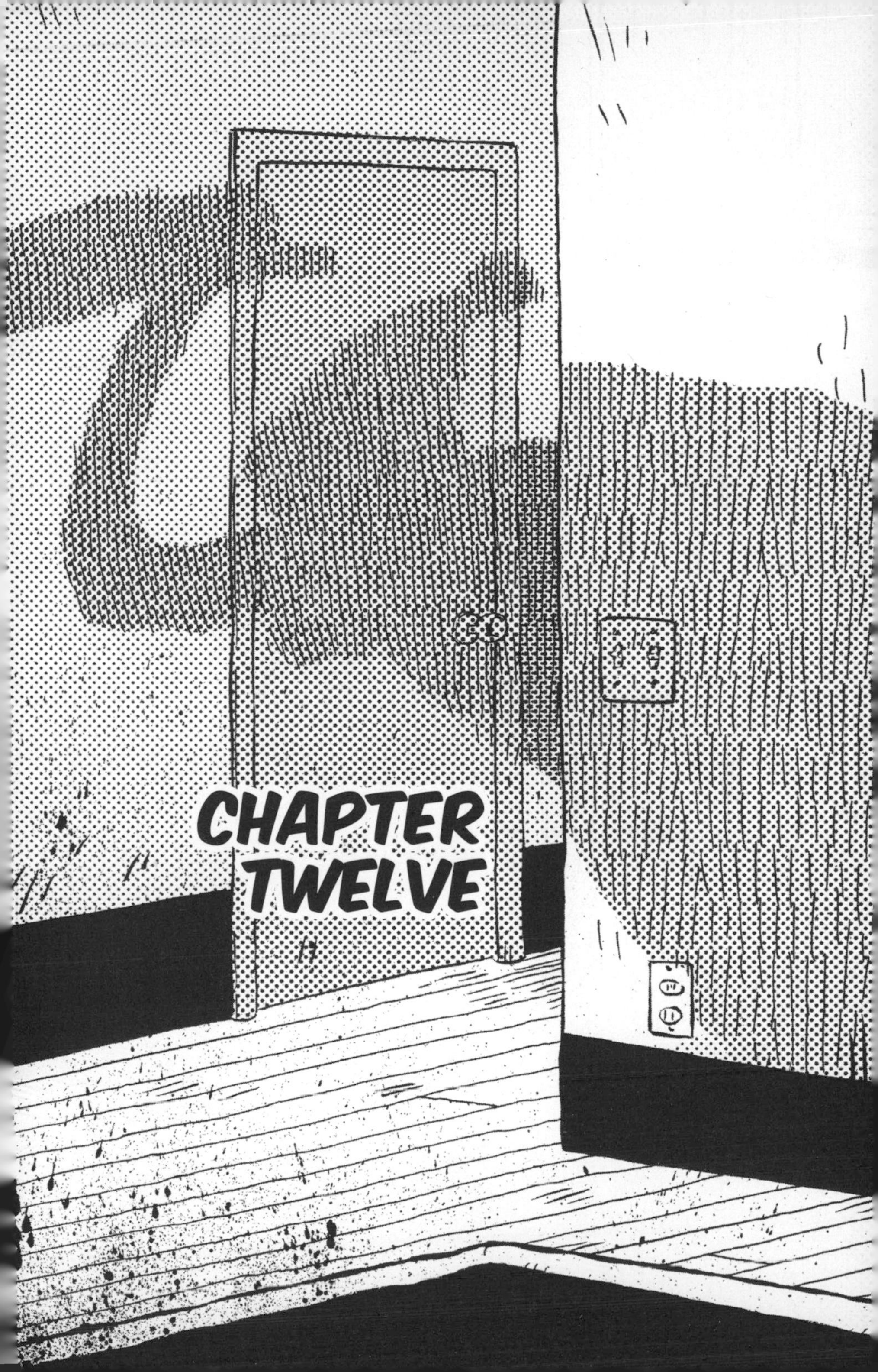
CHAPTER
TWELVE

FALL BREAKS AND BACK TO WINTER

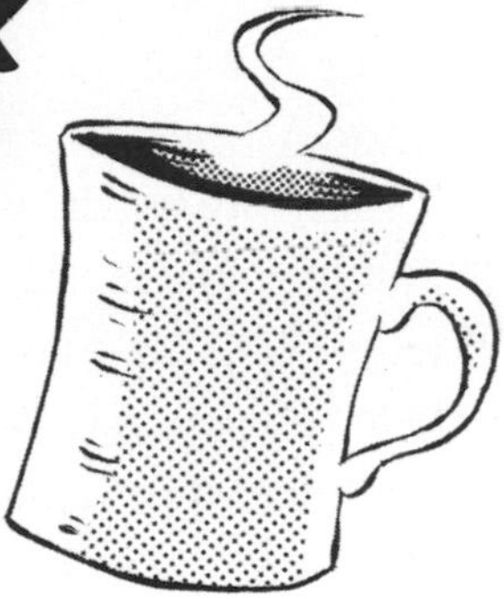

"Mmm, *chamomile*," Lucy said, taking a delicious whiff of imaginary tea. This was her only line for the first scene.

"Maybe you can say it like Sue Sylvester from *Glee*," Tim offered, excited to play director. Tim stood by the kitchen counter upstairs at Marshall's house with Lucy, who was in a soft maroon bathrobe with a golden *M* embroidered into it. Thus, her character's name: Mindy. Lucy had no idea who Sue Sylvester was, so Tim said to just sound angry and sarcastic. Lucy gave it a shot.

"Let's try it as Nicolas Cage," Tim said, and Lucy gave it her best and they laughed.

The kitchen and dining room were joined by the living room area, where Evan sat on the couch in his thirty-dollar Santa Claus outfit. It was duct taped on in most places. Even though he was supposed to be pantsless, he kept the cheap costume pants on between scenes. The belt around his waist was becoming more of a prop than a usable belt, so he held the pants in place with his left hand and stayed glued to the couch. He had a pillow stuffed under his Santa coat and into his pants. With his right hand he was constantly scratching his face and head because of the itchy cheap beard and hat.

"That really fits the contours of your face," Marshall said.

"You're gonna be in that for a while. I'm sorry," Tim said, looking over from where he and Lucy were standing. He giggled. "It's going to take some time to get the lights and audio set up." The living room was full of lights and clamps and wires and large silver sheets and duffel bags full of camera equipment and microphones and more wires and *stuff*.

"*Where is Mrs. Claus?*" Evan shouted in his gruff Santa voice. "Bring me my *cookie baker*! Peppermint Patty, we used to call her, *ho ho ho*. And now she's just Peppermint *Claus*, much less ring to it."

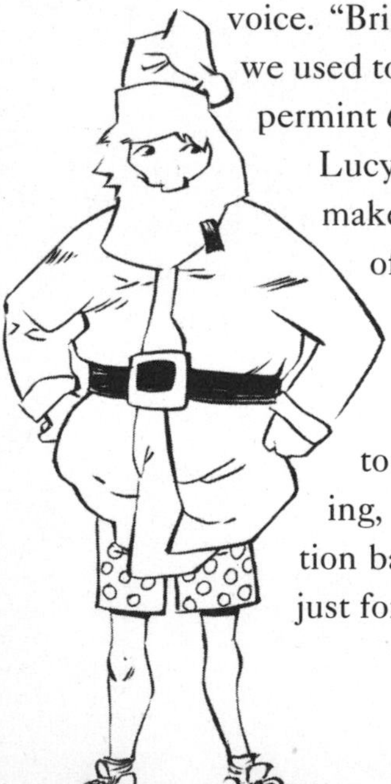

Lucy rolled her eyes as Evan tried his best to make a character of this. She wished he'd held off on putting on that ridiculous costume, seeing as he couldn't really do anything now because of it. He was trying to get her to sit on the couch, where she'd have to listen to that goofy voice. "I'm rehearsing, Ev," she told him, and turned her attention back to Tim. "So what is this thing? Is this just for fun?"

"Well, yeah. It's threefold," Tim said, hopping up on the counter. "For one, yes, it will be fun. Marshall and I love horror movies, so it's just something we've been wanting to do for as long as we've been together. Also, we both want to go to NYU for film school, so you know. If it comes out good, then maybe we can use it as a portfolio piece. And third, it's going to be really fun."

"*Ho ho ho!*" Evan said in Santa-voice. "You said *fun* twice!" He put down his phone, which he'd been playing with.

"Evan, Santa doesn't even talk in this thing. And he's certainly not jovial. You really don't need to get in character." Lucy had a particularly low tolerance for Evan suddenly that she didn't care to explore. She wanted to have a short finished by the end of the day, which was going to take a lot of work, and she was having more fun with Tim and Marshall. They were telling her about the time they had cut school to go to a taping of *The View* in New York. Lucy laughed as they told her about the angry woman they sat next to on the train who kept hushing them.

"She was just jealous because she had to go to her boring job and we were on our way to see Joy Behar," said Tim. And then there was the cute audience extra who got placed next to Marshall and how they tried to follow him around after the show.

"I love how you guys are actually interesting," Lucy said, feeling momentarily bored with everything and everyone else in the world.

"Aww," Tim said, "we try."

"Maybe dropping off toys in every house in the world

isn't interesting to *you*." Santa Evan tried to join in, but his outfit was falling apart even as he sat there glued to the couch. Lucy felt guilty that he had overheard her. She didn't mean to take a dig at him. She wasn't even sure why she was feeling so angry. There was no logical reason. What she wanted was to walk with Evan and talk for hours and empty out her mind, but she couldn't do that, because she couldn't actually tell him anything. Because then he'd be the angry one, if she was honest. If he knew about Ian, especially. She couldn't bear for him to stop looking at her the way he had been. The same look that made her feel so guilty now. It was probably some karma thing, some kind of self-sabotage.

"We're all set," Marshall said, finally ready to film Lucy's big tea scene. Marshall and Tim both got behind the camera, framing everything just so and disagreeing on the direction of light and how close in on Lucy they should be. Tim settled the argument (they went close-up) and, it being Marshall's camera —

"...*Go!*" Marshall said. Lucy figured this was the same as *Action!*

"Mmm, *chamomile*!" Lucy sighed, not as Nicolas Cage, holding a mug of actual tea close to her nose.

"*Cut!*" Tim said.

"That was *so...good*!" Marshall said, and they began the long process of taking all the lights and mics down.

Back in the living room, Evan wasn't thrilled with the brief script he was looking over. "Aww, don't worry," Tim said. "It's just a short movie, no one will think you're really pantsless Santa. It's pretty much exactly what we've talked about all year."

Evan replied that he had been excited to film the short with Lucy but had forgotten that he'd basically be brandishing a knife and a baseball bat and chasing her around the house. Lucy tried to comfort him. "It's just acting, it's not like the cops are going to show up and catch you threatening me with weapons or anything. Don't overthink it."

"This is going to be preserved," Evan said. "I mean we'll probably watch it a million times. What if it's a romance, what if Santa breaks into her house and sweet talks her, and—" This was met with a roomful of jeers.

When it was time for them to film again, about twenty minutes later, the scene involved Lucy hearing a noise and walking into the living room, where she would find a single present sitting on a lamp table. Lucy would pick it up, look at it curiously, and open it, to find Santa's knife thrusting through it from the bottom, beginning *the chase*, which was essentially *the script*.

"We're going to film the living room scene really quick, and then move back to the kitchen for the next part," Tim said.

Evan groaned. "Why don't we just film all the kitchen scenes together?"

"It'll be easier to edit if we shoot it linear."

"Not really," Evan said. "Once it's in the computer, it doesn't make a difference when you shot what. You can drag and drop it anywhere. We're really just losing time here, when we need it."

"Ev, drop it, it's done." Lucy let out a long sigh and headed back to the kitchen with everyone else. Evan stopped her in the part of the hall that branched out where the living room and kitchen areas met.

"Lucy. Is everything okay?" he asked. Lucy felt the guilt like a stab from Santa's knife. He was a puppy dog again, worried about her. She touched his cheek with the palm of her hand. She wished she could choose an emotion and stick with it for longer than fifteen minutes. She leaned in and gave him a kiss, and told him she was fine.

"Are you sure?" Evan asked. "You seem a little off."

That was the theme of vacation this year, she wanted to say. Lucy didn't want any drawn-out conversations, though, not now while they were in costumes and had to run around the house. Maybe they didn't have to have one at all, with this whole back-and-forth that she was feeling, maybe she could just get through the rest of the week and some time apart would be all she needed to figure it out. That sounded really good. *Just have fun now so this kind of talk doesn't happen, and everything else will work out on its own.* Right.

"I'm sure," Lucy said, and tried to change her demeanor. She *was* an actress, now. She smiled and said everything was fine, and that she hadn't planned on the filming to drag on so much. Evan agreed and was satisfied with that answer and went to look for his pants. The lying brought on the guilt again, but she convinced herself that it was better in the end if she carried all the bad feelings herself. She was used to them.

*   *   *

Mel came home while everyone was cleaning up after the big chase scene. Lucy was helping Tim wipe up fake blood, and Evan was sitting at the kitchen table by Marshall. He had taken out the pillow, wearing just the jacket, beard, and hat now. Tim wanted to shoot another scene from early in the script, but Evan was splattered with fake blood that wouldn't come off.

"I hope I didn't ruin your film!" Mel said as he walked in. "If you want, I can come back in. I think I can make a better entrance."

"Hi, Dad," Marshall said. "We're between shots."

"We've been between shots for most of the day," Lucy said, and slumped her head onto the counter.

"Looks like a lot of work," Mel said, taking in the scene. "And a lot of blood. A *Christmas Carol* remake?" He said his hellos to Tim and Lucy. Mel pointed to Evan. "And you must be…the Easter Bunny?"

"Close," Evan said with a smile.

"I understand congratulations are in order," Mel said, and shook Evan's hand. "Marshall tells me you and Lucy started dating since I last saw you. That's wonderful."

Lucy lifted her head and said, "It's complicated." She wasn't sure why she said it, *just trying to be funny*, but she regretted it immediately. This was one of those stupid things she'd say only half-aware she was saying it in the first place, but now it would hover in the air and follow her around. It *was* complicated.

Tim and Marshall looked away. Evan looked at Lucy, but she kept her head down. So much for avoiding conversation.

"I understand how that is," Mel said with a sympathetic grin. "Well, you kids let me know if you need anything."

There was silence and some small awkward chatter after Mel left. *We can leave this to clean later, look at the time.* Everyone worked as fast as possible to get the next scene set up. Evan begrudgingly got in place, but his face was blank. Lucy wished it were anything but.

"And...*go!*" Marshall said.

Evan took a deep breath and exhaled for what seemed like forever. Lucy waited.

"Can we stop?" Evan asked. "I'm just not really in the mood. I'm sorry. We can finish some other time." Evan walked into the living room and grabbed his pants and put them on along with his boots.

"I won't really be around past this week," Lucy said timidly. She wanted to film this but knew it wasn't going to happen now. And she knew they'd have to talk. She knew she had just ruined her shot at this actually working with Evan. She felt horrible, and embarrassed. She wished she'd just played nice and shut up, and she couldn't figure out what her deal was in the first place. She had had this coming all day, and she knew that, too.

"Honestly, Tim, Marshall, it needs work," Evan said bluntly, still wearing his hat and beard. "It needs more thought. It needs *some* semblance of a script, no one just picks up a camera and makes a film, you know? You have to plan it." Evan picked up his gloves and his phone and his notebook. "I'm just being honest. I'm sorry. Not trying to disappoint, but this isn't going anywhere like this. It's not going to make any festivals, and it's not going to get you into NYU." Tone-wise, Evan's lecture reminded Lucy of his dad.

"Yeah, sure," Tim said uncomfortably. Everyone else stayed quiet. Lucy couldn't think of a time in her life when she'd seen Evan lose his cool. She was having trouble picturing him even upset or angry aside from now. She'd wondered if Evan felt like she did, if maybe he had a long-standing crush like she did, or if maybe he'd just been going with the flow and seeing where this would all lead. He felt something strong, though. Lucy knew that now.

"Look, we'll keep working on it. Maybe in the spring. It's not like we were going to finish it by your NYU application deadline anyway," Evan said, shrugging his shoulders, and tossed the hat and beard. "I'm gonna take off." He left his Santa suit on the couch, grabbed his real coat, and walked out the door. A few seconds of quiet passed.

"Are you okay, Lucy?" Tim asked with a frown. "I like Evan and Lucy."

Lucy sighed. "I know, I do, too. Thanks, Tim."

Tim gave Lucy a small hug, and she sat with Tim and Marshall for a minute. No one was sure what to say.

"I want to stay and help clean, but I have the keys," she said, pulling them out of her purse and jingling them. "I drove. So. I'm gonna go get changed."

She walked zombielike into the bathroom and shut the door.

*　　*　　*

The snow was falling faster than it had all day and the roads were a coffee-colored slushy mess, but Lucy floored her dad's

243

car through the dark streets with abandon, desperate to get Evan home before things got any worse. She darted through the back roads, speeding up at any stretch of road and hitting the brakes at each turn. Lucy clutched the wheel and her eyes were open wide in a disturbed panic, her mouth shut tightly. If Evan's mouth could do the same, maybe she could figure out something, anything to tell him that would make things okay. Unfortunately, Evan didn't wait long.

"You know, what is *with* you?" he asked. Lucy stiffened further. She wanted to fix things, but she did not like arguments, or blame, or nasty tones. "Why are you acting so different? It's not just the look. You've been snippy since you got here. I feel like an asshole every time I open my mouth around you. Do you even like me? I feel like you don't."

"You know I do," Lucy said through her teeth.

"Well, then I don't know what's going on. You never used to be this way."

"You're different, too," Lucy said, finding herself quickly getting worked up. The words were going to fly now, and she was worried because she had no idea what they'd be. "Since when are you Mister Settle-Down-and-Have-a-Family, Mister Small-Town-Romance-Junkie? You've changed, too."

Lucy hit a stretch of ice and pumped her brakes and then hit the gas to avoid swerving.

"Who said anything about a family?" Evan asked. "I had a girlfriend for a month this year. You're projecting. Could you drive a little slower?"

244

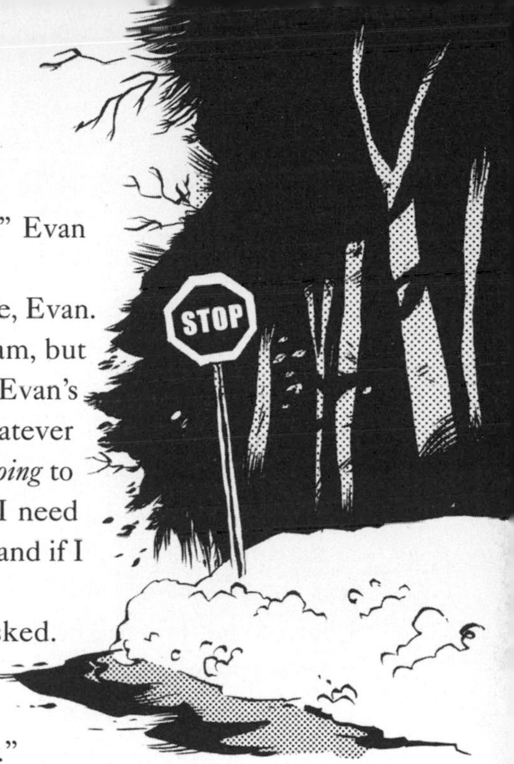
STOP

"No."

"What's going on with you?" Evan asked, still heated.

"I'm not some Stepford Wife, Evan. I don't know what you think I am, but I'm not cute little Lucy, I'm not Evan's bitch, I'm not going to be whatever you feel like I should be. I'm *going* to get angry, I'm *going* to curse if I need to, and I'll *smoke* if I'm stressed and if I feel like it, so *get used to it.*"

"What stress?" Evan asked. "What is going on? Because I feel like this should be a happy time, and you are *not* happy." Evan threw his arm up by the window and rubbed his temples. "You know, I'd like to know how you see me," he said, turning to face Lucy. "You seem to be so angry with me, and I can't think of anything I've done to deserve it."

Lucy slammed on the brakes as a light turned red, and the car skidded for a second before coming to a stop.

"And could you *please* drive slower? I get it, you're pissed."

"You don't get it, that's the problem," Lucy said, shutting her eyes for emphasis. "You haven't had any challenge in your life, you have it so easy, you can't appreciate what others go through, and you definitely can't appreciate me."

"How do you know? It's been, like, two days. What the hell." The light turned green. "And how would you know how easy I have it?" Evan asked. "Just because we don't have the *same* issues doesn't mean I don't have *any*. My family is always expecting something from me. And so are my friends. Tim and Marshall, who I probably just pissed off. I have to deal with my father and his constant micromanaging of my life." Evan's tone changed, it was calmer now. "Sometimes I wonder what it would be like if my parents were split up. Like maybe they wouldn't be so focused on me, and I could just do what I want. Running off to be some kind of artist isn't even an option in my life — my dad couldn't care less about drawings and comics. I have to make straight As, I have to get into the best school, I need to be doing extracurricular work every day, or I'm not meeting my potential. I work *every minute* for a life I don't even know I want! And then you come into town and I try all week, but I can't think of a reason to work on this stupid paper I'm being harped on about. And somehow I have to live up to this character."

"No, you don't," Lucy said, having heard enough of his tantrum. "You need to break away from there. I know it's your family, and they mean well, but listen to you. It's unhealthy."

"You want me to run away from home?" Evan said quietly.

"Not run away, break away," Lucy murmured. They were having a conversation now, and not a fight, Lucy thought. That was good.

"Can I just say, about us? About this? Maybe I don't understand you, but I see you for a few weeks a year. Yeah, we grew up together, but that was a long time ago. I want to get to know you again. Like I did then, but now."

246

Lucy felt calmer now. She felt sad for Evan. But she felt glad, too, and saw that maybe he could change. Maybe they both could still change, and meet somewhere in the middle. They were making some kind of progress now, but she wasn't sure where to go from here because she was still lying to him. There was still so much she hadn't even hinted at that would stop everything if it came out. She couldn't have an honest conversation with him about his future or theirs when she was still lying about everything else. And she couldn't bring those things up until she could trust Evan not to freak out and never speak to her again.

"Can we not fight?" Evan asked. "We have a few more days, and I don't even know what to do anymore. I don't know where this is going or what will happen when you leave, but I don't want to spend this time fighting."

"Yeah," Lucy said, and placed her hand on Evan's lap. "Okay. Maybe we can have an adventure or something," Lucy said, uplifted by the idea. "Something different."

"Okay," Evan said tentatively, "like what?"

"I don't know. Something memorable. All right, tomorrow. *I* get to pick our plans. And you have to do whatever I say."

Evan chuckled nervously. "I told you, I don't want to smoke."

"No, no. That's not an adventure. It'll be something fun. I'll think of something. Just give me tonight." And Lucy got excited.

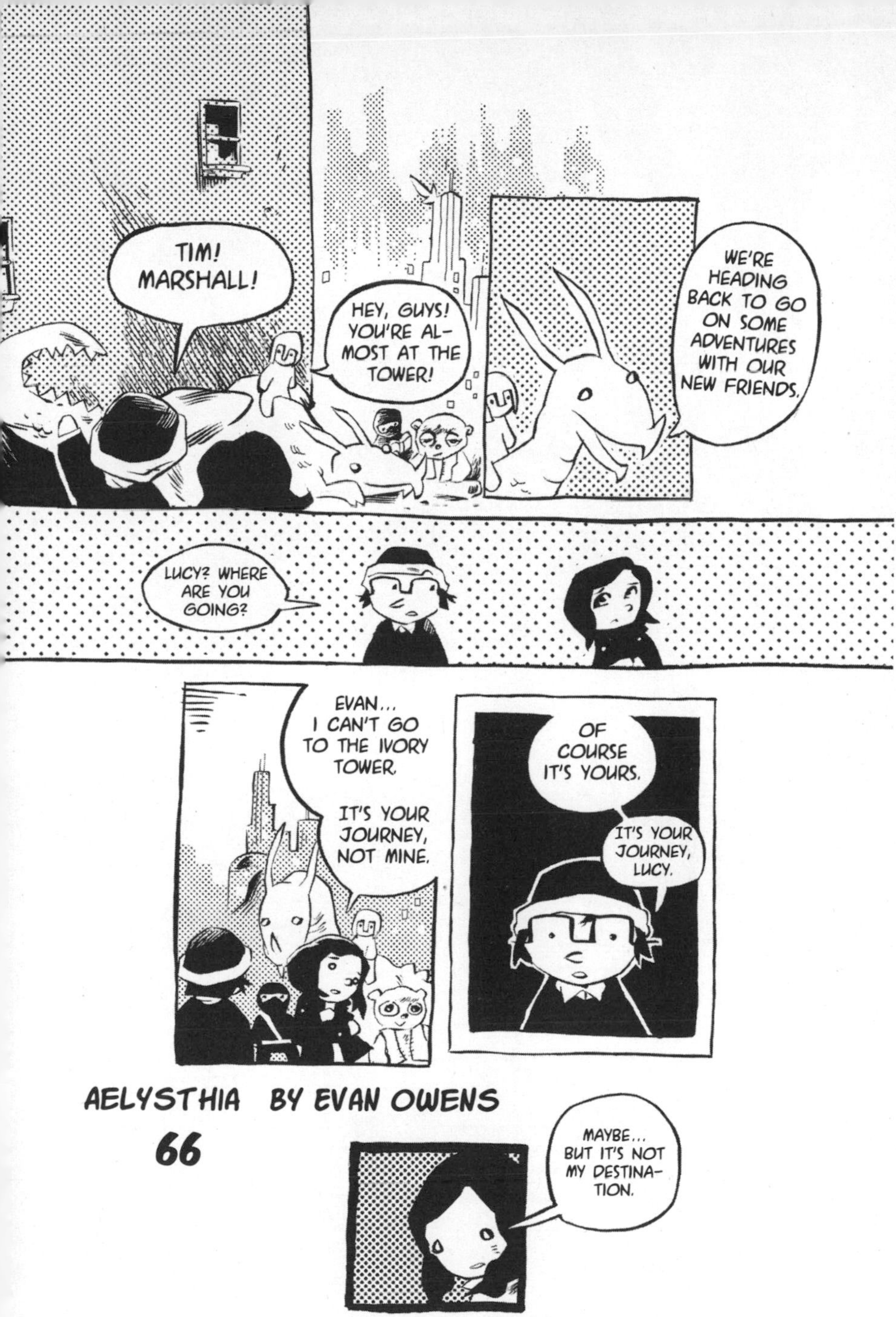
TIM! MARSHALL!
HEY, GUYS! YOU'RE AL-MOST AT THE TOWER!
WE'RE HEADING BACK TO GO ON SOME ADVENTURES WITH OUR NEW FRIENDS.
LUCY? WHERE ARE YOU GOING?
EVAN... I CAN'T GO TO THE IVORY TOWER.
IT'S YOUR JOURNEY, NOT MINE.
OF COURSE IT'S YOURS.
IT'S YOUR JOURNEY, LUCY.
MAYBE... BUT IT'S NOT MY DESTINA-TION.

AELYSTHIA BY EVAN OWENS

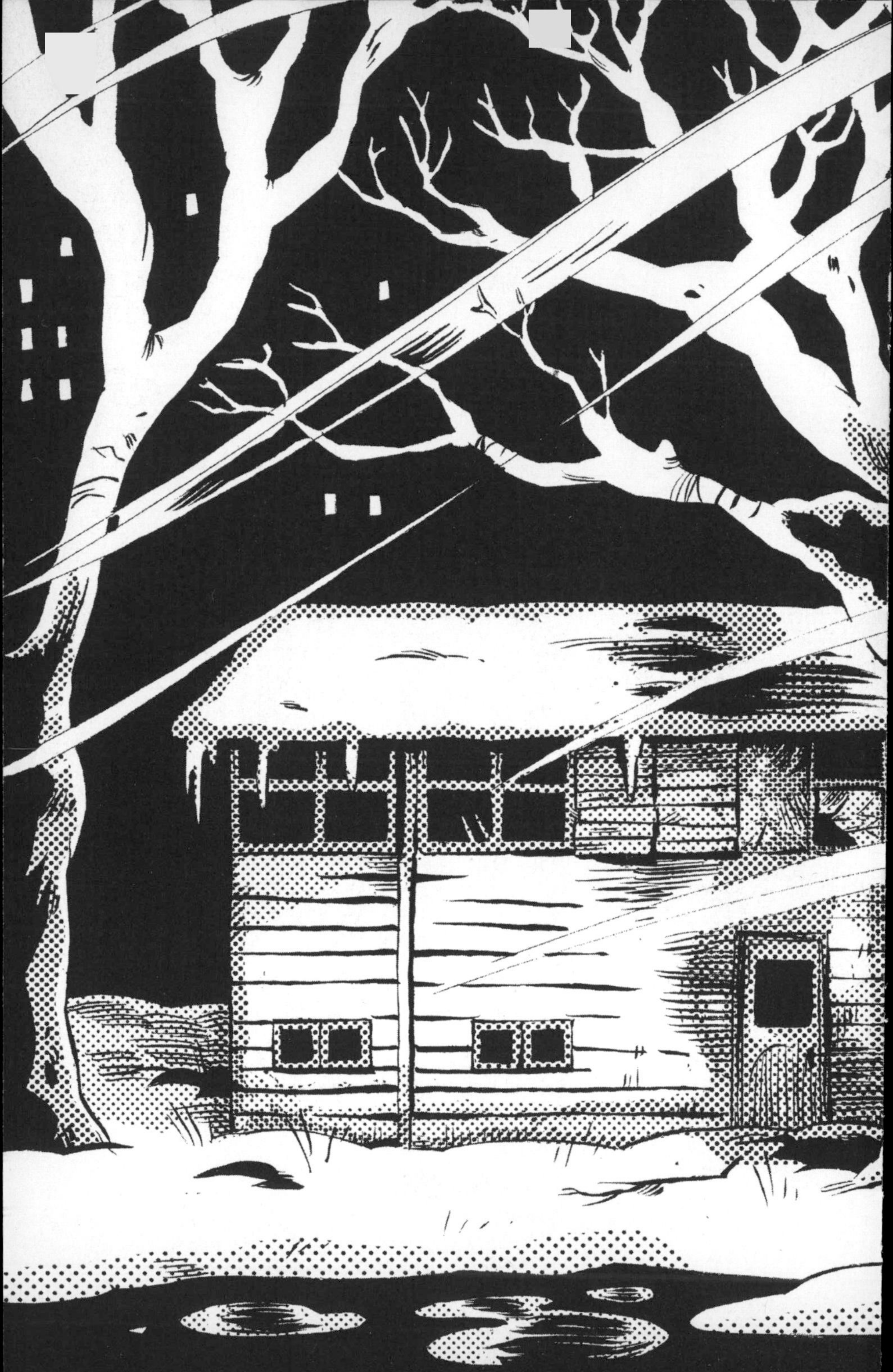

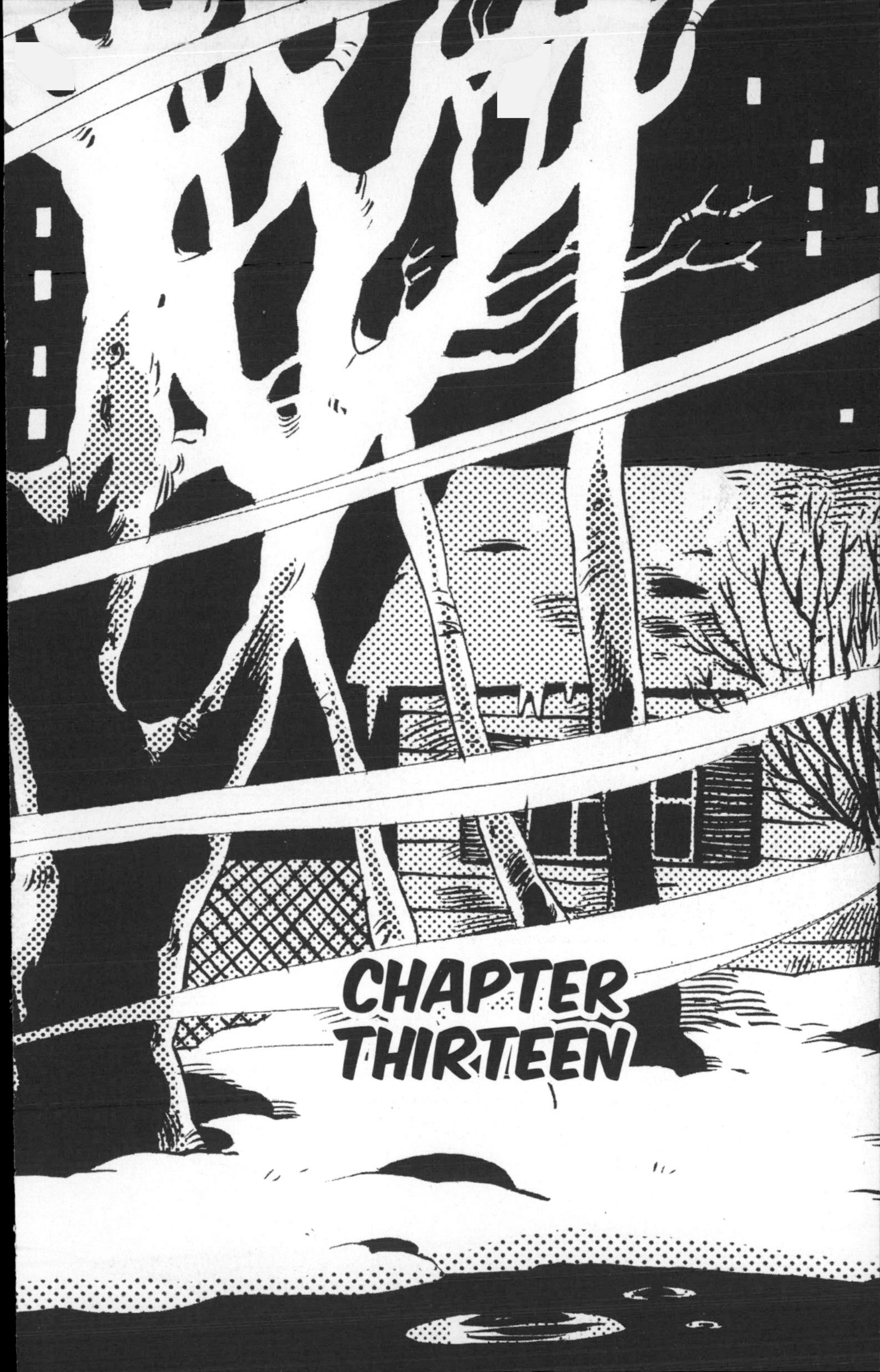
CHAPTER THIRTEEN

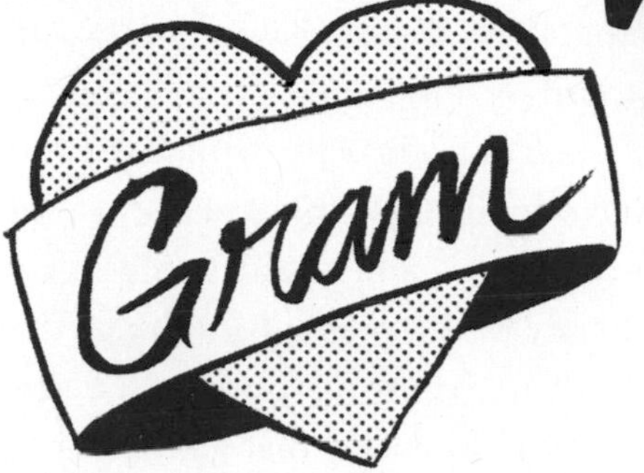
Gram

WIND CHIMES

Twenty-four hours later, Lucy was driving again, with Evan in the passenger seat, and he still had no idea what they were up to or where they were going. He had been told to dress warmly, so he had, with layers of shirt, hoodie, and coat and his winter hat and gloves. Lucy was dressed warmly, too, with a sweater, coat, and her own hat.

"Are we going to lie down on a frozen lake, like in *Eternal Sunshine of the Spotless Mind*?" Evan asked.

"Stop guessing!" Lucy scolded, and not for the first time.

Lucy wanted to have a fun adventure, but she was mostly nervous. She had a plan for the evening. If, in the worst-case scenario, they didn't have fun and she and Evan ended up fighting, then so be it. If the evening went well, and she and Evan got along, then she'd tell him about her summer, and about Ian, and the night would end in failure after that. If they had fun all night, if she told Evan about her boyfriend and the drugs and her mom's boyfriend, and if Evan was all, *Hey, that's cool,* then she'd commit a suicide/homicide. Either way, things were going to go downhill, and she wasn't holding much faith in a positive outcome. If Evan forgave her, a big *if,* she couldn't just numbly live with her problems back home. She'd have to change things, and that was scary—that made her entire body clench. She couldn't run or hide behind drugs or do any of the messed-up things that came easy to her. Not with Evan. Knowing this would end in misery helped in a strange way. It was *hope* that was the problem. Hoping feelings wouldn't be hurt, hoping love would blossom, that was painful. But committing yourself to misery, that was just a dead feeling. It was pulling the Band-Aid and embracing the pain.

"All right," Lucy said, and glanced at Evan. "I told you we were going to do something memorable. So. I'm taking you to a strip club."

"Seriously?" Evan asked as they passed through downtown. He looked out his window, expecting a neon triple-X sign to pass overhead.

"You wish!" Lucy said, and laughed. "Dork."

A few blocks later, Lucy turned into an alley between two buildings and pulled into a parking lot behind them. It was on the outskirts of the downtown area, and not so well lit. There were a few other cars there, but no people, and the area looked like it hadn't been plowed in days. The waterfront was just a few streets away, and visible from the lot.

"*Here we are!*" Lucy said, as if it were the final destination. She got out of the car, and Evan halfheartedly followed suit. It was bitterly cold and windy. The sky was black, aside from the tiny moon, but most of the light came from the yellow light over an unlabeled door, and from the streetlights a few blocks away.

"All right. So this is adventure, according to Lucy," Evan said, looking around. "Are some goons going to pop out and break my arms or something?"

"That's later," Lucy said, as she opened the trunk and took out a large cloth portfolio. She shut the trunk and looked at Evan and wished for the best. "Let's go."

Lucy and Evan walked uphill through the alley and came out into the brightly lit street. They turned right, though, and within a few minutes, they were leaving the busy downtown area behind. The lights all fell behind them, and they walked under a bridge and into a hilly area that they had followed on the long walks they took when they were younger. "I hope we're going somewhere warm," Evan said.

"I told you to dress for this," Lucy said. Her nose was running and her fingers were numb, but a plan was a plan.

"Remember the creepy house down here?" Evan said, and Lucy knew the one he was talking about. They used to pass this tiny abandoned house, its lawn in disarray, the windows either broken or boarded up. They had stopped to poke around one day and were terrified when the angry head of a decrepit old lady swung upward into the window frame and screamed jibberish. Evan and Lucy had run half of the way back home, and later had included her as a crazy old witch in their fantasy stories. She'd grown into legend over the years. And now they were headed to that house.

Evan looked at the house as they stopped in front of it. "This isn't *it*. This isn't your big plan for the night, is it?"

"It's part of it," Lucy said with an accomplished smile. "Yep."

"Are we spending a night in a haunted house? Do we go inside and get eaten by angry old-lady ghosts?"

"First off, ghosts *haunt*, they don't *eat*. And second, no, it's not *haunted*. Although that lady has to be dead by now."

"Does she?" Evan asked, and looked sideways at Lucy. "This is kinda freaking me out."

Lucy took Evan's hand and pulled him along the un-plowed driveway toward the dark house, which was still broken and boarded up. It was two stories but looked like it couldn't hold more than a few rooms. Lucy opened the light outside door and tried to open the main front door, but it was locked.

"Kick it!" she ordered.

"What if that lady really does live here?" Evan said quietly, his eyes glued to the windows, as if he was expecting her shriveled old head to appear. "Maybe she's just poor and can't afford electricity. Or maybe she's homeless and is just squatting here."

"Evan, she was, like, four billion years old. There's no way she's still here. It's abandoned property. We have as much right to be here as she does."

"Which is none. And why would we *want* to be here?"

"Because I said so, and I get to choose what we do." Lucy was staring ahead at the door.

"I'm thinking that was a mistake."

Evan knocked softly on the door and paused as he listened for a reaction. Lucy insisted the door needed a kick. Evan pushed the door with his foot. Lucy explained what a kick was. *Be badass.* Finally, Evan stepped back and gave a forceful kick, and the door swung open, banging against the wall. They ducked inside and closed the door before anyone noticed them, as the houses here were close together. *Good job*, Lucy thought. *Yeah, that was pretty badass.*

"All right," Evan said, as Lucy put down her stuff and turned on a flashlight. "This is creepy. What now? Are we looking for ghosts or something?"

"We spend the night. You know. Together." Lucy put on her vulnerable face. A cute pout. She looked Evan in the eyes.

Evan's eyes darted around the dark room. "Really? *Here?*"

"No, get your head out of the gutter."

Lucy set the flashlight down on a windowsill so it pointed into the empty house. It was more like a garage than a house. It was small. There was a staircase only a step inside, leaving barely enough room to open the door completely. The floor was concrete, covered completely in a thick layer of dust, like nature had installed its own carpet. There was a very small kitchen area and a table, and a bathroom, and that was all there was downstairs. Exploring the house wasn't a part of Lucy's plan, though, so she opened the portfolio and took out a bunch of large sheets of paper and some thick black markers. The slightest movements cast huge splashes of darkness across the walls. She wiped a large spot on the floor with her foot to set the papers down, and did the same so she and Evan had space to sit. She took off her dirty gloves.

"I don't think I'm going to sleep for a week," Evan said. "This place is already giving me nightmares."

"Hush," Lucy said. She dropped down to the floor and popped the cap off one of the markers. "This is the easiest part of the evening. We're going to draw."

"You know"— Evan sat down carefully — "we could have drawn just about anywhere. My house. Yours. The library. Like, any diner or café. You know they have clean tables and everything? Free Wi-Fi. You can even get coffee."

He'd be fine. She took this to be an instance of Evan just liking the sound of his own voice. "This is a secret private drawing. It's just for us," Lucy said, not ready to tell Evan *why* it was a secret private drawing. Lucy had to rest her weight on her knees and lean over the paper to draw. She began their most ambitious jam strip yet. It would take at least five large sheets of paper, fitting only two or three panels per sheet. The first panel, which Lucy drew, taking her time with it, was a fantasy sprawl of Aelysthia. The vomiting sun gave it away. If she was going to do a special jam strip with Evan, it only made sense that it would take place there. The setting made it personal and special right from the start.

"Why so big?" Evan asked. "This could take a while."

"Because that's what I want. And we have a couple hours, tops. Make it good."

Lucy finished her establishing shot, and Evan took over, starting his panel.

Lucy watched Evan draw. The setup probably wasn't the

best. The flashlight lit the room decently, but it also made for dark shadows. Half of Evan's face was indiscernible, and he was drawing in his own hand's shadow, basically guessing at what would come out. When he moved his hand, though, it looked fine. If she hadn't watched him draw it, she'd never have known he could barely see the paper. He was drawing a person with hands coming out of her face. This was a common feature if you lived in Aelysthia; it was like having freckles here. Lucy thought she would put up with the face hands to live in a beautiful fantasy world. She could live in a hobbit hole and eat all day and fight trolls in the woods just fine. In fact, it was a huge disservice to her character that there were *no* monsters at all to battle where she lived. She was positive it was what she had been put on Earth to do. She brought this up to Evan.

"It would be a clean-cut world. Peaceful, scenic towns, baking pies and sleeping 'til noon, then taking your sword and shield and fighting the bad guys. If I could do that and forget all the bullshit, all the school and jobs and complicated relationships, forget about working until I'm sixty-five, forget the economy and all the crap we're going to grow into, that'd be just fine with me. I'll fight trolls all goddamn day."

"It'd be nice," Evan said. "I'm sure we'd just trade our problems for new ones, though. I mean, trolls can't be that easy to defeat. And we'd run through shoes like nobody's business."

Evan had once said he liked fantasy books because of the wide-open worlds you could escape to, where everything was new and the journey was going to be long and take you

259

far. Lucy thought of it differently. Even then, when they were kids. She found the real world to be too open and scary sometimes. And she liked to hide in a book that was comfortable and familiar. Where she knew what she was getting into.

Lucy decided to pick Evan's brain while she had him trapped. She asked about this Jessica girl he had dated. Lucy had been incommunicado during the month when he was dating her and had missed the whole story. She had only heard bits and pieces from his family in the past week.

"You don't want to hear about that, do you?" Evan said, passing the large sheet of paper back to Lucy. There was still space for a smaller third panel in the corner.

"I asked, didn't I? I never hear about these girls of yours. I want to know what I'm getting into."

Evan thought about it for a minute. He didn't sound enthused to talk about her, but began anyway. "Well, it was short. That's the main thing. It was short, and dramatic, and that makes for good teasing around here. All right. So there was this girl named Jessica Lyons. She worked at McDonald's."

Lucy snorted with laughter and covered her mouth.

"What? Why is that funny?"

Lucy didn't know why it was funny that she worked at McDonald's. Somehow she pictured the playpen and Grimace and Ronald, and it just made her laugh.

"All right. So I met her when I went to McDonald's, and she was clearly having the worst day of her life or something because she'd come across as stone cold, like, don't mess with me, I hate my job, whatever. Then she went to get this stack

260

of cups, and she dropped them all over the floor. I thought she was going to kill someone, but she just started laughing, and she seemed like this whole other person. She was really pretty, curly brownish-red hair, bright eyes. Anyway, I started laughing, too. So that was the first time I met her."

Lucy had already finished her panel, and Evan started drawing on the next sheet of paper. The wind was screaming loud and pounding against the house.

"The next time I saw her was at an open mic I went to with Tim and Marshall. She was a singer, and this other girl was playing piano. So that was a game-changer. She wasn't just some cute McDonald's girl, but she was a singer, a musician. Now I was really interested. I knew every guy was going to pounce on her, so I made a point to go look for her as soon as she'd finished. We talked for, like, forty-five minutes. She came with me and Tim and Marshall for our Friday-night routine, which involved going to Kmart and dicking around, basically. Then we started talking at school, and then I asked her out."

"This is really the stuff of fairy tales, Ev," Lucy said, slouched over. She felt a little jealous, which surprised her. *So she sings. Whatever.* "Is she friends with Tim and Marshall?"

"Nah. We mostly hung out alone. So almost immediately things start going sour. I can tell from the first day that she's thinking of when we should break up. She has, like, twelve thousand guy friends that are all in love with her. She disappears for days at a time, always busy. So I know pretty fast that I need to break up with her. I start thinking about how to do it, and when, but she beats me to it. She says we've lost the magic we had at first, which must have been, like, the first night or something because that's when it started going downhill. We dated, we broke up."

"So all the quote-unquote guy friends?" Lucy asked.

"I don't know. I really never found out what she was up to. She never told me. So, whatever, I guess."

"Cold break," Lucy said after they'd drawn another page. There was no source of heat at all, and they had to draw with their gloves off. She put down the marker and crawled over to where Evan was sitting and nestled into him for warmth.

"I think we should finish this comic," Evan said, and wrapped his arms around Lucy and placed his cheek against hers. "We're going to freeze to death if we don't."

"Okay," Lucy said, and closed her eyes. "We have more stuff to do anyway. The night is young, Owens. Be afraid."

They sat quietly for a moment, listening to the wind swirl and slam against the walls. Lucy didn't want to be a Jessica to Evan. She wanted to be honest with him. She almost told him everything right then, but a loud thud hit the door and startled them. Evan held on to her tightly, and they sat in silence, their ears perked. Lucy slowly moved to get the flashlight and turned it off. The wind kept swooshing away, but there was no more *thud*. A car drove by, and a few seconds later a dog barked.

Evan peeked over the windowsill slowly. No one was outside. Lucy looked up through the window and saw a loose tree branch swinging wildly. She settled back down and sighed heavily.

"Okay, let's finish this comic and get going," she said.

* * *

By nine thirty, Lucy and Evan had left the creepy small house and were walking downtown again. Lucy was glad to see the light and people. She held Evan's hand.

"So part two of the plan takes place downtown?" Evan asked, being a good sport about all the secrecy.

"Maybe," Lucy said coyly.

"So we *are* going to a strip club!"

"Ev, what the hell. You've lived here all your life. There are no strip clubs."

A block away, they reached Lucy's second destination: a tattoo parlor. They stopped outside a small storefront with purple neon lighting. The inside looked clean but small. Lucy could see the joy drop out of Evan's face when he noticed where they'd stopped. He let go of her hand.

"Lucy, I don't want to get a tattoo," he said.

"Sure you do. It's art, you love art. Come on, let's go." Lucy gave Evan a playful shove, but he wasn't budging.

"Look, I told you I was on board fully tonight," Evan said. "It's your night. I want to have fun, I want to do memorable stuff, and I want to make you happy. But isn't there anything else we can do?"

"This is supposed to be adventurous, though," Lucy said, resigned. "What's more memorable or adventurous than getting tattoos?"

Evan looked in the window, and Lucy could see the gears turning in his head as he tried to justify getting the hell out of there.

"And I suppose you want me to design something?" Evan

asked. "My art changes every few months. I guarantee a year from now I'll be repulsed by anything I come up with on the spot here."

"Relax, no, you don't have to design anything. I have something in mind. Hear me out?"

There was a lone person working inside, and Lucy could see her patiently watching them debate the tattoos. Evan signaled for Lucy to carry on.

"Remember Christmas?" Evan smiled. He remembered Christmas. "Not that. Though that was nice, too. But remember when we were sitting on the couch, and your grandmother said you were going to get a tattoo for her? And I said I'd get one, too?"

Evan remembered.

"*Ta-daaa*," Lucy sang, presenting the tattoo parlor. "So even though I know you would *totally* do this for *me*, it's also for your grandmother. And besides, I'm getting one, too, so we can have matching tattoos."

"You're really getting a tattoo for *my* grandmother?" Evan asked.

"Yup. But mine won't be on my face, like yours will."

Lucy could see Evan starting to agree with her logic. After all, he was an honest, stand-up guy—and he would do anything for his grandma. Lucy thought very highly of her herself.

When Lucy had come out of the bathroom after playing Zombies, she was embarrassed at how much time she'd spent in there crying and afraid of how Evan's mom and

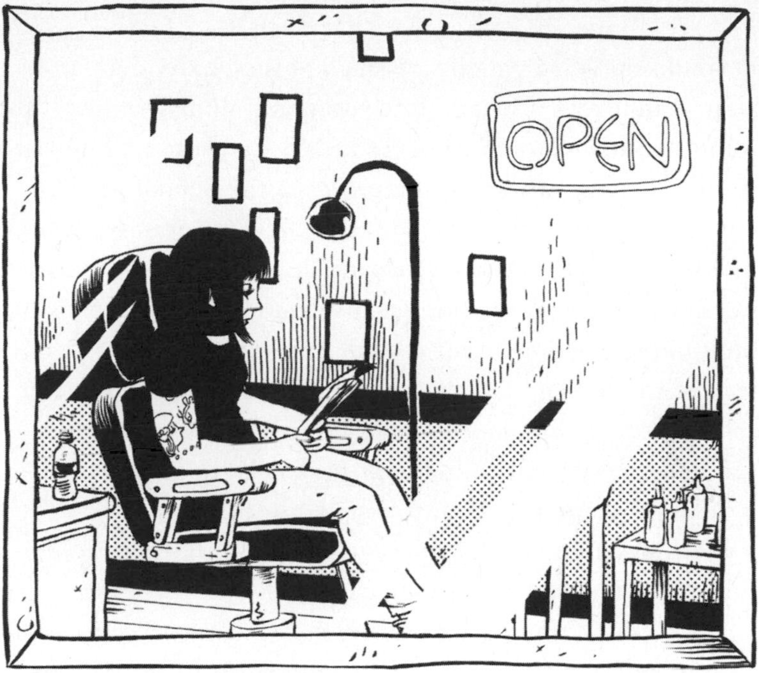
OPEN

Gram would react. Maybe they'd tell her to go home, or maybe they'd call her dad. Instead, she had come out of the bathroom to find lunch being made in the kitchen.

"You're just in time," Gram had told Lucy. "You missed Evan and Barbara already, but I waited because you should have company while you eat." Lucy had looked out the window at the snow falling while Gram made her a sandwich. It was pretty obvious that she was just trying to get her to open up, and Lucy was okay with that. She was tired of not talking. Lucy started by telling her how the game had reminded her of the game nights the Owenses had had every couple of weeks on Sunday nights, with all of their extended family over. And it wasn't long before she was spilling her guts. "It reminded me of when we were kids," Lucy said. "The last thing I looked forward to before going to school on Mondays was game nights over here." Lucy still felt awkward, like Gram must have been judging her quietly. Not because Gram was a bad person but because Lucy had just been sobbing in their bathroom for twenty minutes. "That was what felt weird, though," she continued. "For a minute it was like reliving some childhood memory or something. But then I remembered it's only a memory for *me*. Evan still has these regular game nights. I'm just not a part of them anymore."

"It's a shame you're so far away most of the year," Gram said. "We miss you here, Evan especially."

"We ended up in such different places," Lucy said with an uncomfortable laugh, getting depressed again. Evan had his home and his family, good grades, and a promising future, and Lucy had a broken home, neglect, and a bunch of dead ends to travel. Evan was happy and she was not. Lucy's negative thoughts had been gaining steam but were disrupted by Gram's laughter, which seemed bizarrely out of place.

"I'm sorry, sweetie," Gram said, "but, *where you ended*? You haven't even begun yet!"

"Oh," Lucy said, feeling like a kid. "You know what I mean, though."

"No, I don't," Gram said. "Where you've ended implies that you think this is it, that was life. Or like there's some kind of line you walk, and you took this path and Evan took that one."

"Basically, I guess," Lucy said.

"Listen. From someone who knows, okay? There are so many bends in that path that you couldn't possibly even know about." Lucy thought this was some kind of *Kids say the darnedest things* speech. "Life throws so many curveballs, the tiniest little decision can change everything. And it's not always your decision, either. You just never know."

Lucy sat quietly, unsure what to say. She thought Gram was right but didn't like being lectured to.

"I'm seventy now, and I've been living with my daughter and her husband since I was sixty-five. Lucy, believe me when I tell you this is not where I had planned to be. I still had some good years left with my husband, Evan's grandpa, when he was taken away from me. I could have ended up in our house, living alone, or I could have ended up in a retirement home, or you could say I ended up here, but I don't feel like anything has ended. It's just all a part of my journey. And I don't believe it will end here on Earth. I like to think I'll meet my husband again, and that maybe he's gotten a tattoo for me since he left, and maybe when I see him again I'll be light enough and he'll be young enough to sweep me off my feet. But I don't think for one second that our paths won't cross again."

Gram had known exactly what was bothering Lucy. That's why Lucy really wanted to get that tattoo for her.

"I'd only do this for you," Evan said as they entered the building.

"And your gram," Lucy said.

"And my gram." Evan's words filled Lucy with warm

feelings. They reminded her of Evan stealing his dad's car—she knew he was telling the truth; he really wouldn't do this for anyone else.

The employee-slash-artist working was named Leslie. She was in her late twenties and heavily tattooed. Leslie showed them around, and they looked through books of designs. She had designed several herself, and Evan and Lucy picked one of her designs. It was elegant and nondescript, and wouldn't cost them any future jobs.

Evan went first, since Lucy was afraid if it hurt she'd scare Evan out of it, and then only she would have his grandmother's name on her. And that would be weird. Evan had it done on his arm. Lucy had jokingly insisted he get it on his lower back so everyone could see what a bad boy he was whenever he bent over. He had no desire to get any other tattoos, so he wanted it somewhere out of the way. The upper-arm muscle seemed like the best spot.

"God, this is so permanent," Lucy said. "Isn't it exciting?"

"It's certainly something. Definitely permanent," Evan said. He looked tense and a little light-headed.

"Well, I'll tell you, it's a sweet thing you're getting put on your arm," Leslie said. "Tattoos can be a powerful statement. Your grandmother will know you love her, that's for sure."

"It is powerful art," Evan said, looking at his bare arm flesh, *for the last time*, Lucy thought, riding a high from the excitement. "I'll be looking at it for the rest of my life, so I'd better like it, right?"

"Or you could be the drunk college boy that came in here last night to get a ridiculous tattoo of Garfield taking a bong hit," Leslie said matter-of-factly.

"I'm going to get that one next," Lucy said.

Lucy had hers placed on her ankle. It was easy to hide, and easy to show off, and hurt more than she'd expected. It was worth it, though. Lucy knew now that even if the rest of the night fell apart, they'd be forever linked in some way, to this one happy spot in time.

"Only a year ago we were both nerds," Evan said. "And now I have a tattoo."

"How does it feel?" Leslie asked.

"I don't know. I feel like Popeye," he told her with a smile, and Lucy rolled her eyes. "I feel like going into a bar. And getting into a fight."

"Good. Because that's plan number three: bar fight." Lucy made a fist.

"Seriously?" Evan said, and froze in his tracks.

"So gullible tonight," Lucy said.

Lucy insisted that the next part of her plan was the best part and that Evan would love it. This part wasn't actually part of her plan, but she was feeling impulsive after the tattoo success. It was her night, and spontaneity went hand-in-hand with adventure. She also wanted one last highlight before the third part of her plan, and before she said anything about her summer. She grabbed Evan's hand and pulled him along to a Starbucks across the street. They darted through the flow of traffic going each way, and a driver honked at them for making him brake. Evan and Lucy looked at each other and laughed. Lucy used the Starbucks gift card Gram gave her, and she and Evan ordered their coffee. Gram did say to take a boy out for coffee, after all. They got their order and sat down in comfy chairs in a quiet corner. It wasn't busy, but it wasn't empty, either. Lucy pulled her chair close to Evan's. They took off their hats and gloves, drank their coffee, and warmed up.

"You're right, I like this part."

"This isn't the plan," Lucy said.

"Are you going to tell me the plan?"

Lucy leaned in. "We make out like horny teenagers." It wasn't breaking into abandoned property, and it wasn't permanently marking their bodies, it was kissing. But it got their hearts racing just the same. Lucy put down her coffee and initiated the making out, leaning over to Evan and grabbing his hair and pulling him in. They made out aggressively, and there was fear, arousal, and amusement as they tried not to laugh. They didn't look up to see if anyone was watching, although Lucy couldn't imagine they weren't being stared at. She felt messy from kissing and at a peak high, giddy even.

"See?" Lucy asked, with her nose pressed against his. "Impulses can be good."

"I think I like your impulses," Evan said, blushing deeply and not looking anywhere but at Lucy.

"Good. 'Cause you're not going to like the next one." And now Lucy was the one who looked nervous.

The wind whipped behind them as they walked through the

cold back to where they had parked the car. Lucy considered ending the evening there, with warmth and cuddling and making out. She'd planned the evening out fully, though, and there was a purpose. She knew she had to see it through. This next step was going to be a hurdle, and if Evan could deal with it, she'd come out with everything she had to say. And she knew there was little chance of it flying with Evan, but it had to be done. She rarely felt fear for herself, but the idea of hurting Evan was killing her.

They reached the car, and Lucy opened the trunk and pulled out the portfolio with the large jam strip. She also took out a white bucket and a rolling pin.

"What are we doing with all that?" Evan asked with suspicion in his voice.

"Hold this" was all Lucy said, and she handed him the bucket, which was heavy.

Evan followed Lucy with hesitation, and they walked behind the building they'd parked to the side of. The back of it was lit sparsely—mostly it was dark, but it caught some of a streetlight, and the moon was bright enough that they could see where they were going. The wall they walked along was facing the waterfront, which ran alongside a highway and a frontage road. At this time of night, the streets on this side of the stores were mostly empty. There were roads on either side of the building that ran perpendicular to the frontage road.

"It's called wheatpasting," Lucy said. "We're going to paste our cartoon to the building."

Evan was, predictably, against it. "That's graffiti," he said in an angry whisper. "It's *illegal*!"

It was, but it was also fairly common, more so where Lucy lived. The point of her night was to immortalize the winter when she and Evan began their romance. Whether the romance continued past the winter or ended right here, she wanted it to last in some form. She wanted it to live on in art. Through their tattoos, through their cartoon, through Aely-sthia. The comic was her art and Evan's, it was their personalities and ideas in one big, silly comic. And she couldn't force some company to publish it anywhere, but she could make it seen. No one had to know it was theirs. And Evan was secret enough about his art that he wouldn't get pegged. This was for them.

"The tattoos aren't memorable enough? Jesus, the things are going to be on us for the rest of our lives. Now we need to poster-bomb a building to show we exist?"

"Yeah, basically," Lucy said, upset. "They'll take it down eventually. It's not a big deal. I mean it *is*, to me."

"Anything else," Evan said. "We'll go somewhere warm again and make out. I've been very accommodating. I'm making this one request."

"Ev, please," Lucy said. "I always wanted to do this, but I never had anything good to do it with. And it's especially meaningful if you're a part of it. It's meaningful and memorable. I put a lot of thought into this."

Evan paced back and forth. A car drove by on the frontage road and the headlights shone on them, causing Evan to panic more. The night cold was unbearable and the wind stung. Lucy waited patiently, until Evan stopped pacing and faced her.

"You look cute with your hat pulled down. And your red cheeks," he said, and Lucy smiled. "Do I have to actually *do* it? I mean, can I be the lookout or something?"

Lucy nodded.

"All right, let's hurry up, then."

Lucy really hadn't thought he would go for it. She quickly opened the lid of the bucket, which contained a cheap wheatpaste that she'd made earlier in the day. She dipped the roller into it and started scrubbing the wall clumsily. She watched Evan walk briskly to the edge of the building with his hands in his pockets, looking around the edge. The wind blew one of the pages out of Lucy's hands, so she set the others under the weight of the bucket and chased after it. When she caught it, she studied the wall and decided she should add another layer of the paste.

"Would it be faster if I rolled and you just stuck the art up?" Evan asked from the parking lot. Lucy nodded.

Evan rolled the wall efficiently, and Lucy spread the large paper out onto it and rubbed it into place. She had to hold the comic for a long minute for it to not get blown off, but once it was on, it was on. Evan started rolling more paste onto the wall as Lucy held the first piece down, and when he was done, she held up the second page. The wind was blocked by the building for a while, and it didn't feel quite so cold. A slight flurry started, and with the moon shining, and the snow and the waterfront glittering, Lucy was again feeling a high. Things were working out.

"See, we make a good team," Evan said, and Lucy smiled, glad he was coming around, too. They laid out each of the six pages the cartoon took up, three pages on top and three pages below.

"Not bad," Lucy said, and felt a breathless thrill at it. She looked at Evan and grinned. "I can't believe we did that."

A bright light snapped on and the art installation was illuminated. The light came from the edge of the building. Evan and Lucy turned and saw that a man was holding a flashlight and walking toward them.

"Couple of artists," the man said in a friendly tone. "Did one of you draw this?"

Lucy and Evan said nothing, waiting for more information from the man. "Well?" the man asked.

"We both did," Lucy said very hesitantly.

"Pretty good," he said, admiring the work. Lucy grabbed Evan's hand and held her breath. The bucket was there, the roller, they'd probably even gotten the light-colored paste on themselves by this point. And Lucy knew she looked like someone who should be behind bars.

"Officer Dave Perkins," the man said, pointing the flashlight back at himself. He was wearing a policeman's uniform. "Little cold to be hanging around outside, don't you think?"

Lucy's heart sank. *So this is how it ends.*

Lucy twiddled her thumbs nervously in the back of the police cruiser. Evan was silent. They weren't even handcuffed — they weren't actually being arrested. They were being taken to the station so their parents could be notified and come pick them up. It was a slap on the wrist. Lucy knew her dad would be disappointed or maybe annoyed, but

Evan's parents were going to blow it out of proportion. Evan had been *turned to the dark side*. Evil Lucy came and corrupted him. She fidgeted in her seat, sighed, and finally asked Evan to say something, whatever. Let her have it. She didn't even care at that point. What Evan did say, however, hit her like a punch to the gut.

"Thank God we got caught," he said. "I hope they take that thing down."

"What?" she said coldly. *That thing* was a symbol to Lucy. It was an even mix of Evan and Lucy, past and present, it was love and art and everything she'd been trying to get through to Evan.

Evan was angry, too; she could tell from his tone and speech pattern. "Can you imagine if it gets left up? People are going to *know* I did that, Lucy. They'll figure it out. I do art for the school play. I mean, people know I'm an artist even if I don't flaunt it all the time or anything. You get to

skip town—there's no risk for you—but that's a big framed testament to my night of criminal debauchery."

"Oh *gawd*," Lucy said in an overly dramatic way, and slumped in her seat. "I give up. Go eat your cookies and cry about the evil succubus Lucy. I'll never bother you again. Just run back to your safe little world."

"Yeah, *safe*," Evan said. "Like being home in bed, not riding in the back of a police cruiser. I think I will." He turned to look out the window in a huff. They were driving through downtown, back the way they had come. There was a big space between them in the backseat. "I've been working my entire life to get into a good college and I could have just pissed it away."

"Is that what you want or not? Make up your mind. I can't tell where you end and your dad begins," Lucy said, looking at the back of the passenger's seat. She was angry and sad and emotional, like an inverse of the highs she'd felt earlier. "I know there's a creative, fun, incredible person deep down in there somewhere, and I keep walking up to that door and knocking. I just hope someday you'll let him out."

"Very poetic," Evan said, and then turned to face her. "You know, I'm really tired of that, by the way. This assumption that I'm somehow not who I am, or not living up to my full potential. *This is me*, take it or leave it, but don't think you can just mold me into some optimal Evan."

Lucy remained quiet, stewing in her own anger, thinking up a rebuttal.

"Just because you're not satisfied with your life doesn't mean that it has anything to do with me," Evan continued.

276

"Maybe your family split up and you're mad because mine didn't, or I get good grades so you want me to abandon school and follow art or whatever. But I'm not you. We have different lives and that's okay. I don't have to be you."

"So I'm dragging you down? To *my level*?" Lucy asked, not expecting an answer. "You think I'm, like, trying to sabotage your life or something? Grow up, Evan."

"No, *you're* the one who needs to grow up," Evan said. "And I hope you do."

The police officer told them to quiet down as they approached the station. Lucy thought about all the stuff she had wanted to tell Evan. She thought of all the ways the night could have ended. Or what would have happened if she had just ended the night before the wheatpasting. She thought of only an hour earlier, when they were kissing and happy. She never thought the night would end well and had even planned it not to, but that damn hope came along anyway. Her heart felt so heavy and she wanted to empty it all out, the good, the bad, and the ugly, but now she'd never get to. And they were both thinking such ugly things. There was no turning back.

Lucy sniffled loudly and muttered little sobs. She felt alone.

Evan tried to console her, but Lucy pushed him away. She wasn't going to be some damsel in distress. And Evan was no knight.

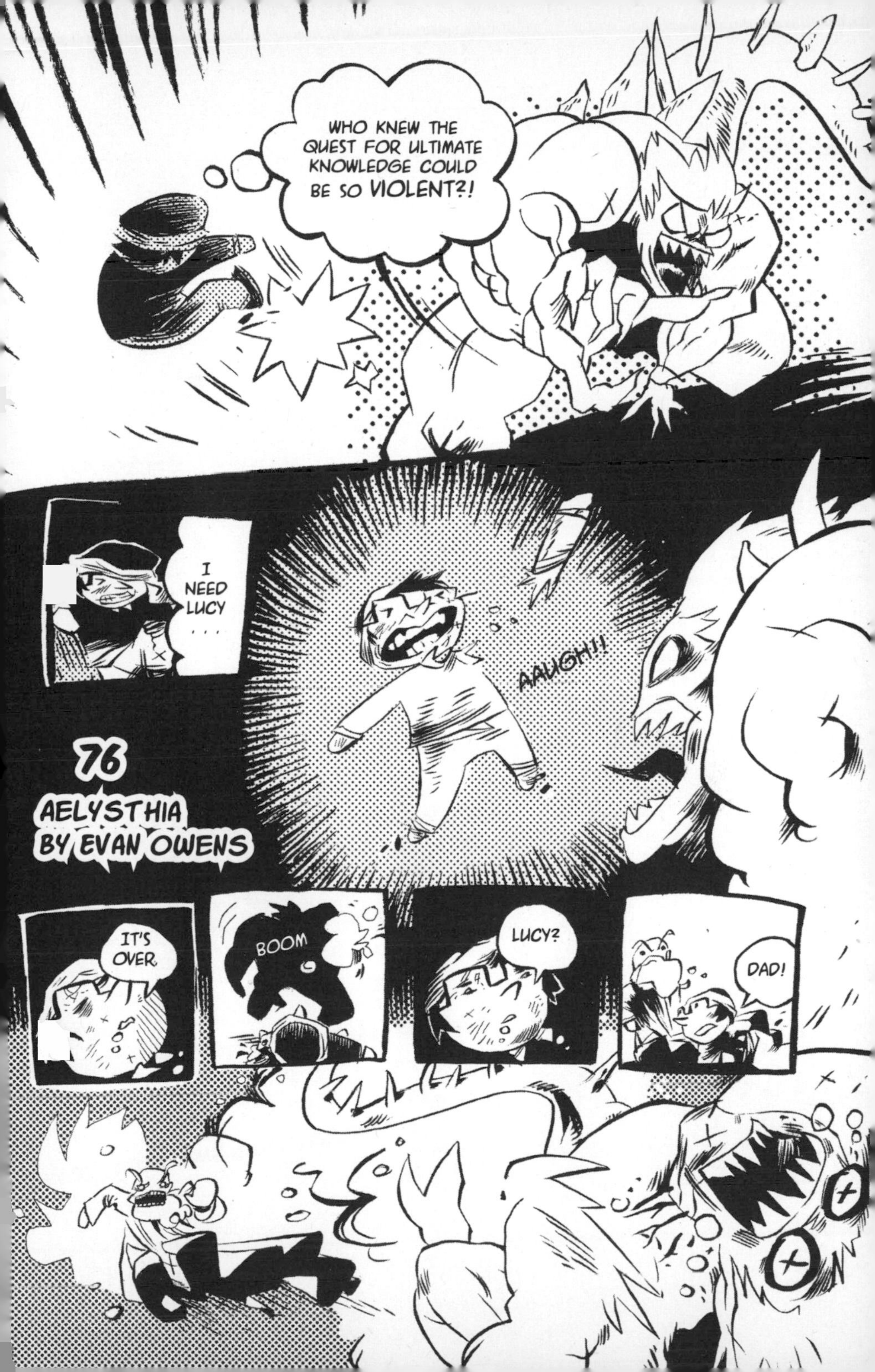
WHO KNEW THE QUEST FOR ULTIMATE KNOWLEDGE COULD BE SO VIOLENT?!
I NEED LUCY . . .
AAUGH!!
76
AELYSTHIA BY EVAN OWENS
IT'S OVER
BOOM
LUCY?
DAD!

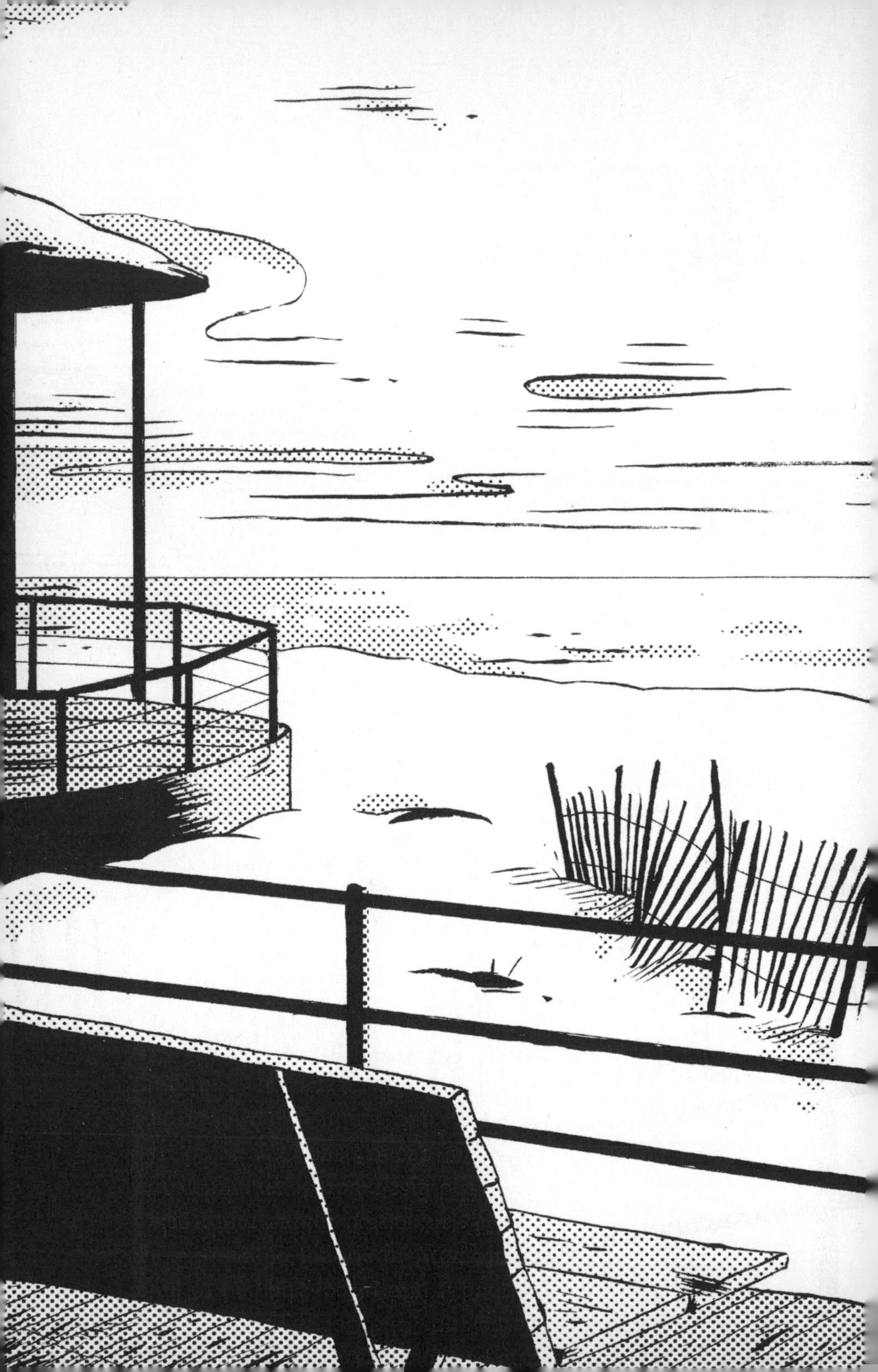

CHAPTER FOURTEEN

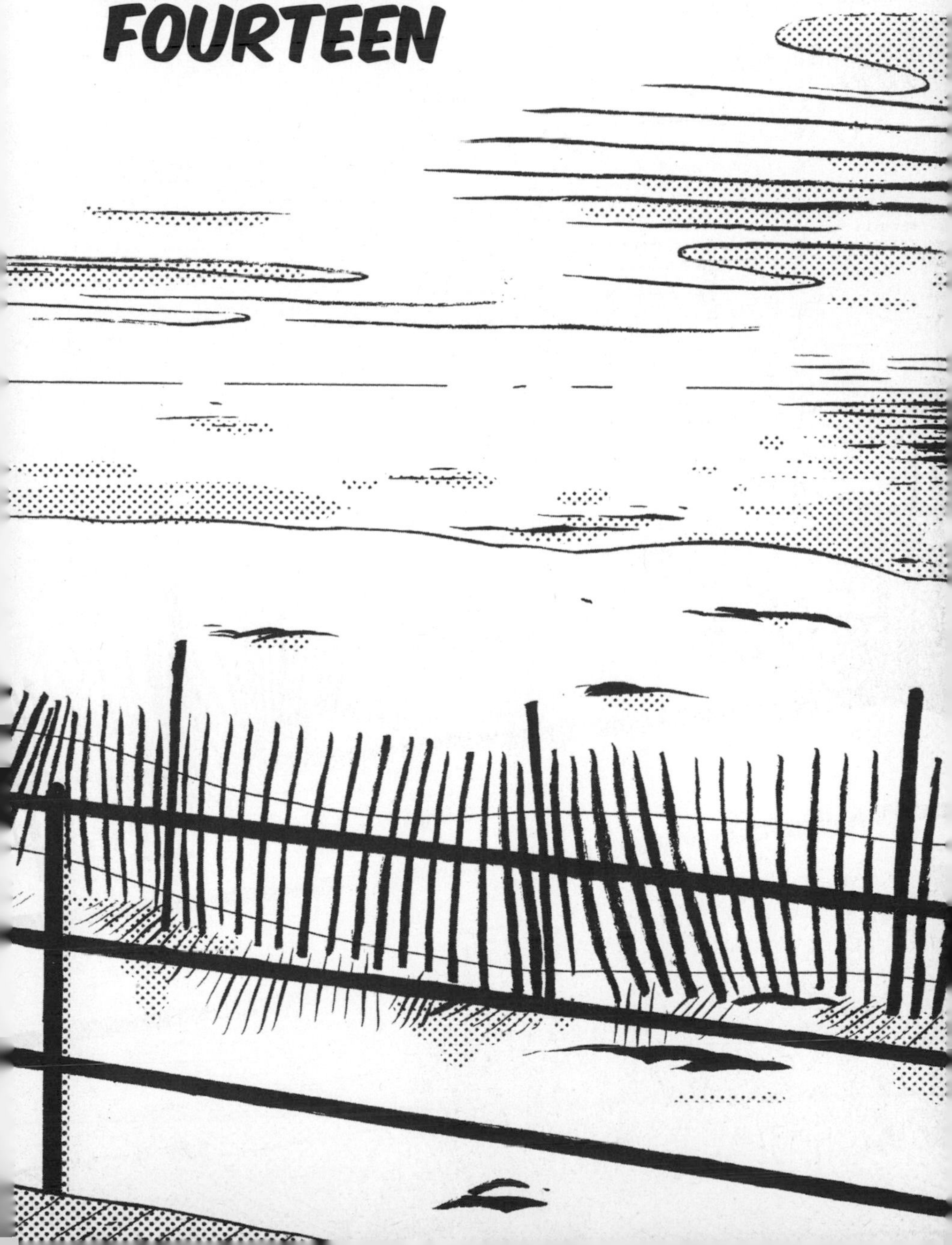

GOD ONLY KNOWS

Dad took Lucy home, and it was a largely silent ride. There were no arguments or loud words or harsh sentiments—he didn't even seem too surprised. He must have gotten all the anxiety out when she'd caused trouble as a kid, back when he'd yell and punish and ask her *Why?* and try to figure out what he could do to help her, to make her happy. She had thought back then that she *was* happy. She had just liked to do what she wanted to do. Maybe she hadn't been happy, though. Maybe doing dumb things had been her way of saying, "Hey, world, I'm not happy."

He did say a few words. "We're together two weeks a year, hon," he said on the ride home. "Could you save the mischief for your mother to handle?"

"Okay," Lucy said, and kept to herself how easy he had

it. She couldn't fit any more drama in with her mom if she tried.

When they got home, Dad jiggled the key and opened the door, threw the keys on the hutch, and turned on the light as they walked in. Lucy took off her coat, dropped it on the couch, and stretched.

"You all right if I go to bed?" Dad asked.

"Yeah, sure, Dad," Lucy said, and Dad went into his room and closed the door.

Lucy decided to do the same and wandered into her own room. She clicked the soft yellow light on, and the white Christmas lights she had strewn about the room a half decade or so ago turned on as well. Nothing in the room had changed much since she was a girl. The same Disney sheets, the flowers on the wallpaper, the yellow book with the smiley face on the cover, the stuffed Totoro doll. When did she like Disney enough to sleep in it? *Is this really me?* she thought.

Grow up, Evan had told her. And she'd said the same to him. And yet, here she stood in a room that was as childlike as it gets, with cobwebs in the corner and dust on every flat surface. That's what she was, a child who aged but didn't change. She thought she wasn't a kid anymore, but she felt here like the seventeen-year-old nightmare version of her ten-year-old self.

Lucy collapsed on her bed and stared at the ceiling while her head continued to race with thoughts. Her brain was a radio with no off button, just a giant volume knob that only went up. She tried to organize, simplify. She knew she couldn't see Evan again. She'd ruined his life enough, and he was furious with her anyway. She wondered if she could get an earlier flight back home. She wondered if she could leave right away. She'd have to pack first. It could wait until morning.

Lucy sat up, took off her shoes, and put on her puffy slippers, which were resting beside the bed. She moved her feet back and forth as if her slippers were stuffed animals, two friends playing together. She looked at her room. She tried to look at it through young eyes, when she had to look up to see the posters on the walls. The last posters she'd put up were from Neil Gaiman's Sandman series. She looked at the giant Pikachu doll on the floor by her desk—Evan had won it for her at a carnival one summer. He didn't win it, actually, but he talked to the man running the game booth and walked away with it somehow. And he gave it to her.

She walked over to it and gave it a little kick. Pikachu fell on his side. On her desk was the drawing Evan gave her for Christmas. Lucy sighed again, trying not to think about the fight they'd just had. It felt like she'd been hopping between alternate universes, one with the perfect loving, creative boyfriend of her dreams and one where everything she touched turned to crap and she had nowhere to go, nowhere she belonged to. She couldn't decide whether she was sad or angry and was gladly letting nostalgia take her back in time and away from everything. She looked at her closet, opened the door, and reached up on the shelf. She took down a shoe box and brought it over to her bed.

This was her secret box. She cringed at the idea of her dad going into her room and finding it. How embarrassing.

If you're gonna snoop in my room, you could at least get rid of the cobwebs, she thought. She shuffled through all the folded-up papers. Mostly notes she and Evan passed in school. Drawings and comics, maps of Aelysthia. There was a ring Lucy had made for Evan in a jewelry-making class she took and never had the nerve to give him. *God, we were such dorks. It's a wonder we've made any other friends.*

Under all the pieces of paper was a small diary she'd kept. Lucy opened it up and flipped quickly through the pages. Lots of book talk. Parents fighting. Running away. Evan, Evan, Evan. Wanting to go to New York, Italy, Paris. She really was the same person. The last entry was about four years ago. She'd written in it since her parents divorced and she moved, but mostly as a novelty. Lucy read the last entry, which was a pretty short one compared with the others.

I hate living in Georgia. I don't have any friends there. I never meet anyone I really like. Thank God for books. I've been into J.D. Salinger, and I think I want to write my own short stories. I mentioned that to Evan, and he said if I wrote anything, he'd illustrate it. But the stuff I'm thinking of writing is like personal stuff. Like I would want to write it for a huge audience, but I wouldn't want Evan to ever see it. Or my mom, or Dad. Or anyone in my school, or my old school. I have this fantasy, though, of writing hundreds of short stories. I want to write the same story over and over but with different faces and different names. And they all end sadly. I know that writing hundreds of short stories is a lot of work, but that's the fantasy. I just have to start with one. I think that would be a good resolution for me this year. Story number one of an eventual hundreds. Maybe they can be published after my death.

Every time I decide to just give up on boys, seeing Evan again makes me rethink it. Look, if I grow old and have lots of cats and write my hundreds of stories, that's still pretty awesome. But if I'm going to date, I hope it's with someone at least like Evan. He's been hanging out with me since I got back here for vacation. We had a long talk tonight, which is, like, rare. We never do that, but I told him about some stuff about my parents and my mom, and it was kinda deep. He wants to help so bad, but what can you do? He's sweet, though. I wish I could bring him back with me. Maybe I'll share one or two of my stories with him.

By the time Lucy turned to the next blank page, she'd decided he deserved some kind of explanation. Whatever happened, she'd just tell him everything. He deserved that much.

Lucy turned off the lights and crawled into bed, and she felt a little calmer, a little more tired. She felt a little bit like thirteen-year-old Lucy. She fell asleep quickly.

Lucy spent the next full day attached to her phone, waiting for a call or text from Evan, trying to muster up the strength to make the call herself. She went over scripts in her mind of what she could say. *Do I apologize? Exactly* what *am I apologizing for? Do I tell him right out that there's a lot I have to tell him? Do I do it over the phone? Can I write an e-mail, so he can't interrupt, so I don't have to see him? Will I chicken out if I try to do it in person?*

She did write, and rewrite, an e-mail. She wrote from the gut in her diary to figure out what she wanted to say. She rationalized the idea of just leaving without a good-bye. It was an easy rationalization. But it was the fact that this was so immensely difficult for her that made Lucy realize she needed to do it. She gave it another night.

Are you free? Lucy finally texted Evan on New Year's Eve, the day before she was flying back. She would do it in person. She would start with "I'm sorry" and she'd let her mouth do the rest of the work. This was not a job for her brain. *Yes*, Evan replied.

Evan met Lucy outside her house twenty minutes later, and they started walking down the hill. Away from the downtown area and toward the ocean. He looked so goofy with his knit hat, and his semismile. It was so hard to stay angry at Evan. Even after everything that had happened between them, she felt like they could look at each other and start giggling. But she couldn't just put this behind them. He deserved to know everything.

They walked in silence for a bit as Lucy tried to figure out what to say. They crossed the fence to the beach, which was understandably empty, what with the cold air and ocean winds. It was cloudy out, a light gray sky. Despite the frigid temperature, it smelled like summer.

"I'm sorry, Evan," Lucy finally said as they walked along the boardwalk, and almost immediately started to cry but fought it back. "I'm really, really sorry. I am so messed up, you have no idea. I'm sorry I dragged you into it."

"You didn't drag me into anything, Lucy," Evan said, and put his arm around her. "I had an awesome time with you. Seriously."

"I didn't want to end things that way," Lucy said.

"I didn't, either."

"No, I mean I at least have to talk to you. We need to really talk." And this was the point of no return. "I haven't been honest with you."

Evan stopped walking and looked at her like she didn't even need to say anything, like he could just read it all in her eyes. Lucy looked down.

"It's just not easy for me to live these two lives in these two places, and the biggest thing in my life, you, I'm only here a couple of weeks each year for. I have this whole other life."

"Lucy—"

"I haven't been honest, because I look up to you *so much*," Lucy said carefully, as if she'd prepared the statement. "I feel inferior to you."

"That's ridiculous, Lucy. You're not at all inferior to me," Evan said, and Lucy knew he wanted to just forget the fight and move on, too, but she had more to tell. "It's the opposite. I *wish* I could be as open and honest with myself as you are—"

"*Please*," Lucy said, and Evan stopped talking. "Can I just say what I need to say?"

Evan nodded once.

"Things haven't been good for me this year," Lucy said quietly. "I was kicked out of my house. Things have been chaos since I got back last year. They still are."

Evan opened his mouth and tried to interrupt, and Lucy knew he was scared and didn't want to hear it, but she kept going.

"My mom started seeing someone new. I guess that's what started it," Lucy said, feeling distant as she spoke, like she was out of her own body. "I didn't like him. *Bill*. And he didn't like me. This guy was a serious asshole, and I tried to explain what he was really like to my mom, and she didn't want to hear it. And I don't even know what happened from there, but she picked him, basically. I mean, that's the short version. She chose this new guy over me, and we basically fell apart from there. Things were uneasy, but I dunno. I always feel uneasy." Lucy looked at Evan now. "I think that's one of my problems with you—you make me feel too stable sometimes, and, like, I'm not used to that. It's hard for me to deal with it. They kicked me out."

Evan looked pale and angry. She continued.

"It gets worse. There was a guy, too. Ian. I was kind of dating him. I kind of am, still."

Evan stopped at a bench and sat down. "Okay. I get it," he said, and sounded beaten.

"No," Lucy said, pained. "There's more. I was with Ian, and we did things, stuff you wouldn't like. The smoking and drinking. And worse things."

"Lucy, okay, I get it. Stop, please."

"I'm not a virgin, either. We had sex." Evan turned his head away from her, but she moved into his sight, tears falling now. "I need to get it all out, Evan. I'm sorry. I had to tell you because if I don't say it now, then I never will. I don't want to lie to you!"

But she'd been lying the whole time. She was never his. Lucy felt like her heart was ready to stop beating. She felt like scum. She'd smiled for him all week. They'd been closer than ever before, and she was *lying*—she was planets away from him. She kissed him when she was in an intimate relationship with another guy, when she knew Evan would never have kissed her had he known. She felt evil. She *was* the evil succubus Lucy. Even as she spoke, she wanted to scrub his brain clean so he'd forget everything she was saying.

Lucy grabbed Evan's coat. "It wasn't right," she said, starting to plead with him, seeing the judgment forming. "My summer wasn't right. It was crazy. I'm not proud of it."

Evan turned to her with a blank look on his face. She was crying now.

"I'm young, Evan. I'm a kid. We have so much growing up to do. Both of us. I need to rein myself in. I know that," she continued. "And you need to run and fall and know pain and get back up. You need to make mistakes, too."

"What?" Evan looked at her as if he'd forgotten where he was. "What's with all this *we*? *You* messed this up. This is all a mess."

"Of course it's a mess. I'm a mess," Lucy cried. She reached to touch Evan's cheek, but he softly pushed her hand away. "I didn't mean for any of this. I just wanted to be together, but it's not the right time. I should never have kissed you."

"We could have grown together," Evan said. "I mean, we did. We grew up together."

"It's not the same," Lucy said. She held her hair to her face and looked at her feet. "You're talking about the whole 'completing each other' thing, and I hate that. It's such

291

Hollywood bullshit. We don't complete each other—no two people do. We just highlight what's missing. We're just two incomplete people."

Evan sat in silence while Lucy cried. She nestled into Evan's side and cried into his shoulder. He let her.

"My heart's broken," he said numbly.

"I know," Lucy said. "Mine is, too."

They kissed, softly and repeatedly, Lucy's face once again a mess of tears and makeup, but this time it wasn't the start of a romance. This time it was the end of one.

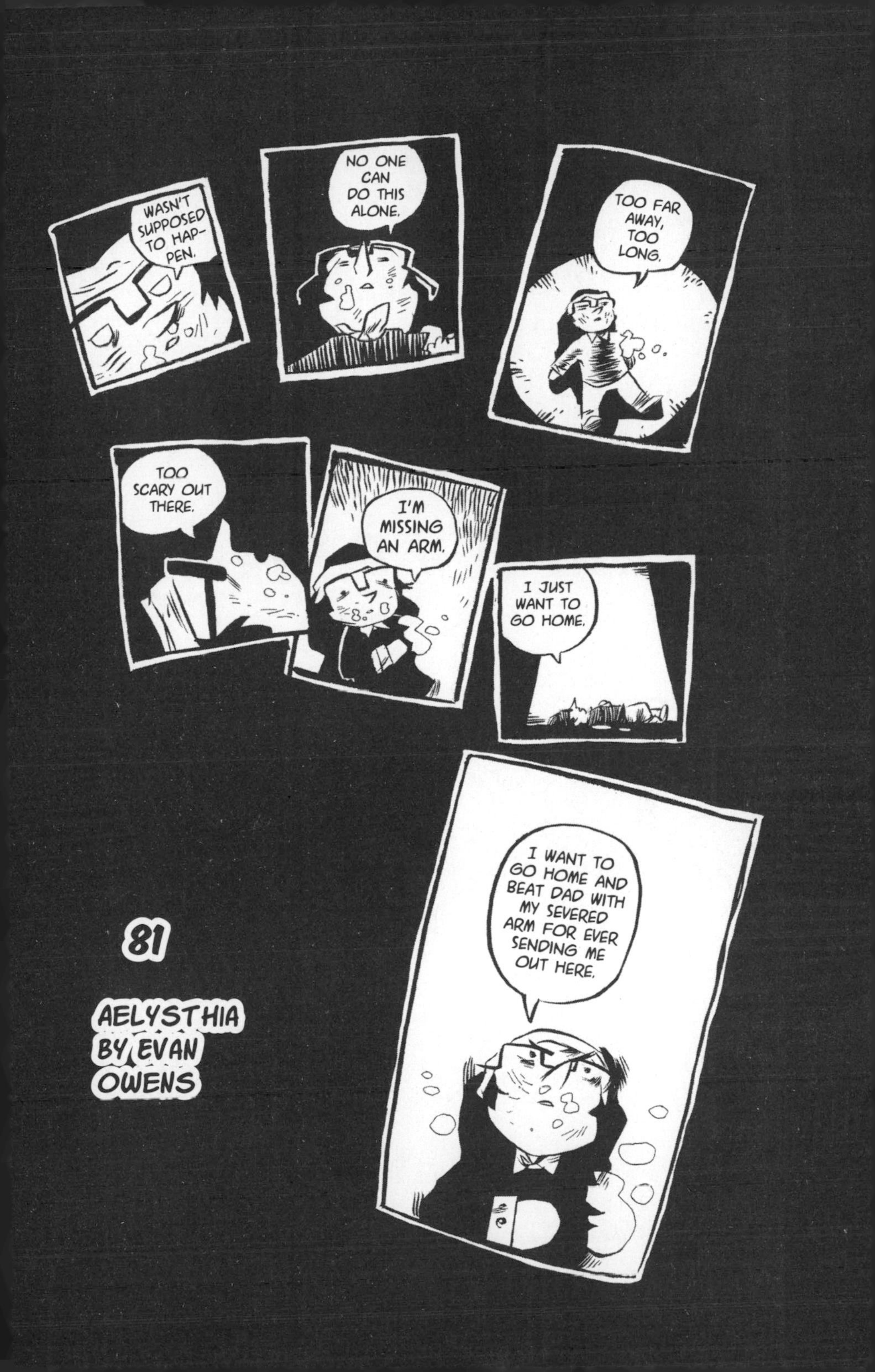
WASN'T SUPPOSED TO HAP-PEN.
NO ONE CAN DO THIS ALONE.
TOO FAR AWAY, TOO LONG.
TOO SCARY OUT THERE.
I'M MISSING AN ARM.
I JUST WANT TO GO HOME.
I WANT TO GO HOME AND BEAT DAD WITH MY SEVERED ARM FOR EVER SENDING ME OUT HERE.
81
AELYSTHIA BY EVAN OWENS

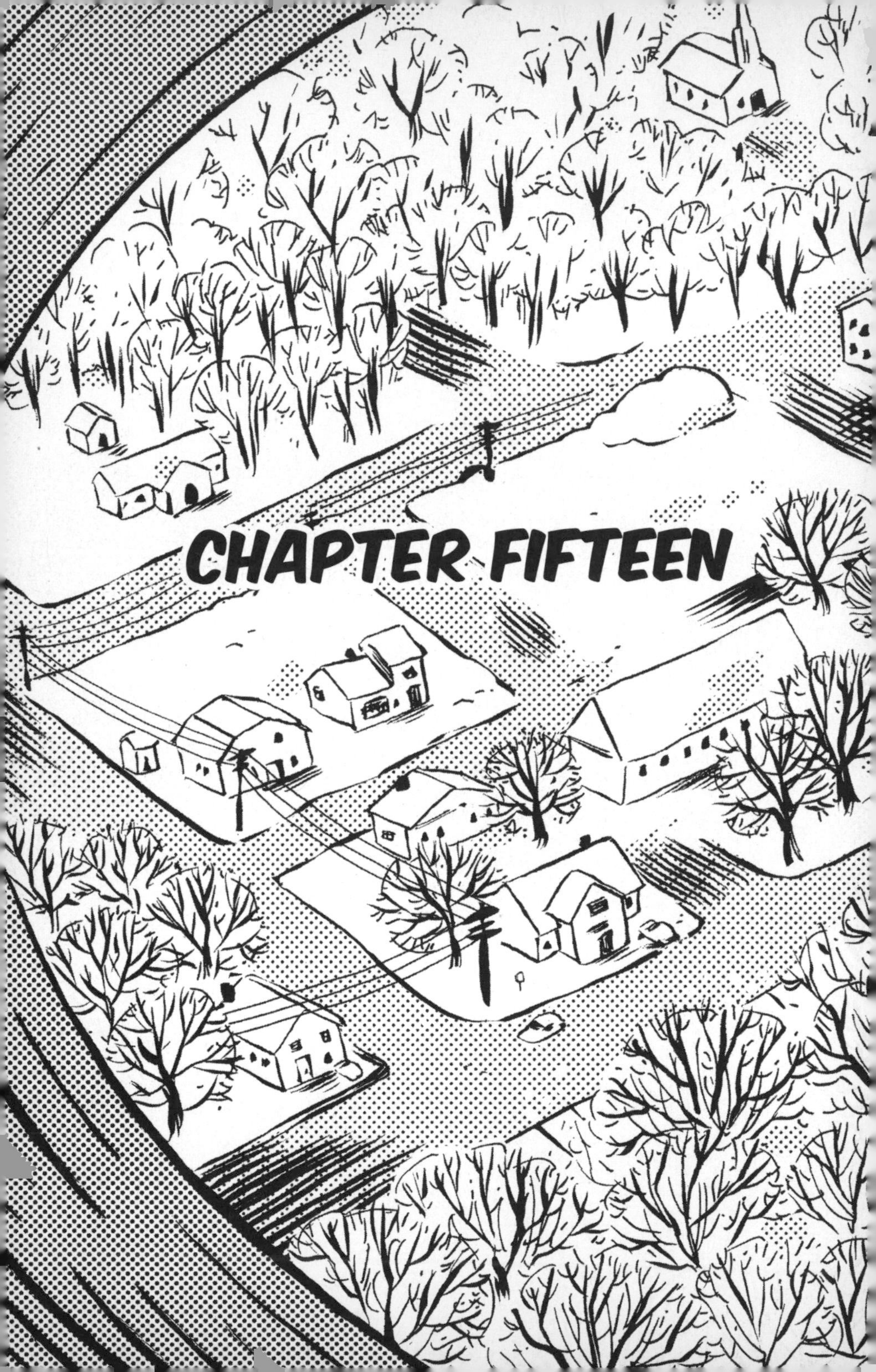
CHAPTER FIFTEEN

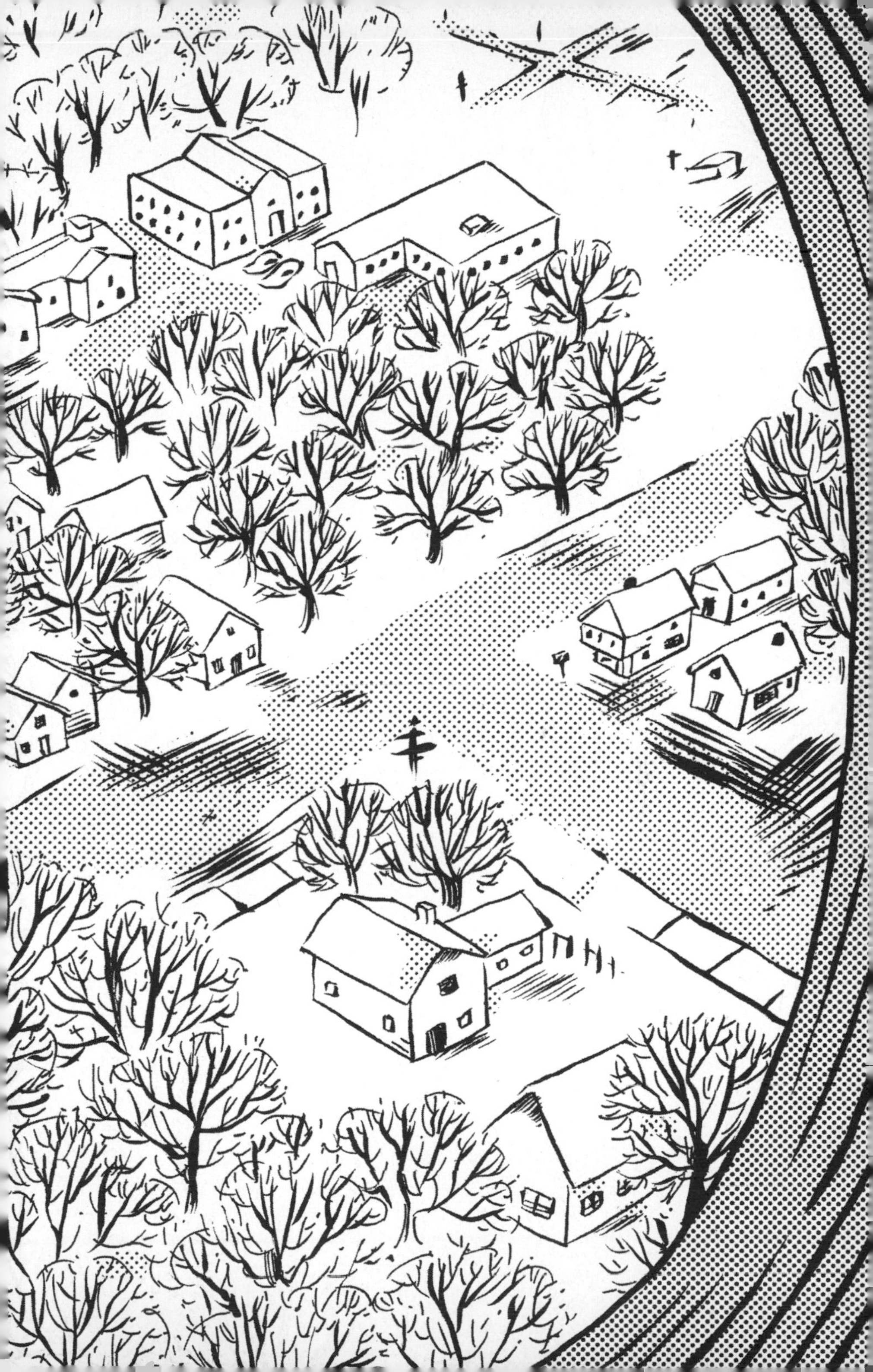

HANG ON TO YOUR EGO

Lucy felt crushingly alone as she sat in the waiting area for gate D-26. She felt sick from eating at a greasy burger place. She had felt sick before and she shouldn't have eaten anything, but her dad had dropped her off too early and there was nothing else to do. Lucy sat lifeless with a twisted frown on her face, looking at strangers' feet as the airport played a string of depressing songs from the seventies. To top it off, they finally played something moderately upbeat, and it was "I Want to Hold Your Hand" by the Beatles and it depressed Lucy even more. She was sure at this point some harsh joke was being played on her; someone, somewhere, was laughing. She was thinking about Evan, doubting every action she'd taken during the past two weeks. She simultaneously doubted that she should ever have kissed him and that she should ever have broken up with him. She should never have left her house and she should never have left his side.

Because now she had nothing. She had this plane to catch, to fly her away to nothing good.

She looked up at the other passengers waiting with her to pass the time. Only the absolute most annoying would be seated next to her on the flight. The most obvious was the young couple with the baby. Sure, the baby looked sweet now, but put him in that tight little space for hours, put that plane in the air, where his ears would pop every few minutes and there was nowhere to move, and it would be only a matter of a very short time before he exploded in tears and screams. That's if she didn't beat him to it. There was the annoying eleven-year-old girl who hadn't stopped talking for the last fifteen minutes. Lucy was sure she'd finally run out of breath and keel over midsentence, and that she'd never get to find out just what it was that Justine said that made Kelly so mad she threw a five-subject notebook at her.

Ten minutes later, Lucy stood in the slow-moving line to board the plane. Claustrophobic. She could feel someone's breath on the back of her neck. Flying was the worst thing ever. She had to do it twice a year, so she was used to it by now. She knew all the sounds to listen for and what they meant. She had her breathing exercises. There was little preparation she could do, though, for when the plane hit

a flock of birds or got struck by lightning or ran out of gas midflight and dropped to the ground in a hunk of flaming wreckage. And that might be the cleanest, most positive outcome. Every ounce of her wanted to run away or scream *This isn't right, I'm not supposed to be here!* She felt like a prisoner, bound and gagged and forced on a long, blazing-hot walk to hell, jabbed repeatedly with pitchforks by a pair of scantily clad Minotaur demons. She had boarded planes regularly for years now with it predecided in her mind that there would be fire, water, or a Gila monster. And so she boarded planes in a state of panic and faintness, and usually with a fair amount of perspiration.

The couple with the baby was two rows ahead of where Lucy was seated. She made brief eye contact with the young boy and his eyes unmistakably threatened a loud and uncomfortable journey for them both. Lucy sat down by the window in row eleven, just ahead of the left wing of the plane. A clean-cut man in his forties stashed his luggage overhead, sat down by Lucy, and took out his laptop and started pecking away. Not bad, as flight-buddies go. And then the sniffles started. *Sniff. Sniff. Wipe. Sniff.* She was seated next to Satan himself. The plane was packed; this was her family for the next few hours. Lucy leaned her head against the window.

The tiniest decision can change everything was floating around in her mind. Lucy wondered what she could change. Her problem was she didn't really believe it was possible. In her head she did, in her head she knew she had choices, but it was this gut feeling, this thing deep, deep inside her, in her heart and in her flesh, that just knew it would all turn to shit.

It was that same voice that was laughing at her when the Beatles came on in the airport waiting area. The same voice that decided she was broken, a failure, that she'd always be painfully shy, that her life would never amount to anything. The voice that had decided that it could never work out with Evan and that he'd never understand her, that he was unable to reach his potential. That he was stuck as a mama's boy.

Lucy played devil's advocate, though, in honor of Mister Sniffles sitting beside her. Things she could change: For one, she could choose not to go home. She could land in Georgia and take another flight somewhere else. Somewhere far. She could see what was available and choose then. Of course, she didn't have the money for the flight. Or for when she landed. She'd be stuck and homeless, and probably turning tricks for food money by the end of the week. She could stay with Tess. Although Tess had an alcoholic, abusive mom and lived in the middle of the ghetto. Maybe she and Tess could get jobs and rent an apartment together. They'd probably still end up in the ghetto, though. Two mess-ups living together, a pair of bad influences, how long could it be before they turned into coke whores, hitting the streets and turning tricks for drug money? She could break up with Ian. Definitely break up with Ian. She'd rather be alone than with him. She could confront Bill, New Dad. Tell him to get out of her family. She could break his nose. She could go to jail. *Hi, Evan, hope you're making some mistakes, miss you.* She'd need a home—that was first. Not with Ian. And preferably not with Tess. And if not with Mom, then somewhere. She thought more about what she could do. She needed a plan, like Evan had plans. Her first goal was to have a plan by the time they landed. It would be like her hundred stories from her diary entry; she had to start with the first one. Not that she ever wrote that.

The plane gained speed and soon found its way off the ground. Lucy felt faint but continued to look out the window. Everything began to get smaller. New England looked like Charlie's winter town. All the little houses and cars shrank beneath her. She knew what was down there, all the dirt in the snow, and the murderous Joeys. Still, it looked pretty and clean from that vantage. From up in the sky, everything looked perfect.

When Lucy landed, it was dreary out. And cold. No one greeted her at the airport. Lucy waited at the luggage terminal with all the reunited families and couples, everyone embracing and jovial. Even the other lone travelers were already on their cell phones. Everyone had someone, somewhere. Lucy had no one. She had herself, dark cloud included. She watched her two weeks' worth of luggage slowly roll out like a piss-poor prize on a game show. Lucy dragged her suitcases and bags along and called a taxi and waited in the drizzle outside.

Lucy's cabdriver annoyed her with inane questions. *Live here? Where are you coming from? Out to see the family? Some weather, huh?* She kept her answers short and watched the scenery pass by like a Flintstones background. Country, buildings, ghetto, repeat. She thought about school. She had only months to prove she was worthy of getting into college.

She could do well. She could study. She was smart. This past year wasn't her—that's what she wanted to prove. And maybe someday she could show Evan. *See? I turned things around. Everything's okay. I'm the same old Lucy.*

Lucy arrived at what used to be her home and braced herself for whatever might answer the door. She felt like she had when she was boarding the plane — tense, hot, flushed, and dizzy — but she tried to swallow it. She had made up her mind that Bill was going to answer the door with her mom and their new adopted kid. She didn't know what she'd do then, but it would be bad, and she knew her family was done for and that her mom hated her—she knew everything was doomed here. But those were just thoughts. She had choices to make, whatever the outcome.

Lucy stood on the sidewalk for a moment, with a cold wind and the taxicab behind her, and her mom's car in the driveway beside her. She took several large paces to the front door, held her breath, and knocked, absolutely terrified of whatever would come next.

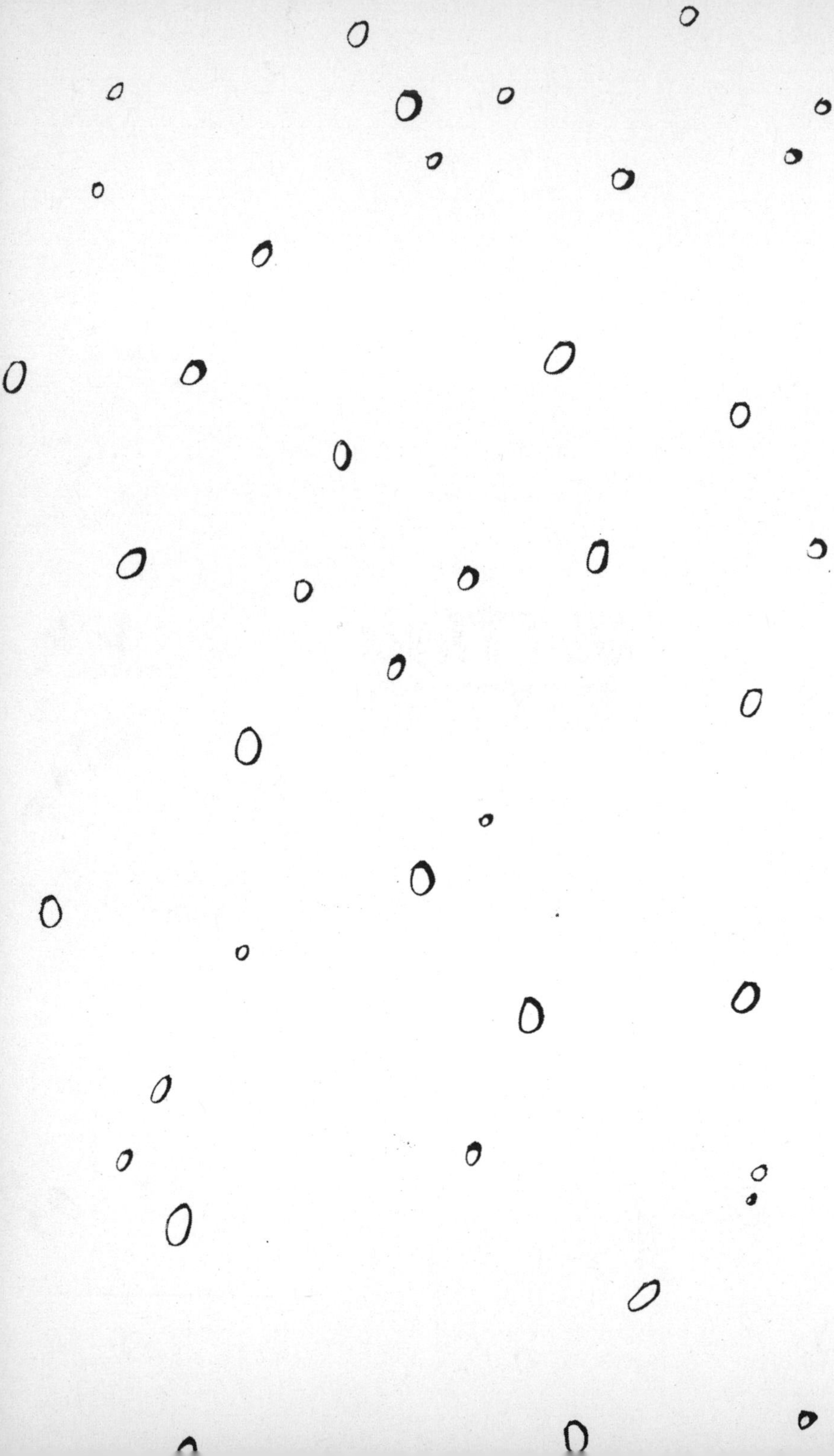

GETTING
BETTER

ONE YEAR LATER

Evan trudged through the snow alone, Nerd Rock blaring in his ears. Fountains of Wayne, the Apples in Stereo, Harvey Danger. He kept a brisk pace, which was no small feat as he juggled his coffee, a large portfolio, and his laptop. It was snowing lightly and it was December again, nighttime, and the sky was dark. It had been almost a year now since he broke up with Lucy, and he hadn't heard from her since. He thought a lot about her, but he didn't have any eureka moments, no answers sprung to him in the middle of the night, and he never figured out what he could have done differently to fix things. His eureka moment was more of a long journey. He was happy with where he'd ended up, though.

A strong wind blew and pulled out a page of art from his portfolio and into the street. Evan started after it but his hands were full, so he looked for anyone who could help him out; no one seemed to be paying any attention, though. He stepped into the road.

"Being the great egoist I am," Evan had stated at the beginning of his valedictory speech, "I've crafted this as a memo to myself, and hopefully you will find some use in it as well." He took the speech seriously and had a lot of trouble writing it. He still felt like he was emotionally in a tailspin after a late winter spent more or less in a quiet and reflective funk. It wasn't until he was accepted into Brown that his father relaxed. With the higher spirits at home, Evan was able to really excel for the remainder of the year. The first draft of his speech was an absurd stream of consciousness that he really did write as a letter to himself, and he asked himself what he honestly thought about going to college, about leaving his family, about what he wanted with these next years of his life. He was amazed to see how much of it connected to his time with Lucy. In the end he wrote a lot about change. He wrote about academia and its place in life, and how it needs to be balanced with adventure, and art, and fun. It became easy when he wrote it this way, when he made it personal. He wished Lucy had been there to see him read it.

Things had been great until Evan decided in the summer that he was, in fact, not going to Brown University. His speech had rung truer than his life did. Again, it wasn't a eureka moment, just a gut feeling that walked with him, that went against every thought he had, but it was an exciting feeling that he couldn't ignore. He told Gram before anyone else.

"It's not easy to hear," she told him as they played cards after dinner, "but sometimes your family are the last people to have your best interests in mind." It *wasn't* easy to hear. Evan had pretty much guided his life on the principle that his family knew what was right. *They're my parents,* he'd thought. *They know what's right and what's wrong and what's worth doing.* "Your mom and dad raised you to do what they know is right, and they've taught you what they learned growing up. Some of it is what they were raised with and some of it is what they learned on their own, but, Evan, you're eighteen now, you're going to college. What they're teaching you is what they know, what they feel safe with. And that's meeting the right girl in college, having a family, and becoming a lawyer or a doctor." Evan listened carefully. Gram spoke like there was something to decode, like this was something important. "They want for you what worked for them. But they aren't in tune with what's going to work for you. And that's what happens when you go away to school—you leave your family and you find your own path, and you're that age now. You need to trust what's in here." Gram placed a jittery finger over her heart. "Or, Evan, you can always trust what's here," and she placed a finger on Evan's *Gram* tattoo.

Evan was lost in thought but almost had his drawing in hand when a taxi slammed on its brakes and laid on the horn. The cabdriver was swearing in some language, Evan was sure. He looked up at the taxi and thought, *This is a new experience.* Evan picked up the portfolio and hopped back onto the sidewalk. A man nearby was working a hot dog cart and caught the scene. He shrugged his shoulders. Evan shrugged his, too, and they shared a moment. *A New York moment?* Evan thought. He breathed in the air and smiled. The streets were busy with students everywhere. It was hard to feel lonely with all the activity. It was nighttime, but the streets were bright. Manhattan was lit up for Christmas.

It was Marshall who had tried to talk Evan into coming to New York with him and Tim.

"I'd like to, believe me," Evan had said on the phone while he was grounded for the summer. He was forbidden from doing anything that didn't involve finding work. He thought back to the excitement he had felt imagining some kind of life in New York with Lucy. It felt like a fantasy, though, not something a person can just wake up and do one morning. "Everything I know is here."

"But everything you *want* is there," Marshall said, and he was right. He was going to be leaving it all behind in months, one way or another. Marshall thought Evan just didn't want to disappoint his family, or face his dad, who would not enjoy this news. He wouldn't be able to get into another school. He'd have to take a year off. It was so *un-Evan.*

"Think of Tim," Marshall said. "He had to tell his family and friends that he was gay. That he wasn't going to be settling down with a nice girl or doing any of the things they all expected him to do. He had to change everything they knew so he could be happy with himself. All you have to do is tell them you want to go to New York instead of Rhode Island."

Mom? Dad? I'm an artist.

Evan knew that every minute he let pass was going to make his family's reaction that much more severe when he finally told them. His anxieties were so much more than this little personal choice, than choosing a school or an occupation or doing what made him happy. Evan was going to disappoint everyone in the name of his own happiness. How could he even *be* happy when he was hurting everyone he loved? He weighed everything in his life on a scale, his mom and his dad, his grandmother, his friends, his school and his grades, his talents. Not one item on the scale could make his decision. He couldn't base his life around any one of them. He had to choose what he wanted deep down. He was going to have to break his father's heart, and he did. At least he thought he did, as there were no tears or mournful talks. There was yelling.

"Do you know how much money we put away for this? Do you know the amount of things we did to make sure you got into a good school? Evan, just look at what you've done the past few years. You're gonna throw it all away?"

"I'm not going to throw it away," Evan said, as scared as he'd ever been around his dad. He'd never heard his voice this loud, and he'd never had his face this close. Mom was in the kitchen, too, when this went down, and Evan remembered her saying *No hitting* to his dad, and Evan wondered if he'd really do it. He didn't know. "I just need more time, maybe a year," Evan said, backed against the counter.

"That's as good as quitting, goddamn it!" Dad yelled with an intense amount of eye contact. Evan was miserable over what he saw in his dad's eyes. "Everything we did for you."

Evan cringed with his eyes shut, certain there'd be some kind of violence or something broken or slammed, but Dad yelled and then there was quiet, a lasting quiet. Dad didn't speak with him for the rest of the summer. There was tension and silence. All the love and joy and Christmas movies and cookies were gone. Evan hadn't just faced down his dad, he'd faced down his entire family, the way they'd chosen to raise him. Evan felt like a traitor, an enemy in his own home. He couldn't apologize, and Gram couldn't make any inroads. He'd effectively broken his own family. He didn't even want to fight. He just wanted to make his own decisions.

Shortly before Evan left for New York, his mom had visited him in his room and given him an envelope with money in it.

"I'm not supposed to tell you who this is from," his mom said, closing the door and sitting on his bed to give him the envelope. "He does love you and he wants you to be safe." She could have been lying, trying to protect them both, but Evan chose to believe her. She'd been hurt by the decision, too. He was going away, he was her only child, and the house would be empty now. He was going away from all of his family, not just the ones he lived with. There was an element of the unexpected, of the *what now?* that threw everyone off guard, that made it seem like there was no plan. The Owenses didn't operate well without plans.

Evan reached the library, his heart still racing from his near-death taxi run-in. He loved it here, the vastness of the place. It had an energy that was completely unlike the sleepy libraries he was used to. It was his preferred spot for working on his comic strip. Evan opened his portfolio and took out his latest page of cartoons and his pencils and brush. He had blown movie night with Tim and Marshall to come draw. He liked to be alone to work on his comic sometimes.

Evan had started doing the comic as a way to hold on to Lucy. He thought somewhere in the back of his mind that maybe she'd see it and write him if he posted it online, which he did, in February. He called it *Aelysthia*. Evan and Lucy were the main characters, and he tried his best to capture her voice, although he always felt it was a pale comparison with the real thing. He wanted it to be good. Epic, and funny. He wanted it to be *big*. But it wasn't; it went mostly unnoticed. Lucy never wrote him; the radio silence continued. Evan had known things were too disturbed to try to write her himself, and he'd figured she must have thought the same thing.

When Evan moved to New York with Marshall and Tim, Marshall started "managing" Evan's comics career. His first move as manager was to get Evan to write a group of online artists he respected and to show them his work. Evan had built a small but consistent archive of comics, and his story was starting to take some fun turns. A few of the artists wrote him words of encouragement, although most of them ignored his e-mail completely. Two of them had linked to his comic, though, and suddenly Evan found himself a small but growing fan base. Around October, Evan's comic took a turn. He found he had more to say than he'd ever imagined. Having his own comic was like having someone to talk to, and then it was like having a therapist. The comic wasn't just stuff to draw, or something he could impress Lucy with, and it was no longer what he thought she'd want to read. It became personal. It was his outlet. Evan learned the joy of self-expression. He fell in love with art.

Evan leaned back in his chair with a satisfied sigh and drank his coffee. He placed his iPod on the table and put in his earphones. He was around people, he felt a part of something, but it was quiet, too. The city was odd because even with the insane number of people around, Evan could feel lonely. Maybe because of all the people. It felt promising, too, like you could meet someone anywhere at any time. Maybe he'd meet some New York lifer who'd be charmed by his cluelessness and show him around. Or someone who'd just moved here like him, and she'd be thrilled to find someone else from a small town. He could meet an artist. Marshall said the city was a magnet to artists. He'd have someone to run around the world's largest playground and explore with. It never happened, though. Evan spent his time with Tim and Marshall or alone, wearing his melancholy like a coat to keep him warm.

Evan liked to people-watch while he procrastinated, and he was doing that when he spotted someone who was all of those things, a city girl, someone who'd grown up like he had, an artist. It started with a woman's leg fidgeting under the table a few rows away. Her head was buried in a large book and her hair was black with streaks of a purple-fuchsia color. She could be cute. And she was artsy. Evan recognized the book as the third Lord of the Rings volume. She was drowning in books—art books, math? A textbook, so she was a student. And she was reading Lord of the Rings. Evan liked her. She looked up briefly and must have noticed Evan staring, because she did a double take and this time their eyes locked. He recognized the girl as Lucy. She was beautiful. The library disappeared and everyone in it turned dark, and all he could see was her, still and emotionless like a fawn in snow. His heart sped up like it had when the taxi nearly ran him over. Evan's face involuntarily spread into a wide grin. He nearly exploded with all the things he wanted to tell her, and he fought the impulse to leap out of his chair and run to her.

Evan stared, grinning, and Lucy's eyes squinted the way they did when she smiled, when she really smiled.

It's different now, Evan and Lucy both thought.

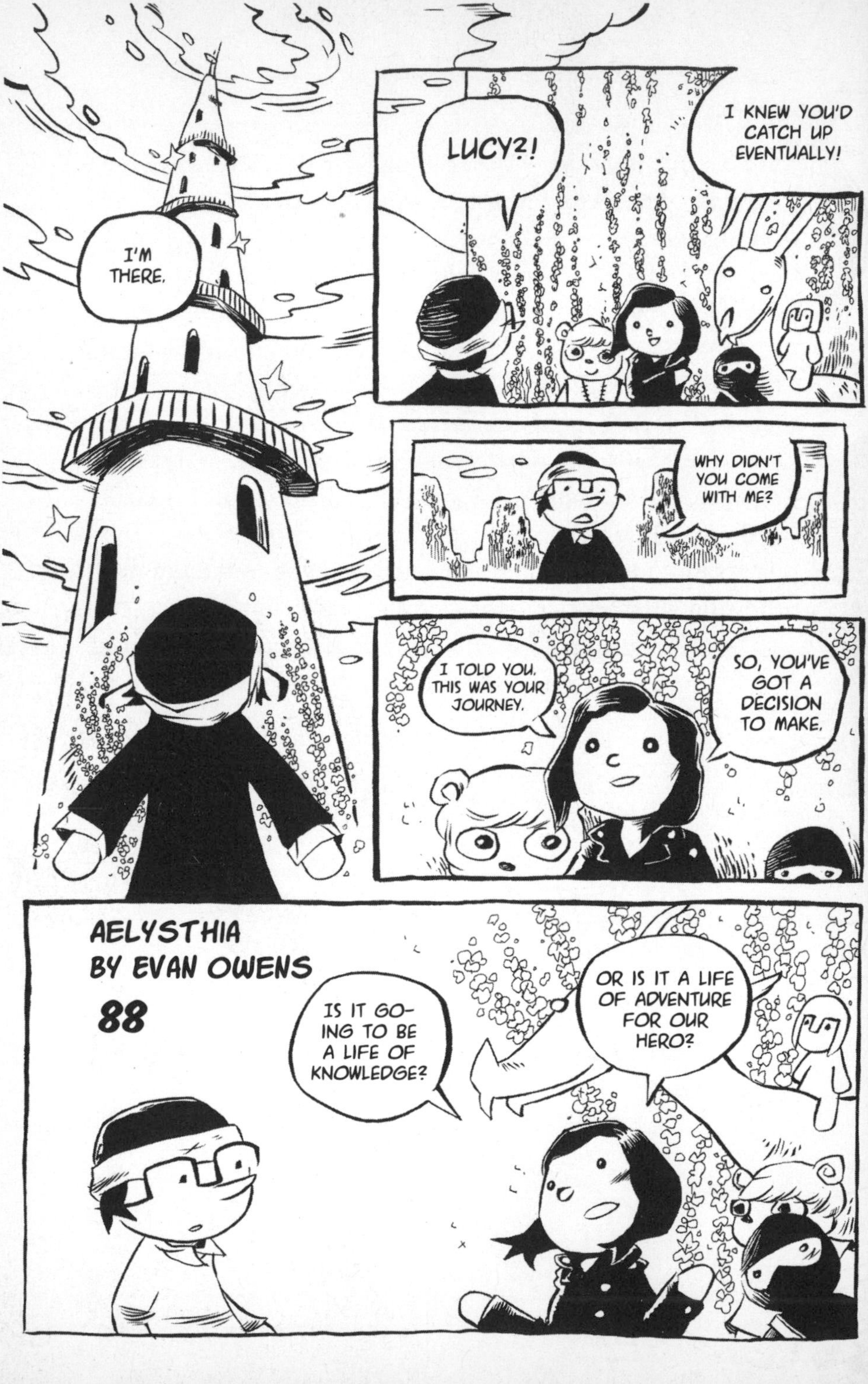
I'M THERE.
LUCY?!
I KNEW YOU'D CATCH UP EVENTUALLY!
WHY DIDN'T YOU COME WITH ME?
I TOLD YOU. THIS WAS YOUR JOURNEY.
SO, YOU'VE GOT A DECISION TO MAKE.
AELYSTHIA
BY EVAN OWENS
88
IS IT GOING TO BE A LIFE OF KNOWLEDGE?
OR IS IT A LIFE OF ADVENTURE FOR OUR HERO?

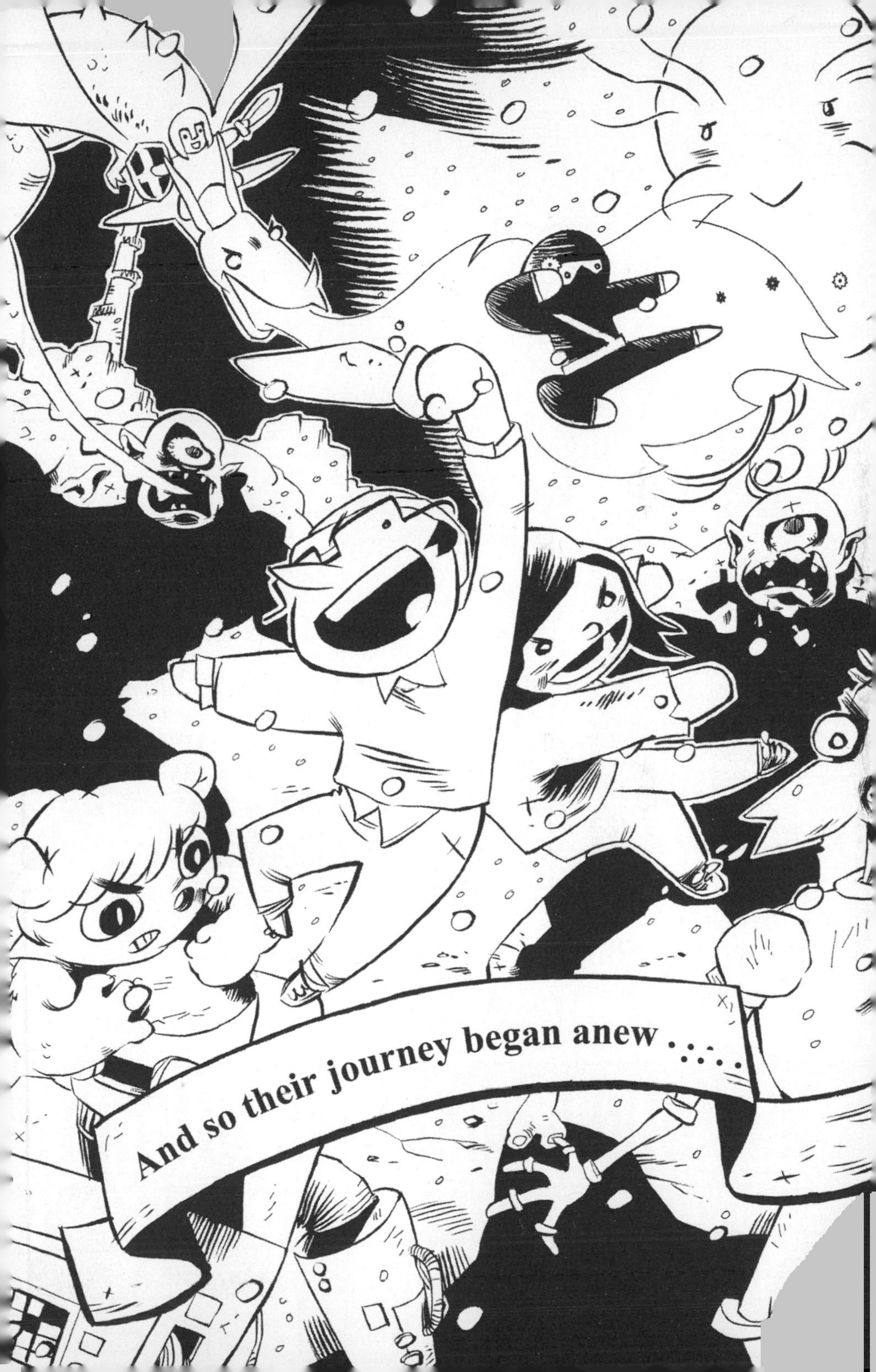
And so their journey began anew . . . . .

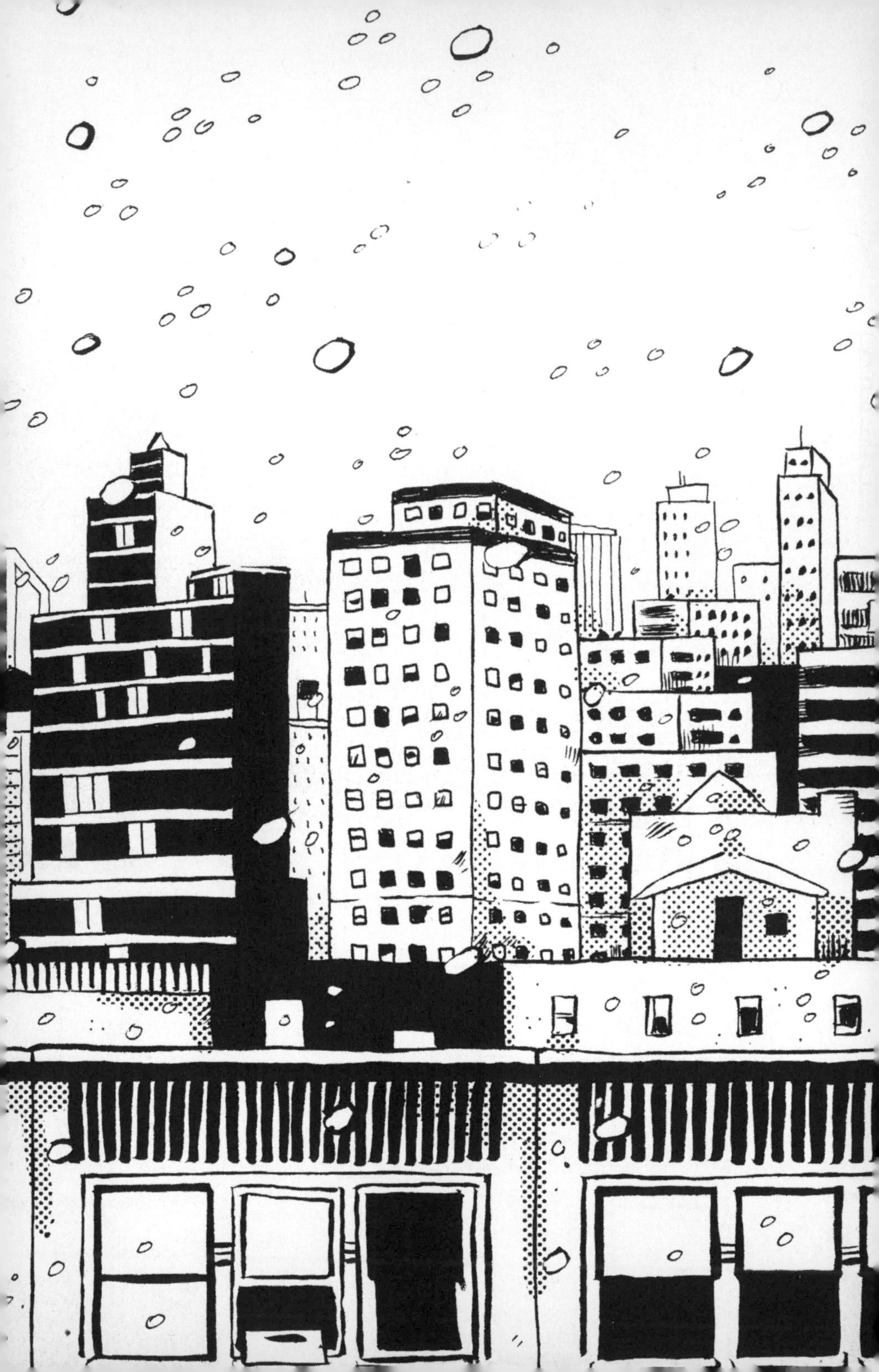

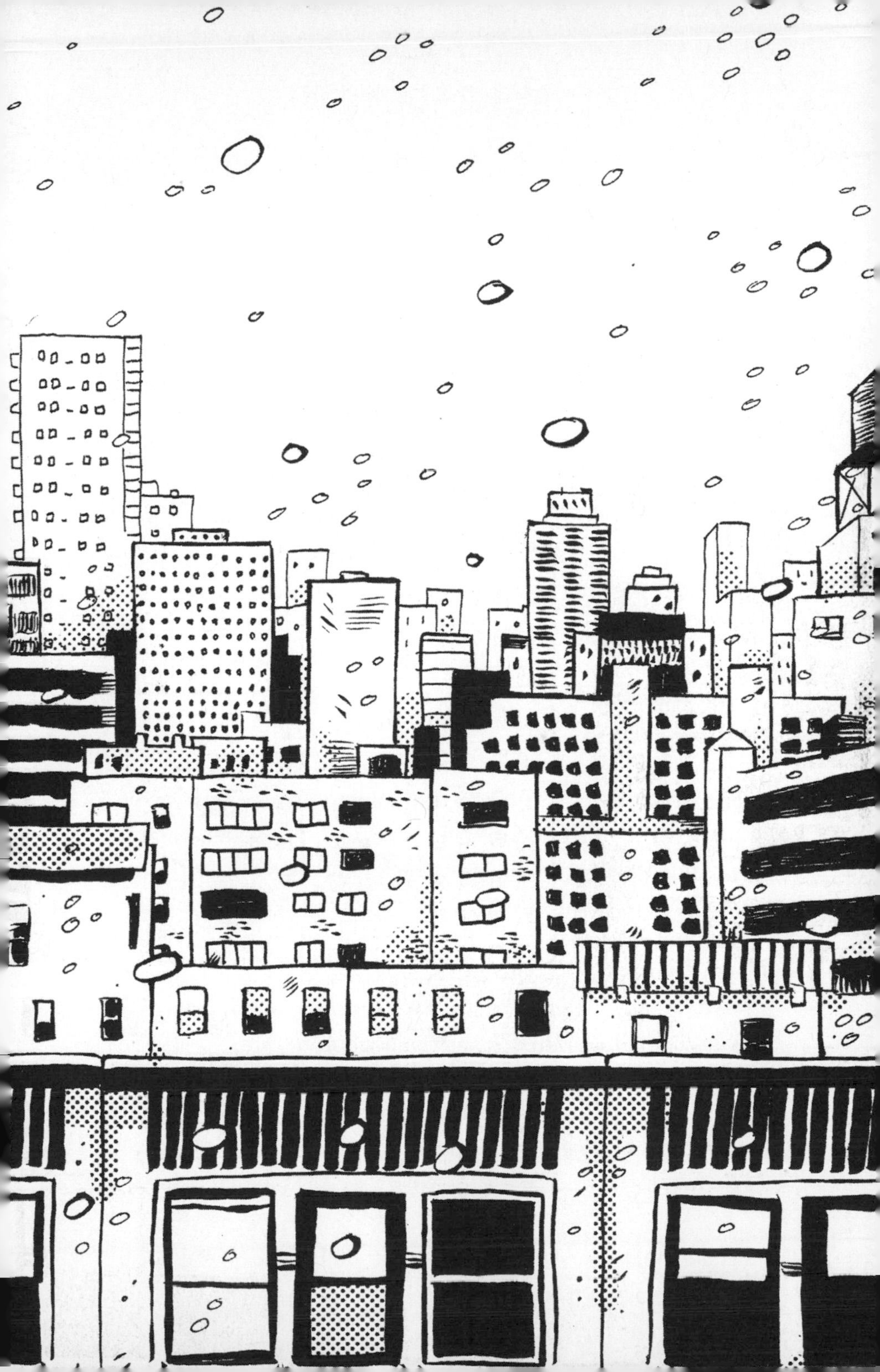

ACKNOWLEDGMENTS

I won't fill up too much space here, but it only feels right to acknowledge a few people who helped inspire this story or helped me while I worked on it. Of course, I want to thank my family, Mom, Mike, Pop and Gram, all my aunts and uncles and cousins — too many to name here, but you know who you are! Elaine Hornby, for being an inspiration in writing this, as well as Jules Bakes — I owe you big time — and my buddy Sara Rhine. I need to thank everyone who listened to me rant and rave: Cori Payne, Bob Jacobsen, Takarra Harrell, Leslie Andrews, Briana Benn. Some other inspirations: Lawrence Degley, Billy Ordynowicz, Mike Attebery, Jack Lilburn. I'd like to thank my agent, Kirby Kim, for working hard on all the stuff I have no brain for.

Thank you to all the Little, Brown folks who have worked on this book with me. Ben Mautner, for the awesome design work and rad cover — we make a good team! Thanks, Alvina Ling and Emma Ledbetter, for reading and offering input, and Victoria Stapleton, Zoe Luderitz, Christine Ma, and everyone else at LBYR for helping to get this book out! An EXTRA SPECIAL THANKS to my wonderful editor, Connie Hsu, for going way above and beyond on this and probably working harder on it than I did. I don't think I could possibly explain how different this book would have been without all her hard work, keen observations, and uncanny insight into my own brain. She seriously knows what I'm thinking before I do. It's scary and it's wonderful.

Thanks to everyone who read and enjoyed *Happyface*. Thanks to all the bloggers and reviewers who said such nice things about that book. I was and am overwhelmed!

And last but certainly not least, thank YOU for reading this.

BONUS SECTION!

HERE'S SOME BEHIND-THE-SCENES FUN STUFF.

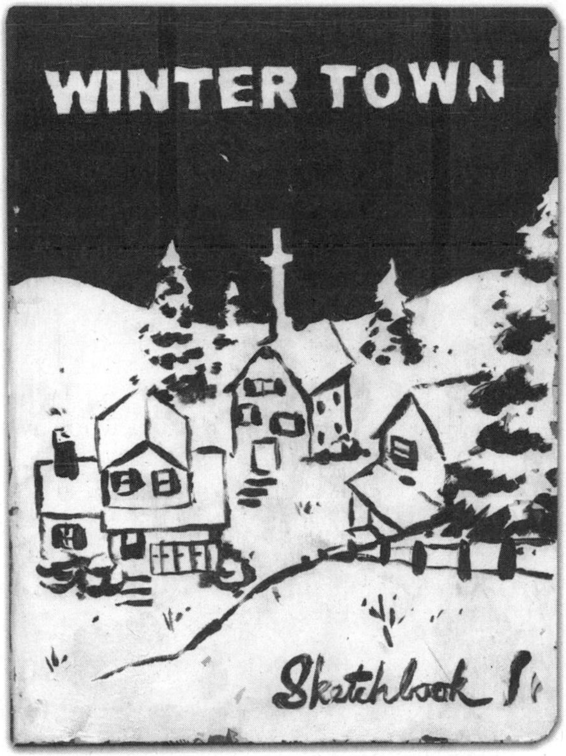
WINTER TOWN
Sketchbook I

Here are a few insights and unused artifacts from the production of *WINTER TOWN*! It's fun for me to share some of this stuff in the extra space I have back here, so I hope you enjoy! Come visit me at www.stephenemond.com for more behind-the-scenes goodies and to say hello, ask any questions, or let me know what you thought of the book.

On to the treasure!

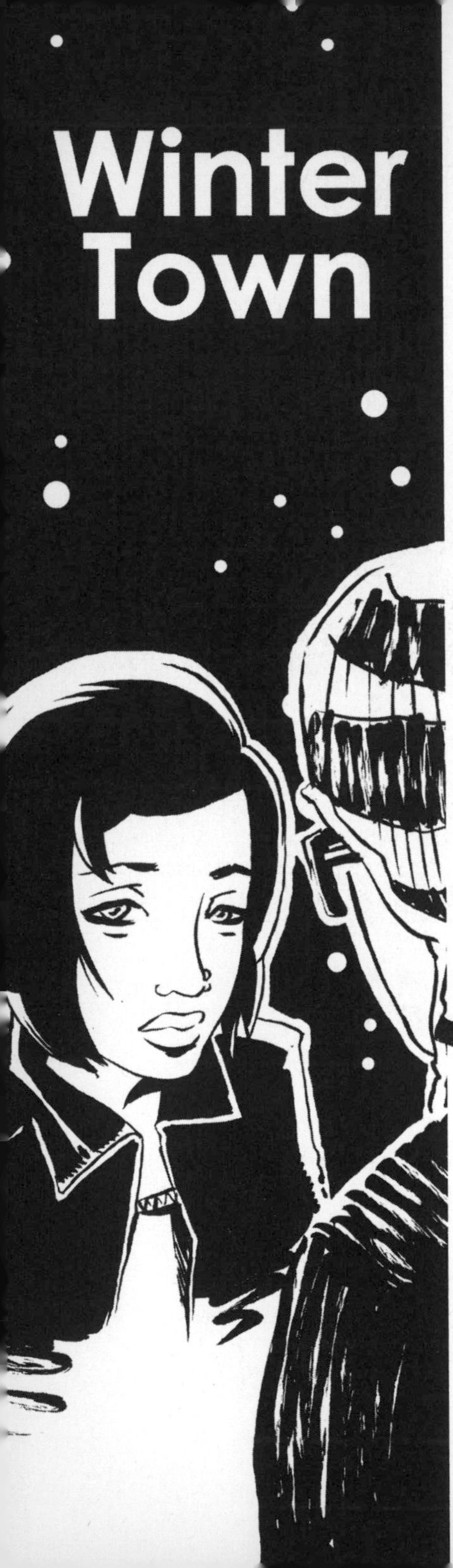
Winter
Town

1 These are some sketches I used to find the characters and to set the tone with the scenery drawings, as well as a few pieces from my original sample pitch.

2 Originally Evan's comics were going to be three-panel strips that would be interspersed throughout chapters. I offered to do an actual Web comic "by" Evan for a year or so around the book release, but my energies were better spent on the book.

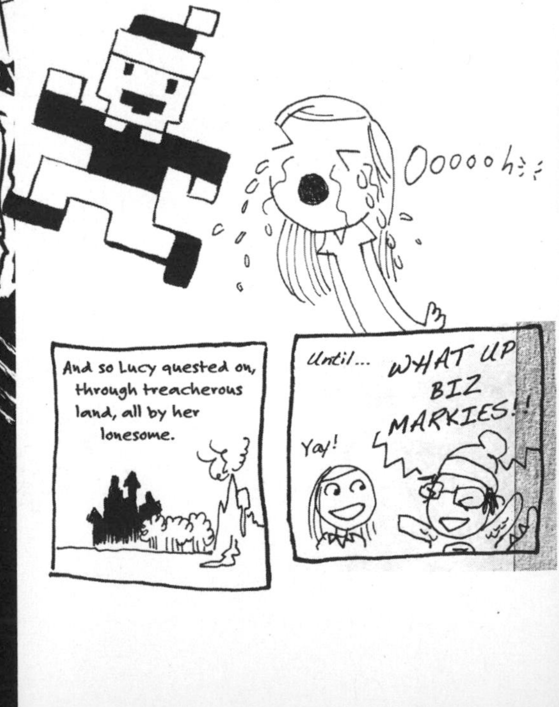
Ooooooh
And so Lucy quested on, through treacherous land, all by her lonesome.
Until...
WHAT UP BIZ MARKIES!!
Yay!

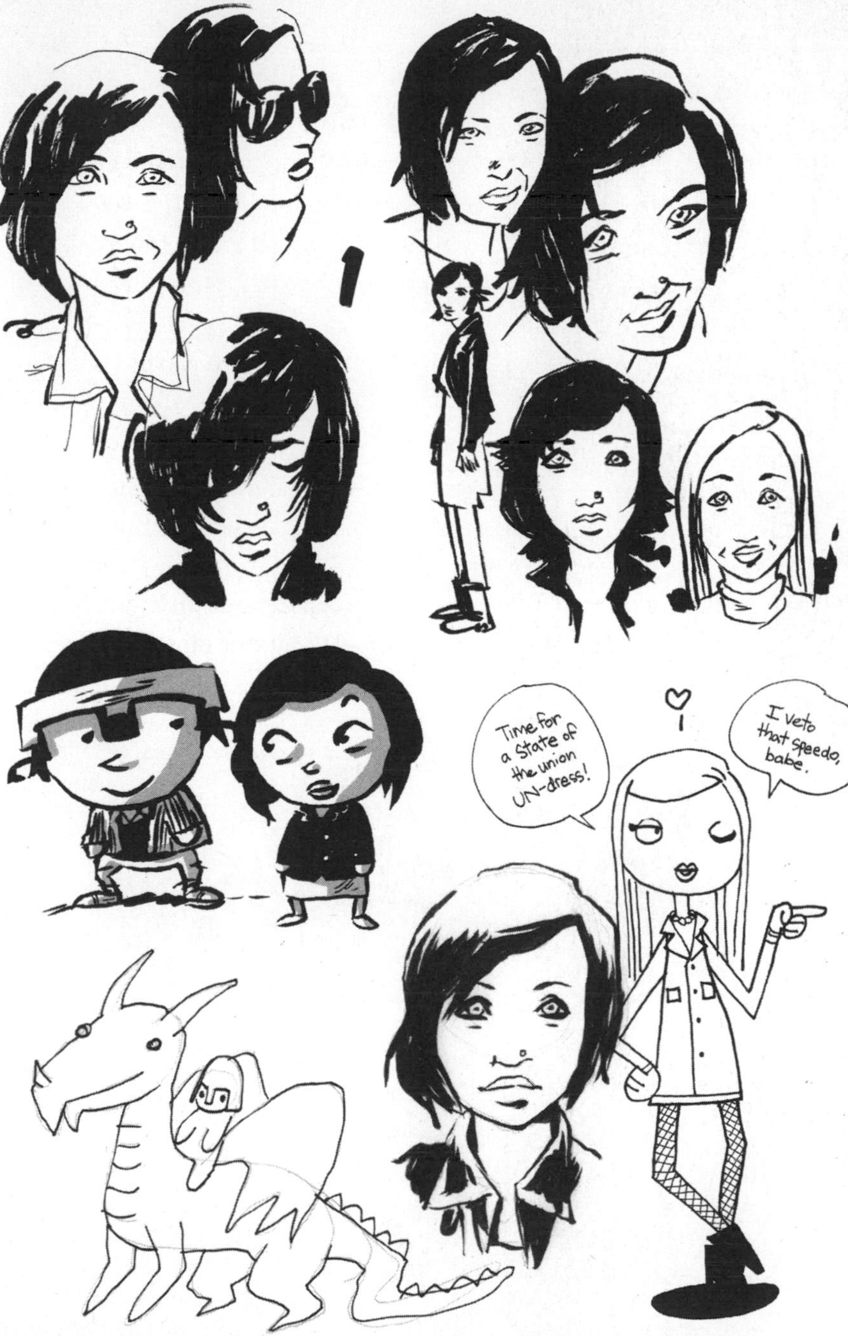
Time for a State of the union UN-dress!
I veto that speedo, babe.

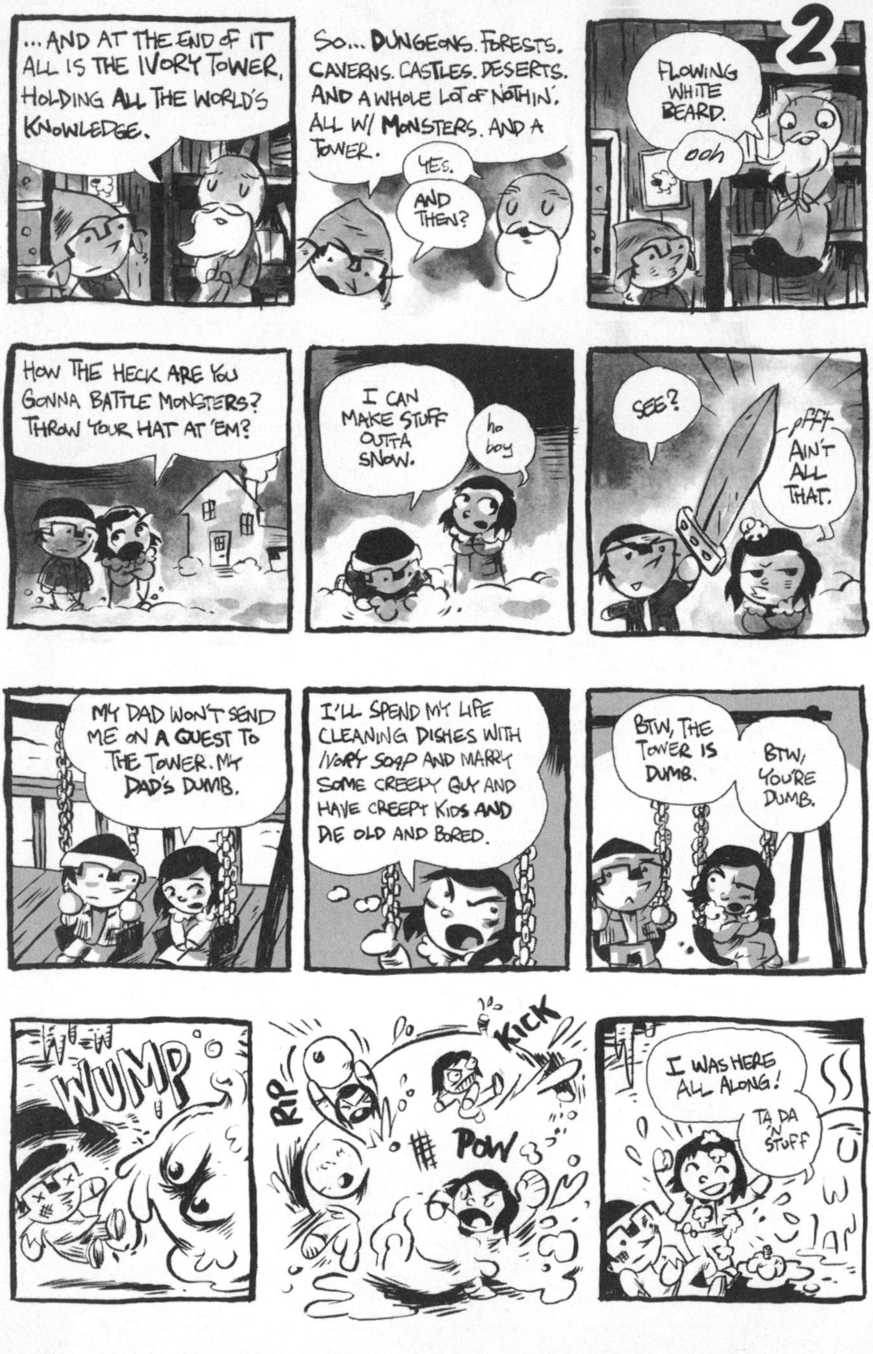
2
...AND AT THE END OF IT ALL IS THE IVORY TOWER, HOLDING ALL THE WORLD'S KNOWLEDGE.
SO... DUNGEONS. FORESTS. CAVERNS. CASTLES. DESERTS. AND A WHOLE LOT OF NOTHIN'. ALL W/ MONSTERS. AND A TOWER.
YES.
AND THEN?
FLOWING WHITE BEARD.
ooh
HOW THE HECK ARE YOU GONNA BATTLE MONSTERS? THROW YOUR HAT AT 'EM?
I CAN MAKE STUFF OUTTA SNOW.
ho boy
SEE?
pfft AIN'T ALL THAT.
MY DAD WON'T SEND ME ON A QUEST TO THE TOWER. MY DAD'S DUMB.
I'LL SPEND MY LIFE CLEANING DISHES WITH IVORY SOAP AND MARRY SOME CREEPY GUY AND HAVE CREEPY KIDS AND DIE OLD AND BORED.
BTW, THE TOWER IS DUMB.
BTW, YOU'RE DUMB.
WUMP
RIP
KICK
POW
I WAS HERE ALL ALONG!
TA DA 'N STUFF

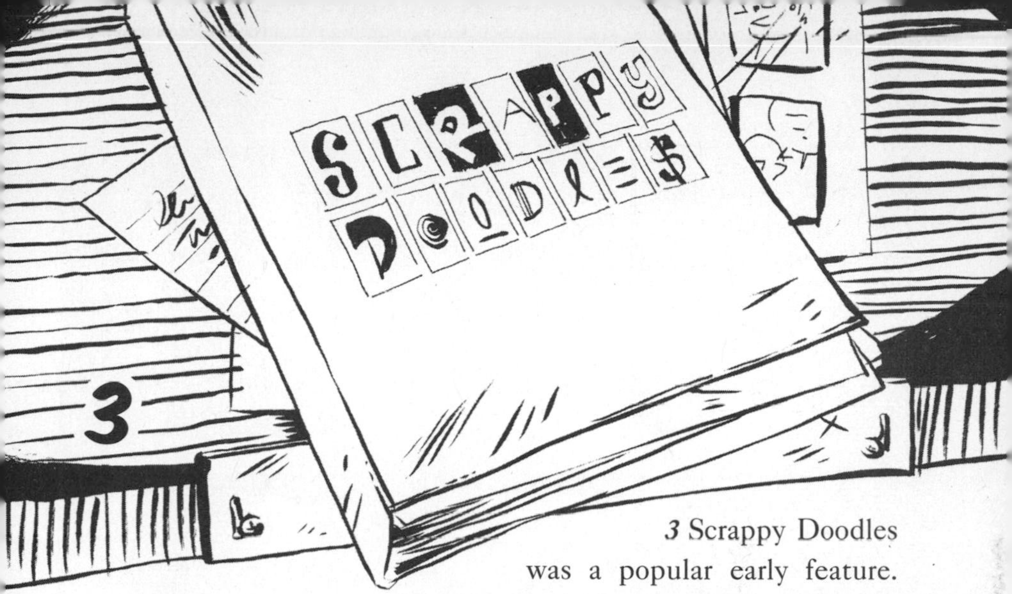
SCRAPPY
DOODLES
3

3 Scrappy Doodles was a popular early feature. Evan and Lucy were supposed to communicate midyear only through this scrapbook, through letters and photos and comics. I did six sample pages, but ultimately they felt redundant and did not offer enough that the main story didn't cover.

4 Before the Aelysthia comic was thought up, I was going to have Evan draw these autobiographical comics throughout the book. I like drawing him better in cartoony form, anyway.

5 I started and ended the book in third person, but I did try out a first-person exercise. This wasn't very good, but was helpful in finding the characters and the world they live in. I did a full chapter in this style before moving back to third person.

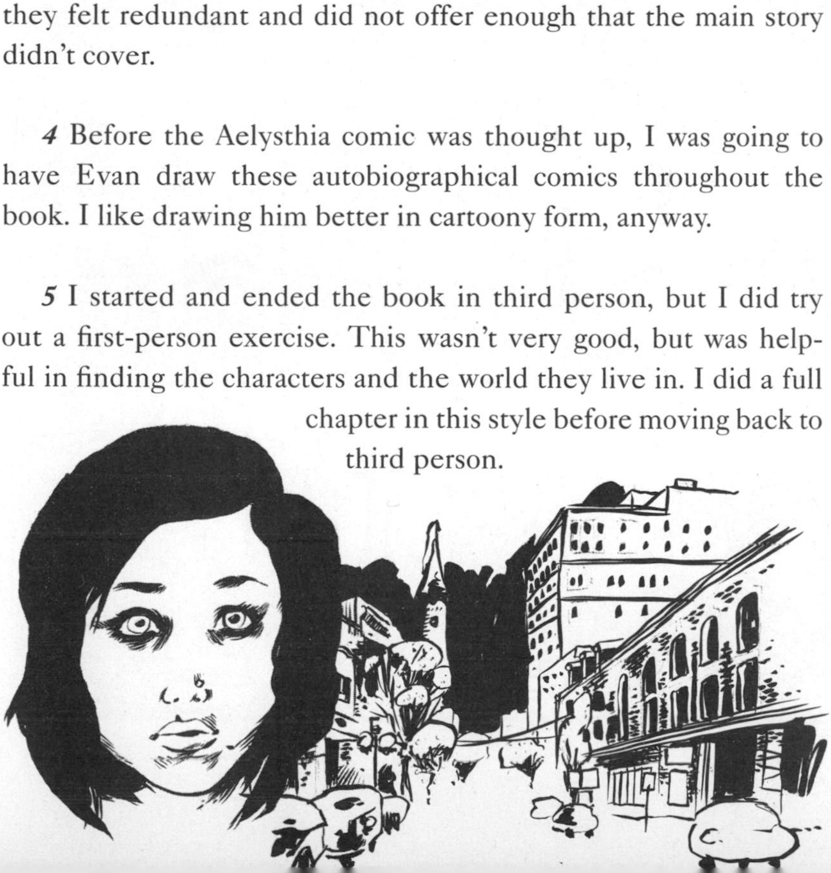

Grade 9
3
EVAN
Unkempt hair from too much hat-wearing.
Eyes go in different directions.
Ear gnomes
Always boogers
Adam's apple = tranny
Spittle in corners of mouth
You are so in love.
FLUSTERED

Dear diary,

So are we supposed to write letters and stuff in this thing? I have to admit, it's kind of boring here without you. I might even miss you, a bit. My parents seem to think that you moving away means more time for school and activities. Not that there's much else to do anyway. So yeah, how much for you to come back here? Just name a price and I'll make it happen. Anything? Please? Y

Anyways this seems as fitting a wa

scrap book. "Scrappy Doodles?" Se

Evan

Dearest Evan,

How dare you sully Scrappy Doodles (YES SCRAPPY DOODLES) with sentiment! I demand blood- soaked elves.

Yours,

Zombie Luc

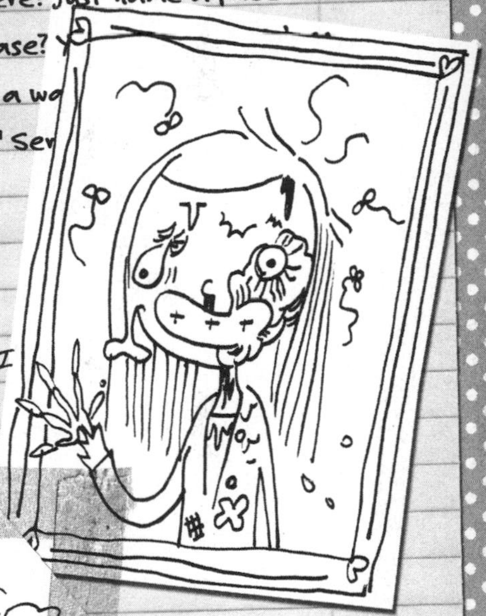

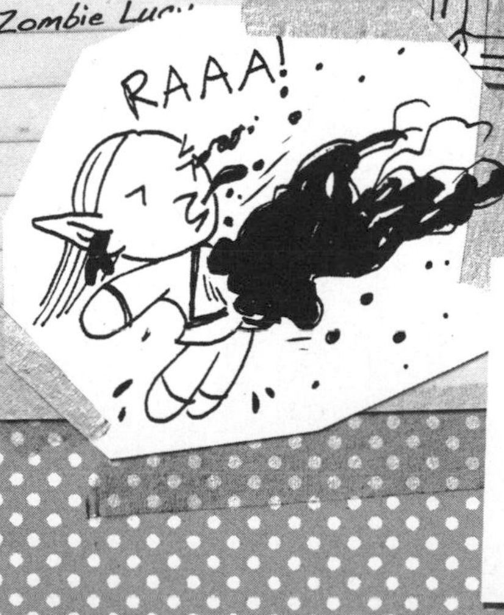
RAAA!

Thank yoooooooou ♡

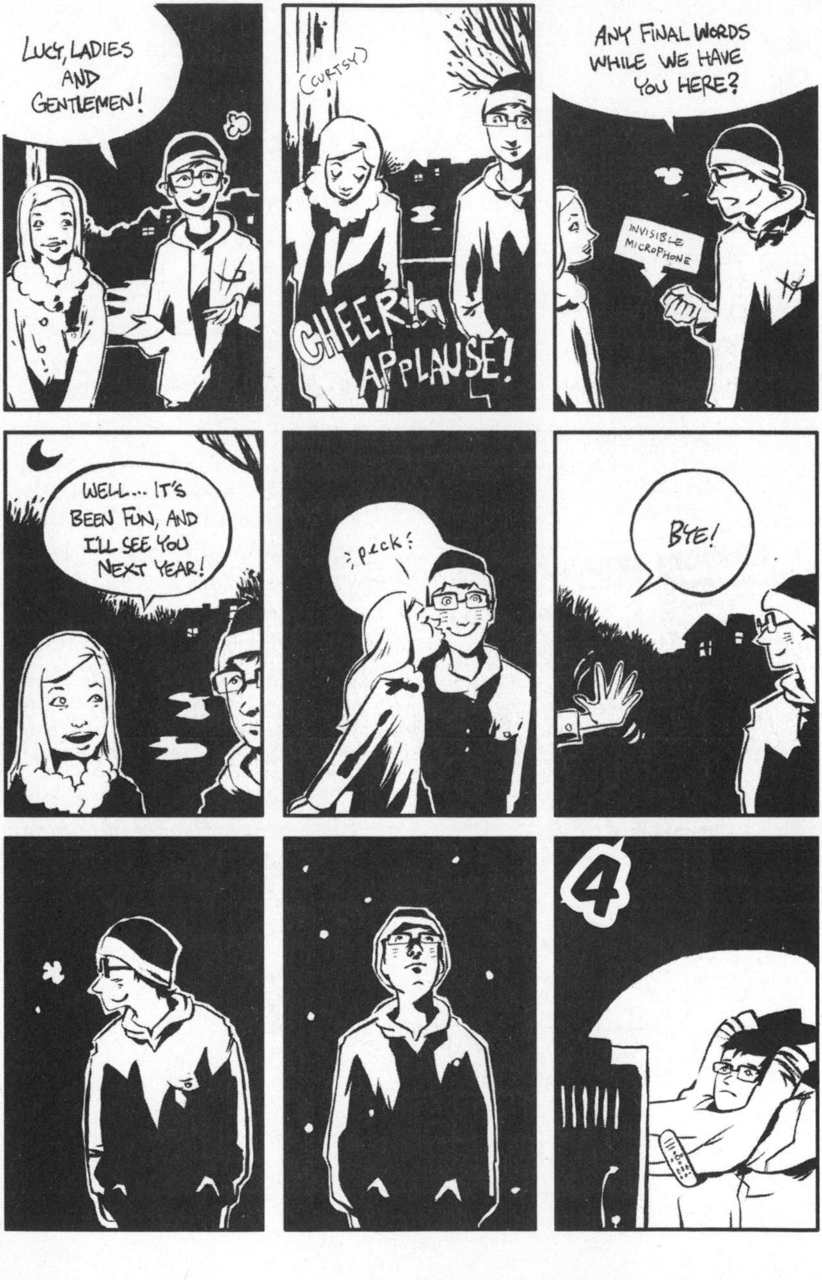

LUCY, LADIES AND GENTLEMEN!
(CURTSY)
CHEER!
APPLAUSE!
ANY FINAL WORDS WHILE WE HAVE YOU HERE?
INVISIBLE MICROPHONE
WELL... IT'S BEEN FUN, AND I'LL SEE YOU NEXT YEAR!
peck
BYE!
4

5

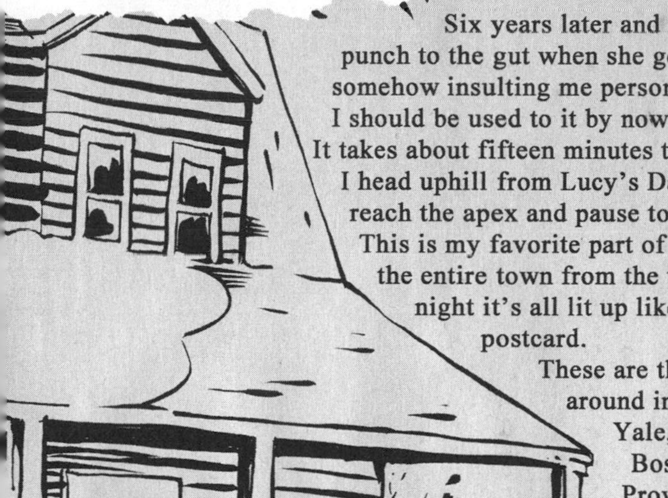

Six years later and it still feels like a punch to the gut when she goes. Like she's somehow insulting me personally by not staying. I should be used to it by now, you'd think.

It takes about fifteen minutes to get back home. I head uphill from Lucy's Dad's house until I reach the apex and pause to absorb the view. This is my favorite part of the walk. I can see the entire town from the top of that hill and at night it's all lit up like my own little postcard.

These are the names bouncing around in my head: UConn, Yale, Boston University, Boston College, Brown. Providence. Amherst.

This is life. It's not really better or worse than when Lucy is here, it's just different. Lucy's still Lucy. She's fun, she's a whirlwind of jokes and sarcasm and pretending, and art. She blows through town for a few weeks, and then she's gone. And everything settles.

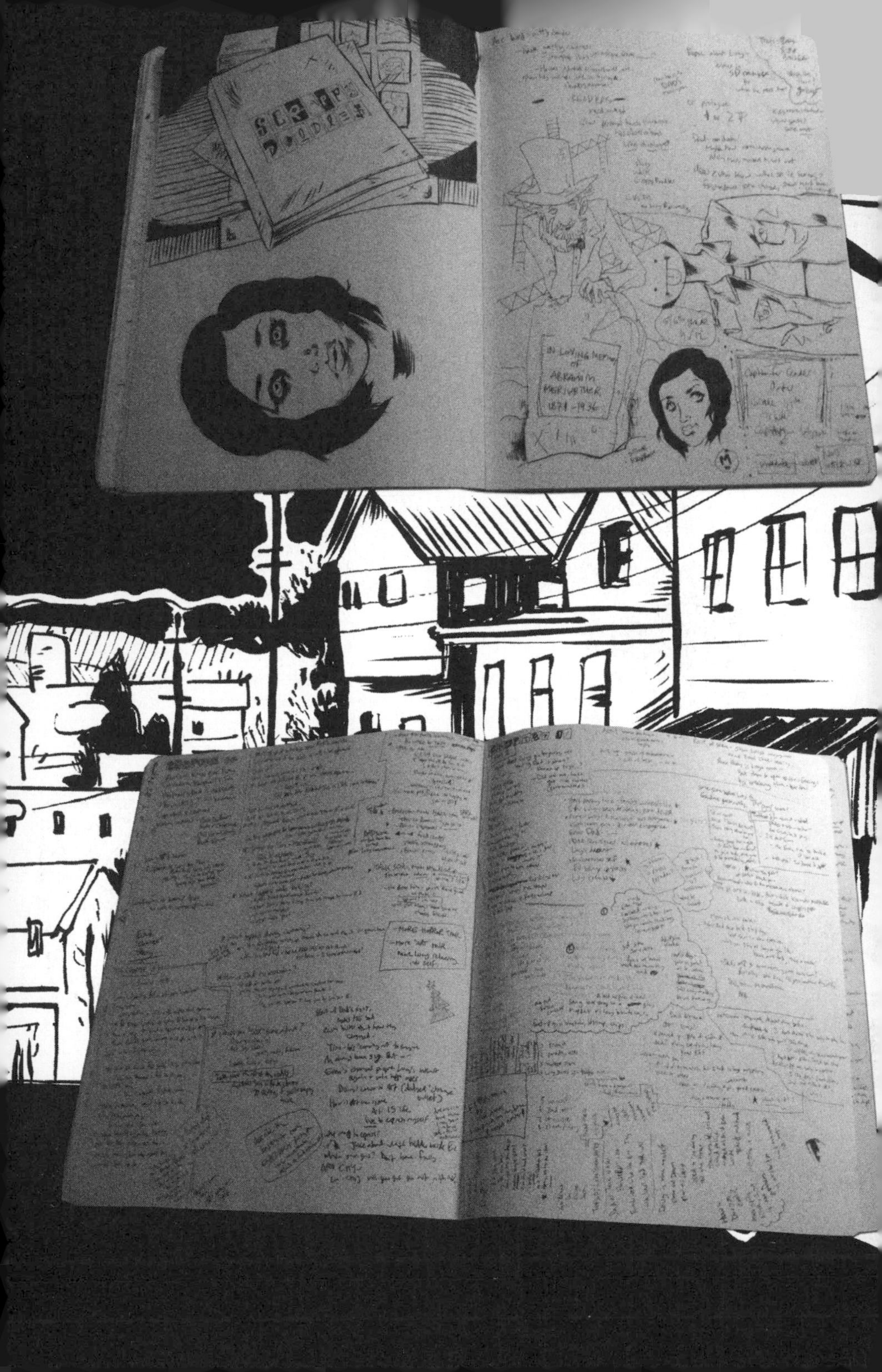
IN LOVING MEMORY OF

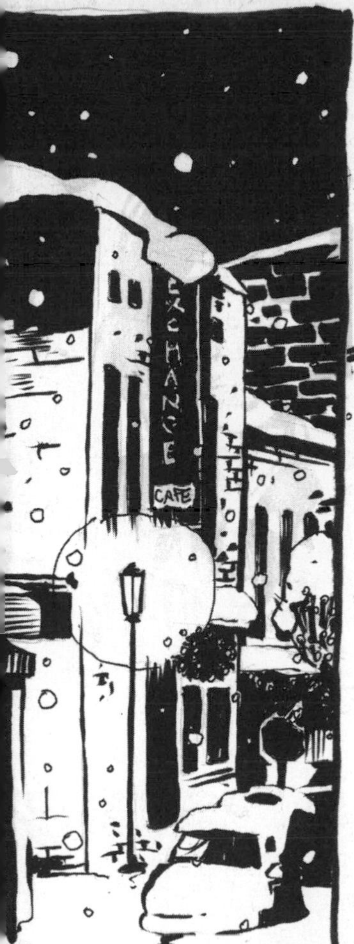
EXCHANGE
CAFE

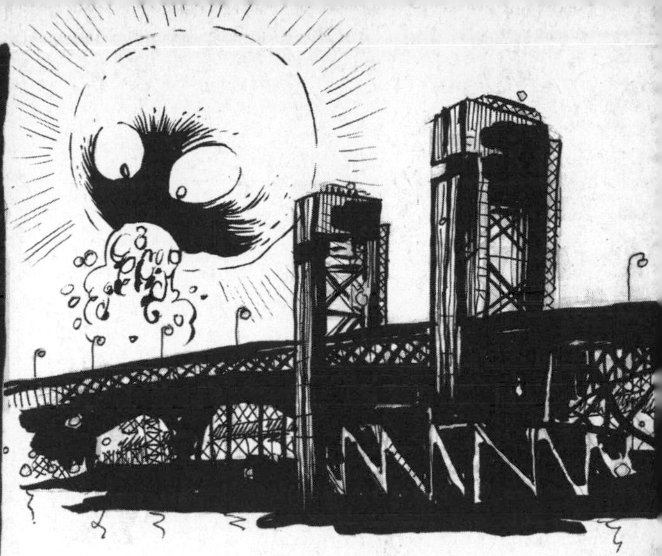

Well, I'm out of room. Thank you so much for reading this. Let me know what you think at my website, stephenemond.com, or via e-mail—emoboyrocks@yahoo.com.
'Til next time!

Steve

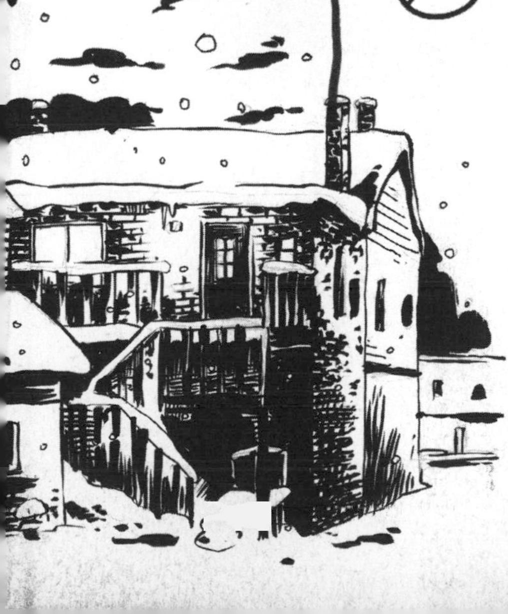

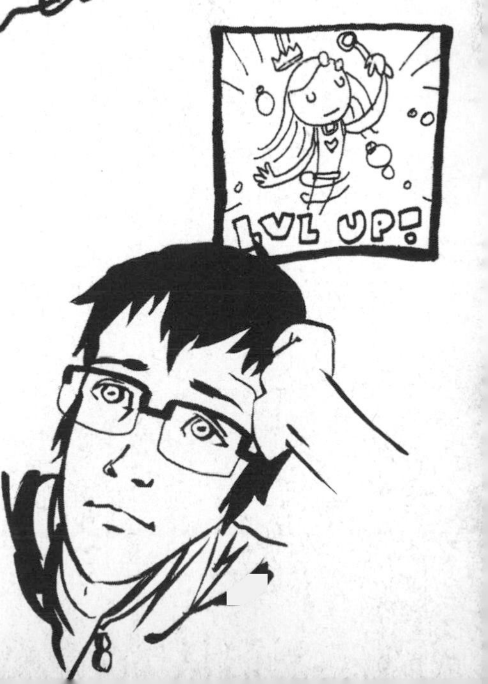
LVL UP!